*the*
two-
date
rule

# *the* two-date rule

USA TODAY BESTSELLING AUTHOR

# TAWNA FENSKE

## ALSO BY TAWNA FENSKE

Preview of *The Trouble with Christmas*
Copyright © 2019 by Amy Andrews

Entangled Publishing, LLC
10940 S Parker Road
Suite 327
Parker, CO 80134
Visit our website at www.entangledpublishing.com.

Amara is an imprint of Entangled Publishing, LLC.

Edited by Liz Pelletier and Heather Howland
Cover design by Elizabeth Turner Stokes
Cover art by
G-Stock Studio/Shutterstock
dcwcreations/Shutterstock
Michael Macsuga/Shutterstock
Interior design by Toni Kerr

Print ISBN 978-1-64063-7436
ebook ISBN 978-1-64063-7443

Manufactured in the United States of America

First Edition March 2020

AMARA

*For anyone who responds to "Great shirt!" with "Thanks, I got it at a thrift store for $1," you are my people. Rock on with your bargain-hunting selves. This book is for you.*

# CHAPTER ONE

"This is complete insanity."

Willa Frank turned to see what her best friend, Kayla, had deemed insane.

The mile-long line for the ladies' room?

The fact that the bar was charging twelve bucks for a gin and tonic because they'd renamed it "The Panty Dropper" and added a penis straw?

Or the fact that grown men were writhing half naked on the floor just twenty feet away?

Not that Willa couldn't appreciate the aesthetic. The man currently gyrating in a police uniform—er, there went his pants—was easy on the eyes, and so was the guy across the room wearing a cheetah-print loincloth and beating his bare chest.

But she had at least twelve million more pressing things to do, starting with that marketing plan for the Cartland deal and the proposal for that new client from—

"Oh, look." Kayla tossed her long, dark hair and pointed to the far corner of the room. "That guy's getting ready for some kind of cowboy-themed show."

Aislin peered over Willa's shoulder, blond curls tumbling around her bare arms. "Giddyup."

Willa stifled a sigh. "I can't believe I let you drag me to this."

She'd only agreed because they were celebrating Aislin's birthday, which was technically three weeks ago. Totally Willa's fault for postponing to deal with client projects for her fledgling web design business.

When had she become such a lousy friend? It wasn't this bad when they met in college. Or, hell, maybe it was. Willa recalled being dragged from her dorm when Aislin and Kayla decided she'd had enough studying and needed more fun.

*Fun.* She should focus on that now.

She glanced at the shirtless guy with abs so grease-slicked, they flickered under the disco lights. How long did it take him to scrub that off every night? And did he have to pay for his own grease, or did this touring stripper group—The Bone Yard Gang, *ugh*—buy it for him? Olive oil would be expensive, but maybe something like Crisco or even used cooking grease from—

"Hello, earth to Willa."

She turned back to see Aislin doing the potty dance in mile-high stilettos. It was a more impressive feat than whatever the hell Greased Abs was doing behind her, so she kept her focus on her friends.

"Half the audience is standing in this bathroom line right now," Willa said. "That has to cut into the performers' profit margins."

"Ugh, I'm dying here." Aislin tried to cross her legs and toppled into Kayla.

"Cut it out," Kayla protested. "You're bumping my bladder."

Willa nudged them gently upright and glanced at her watch. "It's been twenty minutes already." She stood on tiptoes to see over the sea of female heads separating them from the ladies' room at the end of the hall. There had to be four dozen women in this line, and the cloud of flowery perfume was making her eyes water. "At what point do we go outside and squat behind a dumpster?"

Kayla peered around her to see over a blonde in a skintight minidress. "Maybe someone died in there."

"No, we're moving." Aislin did a delicate side shuffle with her legs pressed together, which was no small feat in those shoes.

"At the rate we're going, it'll be Christmas by the time you two get to pee." Willa edged forward with the crowd.

She didn't even have to go, not really. But standing in line with her best friends felt like a better alternative to sitting out there alone watching The Bone Yard Gang gyrating like plucked peacocks having a seizure.

As much as the three of them worked—okay, fine, as much as *Willa* worked—it was tough to find a time when they could all go out for girls' night. These two had been by her side through thick and thin, so yeah, she owed them a fun night on the town. She owed them more than that, honestly.

Aislin stepped up the tempo on her potty dance. "Come on, come on, *come on*."

"Okay, seriously." Spurred by her friends' suffering, Willa glared down the hall. "If we don't hit the front of the line in five minutes, I'm dragging you down the street to the Laundromat. They've got bathrooms, and the bar next door has gin and tonics for five bucks."

"Without the penis straw," Kayla argued. "And without the scenery."

Applause exploded behind them, and Willa avoided turning to see who'd doffed which article of clothing. Or donned it. It always felt creepier watching someone get dressed after stripping than it did watching them take their clothes off in the first place.

Not that Willa had tons of experience at strip clubs, though this wasn't technically a strip club. Who even knew the Boyton Ballroom hosted stuff like this? Maybe she should talk to them about revamping their website to reflect a broader range of offerings. She could design an event calendar for them that would be easy to update with—

*Stop it. You're not here to work.*

Ha. Like shutting off work mode was simple. For Willa, it took an act of God, and maybe a crowbar.

"Hottie at six o'clock." Aislin nudged Willa with her elbow. "Check it out."

Kayla bounced up on her toes to look. "Ohh, he must be planning some kind of fireman thing," she said. "Yummy."

Willa turned, already hating herself for doing it.

And okay, fine, her friends had a point. The guy was hot as hell. He had that ten o'clock scruff going on, complete with ashy smudges on his arms and forehead meant to look like he'd battled a house fire. Nice touch. She couldn't make out all the words on his tight gray T-shirt, but she caught something that looked like "smokejumper" across a chest so broad, it deserved its own zip code. Nice eyes, too. Sort of a smoky gray lit from behind, the way the Central Oregon sky looked at sunrise during wildfire season.

Watching Smokey bare it all wouldn't be the worst thing in the world...

*Smokey the Bare.*

Willa stifled a snort laugh at her own joke.

"Ladies." Smokey edged past them, probably en route to the men's room, which never had a freakin' line. So unfair.

"Excuse me, sir?"

Smokey the Bare stared right at her, and Willa realized she'd been the one to speak.

Well, shit.

She cleared her throat and pressed on. "Look, I've got thirty bucks in ones that these two made me get so I could stuff them in someone's G-string," she said, "only we can't do that because we're stuck in this damn bathroom line."

Smokey stared at her. "Uh—"

"So I'll make you a deal," Willa continued, aware of her friends giggling beside her. "If you can get us access to a bathroom in the next two minutes—"

"Like maybe an employee restroom or something?" Kayla suggested.

"Or an outhouse in back?" Aislin crossed her legs again.

"Or a chamber pot," Willa added. "We're not picky."

"Um, look—" he started, but Willa pressed on.

"If you can do that for us, Smokey, I'll stuff my whole wad of ones in your pants."

*And as a bonus, I'll get out of here earlier.*

She didn't say that part out loud. No sense offending one of the entertainers. These guys were working hard, and besides, Smokey was hot.

So Willa shut her mouth, but she wasn't the only one. Smokey had been rendered mute, staring at her with those stormy gray eyes and a look that was somewhere between befuddled confusion and *hello, I'd like to lick butterscotch syrup off your body.*

He folded his arms over his chest, and Willa caught a faint hint of wood smoke. Damn, this guy committed to the role.

"Let me get this straight," he said. "If I get you into a restroom, you'll stuff thirty bucks in ones down my pants."

"Yes."

"And all I have to do is get you into a bathroom in the next two minutes."

"Correct."

Smokey tilted his head to the side, considering it. "How about we skip the ones and you have dinner with me?"

• • •

Grady Billman stared at the green-eyed brunette and waited for her answer.

He'd swung by Boyton Ballroom on his way back into Hart Valley after five days fighting a blaze out in the Siskiou National Forest. Normally he'd go straight home for a shower, but the club owner had left a message bitching about how the bass player hadn't picked up the amps after their last performance. Fucking Nielson. Or wait, fucking Jensen—it was his turn to haul gear, since Nielson was out on that Crater Lake fire. Was there anything less reliable than a rock band comprised entirely of smokejumpers and Hotshot wildland firefighters?

"Dinner," he repeated to the brunette, who was staring at him with her mouth open. "I've been dying for a good meal. Something that isn't freeze-dried or out of a can. I've heard good things about that new Italian place, or maybe something downtown?"

Five days of MREs had left him starving for a quality culinary experience, and he sure wouldn't mind sharing it with this brunette. She had spunk.

She closed her mouth, then opened it again. "If I go to dinner with you, you'll have us into a bathroom in less than two minutes?"

"Yes."

"Deal."

Grady started to stick out his hand, then thought better of it. He really should have scrubbed up before coming here. His nails were caked with soot and dirt that he hadn't been able to get rid of at that campground water pump. He needed at least a twelve-hour shower.

But the brunette grabbed his hand anyway, lifting an eyebrow at the sight of the ash-smeared chest of his T-shirt. "Nice touch," she said. "A tad over-the-top maybe, but I like the attention to detail."

"What?"

"Nothing. Okay, Smokey the Bare—"

"Huh?"

Her smile turned a little sheepish. "*Bare*—you know, because, um, you bare it all for a living?"

He stared at her, realization seeping slowly into his subconscious. Five nights of sleeping on the ground might have dulled his brain, but he was slowly catching on. Did this woman actually believe—

"You think I'm a stripper." He should probably be annoyed but could only muster up flattered.

"Hey, I'm not judging," she said. "I mean, obviously I'm here. And it looks like hard work."

A grin spread slowly across his face, and Grady could hardly hold back his laughter. Oh, man. This was too good. Wait till he told the rest of the crew. And hot damn, the brunette was smokin'. A killer body and eyes that reminded him of the forest. Sort of a swirly blend of green and brown with spots of amber sunlight mixed in. "Wait right here."

He didn't stick around for a reply. Just turned and wove through the sea of bodies toward the men's room. Shoving the door open, he peered inside to make sure the coast was clear. Not a dude in sight, which wasn't surprising. Most guys he knew steered clear of Boyton on a night like this.

Grady turned back to the brunette and her friends and gave them a wave. "Come on," he said. "I'll stand guard."

The brunette hesitated, but her friends pushed ahead of her. As they scurried past, they murmured words of desperate gratitude. Three more women followed, but Grady kept his eyes on the brunette. What was she waiting for?

"Can't say I blame you," he said. "Guys are gross. I probably wouldn't go into a men's room by choice if I didn't have to."

At last, she moved toward him, taking her time, eyeing him with a guarded expression that made him slouch a little. At six four, he was used to shorter people feeling skittish around him, but something told him that wasn't this woman's deal.

"I, uh, don't have to go." She swiped a shock of golden-brown hair behind her ear, and Grady wondered if it was as soft as it looked.

The rest of her looked soft, too, especially those curves under her silky-looking pink shirt. "So you were just looking out for your friends?"

"Pretty much," she said.

"That's very generous of you," he said. "Your willingness to shove thirty bucks down a stranger's pants for the good of others shows an admirable level of self-sacrifice."

That got a little lip twitch from her. Not quite a smile, which was okay. He'd just as soon earn that.

"Thank you," she said. "Kayla's got my cash in her purse, so—"

"What's your name?"

"My name?"

"Your name." Grady smiled. "If I'm choosing a date over the thirty bucks, I'd like to know your name."

"Oh. Willa," she said. "Willa Frank."

"Willa," he said, trying it out. "That's pretty."

"Thanks. It's short for William."

He cocked his head at her. "Your real name is William?"

"Long story." She winced. "Don't ask."

Okay, he wouldn't. Not tonight, anyway. But he would on their date. He'd ask a lot of things on their date if it meant getting to know her. His job made relationships impossible, but spending quality time with a beautiful woman was a great way to enjoy rare moments between fires.

"So, Willa," he said, leaning against the wall as two women shuffled out of the men's room and two more went in. "You like Italian?"

"To eat?" She bit her lip. "Of course you meant to eat. You're not asking me about Italian men or shoes or—"

"You're adorable."

Her cheeks flushed pink. "There's a word no one's ever used to describe me."

"No? What words do they use?"

She frowned and looked up at the exit sign. "Efficient. Hard-working. Dedicated."

"That sounds like a herding dog, not a human."

There was that lip twitch again, almost a full smile. "Guilty as charged," she said. "I own a web development company, so I'm pretty much married to my work."

"As long as you're not married to anyone else, we're good."

"What? Oh, no—not married." She gave a startled little laugh. "Definitely not married."

"That's good news." Not that he trusted everything someone told him, not after the last woman he dated turned out to have a husband and two kids. But Willa seemed sincere.

"So, Italian," he said. "That new place is down by the river, or Briana's is always good. Are you okay eating late?"

Her soft gold-brown brows lifted. "You don't mean tonight, do you?"

Right. He should probably go home and shower. And sleep. Five nights in a tent on the ground had been killer on his back. "I suppose I should get cleaned up for our first date." He lifted the hem of his T-shirt and sniffed. He'd put on a fresh one when he got to the pickup point, but it still smelled like smoke. Everything in his pack probably did.

He glanced back at Willa in time to see her jerking her eyes off his abs. Excellent.

"All right, no rush," he said. "How about tomorrow night?"

Willa frowned. "How long are you in town?"

"A couple of days," he said, though admittedly that could change if they got a call on another fire. "Mid-season like this, there's not a lot of downtime."

"There's a season for— Oh my Lord, what is that guy doing with his hat?"

Startled, Grady followed her gaze to where a performer was doing some sort of cowboy routine. Well, assuming cowboys made a habit of getting carnal with their headgear.

He looked back at Willa, preferring that view. "I don't have the most reliable schedule in the world in the summertime."

Willa tucked a lock of hair behind one ear. "What time do you go on?"

"On?" Oh, right. She still thought he was a stripper. Amusing as that was, he should probably let her off the hook. "The band's playing next Friday night, assuming we've got enough of us in town."

"What?"

He pushed off the wall and slipped a hand into his pocket. Pulling out a business card, he slid it into her palm, letting his hand linger a few extra seconds against hers. "That's when my band plays here again. The Smoky Blues Boys?"

"Your band." She stared at him, then at the card. "You mean you also—"

"I'm also a smokejumper with the Hart Valley

Air Center," he said. "A bunch of us formed a band, and we play here when we're not out jumping out of airplanes into forest fires."

She stared at the card, which had his phone number, email, website—

"Grady Billman." She looked up at him, confusion in her eyes. "Lead singer and guitarist."

"Also a master rigger, which sounds a little stripper-ish now that I'm saying it out loud." He grinned, hoping she wasn't too disappointed to be going out with a musician/smokejumper and not a stripper. "So how about tomorrow night? I can pick you up around seven."

She stared at him, a whole forest of color in those eyes that he honest-to-God couldn't read. He didn't breathe, didn't move at all, wondering if she was about to bolt.

"It's a date," she said and offered up the smallest smile that lit up the whole hall.

# CHAPTER TWO

Willa glanced at her watch as she parked her Toyota sedan in front of Briana's Fine Dining on the edge of downtown Hart Valley. She'd nearly hyperventilated when Smokey—er, *Grady*—had suggested the nicest restaurant in town as the scene of their first date.

First and *second-to-last* date, since they were only doing this twice. Or once if it didn't go well, though Willa felt optimistic. Grady seemed nice. And funny. And sexy. It was almost a shame she'd chosen to forego relationships so she could focus on her business.

So two dates. That's what she hoped would come of tonight. Nothing more, nothing less.

Aislin and Kayla called it her "two-date rule."

Staring out the car window at the restaurant's swanky facade, Willa bit her lip. Maybe this was a bad idea.

"That's too expensive," she'd protested on the phone when he called to set the time and place.

After a long pause, Grady had cleared his throat. "Call me old-fashioned," he'd said, "but where I'm from, the person who invites someone on a date is the one who pays."

Still worrying about money, Willa had scrolled through the Yelp reviews. "It has four dollar signs, which means entrees are more than sixty dollars a person."

"I've spent the last five days eating Spam and

rehydrated beef stew," Grady had said. "Not that I don't appreciate a good ramen Spam burger, but when I'm in town, I like to eat well."

And he wanted her to join him. Good Lord, she was still blushing about the whole stripper misunderstanding. He'd laughed it off, but Willa apologized so many times, he finally told her to can it.

After she gave up apologizing and fretting about the cost of the restaurant, she'd pawed through her closet, looking for something nice to wear. The few fancy clothes she owned were business suits and one nice dress she'd worn to the bank the day she'd signed papers for the small business loan that started her company.

Since that was more than six years ago, Kayla put the kibosh on that dress and came over with a whole armload of little black dresses for Willa to pick from. But none of them looked quite right, and besides, that felt too much like charity. In the end, she prowled the racks at her favorite consignment shop until she found a fitted green dress with cami straps and a little flounce at the hemline.

Glancing in the rearview mirror, Willa fiddled with the neckline and wondered if it was too low. Too late to do anything about that now. She scraped at a fleck of mascara under one eye, then glanced at her watch.

Six forty-five. Being punctual was one thing, but this was probably ridiculous.

It was better than being late. God, how she hated being late. She could still taste the shame of walking into her third-grade classroom in hand-me-down jeans with her Minnie Mouse backpack held together with duct tape. Everyone had turned to stare as she muttered something about the car not starting.

"Willa smells," Ashley Deek had hissed as Willa shuffled by. "Like old cheese and cigarettes."

Tears had stung Willa's eyes, but she'd held her head high as she moved past the teacher, who sighed and scrawled another tardy slip.

Even now, all these years later, Willa recalled the flush of humiliation. The way she'd pleaded with her father to buy her a bike or a bus pass so she could cover the five miles to school faster. Or maybe if they had a car that ran reliably…

But her dad had been on another bender, so there'd been no point in talking to him. Instead, she'd locked herself in the bathroom and soaked in the tub until the water turned cold and her skin got all wrinkly. She'd washed her clothes in there, too, since there were no quarters for the Laundromat.

Afterward, she'd toweled her hair and covered herself in baby powder, desperate to mask the scent of secondhand smoke, fried potatoes, and poverty. She'd stared at herself in the mirror for a long time, mouthing the words she'd committed to memory.

*You can get out. You can be someone.*

She'd repeated the words again and again until her father banged on the door and asked if she was alive, if she wanted to go out stargazing with him, which of course she always did.

*Bang-bang-bang!*

Willa jumped, startled from her memories by a real-life intrusion. She peered through the window to see Grady standing beside her car. He wore gray jeans that fit like a dream and an apologetic smile.

"Sorry," he called, holding up his hands in

apology or surrender. "Didn't mean to scare you."

Willa yanked her keys out of the ignition, shoved them in her purse, and opened the door.

"I saw you out here killing time," he said. "Figured we could kill it together."

"You're early, too?"

"Yeah, I had some errands to run in town," he said. "Misjudged the time a little and ended up getting here way before I meant to."

Interesting. She wasn't sure whether to take that as an admission of chronic earliness—Willa's problem, to be sure—or a scatterbrained quality about his schedule. Either way, it didn't matter much. It wasn't like this was going to turn into a relationship.

Not even with a hottie like Grady.

Surveying the cleaned-up version of the man in question, she couldn't help noticing his expensive watch and nice shoes. Was that a Rolex? She had no idea what one looked like, but it seemed pretty fancy.

*Out of your league*, the voice whispered in the back of her head. *Or a big spender. Either way, he's not for you.*

Willa smoothed her hair back and glanced toward the restaurant. "Are we too early?"

"I've already got our table." He smiled, and something shifted in her gut. "Figured I was here, so I might as well grab a drink."

She leaned against her car, savoring the late-evening sunlight that sprinkled her bare shoulders with little dots of warmth. She recalled what he said earlier about running errands in town. "You don't live in Hart Valley?"

"Nah, I'm about fifteen miles east, out past the air base."

The air base, of course. He was a smokejumper, not a stripper. "I'm sorry again about the misunderstanding at Boyton," she said. "What I said about—"

"If you apologize one more time for calling me a stripper, I'm going to start taking my clothes off in the parking lot while I sing 'I'm a Little Teapot' at the top of my lungs."

Willa dared a glance at his chest, which was sculpted and broad under the gray Henley that matched his eyes. Honestly, the striptease wouldn't be so bad…if it were in private.

"What's that smile about?" he asked. "I noticed you don't smile too easily, so I'm making notes about which jokes work."

"Come on," she said, wondering if he knew it wasn't his joke at all. "Let's grab our table."

He offered his arm, and Willa took it, feeling only a little silly. As they started toward the restaurant, she sniffed him as discreetly as possible. He'd mentioned having a drink but didn't smell like he'd bathed in a beer can the way her father did after hitting the bar.

Grady smelled like soap and something woodsy. Fresh smells, pleasant smells, not like cigarettes or booze or anything but clean, well-dressed man.

"I hope you don't mind that I asked for a table outside," he said as he led her to the patio, to a table in the corner with a cheerful bouquet of daisies and a candle flickering in a glass holder.

"It's perfect, thanks."

"They've got heaters if it turns chilly."

"I have a sweater in the car." She sounded stilted and out of practice, even though she wasn't. Not really. She'd had plenty of first and even second dates. There was nothing different about this one.

She tucked her purse under her chair and folded her hands on the table. The air held no hint of impending chilliness. Summer sunlight dappled the white tablecloth, making the silverware sparkle.

Completing her survey of the flatware, Willa looked at Grady. Really looked at him this time, not through a car window or a haze of disco lights and perfume or from the side as they walked.

"Wow," she said. "You're way better-looking than I thought you were."

"Um…thanks?"

Shit. That came out wrong.

"I just meant—"

"Let me go out on a limb here," Grady said, grinning as he picked up a sweating glass of ice water. "You have a habit of saying whatever pops into your head without first running the words through a filter."

"I—" She thought about arguing, but what was the point? "Guilty as charged."

"I think it's adorable."

Willa rolled her eyes. "There's that word again. 'Adorable.' Are you trying to be patronizing?"

"What? Of course not." He shook his head, looking bemused. "I like that you say what you think and I don't have to play guessing games about what you really mean."

Willa watched him for a second and decided he was sincere. "That's true." She picked up the wine list and pretended to study it. "So how about you? What's your flaw?"

He laughed, a warm, rich baritone that made her arms feel fuzzy. "I appreciate that you think I might have only one."

"Top three, then."

He took a sip of water, considering it. "Is this like in a job interview where they ask about your flaws and you're supposed to say something like 'Oh, I'm a workaholic' or 'I'm just so *driven*?'"

Willa smiled and set down the wine list as her shoulders started to relax. "What's the dating equivalent of that?"

"Hmm. Maybe something like, 'I'm too open in communicating my feelings, and I'll want to stay up all night just talking.' How's that?"

Willa made a face. "That sounds awful."

He cocked his head to one side. "You don't want to stay up all night talking about your feelings?"

"Do you?"

"Hell no."

"I rest my case." Willa took a sip of her water, studying him over the rim of her glass. He really was well put together with thick, muscled arms and broad shoulders. What would those feel like under her palms? Broad and solid and—

"Do you know what you want?"

She blinked at him. "What?"

He tapped the wine list. "Did you decide on something, or you need another look at this?"

"Oh. Um, water's fine."

"Really?"

All right, she was being lame. It's not like she

didn't drink, and a chilled glass of white wine *would* be nice. "The house Pinot Gris, then."

He gave her an odd look. "Because you actually want the house Pinot Gris, or because it's the cheapest thing on the menu?"

Willa felt her chin lifting, her hackles rising. "Does it matter?"

"I'd just like you to get what you really want," he said. "You made such a big deal about the prices here, I thought—"

"The Pinot Gris is only seven dollars a glass."

"Which is terrific if that's what you're really craving," he said. "But please don't worry about the cost. Get whatever you want."

Was it what she wanted? Willa bit her lip. She wasn't in the habit of thinking that way, not even when someone else was paying. What was affordable, what was practical, sure, but what she *wanted*?

Grady held her gaze. His blue-gray eyes were open and friendly, and there was nothing at all threatening there.

"I want—" Her mouth felt dry, and the ending of that sentence took absurd forms in her mind.

*I want to know what you look like with your shirt off.*

Now, where had that come from? She must still have male strippers on the brain, that was all.

She ordered herself to focus as she fingered the necklace at her throat. "What I want," she said slowly, "is to conclude this date not worrying that anyone's going to need to take out a second mortgage to pay for our meal."

He grinned. "I think I can afford a ten-dollar

glass of wine. Or even a twenty-dollar glass of wine, but I'll let it go." His smile was warm and open, and Willa felt herself relax again. "That's a pretty necklace," he said.

She glanced down to see she was still touching it. "Thanks," she said. "My father gave it to me years ago. I was eleven, I think."

"I like that. Can't tell if those are stars or flowers—"

"Stars," she said a little too quickly. Her dad wasn't the best topic of conversation, so she picked up the wine menu again. Frowning, she skimmed for the second-cheapest option. "The pinot blanc is pretty reasonable. That's nine dollars a glass."

"You take the budget-conscious thing to the next level."

When she looked up, there was no judgment in his eyes. Just curiosity.

"Truth," she said. "Be glad I didn't ask to use coupons when I volunteered to stick money down your pants."

He burst out laughing, scraping a hand over his chin. "Good point. I'm still waiting for that, by the way."

"You picked dinner over the cash, remember?"

"Still a damn good choice."

Willa folded her hands on the table. "I'm not sure if it's an asset or a flaw, but we can put my cheapness in the flaw category if you want."

"What?" He looked genuinely baffled.

"The three flaws I asked you to share about yourself? You haven't told me any of yours yet, and I've shared two of mine."

"The money thing and—?"

"Lack of filter," she supplied. "Which allows me to point out that you're totally stalling on the flaws."

Grady laughed. "This is turning out to be a very strange date."

She'd have bristled at his words if he didn't sound charmed by it, and he kept talking anyway, so she didn't have a chance to interrupt.

"So far on this date, you've sniffed me to make sure I showered—yeah, I caught that," he said when she opened her mouth to protest. "You've implied that I'm broke," he continued before she could argue, "and suggested we make small talk about everything that's wrong with us. If this is your idea of a first date, I'm dying to know what a second one is like."

The weird thing? He didn't sound annoyed. He sounded...*intrigued*?

Willa sipped her water. "We only get two dates, so I like to make them count."

Grady looked befuddled, but before he could ask questions, the waitress rushed over. "Sorry to keep you waiting," she said. "Can I get you something to drink?"

Grady gestured for her to order first. Willa hesitated. Picked up the wine menu. "What can you tell me about the Gruner Veltliner from Illahe Vineyards?"

"Very crisp," the waitress said. "Notes of peach and honeycrisp apple. It's partially fermented in acacia barrels, so that lends some nice herbal flavors and a really bold mouthfeel."

She didn't understand half of that, but the wine was nine dollars a glass, so she nodded. "I'll try that."

"And you, sir?"

Grady picked up the wine menu. "That Gruner does sound good," he said. "I was leaning toward red wine, but I haven't had a good white for a long time. You wouldn't want to share a bottle, would you?"

"I'm only having the one glass," Willa said. "I have some work to finish up tonight."

Grady nodded but didn't comment, which Willa appreciated. He ordered some complicated-sounding Pinot Noir, and Willa tried not to notice the price—*eighteen dollars a glass!*—while the waitress described the specials. Something with salmon and a pork dish of some kind. Why did they never give the prices when rattling off all the details of a dish?

*If you have to ask, you can't afford it.*

Her personal motto, one of them at least. Willa listened politely, then ordered a pasta dish that sounded filling and wasn't too pricey.

Grady put in an order for cherry-glazed duck breast with a bunch of fancy-sounding side dishes. He handed the menu back to the server, who turned and hustled back to the kitchen.

"What did you mean earlier?" He turned that stormy gray gaze on Willa. "That comment about only getting two dates?"

She uncrossed her legs and spread her napkin over her knees, even though they were a long way from getting their dinner. "Just that," she said. "I don't date anyone more than twice. It's a personal preference."

He stared at her for so long, she wasn't sure he'd heard her. "You're kidding."

"Nope. Dead serious."

"Two dates? That's it?"

She nodded, surprised he'd care. The guys she'd been with usually didn't. "Sometimes it's just one date, if there's no chemistry," she admitted. There was chemistry here, though. She'd noticed that the first night, and it seemed hotter now. "Anyway, it doesn't matter. Two's the limit."

"Why?"

She shrugged before turning to accept her glass of wine from the waitress, waiting until the woman was out of earshot to reply. "I'm not really looking for a relationship," she said. "And more than two dates starts to imply relationship, so…" She shrugged again, expecting that to be the end of it.

"I don't get it." Grady shook his head. "What happens if you're really into someone?"

He sounded more curious than judgmental. She hated to admit it, but she kind of liked his interest in her thought process. "At this stage in my life, career comes first," she said carefully. "I've worked hard to build my company. To build a safety net and a stable income stream. I'm not about to blow that for some guy."

*Some guy.*

Some guy like her father, the kind of man who made her mom throw away everything to travel clear across the country for a life with a vagabond dreamer whose gambling problem meant they never had any money. And then later, much later, after her mother left—

*Stop it.*

Willa ordered herself to stay focused on the conversation, on Grady. Might as well make the most of their first and possibly *only* date.

The thought of having only one date with him bothered her more than she expected. It was silly, really. She hardly knew the guy. But there was something intriguing about him. Something that made her want to know more.

She swallowed back her overanalysis and concentrated on Grady. "How about you?" she asked. "You're, what, late thirties?"

"Thirty-two," he said, offering a wry grin. "Jumping into fires for a living tends to age a guy. Thanks for noticing."

"Sorry." She traced a fingertip through the condensation on her water glass. "So what's your story? Divorced, never married, what?"

"Never married," he said. "Never planning to get married."

"Really?" Wasn't that interesting. She took a sip of her wine. "May I ask why?"

He shrugged and swirled his own wine in the glass. "I'm gone for weeks at a time for most of the summer," he said. "And when it's winter here, it's summer in Australia, and I usually go there to work their season."

"Sounds busy." What wasn't he sharing?

"It can be," he said. "It's better now than it was when my old man did the job."

"Your father was a smokejumper?"

Grady nodded. "A couple of my brothers are, too."

"Sounds like quite the family affair."

"Yep." He cleared his throat. "Back in my father's day, they were gone the whole summer. Literally, no days off. Made it tough on my mom with ten kids to raise."

"There are *ten* of you?" Holy cow. And Willa thought Kayla came from a big family with four of them.

She started to blurt a nosy question about birth control, but stopped herself and focused on him instead. "Nine brothers and sisters," she said. "What was *that* like?"

He laughed. "Exactly as nuts as it sounds. I don't think I slept in a room by myself until I was eighteen years old. How about you, any brothers or sisters?"

Interesting. Willa jotted mental notes.

*Doesn't like talking about himself.*

*Still hasn't answered the question about flaws.*

*Has lips that look like they're made for kissing, lush and full and—*

"Only child," she said. "I lost my mother when I was little, so it was just my dad and me."

She did her best to keep her tone breezy, like they hadn't just tiptoed into a minefield of uncomfortable memories. Like she wasn't remembering the sound of her grandfather's strained baritone explaining that Mommy was never coming home. Like her nostrils didn't prickle with the smell of cheap beer and her father's desperation, her constant companions in the years following the loss of her mother.

Grady was studying her with such intensity, she had to look away.

"You still haven't answered my question," she teased with as much cheer as she could muster. "The one about flaws."

Now who was avoiding talking about themselves?

He smiled and took a sip of his wine. "Not great at small talk. There's one. How's that?"

She picked up her wineglass and clinked it against his. Something they had in common. "Cheers to that."

The tiniest flicker of relief played across his handsome features. "First-date conversation is always a little awkward, isn't it?"

"Tell me about it." It felt nice to have him admit it. "I guess we're supposed to keep asking each other questions about ourselves, right? That's how the first-date thing goes."

"Great idea." He looked thoughtful. "What's it like jumping out of airplanes for a living?"

Willa snorted. "Um—"

Grady grinned and fingered the edge of his wineglass. "I figure both of us have the standard first-date questions other people ask us," he said. "That's a little tired and boring. Maybe we should ask each other instead."

"You're so weird." Weird but creative. This was definitely a first.

"So take your best shot at it," he said. "What's it like jumping out of an airplane into a forest that's blazing all around you?" he asked. "You're hundreds of miles from the nearest town, and you know there's a chance your chute could get caught in a tree and you'll have to climb a hundred feet to the ground before you can start revving your chain saw."

Willa looked at him—really looked at him, hard—and considered what sort of guy he was. What it might feel like to do his job. "It was scary at first," she said. "Airplanes are a little terrifying to me, actually. I've never even flown." She cleared her throat and offered a shy smile. "Before I was a smokejumper, I mean."

"No kidding?"

She nodded, not sure whether to stay in character as herself or pretend to be him. "But I got used to it," she said. "Jumping out of planes is kinda awesome, and I like being a hero. Eventually it became like any other commute."

Grady laughed. Picked up his wineglass and took a sip. "I'm definitely no hero, but for someone who just met me—and hasn't been in an airplane—you're not too far off with the rest of that."

His grin was disarming, and so was this silly game. She should probably keep her guard up, but this was more interesting than any first date she'd had in… well, she couldn't remember. But she was having fun, and that was saying something.

"Why'd you go to that stripper show the other night?" she asked.

Such a bizarre question to ask, and she watched him process it. She wanted him to guess why someone like her—frugal, serious, not at all a party girl—would have ended up at a bar with men taking their clothes off to music.

"My friends," he said. "Kayla and Ainslie—"

"Aislin," she supplied, surprised he'd even gotten close.

"Right, Kayla and Aislin," he said. "We're really close, though we don't see one another as much as I wish we did. They wanted to go, and I like spending time with them, plus I like to keep an eye out in case someone tries to slip something in their drinks or they need a wingman to rescue them from some douchey guy."

"Wow." She stared at him. For a man who'd known her less than an hour, he'd gotten pretty damn close to her reality.

He grinned. "How'd I do?"

"Very nice." She cleared her throat and waited for his next question.

"I hear you did two years in the military right out of high school," he said. "What was that like?"

Willa bit her lip and considered him carefully. She'd figured out fast that he wasn't the type to open up easily, so the fact that he was sharing seemed noteworthy. "Everyone just assumed I'd be a smokejumper like my father." A total guess, but she could tell from the lift of his brows that she wasn't far off. "I wanted to try something different. Shooting guns and beating people up—"

"That's totally what the military's all about."

She grinned and kept going. "Anyway, I eventually realized I was meant to hurl my body out of airplanes for a living. The rest is history."

He gave her a smile that held equal notes of surprise and approval. "Well done."

"Thank you." She grinned and took a sip of her wine. "My turn."

She flipped through the notebook in her brain. What would she like him to guess about her? "Tell me what you like and don't like about owning your own company."

Grady twisted the stem of his wineglass, spinning it on the table without taking his eyes off her.

"Having control is nice," he said. "Being in charge of my own destiny, making all the decisions, being self-reliant." His huge hand made the wineglass stem look like a toothpick, but it wasn't his hands taking her breath away. It was how close he'd gotten to her truth.

"I like having control," he continued. "But it's also my least favorite thing."

She swallowed hard, wondering how he'd read all that about her. How he'd guessed so accurately. "Sounds like a lot of responsibility."

"It is, but I enjoy it," he said. "I like what I do for a living. I just wish I could relax a little sometimes."

Willa bit her lip. Was that a wild guess on his part, or was she really that transparent?

She picked up her water and took two big gulps, figuring that was safer than chugging the wine.

"How about you?" he asked. "I understand you really love baking. That you've thought maybe when you stop jumping out of airplanes someday, you'd like to open a pastry shop."

Willa laughed, charmed by this new insight into Grady's life. "Oh, I love to bake," she said, even though she knew as much about baking as she did about jumping out of airplanes. "All that flour and butter and sugar and"—what the hell else did people use for baking?—"baking powder," she said, taking a wild guess. "Can't get enough of the baking powder."

Grady snort laughed into his wineglass. His gray eyes were twinkling, and Willa had the sudden urge to ask the waitress to box up their meals so they could go back to her place and get comfy. What would it feel like to kiss him? Or more, maybe—

"Maybe if I play my cards right," Grady said softly, "I could come over sometime and you could make me your world-famous lava cake."

Willa's mouth watered, though it wasn't for the lava cake. It was the thought of Grady in her kitchen, that broad chest stretching the front of an apron. Damn, this man did things to her brain. And her body. She uncrossed her legs, conscious of the clamminess of her palms.

"Lava cake." Willa swallowed to keep from drooling on the table. "That sounds amazing."

She glanced toward the restaurant and wondered what was taking so long with the food. Was it bad to admit she wanted to get out of here? That she really did want to take Grady home with her, and not just for the lava cake.

That was the thing about the two-date rule. If she decided early that she wanted to sleep with a guy, there was no playing games and waiting till the third date. She could go after what she wanted on date one with no worry about how it would affect things later in a relationship.

What would Grady say if she suggested it?

"I actually don't live all that far from here," she said. "And I'm pretty good with sharing my kitchen and my baking ingredients."

Good Lord, that sounded like a lame entendre. She hadn't meant it that way, but Grady smiled like he'd picked up the vibes she was laying down.

"Well," he said slowly. "I think we could arrange to—"

*Squeeeeeeeeeee!*

His eyes blazed wide, and Willa jumped in her

seat. Grady sat up straight, scanning the restaurant door.

Was that smoke she smelled?

Grady leaped to his feet, knocking back his chair.

Willa was two beats behind him, trying to identify the sound.

"Fire alarm," he called over his shoulder as he strode with purpose toward the restaurant. Toward the smoke getting thicker by the moment.

Into it, not away from it, and that told her a helluva lot about Grady Billman.

# CHAPTER THREE

Grady smelled smoke before he made it inside, but it hit him full force in the face as he burst into the dining room. The other customers—all two dozen or so—were lurching to their feet and rushing toward the door, a few of them grumbling over the screech of the smoke alarm.

He ignored them, focused on locating the fire. It didn't take long.

Smoke billowed from the private dining room off to the right. He knew the space well, since he'd helped a bandmate propose by serenading the girlfriend over dinner. It looked empty at the moment, minus the tower of fire erupting on a table. What *used* to be a table. Flames danced across the surface, licking their way up the curtains.

Off to Grady's right, the waitress flew in from the kitchen and gasped. "Oh my God. The candles. There's a proposal and—"

"Fire extinguisher," Grady barked. There had to be one in the kitchen. "Find it. Please."

She spun around and sprinted away as Grady moved forward. Spotting two pitchers of ice water on the bus station, he grabbed both and made for the table.

"Grady, be careful." Willa's voice came from behind him, but he didn't turn. Didn't lose focus.

"Stay back," he called as he tossed the first pitcher at a patch of carpet where the fire was just getting started. The baby flames sputtered out in a furious burst of smoke while the bigger ones kept rising.

"See if there's a mop in the kitchen," he called over his shoulder. "Or a broom, anything with a handle."

He had to get those curtains down to keep the flames from spreading. God, the smell. Fucking polyester tablecloths. He yanked up the hem of his T-shirt and pulled it over his mouth and nose. Then he tossed the second pitcher of water at the table.

*Tssssssssss!*

The flames gave an angry sizzle, and a few flickered out. Most didn't, and the fire kept climbing the curtains, its greedy orange fingers clawing at the ceiling. Didn't this place have a damn sprinkler system?

"Here! I found a broom by the door," Willa called from behind him.

Grady tossed the empty pitcher aside and held out a hand. "Thank you." He caught the handle and pulled it to him, grateful when Willa scuttled back to safety.

Holding the broom handle out like an extension of his arm, he took a swipe at the curtains. *Miss*. He tried again, desperate to keep those flames from spreading.

"What the hell is— Oh shit."

Grady glanced behind him to see the chef staring open-mouthed. His jowls wobbled, and his white chef's coat was spattered with something. "Extinguisher!" the man shouted.

"Right here." The waitress popped up behind

him, coughing as she made her way toward Grady.

He held out his hand for it as one of the curtains dropped to the floor like a dying butterfly. Ash billowed around it, fleeing the scene of the crime.

"Get back, please." He yanked out the pin, breaking the tamper seal. A good sign it was in working order. So many of them weren't. Clutching the hose in one hand, he aimed it at the base of the flames.

"Be careful." Willa's voice again, and Grady felt an odd surge of affection.

He aimed low, nozzle pointed at the puddle of flaming chiffon that had once been a curtain. Gripping the hose tighter, he gave a sharp squeeze.

*Whooooosh!*

Flames spit and jeered in protest, then fluttered out. Sweeping side to side, Grady blasted the floor, then up to the table with steady, even strokes. Retardant whooshed out, smearing the table and wall with foam. The fire fizzled and hissed and vanished under a blanket of white. It was like flocking a Christmas tree, if the Christmas tree were on fire.

Grady thought he heard Willa's voice say the word "firefighter" behind him but couldn't be sure. Not like he spent a lot of time putting out little candle fires like this one, though in some ways, that's what being a smokejumper was all about. Being on the front lines at the very start of the fire and fighting like hell to keep it from getting bigger.

He aimed for the last curtain, blasting it down into a soggy heap of charred cloth and sizzling embers.

And then it was over. He surveyed the wreckage, looking for straggling embers or hot spots. Nothing. No sign of flare-ups. The fire was out.

Lowering the fire extinguisher, he turned to face his audience.

Willa's eyes were the first ones he locked with, and he stared into those green-brown depths and felt his chest clench. Bringing her hands up, she began to clap. The waitress followed suit, and so did the chef. The rest of the customers joined in, too. Cheesy as hell, but Grady only saw Willa. Saw the wonder in her eyes, the ripple of her hair around her shoulders, the gentle curve of her breasts in that killer green dress.

He couldn't have broken eye contact if someone ripped his eyelids off with pliers, so he was glad she did first. Her gaze dropped down his torso and stayed there, eyes flickering with interest. Had he spilled food on his shirt?

"Oh." Right. His shirt was still serving as a mask, leaving his chest bare.

The hunger in Willa's eyes made him want to leave it there all night, but he yanked down the hem so he could look like a gentleman in this fine-dining establishment. He set down the fire extinguisher, too, as the chef stepped forward to shake his hand.

"Dinner's on the house tonight, son—"

*Screeeeeeeeeech!*

The chef blanched, then yanked his hand back and ran for the kitchen. Grady glanced at the waitress, who'd gone considerably paler.

"Just a hunch," he said, "but I'm guessing dinner just got charbroiled."

The waitress nodded. "Good guess." She offered an apologetic smile. "Sorry about your romantic dinner."

"It's okay." Willa stepped closer and gave him a wink. "The night's not over yet."

Grady had to breathe deeply to keep his chest from exploding with excitement and lust and a healthy helping of pride.

"How about I make sure the kitchen's not on fire?" he said. "And then we continue our date night somewhere else."

Willa smiled, her green-brown eyes flashing. "Deal."

• • •

An hour later, Grady shoved half a slice of pizza into his mouth. The crust was garlicky and crisp, with gooey cheese oozing off the edges. "Best idea ever," he said around a mouthful of pepperoni.

Willa laughed and tossed him a napkin. "Probably should have started out here."

He could tell that wasn't a jab at his date-planning skills, so he didn't take it as one. Dinner at Briana's wasn't a bad idea, but this was better. Lounging on Willa's sofa with their sock-clad feet side by side on her coffee table was a damn fine way to end the night.

The television blared reruns of *Whose Line Is It Anyway?* which was pretty much his favorite show. She'd been the one to pick it, flicking the remote until she found the right channel. He liked that they had this in common.

Grady grabbed the napkin and wiped his fingers one at a time. "Would you really have been into it if I'd suggested lounging in pajamas at your place for a first date?"

Willa chewed her bite of pizza and looked thoughtful. "Maybe. It would have given Stevie a chance to check you out and make sure you're not an ax murderer."

Hearing his name, the spotted white greyhound mix heaved himself off the dog bed beside the window and lumbered over to them. The dog looked like a cross between a giraffe and a lean polar bear, and Willa held out a piece of Canadian bacon for him.

"Good boy." Stevie bumped the edge of the coffee table with his leg and snuffled at the arm of the couch before locating the scrap she held out to him. He gobbled it down, then nosed Grady in search of more.

"It must be tough having a blind dog." Grady patted Stevie's rump as the pup's cloudy eyes fixed sightlessly on the pizza box. His sniffer worked just fine.

"He can see some shapes and light, I think," she said. "The vet says his vision is probably like if you took a pair of sunglasses and smeared the lenses with a thick coat of Vaseline."

Grady reached out to scratch behind the dog's ears. "He gets around pretty well, considering."

"He's learned to trust me." Willa reached out to scratch the dog's other ear, earning a groan of pleasure from Stevie. "I have a special short leash that makes it easier to go on walks, and he knows

I'm not going to run him into any trees or telephone poles."

"Smart dog." Grady was only just getting to know Willa, and he could already tell she was one of the most trustworthy people he'd met.

"The three-legged cat, on the other hand," Willa continued, "has been a challenge. The litter box thing took ages to figure out. And the deaf cat has her own set of issues."

Grady snorted. "You have a deaf cat and a three-legged cat?"

She nodded around another bite of pizza. "Earmuff and Wheelbarrow," she said. "Barrow for short. They're around here somewhere."

He shook his head in amazement as he grabbed another slice of pizza. "That's impressive," he said. "So you're a rescuer."

Willa shrugged. "They're the animals who needed homes the most," she said. "I happen to have a home."

She was so matter-of-fact about it that Grady might have thought it didn't matter. But it did matter. He'd seen the way she snuggled and cooed at Stevie when they'd arrived, prompting the dog to flop at her feet and groan in adoration. And she'd refused to sit down and eat until Stevie was fed and watered and had all his meds on board.

That was love. And seeing what it looked like in Willa made him even more interested in her. True, the fire had made for a bumpy first half of the date. But this... This was nice.

Way better than nice.

"Do you have any unbroken animals?" he asked.

"A beta fish named Carl," she said. "Well, he's unbroken now. He had his tail chewed to shreds by another beta, but it healed up once I got him out of that pet store. He sits on my desk when I'm working."

"Rescuer," Grady said again, more definitively.

"Human," Willa countered.

Grady shrugged, then bit into his next slice of pizza and surveyed the living room, trying to figure out what her home said about her. The little midtown bungalow was small but immaculate. The furniture showed its age, though someone had taken very good care of it. Every chair, every end table, looked like it had been polished and buffed and lovingly upholstered to be the very best version of itself.

The leather sofa where they sat was worn, but in a way that made it soft and smooth. The cushions wrapped around them like a hug, and Willa had dotted the corners with turquoise throw pillows and a bright-orange afghan draped over the back.

Grady returned his attention to Willa, who was a lot more interesting to look at than furniture. She'd changed out of her dress and into pale-blue leggings and a yellow tank top. He'd never say this to her, but she looked even hotter like this than she had in the fancy dress. Her hair was loose around her shoulders, and it was possible she'd ditched the bra when she ducked into her bedroom to change. He was trying not to stare.

"Can't say I've ever had a first date that involved a fire extinguisher," he said, biting into his slice of pizza. "Definitely one of my most memorable."

"The secondary grease fire was a nice touch," she said. "Too bad about the waitress's eyebrows."

"Sometimes casualties can't be helped." Grady polished off his pizza and wiped his hands on a napkin. "So have I earned a second date?"

Bored with the conversation and lack of pizza, Stevie the blind dog trudged away and settled onto his bed in the corner. Willa took another bite and made a big production of pretending to consider the question.

"Hmm." She finished chewing. "Pleasant conversation: check. Good meal: check. First-date heroics: check. I'd say your second date odds are good."

He laughed and reached for another slice. "You're a fan of heroics. Good to know."

"Only when well executed," she said. "And they have to be the right kind of heroics. If you'd gone around beating your chest over getting a good parking spot, I'd have been less impressed."

Grady gave her a grave nod. "How about opening a tight jar lid?"

Willa shook her head, lips twitching the way they seemed to when she fought back a smile. "Nope."

"Pulling on a black shirt without getting deodorant marks on it?"

She giggled, and it was the best damn sound Grady had ever heard. "Not heroic enough."

Grady pretended to frown. "How about replacing the toilet paper and making sure it's going the correct way."

Willa lifted one brow. "Which direction—over or under?"

"Over, of course," he said. "What do you think I

am, a savage?"

She laughed and shook her head. "That's certainly heroic, but no," she said. "Only true heroism counts. Like what you did tonight."

His ego shouldn't love that, but it did. So did the rest of him. "Good thing I paid the waitress to light the table on fire," he mused. "That was money well spent."

She laughed and tucked some stray hair behind her ear. "Well done, Smokey. Don't feel like you need to replicate it. I'd rather keep my furniture unburned."

"Noted." He picked up the bottle of beer she'd found for him in her fridge. It was an IPA, one of his favorites, but Willa was sticking to soda.

She nodded at the empty bottle. "You want another one?"

"I'm good." More than good with Willa cozied up next to him, so close her thigh brushed his. He wouldn't have minded another beer, but no way in hell did he want to lose the warmth of her body.

He glanced at his watch, grateful he didn't have to be at the base tomorrow. Three whole days off. It seemed like a luxury. Maybe he could sleep in.

When he looked up again, Willa was watching him. "Watching" wasn't the right word. *Studying*, like she was trying to peer inside his skull. He remembered their conversation back at the restaurant, the one about flaws. He hadn't ever answered, had he?

"I'm not good at saving money."

Willa blinked. "What?"

"That's one of my flaws." He tossed the napkin into the empty pizza box, then shifted on the couch so they faced each other. "I make decent money doing what I do, and the benefits are solid. That's an upside of a government job with the Forest Service."

"Okay," she said, tense all of a sudden.

"It's not like I have tons of debt or anything, but I'm not a great saver," he said. "I know I should be socking cash away in a money market account or something, and I know I should have a better plan for my future. I can't be a smokejumper forever."

Willa nodded. Her eyes held his, but they seemed guarded now. Shit, had he said too much? He was just trying for honesty, trying to spell out his faults as best he could.

"I'm sort of the opposite," she said. "A neurotic saver. A tightwad."

He waited for her to say more, but that was it. She wasn't meeting his eyes anymore, and he sensed he'd hit a tender spot. Something she didn't talk about with many people. Was this why she'd wanted to order the cheaper wine? And he'd kept pushing her, thinking she was just trying to be nice because he was paying. Apparently it went deeper than that.

*Way to kill the first-date vibe, asshole.*

But then she looked up at him and offered a small smile. "Probably a good thing we're only having two dates."

"Why is that a good thing?"

"Because we'd argue all the time about whether to go out for fancy meals or stay in and cook Top Ramen."

"Please." Grady snorted. "For most of the year, I eat Spam and freeze-dried meals out in the field. I can handle Top Ramen just as well as a fancy meal, as long as the company's good."

"And is it?" She held his eyes like this was a real question. Like she truly wanted to know.

"Tonight?" He set his empty bottle on the coffee table. "This goes down in my book as one of the top first dates in history."

"Really?"

"Yep."

She seemed to hesitate, dropping her gaze for an instant. When she looked at him again, something shifted. "Same," she said. "You're good company."

Well, that was something. A start. Not a promise of more than two dates, but why the hell would he want that? She was every guy's dream—the chance to have a nice time with a beautiful woman without being pulled down by the anchor of commitment.

How many times had he wished for exactly what Willa was offering? No strings, just a few good dates and then gone. He should be ecstatic. He should be putting the moves on her. He should be wooing her with stories about what a hero he was and—

"I'm an asshole in the morning," he blurted out.

So much for wooing. Or heroics.

Willa lifted an eyebrow. "What?"

"That's another one of my flaws," he said. "I'm a sound sleeper, and I hate waking up. Until I've had at least two cups of coffee, I'm like a grizzly bear with its leg caught in the door."

She laughed and set her soda down on an end table. "Good to know." She shifted on the couch, bringing one knee closer to his. He could touch it if he wanted to. Just reach over and cup her knee through the thin cotton of her leggings. He ached to do it. Just slide his hand up and—

"I mean, it really is handy information." Her voice had turned husky, and he looked up to see an unexpected heat in her eyes. "In case we ever have occasion to wake up together."

*Holy shit.*

Grady swallowed, not 100 percent sure he was reading this right. He could be a presumptuous asshole sometimes, which he probably should have listed as one of his faults.

"I didn't mean to imply—"

That's all he croaked out before Willa leaned in and kissed him. It started slow and gentle, giving him a chance to pull back if he wanted.

Like hell.

His response was primal. He forked a hand into her hair, kissing her hard and deep and leaving no question how much he wanted this. Wanted her.

Somehow, his hands found their way to her waist, and then he was lifting her up and pulling her onto his lap. She came willingly, thighs falling open on either side of him as she shifted so her perfect ass settled on his lap. He cupped it through her leggings, tracing the edge of her thong with his thumb. He must have been very, very good in some past life, because God, she felt amazing.

"Willa," he groaned against her mouth, and it sounded more like a desperate sigh. She murmured something back, circling her hips to grind against him. The leggings were so thin, he could feel the heat at her center, could sense her need as burning as his own.

He kept kissing her, tasting grape soda and spice

and the low simmering passion he'd felt stirring in her all night. If Willa Frank was serious about the two-date thing, she sure as hell made every date count.

Lucky him.

"You feel unreal." He broke the kiss to get those words out and to kiss his way down her throat. Her silky skin rippled under his tongue as she let her head fall back. He licked the hollow of her throat, hungry to taste more of her. To have his mouth on those lush breasts he'd been admiring all night.

She clutched the back of his head with an urgency he could read like subtitles on a skin flick. She wanted this as badly as he did.

"Grady," she said, and his name was a hungry growl. He peeled the straps of her tank top down both shoulders, baring her to him. What perfect breasts. Round and full and exactly the right size to cup in his hands. Her nipples pebbled with his breath, then tightened as he swirled his tongue around one and then the other. He moved between them, growing dizzy with sensation and heat and the haze of his own need. Fuck, she tasted sweet.

"More," he growled, gripping her hips.

She gave a soft squeak as he lifted her off his lap and eased her back onto the couch. Her hair fell over one eye, and she peered at him through the golden-brown curtain, looking rumpled and hungry and thoroughly debauched.

"I like where this is going." She grinned at him, tossing her hair.

"So do I." Boy, did he.

He gripped the waistband of her leggings,

drawing them slowly down her thighs. Her panties came along for the ride, baring her inch by glorious inch. Jesus, her skin was flawless.

He paused with the fabric bunched at her ankles, giving her a chance to halt things, to tell him he was moving too fast. He could slow it down if he had to. Hell, he could take all night.

*All fucking night.*

Willa tossed her hair again, letting her thighs fall apart. "I want you."

Or that.

Grady's mouth watered. He wanted her, too. Her sex was slick with the same need that had his cock straining at the front of his jeans. He'd never seen anything so fucking beautiful in his life.

Part of him wanted to rip the condom out of his wallet and bury himself to the hilt in ten seconds. The other part of him wanted to hit the slow-mo button, to savor her for hours…days, even.

Somewhere in the middle felt just about right. If their time together had an end date, he'd damn well make every minute count.

"I want to taste you." He tossed the leggings aside, checking to make sure he hadn't thrown them over a candle or hit a cat or something. It'd be just his luck after how the evening started. The urge to devour her overpowered him, and he was having trouble seeing straight. The only thing he wanted in the world was to bury his face between her thighs, then the rest of him if she was down with that.

He shouldered her thighs apart, lunging for her like a starving man.

"Oh, fuck, Grady." She gripped the back of his

head, clutching at his hair as he stroked the length of her with his tongue.

He ordered himself to tease, to take it slowly. But Christ, she tasted so sweet. And the way she was moving, arching her back like she was fucking his mouth. He couldn't get enough.

"That's it," he murmured as he teased her clit, gripping her hips as she bucked against him. "Show me how you like it."

She liked it fast and hard, apparently, and Grady was glad to oblige. Thrilled to devour her with the sort of hunger he couldn't hide if he wanted to. He sucked her soft folds, committing everything to memory. Her taste, her scent, the feel of her in his mouth. *Everything.*

When she tensed in his hands, he knew. It was crazy fast, but that was hardly a problem. He let go of her hip and dropped a hand between her thighs. As he slipped one finger inside her, Willa exploded.

"Grady!"

*Yes.*

He drove two fingers into her, feeling for that spot. The one he knew would take her to the next level. When he pressed against it, she shrieked and clutched his head.

"Oh my God—"

Her tight walls clenched and pulsed around him, squeezing his fingers as he fluttered his tongue over her until she went still in his hands.

*Holy smokes.*

He started to kiss his way up her body, to pull her against him for a breather. He was a helluva good snuggler, and pulling her soft and warm and pliable body against his chest sounded like a damn fine idea. He'd let her come down slowly.

But that's not what Willa wanted. She sat blinking at him through lust-crazed eyes, lips bee-stung and parted. She didn't bother bringing her legs back together, and Grady feasted his eyes on her, memorizing every curve, every ripple of muscle, every glorious, naked inch.

He'd never seen a more beautiful woman in his life.

Willa smiled, and his heart damn near melted.

"Tell me you have a condom," she breathed. "Because I need you inside me right now."

# CHAPTER FOUR

*I need you inside me right now.*

She sounded like a porn star. Willa couldn't believe the words coming out of her mouth, couldn't believe what she'd just done with a guy she barely knew.

But she couldn't stop doing it. Couldn't ignore the desperate need still plucking at her insides like fingers tugging threads from a sweater.

"I have a condom." Grady slid a hand into his back pocket to pull out his wallet.

A flush moved through her body as Willa realized she was practically buck naked, save the tank top shucked tubelike around her middle. Meanwhile, Grady was fully clothed. Even his shirt was unrumpled.

Better fix that.

Grabbing the hem of it, she pulled him down like a spider reeling in dinner. Grady laughed and let her tug the shirt up.

"I dig that you know what you want," he said as he helped her strip the shirt over his head. He handed her the condom and dragged the shirt over his arms, then reclaimed the prophylactic and tore it open.

"You're sure?" He held her eyes as he reached for his belt buckle.

Willa grabbed his button fly and yanked. "Do I look like I'm fighting you off?"

Still grinning, he helped her push the jeans down over his hips and toss them aside. "Just checking," he said. "Enthusiastic consent and all that."

She wrapped her legs around him as he rolled on the condom. "Is this enthusiastic enough for you?"

Digging her heels into the backs of his thighs, she drew him to her slippery center. He hovered there for a moment, the thick tip of him brushing her swollen folds.

"Willa," he groaned. "I've never known anyone like you."

*You don't know me now*, she thought as she pulled him inside.

He filled her in one slick stroke, and she gasped. He was big. It hadn't been obvious until he buried himself all the way, and she cried out from the shock of it.

"You okay?" he breathed and held still.

"Don't stop."

She gripped his shoulder blades to make sure of it, holding him to her as he moved in and out, setting a slow rhythm. He felt so good. It had been so long—

"Grady," she gasped as he stroked something incredibly sensitive inside her, and her body responded with shock waves of such intensity, they pulsed all the way to her toes. She bit down on his shoulder, so filled with pleasure, she thought she might burst.

This wasn't like her at all. Yeah, she'd had lovers. Not a lot, but enough to know a good one from a not good one.

Grady was more than good. He was...*holy fuck*.

Her subconscious fought the urge to think of him as different, special. He was just another guy. That was the point of the two-date rule. No attachment. Just no-strings fun, the way it should be.

So why was she here, gasping and groaning and writhing against him, feeling this unexpected base-level connection?

She dug her nails into his back, willing herself to get out of her head and into her body. There was too much sensation here to waste it, to spend even a second dwelling on scary thoughts.

The way he moved. And the things he was whispering in her ear, words she couldn't make out but understood on some primal level.

He drove in deeper, and Willa felt the tension building inside her, with every nerve in her body preparing for the inevitable. Already?

"I'm close," she gasped, as surprised by her own words as she was by the sensation itself. Christ, who was this wanton woman with a hair-trigger orgasm switch?

"That's it," he groaned. "Yes, Willa."

She cried out. Eyes closed, full-throated screaming with her head thrown back and white-hot flames blazing behind her eyelids. Sparks burst in the center of her chest as she clenched her thighs around him and screamed. *"Grady."*

He thrust deeper with a groan, and she realized he was right there with her, the same rhythm as the pulsing deep inside her. He drove in again and again as the waves of pleasure rippled outward like a brick tossed in a pool of molten lava.

She clung to him, and he carried them through the inferno and out the other side, both of them breathless and panting.

Then he went very, very still.

Willa breathed in. Out. In again. She lay there beneath his motionless body, wondering if he'd fallen asleep. Or died. Was he breathing? Definitely breathing. Should she check his pulse?

Grady drew up on his elbows and looked down at her. "What are you thinking?"

"Wondering if you'd died."

He laughed and rolled onto his side, pulling her with him so they faced each other on the couch. "I'm very much alive," he said, planting a kiss on her forehead. "Thank you for that."

"Thank *you*." She sounded like a restaurant patron accepting a soda refill, not like a woman who'd just had the best sex of her life. "Thank you very much."

Grady grinned and shifted away from her for a second, getting rid of the condom. She'd have to remember to toss that pizza box before one of the pets got to it.

He reached behind them and found the crocheted afghan she kept folded on the back of the couch. It was one of the few things Willa owned that her mother had made, one of the few precious mementos from her former life.

It felt like a hug as Grady wrapped it around them.

"You warm enough?"

She nodded and rested her head on his biceps. "Perfect."

They lay there together in silence for a long time, and Willa let her eyes drift shut. Somehow she synced her breathing with his, not even aware she was doing it until her breasts pushed forward at the same time that his chest moved into hers. As her heartbeat slowed, she decided this was as close to bliss as she'd been in a long time. Maybe ever.

"So you never make an exception?"

She blinked her eyes open, wondering if she'd drifted off and missed part of a conversation. "What?"

"To the two-date rule," he said. "You said at dinner that it's an ironclad rule, but I wondered if you ever let it slide to three or four or—"

"No," she said a little too abruptly. "Nope. Nuh-uh. Never."

She cringed at her own words, sure she'd offended him.

But he didn't look offended. Just curious. "How come?"

"It's easier that way," she said. "Less complicated when no one gets attached."

He lifted one eyebrow. "So you've never had a long-term relationship."

She hesitated, then gave him a ridiculous combination headshake and shrug. Sort of an unsure negative, which got a reaction.

"Seriously?" he said. "Not once in your— How old are you?"

"Thirty-one," she said, smacking him on the shoulder. "Didn't your mother tell you it's rude to ask a lady her age?"

"Since I just had sex with the lady, I'm thinking we've crossed into age-asking territory." He stroked a hand down her arm and back up again, making her shiver. "But really, you've never had a long-term relationship?"

"Once," she said, not sure how much to volunteer. Wasn't it bad manners to talk about other guys while lying naked with a man? "In my early twenties, way before I set the rule in stone."

He stroked her arm again, calling the goose bumps to the surface. "What went wrong?"

A shank of hair fell over one eye, and she blew it off her sweaty forehead. "Why do you assume something went wrong?"

And why did she feel defensive all of a sudden? She ordered herself to relax, to enjoy the pillow talk while she could.

"Well, you're not still with the guy," Grady pointed out. "So either you broke up for some reason or you lopped off his head with a cleaver and stuck it in your hall closet."

Willa glanced toward the foyer, which saved her from having to look him in the eye. "I told you not to look in there."

He laughed and stroked her arm again. "All right, I'll take the hint. You don't want to talk about old boyfriends."

"It's not that." She lifted her head off his arm, putting a tiny bit of distance between them. "I guess I just felt myself getting derailed."

"How?"

"By dating," she said. "By relationships, I mean. One or two dates and you can move on with no hard feelings. But take it beyond that, and things get messy."

"And you're not a fan of messy?"

"I'm not a fan of losing myself," she said. "Of losing sight of my goals or losing track of what I want out of life."

*I'm afraid of becoming my mother.*

*I'm afraid of dating my father.*

*I'm afraid of the unstable life their love created.*

She dropped her gaze from his so he couldn't read what she was thinking.

"Fair enough," he said, brushing the hair off her forehead. "I'm okay with the two dates."

"Good," she said. "Thanks."

The word sounded hollow, much different from the sex "thank-you" only a few minutes earlier.

"We've got one more to go. Better make it count." He planted a kiss on her forehead, then shifted against her. That's when she felt it. That slow thickening between them, the sign that Grady was ready to go again. With a start, she realized so was she.

*I should push him away*, she thought, even as she drew him to her. How the hell could she want him again?

Thank God she had condoms upstairs.

"So we'll make the most of our two dates," Grady said, kissing his way down her throat. "And then we'll shake hands and say goodbye."

"Perfect," Willa said, almost able to believe it.

• • •

"So you slept with the hottie firefighter." Kayla smirked as she reached across the table and swiped two of Willa's truffle fries. "Tell us everything."

"Don't leave out any details." Aislin grinned and stabbed her Caesar salad. "Especially the sex stuff."

"I'm not giving you details." Willa ignored the heat in her cheeks and swatted Kayla's hand away so she couldn't grab another fry. "I can't believe I even told you he spent the night."

Which was odd… Well, not odd that she'd told her girlfriends about knocking boots with Grady. Kayla lived just two blocks away, and the route for her morning run zipped right past Willa's house. Since it happened to be a morning Aislin had agreed to run with her, both ladies had been treated to the sight of Grady's truck pulling out of Willa's driveway at an hour that left little to the imagination.

She couldn't believe she'd let him stay over. *That* was the odd thing. While it wasn't one of her rules, it also wasn't something she usually did. Neither was first-date sex. None of this was like her.

So why the hell was she smiling?

"It was a good first date," she said carefully, taking a sip of her iced tea to cool the flames rising in her face.

"Which is why he'll get a second one." Kayla nodded her certainty, but Aislin's brow furrowed.

"And then what?" she asked.

Willa shrugged and picked up her burger. She took a big bite—ridiculously big—so she wouldn't have to answer right away.

But her friends weren't letting her off the hook. They sat watching her, Kayla with her chin in her hand and dark hair framing her face. Aislin's blue eyes stayed fixed on Willa, like she thought she might miss her response if she blinked.

Willa took another sip of iced tea. "So I was thinking if I get this RFP together for Tranquility

Villa, maybe the two of you could help me out with—"

Kayla smacked her palm on the table, jostling the ice in their glasses. "Oh no you don't. What happens after the second date?"

Willa sighed and reached for her burger again, but Aislin caught the edge of her plate with one manicured nail and dragged it out of reach. "Come on, Wills. When was the last time you let a guy stay over?"

"Or let a guy get past second base," Kayla added.

"Or got this moony look in your eyes when—"

"Stop." Willa grabbed her plate back, and Aislin didn't fight her. "Come on, you know the rule."

"Does he?" Aislin picked up a napkin and dabbed the ketchup Willa had dropped on the table without noticing.

Blame it on distraction. Blame *that* on Grady. She hadn't stopped thinking about him since—

"I made it pretty clear," Willa said. "He knows I don't get involved."

Kayla leveled her with a look. "Yeah, that part where you shagged him silly totally underscored how uninvolved you are." She swiped another fry, expertly dodging Willa's smack. "Way to hammer the point home."

Aislin snickered, while Willa did her best not to blush again. She *had* made it clear, right? And even if she hadn't, it wasn't a big deal. Most dudes saw the upside of not getting tied down. They seemed relieved when they learned she wouldn't be hounding them with texts or turning clingy. This was good for everyone, right?

Possibly recognizing Willa's need for a break—or

maybe just hell-bent on trying another tactic—Kayla changed the subject. "His band is playing again on Friday night at Boyton Ballroom," she said. "I saw it on the schedule. I've heard they're pretty good."

"That wouldn't count as a date," Aislin put in. "Just a bunch of girlfriends going to see a concert."

"It wouldn't count as a date," Willa agreed. "But I'm not going, so it's a moot point."

Both women scowled at her.

"Why wouldn't you go?" Kayla demanded.

Willa sighed and picked at her fries. Salt seeped into the paper cut on her pinkie finger, but she made a point not to flinch. "Because I have three proposals to finish before next week," she said. "This isn't a good time for me to be risking potential business."

Kayla and Aislin exchanged a glance. Willa knew that look well. It was the look that preceded these two dragging her to yoga or breathing classes under the pretense of needing to relax. She knew damn well they were only doing it for her.

"What?" she demanded, ready to get it over with. "Are you going to lecture me again about working too much?"

Aislin held up her hands in mock surrender. "Far be it from us to tell you how to run your life," she said. "But do you ever think there will be a point where you can ease up a little?"

"You've said yourself that you might be at max capacity with clients," Kayla added. "That you already have enough work to keep you plenty busy."

"And keep a roof over your head," Aislin added more softly. She stretched a hand out, and for a second, Willa thought she was going for the fries, too.

But she touched Willa's hand instead, offering a squeeze. "We're proud of you, Wills."

"For work stuff," Kayla added. "But also for boning the smokejumper."

Aislin grinned. "Especially for the smokejumper."

Willa tried not to show how much her friends' words meant to her. Not the stuff about shagging Grady. The part about her childhood. They knew where she'd come from—maybe not the depth of the poverty but the gist of it. They didn't know specifics about her mom. No one did.

She'd kept that secret to herself.

But they knew she'd grown up motherless. Penniless. Scared.

Which meant they understood why her career mattered so much. Mattered more than anything.

"So Friday evening." Willa sighed, already regretting throwing them a bone. "What time are we going to Boyton?"

Both women bounced in their chairs, excited as kids on Christmas morning. "The band goes on at seven," Aislin said. "If we get there early, we'll be able to ogle the smokejumpers from the front row."

"Grady plays lead guitar, right?" Kayla asked.

"Yeah," Willa admitted. "And sings. The rest of his bandmates are smokejumpers, too."

"Yummy." Aislin grinned. "So we'll go and hear some music and have a few drinks and keep it simple."

"Absolutely." Kayla nodded.

"All right," Willa said, wondering if she was already long past the point of keeping it simple.

# CHAPTER FIVE

Grady was halfway through the bridge of Bruce Springsteen's "I'm On Fire" when he spotted her.

Willa, out there in the crowd, flanked by the two women she'd been with the first night he met her. Crap, he'd forgotten their names. Kayla and—something with an A?

It didn't matter; his eyes were glued to Willa. She could be standing between Beyoncé and the Cookie Monster for all he knew. A surge of adrenaline rippled through him, and he closed his eyes, channeling all that energy into the song. His fingers flew over the frets as he wailed into the mic about longing and lust and desire so strong, it left you sleepless.

Basically, all the things that had been simmering under the surface of his skin since the night he slept with Willa. Since he left her house after a lazy pancake breakfast and a promise to call sometime.

That usually meant a few days, but idiot that he was, he ended up texting her two hours later. A text that went ignored until the following morning when she dashed off a perfunctory note about being really busy with work.

He thought she was blowing him off. Had still thought it up until the moment he spotted her in the crowd at his show. She wore a fitted black tank top and a little jean skirt, and the look she was giving him said this wasn't a coincidence. She'd come here to see him. To watch him play.

He leaned into the mic and delivered the song's final notes with gusto, mouth watering as he watched her hips sway to the music. She smiled at him, and Grady's voice wobbled as he remembered what it felt like to sink inside her.

*Damn, she's beautiful.*

The song wound down, and the drummer finished out the set with a flourish. Grady sang the final notes in a lust-fueled haze.

"That's all for this set," he said into the mic. "We're gonna take a quick break and we'll be back in a few minutes."

He turned to put his guitar in the rack, wondering if he should play it cool. His bandmates headed for the bar where the flirty waitress had been hooking them up with free drinks all night. Maybe he should wander over there and let Willa come to him.

But his feet carried him halfway across the floor before he could give them other orders, and suddenly, he was standing next to Willa and her friends.

"Hey, it's Smokey." The dark-haired one nudged Willa in the ribs and grinned. "We haven't been properly introduced, but I'm Kayla. Is it okay if we just keep calling you Smokey the Bare?"

Grady grinned, already liking Willa's friends. "I'll have it stitched on the back of my jump suit."

The curly-haired blonde laughed. "Gotta love Willa's gift for wordplay. I'm Aislin, by the way. Smokey does have a nice ring to it."

Willa looked ready to run and hide in the bathroom, but she managed a nervous eye roll instead. "Very funny," she told them. "You know damn well his name is Grady."

Kayla made a half-hearted effort to wipe the smile off her face, but her somber look wasn't too convincing. "That's about *all* we know."

"Willa's not the sharing sort," Aislin put in. "But we saw your truck pulling out of her driveway and put two and two together."

Grady glanced at Willa, on the brink of commenting that he found her to be pretty damn sharing, but the discomfort in her eyes had him holding back. "I don't kiss and tell."

Willa glared at her girlfriends. "Weren't you two headed to the bar?"

Kayla eyed him some more while Aislin glanced back toward where his bandmates had headed. "The line's not bad yet."

"It will be," Willa insisted. "Better hurry."

Aislin winked at him. "We can take a hint." Still grinning, she grabbed Kayla's arm and towed her away before Grady could pepper them with questions about Willa.

Did it mean anything that she'd talked with them about him? Not much, clearly, but if she was as tight-lipped as they claimed she was, maybe it meant something that they were treating him with friendly flirtation.

*Stop grasping at straws.*

"Sorry," Willa offered as soon as her friends were out of earshot. "Does the Smokey the Bare humor annoy the crap out of you?"

"Not at all." He stuck his hands in his pockets, determined to play this as cool as she was, though he had a killer urge to touch her. "Did you know it's actually just Smokey Bear?"

Willa frowned. "What?"

"Smokey Bear, not Smokey *the* Bear," he said. "That's the name of the Forest Service mascot."

She stared at him, those deep green eyes perplexed. "Did you just mansplain a fictional bear to me?" Her words were more teasing than offended, and she cocked her head to the side and looked at him. "Wait, is there seriously no 'the' in the title? It's just Smokey Bear?"

"Yep," he said, wondering if his knowledge of fire-suppression geekery made him more or less interesting · to her. "The Forest Service launched Smokey Bear in the early forties to urge people to help prevent wildfires," he said. "In the early fifties, Eddy Arnold had this big hit song called 'Smokey *the* Bear.'"

"See? I knew I'd heard it with a 'the' in there." Willa shifted a little, moving close enough that he could graze her elbow with his fingertips if he wanted to. God, he wanted to, but he held back. No sense acting like a possessive douchebag.

"Apparently, the songwriters just thought the rhythm flowed better with 'the' added," he said. "But the Forest Service is always reminding people that's not the real name. It's just Smokey Bear." He grinned, fully aware he sounded like a dork but finding it hard to care. "It's one of those PR things that drives people batty."

She laughed, and the sound gave Grady a warm glow in the pit of his stomach. "You're a font of useful trivia, Smokey."

"I do my best."

Willa tipped her chin toward the stage. "You

sounded really good up there. You're a man of many talents, huh?"

"So it was good for you, too?" He grinned as her face turned pink again. "Or were you not making a sex joke?"

"No, I wasn't." She glanced around, a tiny ghost of a smile tugging the edges of her mouth. "But yeah, it was good. Stupendously amazing, if you want the truth."

*Hot damn.*

It was all Grady could do to refrain from doing a fist bump or asking why she hadn't called him back. None of those things would win him any cool points or get him any closer to setting that second date.

"When do you fly out again?" she asked, seemingly eager to change the subject.

"I'm on duty at the air base in a couple of days," he said. "Whether I fly out depends on whether fires start popping up, but this time of year, they always do."

"How long are the shifts?"

"Eight hours a day on base, but we'll go for twenty-four hours straight if we're out on a fire," he said. "Sometimes longer. Forest fires don't exactly follow a time clock."

"Sounds brutal," she said.

"It can be," he admitted, shuffling his feet to stand just a half inch closer to her. "We're on duty for twenty-one days at a stretch, but if we're out on a fire, they don't want us going more than fourteen days without a break. Usually just a day or two, but it's something."

"And you do that all summer?"

"Longer than that." The crowd bumped him from

behind, pushing him closer to Willa. It was his first time feeling grateful for being jarred. "The season starts early, sometimes in March. And the way the climate's been lately, I can get sent out to fires in California as late as December."

"Wow." She sounded genuinely shocked. "That's a long time to be on."

"It's even longer when I do Australia's fire season," he admitted. "I could pretty much work all year if I wanted to."

"Do you want to?"

"Sometimes." He shrugged. "I love the job. I love traveling around the country knocking out forest fires before they can get bad. I love the camaraderie. And I love the feeling of jumping out of the plane, having the world spinning around me and the wind howling."

Someone jostled her from behind, and Willa tipped forward into him. He caught her easily, thrilled by the excuse to touch her. He took his time letting go.

"Jumping out of a plane sounds terrifying," she said.

He smiled. "There's this moment right after the chute deploys, just after the bounce, when everything goes silent… You're just drifting through space with nothing but the sound of your heartbeat thudding in your ears."

"I can't imagine that." She shook her head. "You couldn't pay me enough to jump out of an airplane."

"It's a good job," he said. "Just not one I can do forever."

"Physically, you mean?"

"Yeah." He shrugged, oddly self-conscious about discussing his career with her. "Smokejumping's a young man's gig. It's rough on your body, so you've gotta think ahead to what you'll do when the aches and pains make it too dangerous to keep jumping."

"And what will you do?"

He thought about what he'd admitted during their first date. His silly fantasy about running a bakery. It was more a joke than anything, just something to amuse himself with on sleepless nights.

The truth was a lot less amusing.

"I don't really know." His voice sounded tight, and he ordered himself to ease up. "I'm not big on making plans."

She stared at him like he'd just spoken Yiddish. "Like—for your future?"

This seemed not to compute for a woman hell-bent on planning everything, even the number of dates she'd grant a guy before they'd had even one.

Grady shrugged, wondering how quickly he could change the subject. "Some guys end up becoming pilots when they're done jumping. It's a natural transition, and you get to keep your benefits."

He was just spewing words now, and the way she watched his face told him she knew damn well there was more to the story.

More, like the fact that planning for the future scared the ever-loving shit out of him. Like the fact that somewhere in the back of his brain, he knew a job as dangerous as his meant there might not *be* a future.

It was all he could do to keep his face impassive, to let none of that fear show in his eyes. "Anyway, I'll keep working the double seasons as long as I can," he said, raking his fingers through his hair. "Summer season here, then southern hemisphere in the off-season. The money's good."

Willa nodded. "Gotta build up that nest egg."

Before he could respond, her friends reappeared, each of them clutching two glasses.

"The waitress asked me to give you this," Aislin said, handing him a glass. "Said it's your favorite."

"Thanks." He took a sip and yep, it was his favorite IPA.

"Tell us about yourself, Grady," Kayla chimed in. "We're dying to know more about any guy who gets into Willa's pants on a first date."

"Not an everyday occurrence, in case you're wondering," Aislin said. "You must be something special?"

She posed it like a question, and Grady couldn't figure out if he was expected to rattle off a list of things that made him special. He couldn't come up with anything, so he was grateful when Willa rescued him.

"Cut it out." She whacked her friend on the shoulder, making her slosh some of the drink she gripped in one hand. "You're embarrassing the guy."

Unembarrassed, Grady appreciated the rescuing anyway. "Willa's amazing," he said, resisting the urge to slip an arm around her waist. That would be too relationship-y, and they weren't doing that.

But still, he brushed her hand with his. "The job keeps me gone a lot, so I don't have a lot of time for dating."

Aislin studied him as she handed one of the drinks to Willa. "Then the two of you should get along great," she says. "Willa's not big on relationships."

"So I've heard." He smiled at her and felt his chest squeeze when she smiled back.

Kayla made a clucking sound. "That look right there confirms you weren't sleeping on her couch the other night."

Aislin laughed. "Like there was any doubt. You think he slept over so he could reboot her computer or organize her spice cupboards?"

Kayla smiled and sipped her drink. "So that's what the kids are calling it these days."

Grady gulped his beer, enjoying this a helluva lot. They were teasing her, sure, but he didn't get the sense she minded all that much. And from what he knew of Willa, she had to be every bit as good at dishing it out.

He looked at her over the rim of his glass. "The band's all going to the Ramble Inn after the show," he said. "You three are welcome to join us."

Aislin shot a look toward the stage where the drummer—a third-year smokejumper named Ryan—was adjusting something on his kit. "If your friends are coming, I'm in."

"I'm game." Kayla eyed Tony, the bass player and one of Grady's best friends on the crew. "You boys have obviously been eating your Wheaties."

Grady laughed. "Blame the hour of mandatory PT every morning." He glanced at Willa. "So how about it? Is it a date?"

Willa quirked an eyebrow at him. "We're having our second date at a dive bar?"

Wait, no.

Shit.

Grady glanced at Willa's friends, hoping they'd back him up on this. "Actually, it wouldn't be a real date," he said. "Your friends will be there; my friends will be there—it's really more of a group hangout."

"Excellent point." Aislin flashed him a smile. "It's no different than what we're doing right now, and obviously *this* isn't a date."

"Obviously," Kayla agreed.

He'd have to remember to send flowers to both of them. Or maybe just introduce them to his buddies.

Willa folded her arms over her chest, pushing her breasts up in a deliciously distracting display. "So this *won't* be a second date?"

"Nope," he said. "Guess we'll have to do that some other time. Maybe when I'm off again in a few weeks?"

"All right." She eyed him oddly, and he honestly couldn't tell if she was annoyed or excited about the prospect. Maybe a little of both.

From the corner of his eye, he saw his bandmates reassembling onstage. It was time to get his ass back up there. "Will I see you at the Ramble Inn?"

"Maybe." Willa surveyed the rest of the band. "As long as you tell me those guys are all fine, upstanding citizens who won't roofie my friends' drinks or grope them without consent."

"There will be no roofie-ing and no nonconsensual groping," he assured her. "Mostly because they're not like that, but also because I'd junk-punch anyone who pulled that kind of shit."

"Then we have a date."

"No," he said, backing toward the stage. "Definitely not a date."

She saluted him as he ran back and hopped up onstage. He strapped on his guitar and started for the mic, then stopped himself. Turning back to his bandmates, he gestured them to huddle up.

"What?" Tony muttered, adjusting his bass.

"Slight tweak to the set list," he said. "Help me out with this one."

He named the song, promised to buy all the beer at the Ramble Inn if they went with it, then turned and stepped up to the mic.

"This next one goes out to Willa Frank," he said.

He strummed a few chords, finding the right key. Then he hit the pedal and cranked it up to eleven with a metal version of "Smokey the Bear."

Finding Willa in the crowd, he locked eyes with her as he belted out the words. "Smokey the Bear," he sang. "Prowlin' and a growlin' and a sniffin' the air."

What had started as an innocent kids' jingle became something altogether sexier as he howled the lyrics against the scream of the electric guitar. Out on the floor, Willa was laughing, but there was heat in her eyes. If she were any other woman, he'd be patting himself on the back right now, thinking his odds of getting laid were strong.

But she was Willa—beautiful, unpredictable, totally unique Willa—so all the rules flew out the window.

Grady closed his eyes and delivered the next verse with his heart pounding in his ears.

• • •

As it turned out, only Tony and a young rookie named Jimmy could make it out that night. Ryan had a date, Pete was coming down with something, and Archer was dead on his feet after ten days working a fire in Southern California.

Grady herded Tony and Jimmy inside like a prison guard escorting his charges into the cafeteria.

"Tell me again why it's so important we go on this date with you," Jimmy grumbled as they headed for their usual table in the back corner of the bar.

"It's not a date," Grady said. "It's a gathering. Come on, we do this every time we play Boyton."

Tony snorted. "Yeah, but you're not usually this jacked up about it."

True, though it annoyed Grady that they'd noticed.

"Whoa, the new bartender's hot." Jimmy nodded at the cute redhead behind the bar, who smiled back even bigger when her gaze snagged on the "Hart Valley Smokejumper" logo printed across his T-shirt.

Grady resisted the urge to whack Jimmy on the back of the head. The kid was still at that newbie stage where he got off on having women swoon when they found out what he did for a living. He hadn't reached the stage yet where the girlfriends dropped like flies after discovering just how seldom a smokejumper stuck around. Being alone all the time was a definite downside of latching on to someone in this profession.

So was the constant worry that your significant other might not come home at all.

"Isn't that your girl?" Tony's voice jarred Grady's attention off the bartender and over to the opposite side of the room.

Willa strode through the door, and Grady's heart lurched into overdrive. Kayla and Aislin strolled in behind her, but Willa stole the show as far as Grady could see. Cheesy as hell, but it was like a spotlight shone down on her, illuminating her path from the door to the bar. He stared, admiring the sway of her hips, the fullness of her mouth, the way her hair brushed shoulders bared by the black tank top she wore. He couldn't see her eyes from here, but he didn't have to. The precise shade of sunlit greenish-brown had been burned into his brain.

"She's hot." Jimmy grinned and waved the women over. "They're all hot. Which one's yours, Grady?"

He glared at the younger man. "They're not property, asshole."

"Brunette in the black top," Tony supplied. "She's the reason we're not calling this a date."

Jimmy looked confused. "She boiled his bunny or something?"

"For fuck's sake," Grady muttered and started toward the women. Toward Willa.

Her eyes found his before he got halfway across the room, and a slow smile spread over her face. "Hey," she said. "Got a table?"

"Over in the corner." He hooked a thumb toward the big booth he and the guys usually nabbed after a show. "Can I get you something at the bar?"

"Beer," Willa said, and Grady liked her even more. "I'll come with you to help carry."

"Let me give you cash." Aislin dug through her purse and pulled out a twenty. "You want beer, too, Kayla?"

"Yes, please." Kayla's attention was fixed on Tony, and Grady couldn't tell if her response was for the beer or for the tall smokejumper with rumpled black hair and dark eyes that seemed to make women crazy.

Good. Maybe if their friends were distracted, he could spend more time chatting up Willa. She'd already started for the bar, making a beeline in that direction, tempted to put his hand on the small of her back. They'd been naked together, so physical contact wasn't outside the realm of possibility.

But something in her posture had him shoving his hands in his pockets. Something about the way her eyes swiveled back and forth, surveying the bar like she expected a pack of zombies to leap from behind the jukebox at any moment.

"You okay?" he asked.

"Yeah, great." Her response was a little too bright. "This place used to be something else, didn't it?"

"Years ago," he said, surprised she remembered. "Some kind of lottery machine dive bar, I think. More dive-y than it is now, if you can imagine."

"It's not so bad. They're obviously trying to spruce things up with the fresh paint and flowers on the tables."

Her voice had gone tense and brittle. Grady watched her face, trying to understand the shift. Did she remember this place?

She must have read the question in his eyes. One bare shoulder lifted in an odd little half shrug. "My dad used to come here when I was little," she said. "I had to wait in the car when my mom went in to get him."

Which would have made Willa tiny, since she'd mentioned losing her mom when she was young, and he knew for a fact that this place ditched the lotto games about twenty-five years ago. The tension in her shoulders was a good indication these weren't happy memories she was dredging up here. "We can go if you want," he said. "Find someplace else."

"No, it's good." She straightened her back. "Let's order."

They stepped up to the bar, and Willa leaned in, studying the tap handles. "I'll have three of the Boneyard IPAs, please."

"Make it six," Grady said. "Keep it simple and hoppy."

He pulled out a credit card while Willa handed over Aislin's cash and some of her own. She left a generous tip, which impressed him again. She might be a self-professed tightwad, but she didn't scrimp when it mattered.

"Did you put this on?" she asked.

"Put what on?"

She nodded to the jukebox. "'Light My Fire.' The Doors, right? Seems like a smokejumper kinda song."

He laughed as the bartender handed them two trays—one for him, one for Willa. "We're usually more interested in putting them out," he said. "But I get your point. You're talking about the Springsteen song we did back at Boyton?"

"Right. 'I'm On Fire.'" She grinned. "I guess it takes on a different meaning when you've got a bunch of smokejumpers playing it."

"You're giving me ideas for a set list," he said as

they started toward the table, each of them carrying a tray. "Maybe 'Light My Fire' by The Doors, followed by 'Sex on Fire' by Kings of Leon."

That earned him a devilish grin from Willa. "How about 'Burning for You' by Blue Oyster Cult?"

"I like it," he said. "We could kick in a little country with some Johnny Cash, 'Ring of Fire.'"

"Or embrace your feminine mystique with Barbra Streisand's 'Smoke Gets In Your Eyes,'" she suggested. "Maybe follow that up with Diana Ross's 'Fire Don't Burn.'"

"I don't think I have that kind of vocal range, but I admire your faith in us."

They'd reached the table, and everyone shifted around to make room. Kayla was cozied up to Tony in the middle, while Jimmy straddled a chair he'd stuck at the head of the table, chatting up Aislin.

There was an open gap on one end of the round booth, so Grady slid in first to make room for Willa beside him.

"Nice," Willa said as she took a seat. "Letting me have the end so I have unrestricted access to the jukebox and bathroom."

"Who says chivalry is dead?" He handed out beers as Tony accepted a heaping basket of Cajun tots he must have ordered from one of the circulating servers. He set them in the center so everyone could reach, then stuck his hand out to Willa.

"Tony Warren," he said. "Kayla was just telling me you do web design?"

"That's right," she said. "I own Frank Solutions. I've been running it for about six years."

Tony whistled. "Impressive. We've been thinking

about doing a website for the band. You have samples we could check out sometime?"

She smiled and pulled a business card out of her wallet. "There's a whole gallery you can browse," she said. "I offer friends and family discounts, too."

"She did mine for my photography business," Kayla put in. "She figured out more than seventy percent of my web visits were coming in from mobile devices, so she did this whole mobile optimization thing and presto—bookings are going through the roof."

Tony pocketed Willa's card. "I'll check it out."

Willa smiled and took a sip of her beer. "All three of you are smokejumpers?"

"Yes, ma'am." Jimmy grinned, laying on the small-town charm as thick as he could. "I was a Hotshot for five years out of college. Got an opportunity to join the smokejumpers last year, so I jumped at the chance."

"Pun intended?" Grady put in dryly.

"Right." Jimmy directed his aw-shucks smile at Aislin, whose focus was still half on her phone. "I'm technically a snookie this year."

"Snookie?" Aislin cocked her head. "Like Jersey Shore?"

Jimmy laughed. "Second-year rookie. There were only three of us brought in last year. It's pretty competitive."

Aislin looked appalled rather than impressed. "There are that many guys lining up to jump out of planes into fires?"

"You'd be amazed." Jimmy shrugged and lifted his beer. "And we're not actually jumping *into* fires.

Just near them."

Tony grabbed a tot from the basket. "'Course, all it takes is a shift in the wind and—"

"We do a lot of training," Grady interrupted, noticing Willa had gone pale. "To prevent accidents. The safety precautions we all take are pretty over-the-top."

A little color returned to her face, but she still looked unsure. "How long have you two been doing it?"

The question seemed directed at Tony and him, and since Tony had just shoved two tater tots in his mouth, Grady took it.

"We've worked together more than a decade," he said. "Four years on a Hotshot crew, then this."

"I spent an extra year with the ground crew," Tony added. "Got a little brother who spent two years with the Hart Valley Hotshots, so I stuck around to make sure he got settled in."

There was more to that story than Tony had shared, but Grady knew better than to offer it up. It wasn't his place.

Aislin picked at a tater tot. "So all the guys in the band are smokejumpers?"

"Yep," Tony said. "Pete, the other guy on guitar—he's the base manager—he's been there the longest. Coming up on fifty and still jumping."

"And Ryan's the drummer," Grady put in. "This is his third year jumping."

Tony took a drink from his beer. "There are other guys who fill in when they can," he said. "Bobby McKillop wasn't there tonight—he's out on a fire in Nevada—but he plays stand-up bass. He's usually there when I can't make it, or sometimes we're both there for an extra thumpin' show."

"Impressive." Willa looked at Grady. "So you all just happen to be musical, or are musically inclined people just drawn to smokejumping?"

"I never really thought about it." He spun his beer on the table, wishing they were alone together. Maybe in her living room with her dog and a pizza and her bare feet on his lap while he stroked his hand up her thigh. "I guess it's one of those things that helps break up the tension," he said. "Gives us something to occupy our minds while we're waiting to get called out."

"Beats knitting?" Her smile told him she was kidding, which meant she didn't know how smokejumpers really spent most of their downtime.

"Come visit the base sometime," he said. "We'll show you our needle skills."

"Oh?" Her smile was flirty. "Is this like showing me your etchings?"

"Pretty much."

There was still tension in her shoulders. He suspected it had something to do with what she'd said earlier, about her mother dragging her dad out of this place. What kind of memory must that have created for her as a kid? He wanted to ask, but now didn't seem like the right time.

"You guys come here a lot?" she asked.

"Whenever we play Boyton," Grady said. "Which is pretty often. This was sort of an anniversary for us."

"How so?" she asked.

"Our one hundredth time playing there."

"Oh shit." At the head of the table, Jimmy blanched. "Fuck."

Grady frowned at him. "You okay?"

"A-Anniversary," he sputtered, jumping out of his chair. "Shit, today's my one-month anniversary dating Baylee."

Tony cocked his head. "You mean Braylee?"

"Braylee," Jimmy amended, shoving in his chair. "Fuck, I've gotta go. I promised we'd do something."

If Aislin was annoyed, she didn't show it. Instead, she grabbed the mason jar of flowers off the center of the table and waved to a passing waitress. "How much are these?"

The waitress blinked. "They're not really for sale."

"Twenty bucks?" Aislin nodded to Jimmy, who obediently took out his wallet.

"I'll give you forty if I can keep the jar," he said.

The waitress shrugged and pocketed the cash. "No skin off my nose," she said. "It came from The Dollar Store, I think."

"You're a lifesaver." Jimmy grabbed the vase and offered a sharp salute meant for all of them. "Good meeting you. Grady, I'll see you at the base next week."

"See ya."

And then he was gone, leaving Grady with one less wingman.

Tony laughed and went right back to chatting with Kayla. Aislin picked up her phone again and started typing like crazy, so Grady turned his attention back to Willa.

"How's Stevie doing?" he asked.

Willa smiled, her face lighting up at the mention

of her dog. "He's great. Had his annual vet visit yesterday. He knocked over a bowl of biscuits and ate about twenty of them before the vet tech got him corralled."

"Atta boy." Grady stretched his arms out over the back of the booth, aware of Willa's hair brushing his hand. "I never did get to meet your cats," he said. "Earmuff and Barrow?"

She smiled and sipped her beer. "Meeting cats is a big step," she said. "Meeting the fish is even bigger. Really more of a second-date thing."

"Which this isn't," he reminded her. "This doesn't count toward your two-date rule."

"Noted," she said as she set down the beer.

It occurred to Grady that the rest of the table had tuned them out. Aislin's thumbs were still flying over her phone, texting someone less boring than them. Kayla was practically on Tony's lap, talking intimately about music and favorite bars and the normal getting-to-know-you stuff.

Grady smiled, recalling how he and Willa had flipped that practice on its head. Such an epic first date. Was it any wonder he wanted another? And another and another and—

Willa shifted, and her hair brushed his hand like silk. She leaned close, and Grady leaned, too, so near he could smell her perfume. "Is Tony single?" she whispered.

"Yeah. As far as I know."

"Because obviously the other guy—"

"Jimmy?"

"Right." Willa cleared her throat. "Jimmy turned out to have a girlfriend, so I wondered about Tony.

He's a good guy?"

An unexpected bubble of jealousy wiggled up through his chest. "Yeah," he said. "The best."

He tried not to picture Willa out on a first date with him or a second—

"Seems like he and Kayla are hitting it off," she whispered. "So I wanted to make sure."

Oh.

*Dumb-ass.*

He picked up his beer and took a slow sip. "Tony's great," he said. "I'd trust him with my life."

"Good," she said. "That's good." She glanced at Aislin, who was still fiddling with her phone. "Kayla—uh—got pretty burned."

Aislin snorted but didn't look up. "Might have to clarify there, Wills. You're talking to a firefighter."

"Burned by love," Willa added, shooting a sheepish look at Grady before glancing at her friend. "So I want to make sure Tony's not going to pull some dick move like stringing her along and ghosting her or something."

"He's one of the nicest guys I know," he said. "She's in good hands."

"Good hands," Aislin repeated, still staring at her phone but clearly following the conversation. "That's a selling point for Kayla."

Willa smiled and grabbed a tater tot from the basket in the middle of the table. Her gaze shifted to Grady's hands, which were wrapped around his glass. She stared for a moment, and Grady wondered what she was thinking. Did she remember the way his hands had felt gliding down her body, moving between her legs—

"No way!" Across the table, Kayla shot up straight in her chair. "You're not serious."

"Dead serious," Tony said. "They're playing at the Polka-Dot tonight. They're going on late, maybe nine?"

"How did I not know this?" she said. "They're, like, my favorite band."

Willa frowned. "Who?"

"Polydactyl Pumpkin," Kayla said, shaking her head at Tony. "I've been following them for years. They're seriously in town tonight?"

Tony glanced at his watch. "We could hurry and make it."

Kayla glanced at Willa, biting her lip. "I don't want to ditch everyone."

"We'll be fine," Willa said. "It's not like we need a babysitter."

"You're sure?"

"Positive."

"Go," Aislin said, glancing up from her phone. "That's been your bucket list band for years. You'll regret it if you don't."

"Come on," Tony said. "The owner loves me. I'll bet I could get us backstage if you want to meet them."

"Holy crap, I can't believe this." Kayla jumped up, and Tony followed, looking downright joyful.

He glanced back at Grady. "Catch you at the base later?"

"See you there."

And then they were gone. Willa stared at the door for a moment, then looked at Aislin. "Everything okay with you?"

"Yeah," she said. "Well, no. It's my sister."

"Ugh. Sorry." Willa made a face, which told Grady everything he needed to know about that relationship. "What does she want?"

"To stay with me tomorrow," Aislin said. "Which means I should probably get home and clean."

"Wait." Grady sat up straight. If Aislin left, he'd be alone with Willa. He liked the idea in theory, but wouldn't that make this a date?

He was just getting to know her. Even if this had no chance of getting serious, no way was he ready for Willa to walk out of his life.

"We haven't even been here thirty minutes," he pointed out. "Can I get you another beer?"

Aislin frowned. "What?"

"Another beer, or how about some french fries?" He tried to catch the server's attention, but no dice. Shit, Aislin couldn't leave…

"Tell me about yourself," he said to Aislin, conscious of Willa exchanging a baffled look with her friend. "Willa said something about skincare?"

"Yes," Aislin said slowly. "Did you want to make an appointment for a facial?"

If that would keep him from wasting date number two like this, he'd subject himself to any manner of services. "Uh, sure—that sounds…great."

Willa grinned. "Maybe you can do a firefighter special."

Aislin quirked an eyebrow and studied him appraisingly. "I do have some special soap made with volcanic ash," she said. "I also offer a pedicure called Fire and Ice."

"He can make it a spa day," Willa said, grinning

like she was enjoying this way too much.

Grady tried to think of something else to talk about. "Movies," he said. "Seen any good movies lately?"

Aislin looked at him, then at Willa. "Is this some kind of setup for a threesome?" she asked. "Because Willa's my friend, and I think it would be weird to—"

"What?" Grady jumped. "No, that's not it."

Willa burst out laughing. Grady turned to see her shaking her head at Aislin. "Just a guess, but I don't think he's trying to get into your pants, Ais." She swiped at her eyes, still laughing. "If you leave, it'll just be the two of us."

Aislin frowned. "And?"

"And that makes it a date."

"Oh. *Ohhh.*" Aislin's expression softened as she glanced back at him. "Awww."

"Shit," Grady muttered, raking a hand through his hair. "This is dumb."

Aislin grinned. "No dumber than you thinking I should stick around and be your chaperone. What is this, Regency England?"

Willa gave him a teasing smile. "I mean, technically, being alone in a bar would be a date…"

"Help me out here, Aislin," he said. "I'll buy you another drink to stick around. Or dinner. Have you had dinner?"

"Hmm." She seemed to consider that. "How about your drummer's phone number?"

"Deal." He yanked out his phone, already scrolling for Ryan's number.

Willa snorted. "Are you seriously pimping out your friend?"

"It's no biggie; Ryan's single." He located the number and looked at Aislin. "What's your number? I'll text it to you."

She ignored him and looked at Willa. "Are you messing with him right now, or can I leave?"

Willa shrugged and looked at him. "I guess it wouldn't be a date." She bit her lip, ready to second-guess herself. "We'd just be finishing our beers and calling it a night."

Grady nodded, vowing to drink his as slowly as possible. "Definitely not a date."

Aislin stood up, shaking her head. "You two need some serious therapy."

And then she was gone.

And then they were alone.

But not on a date, dammit.

"You want to go back to my place and meet my cats?" Willa smiled.

Grady shook his head. "Nope."

"Really?"

He picked up his beer and took a sip. "You said earlier that meeting cats was a second-date ritual."

"I was kidding." She leaned back against him, snuggling closer and making his pulse kick up.

"I'm sensing a trap here." Grady resisted the urge to touch her hair. "Besides, if I leave you wanting, doesn't it up my odds of more dates?"

She folded her arms over her chest and stared at him. "No, but why do you even want more dates? You said yourself you're not looking for anything serious."

He had said that, hadn't he? But that was before he'd gotten to know her. He *still* wanted to know her.

To find out more about what made her tick.

"I'm not after a relationship, if that's what you're worried about." He clutched his pint glass, not sure if he was reminding himself or her. "The sex was good, right?"

Willa blinked. "Um—"

"Actually, I believe the words you used earlier were 'stupendously amazing.'"

"Well, yes, but—"

"And I agree," he said. "So we should either negotiate for more dates, or make sure we never actually hit that second date."

"You're a strange guy, Grady Billman." She didn't sound too upset about that.

"Maybe." Grady breathed in the scent of her hair, loving the chance to be alone with her at last. "But I'm not taking any chances on canceling out our last date."

"For a guy who jumps out of airplanes for a living, you're very risk averse."

"Only with the things that matter." He drained the last of his beer and signaled the waitress, determined to settle in. Determined to make this the best non-date either of them had ever had.

# CHAPTER SIX

Less than two weeks later, Willa gripped the steering wheel and turned off the highway toward the airport, wondering what the hell she was doing.

*You're getting attached.*

The warning from her subconscious was both unwelcome and untrue. Come on, this was just a friendly visit. Grady—her *friend* Grady—had mentioned how the Hart Valley Air Center was open for public tours, and had she ever been out to see it in person?

Willa had not. And as a resident of Hart Valley—and a citizen with an interest in public safety—she owed it to herself to take a tour, to get a sense of how the base operated and what was involved in fire suppression efforts launched from this Central Oregon base.

*Keep telling yourself that.*

"Shut up," Willa muttered as her phone buzzed on the passenger seat.

She glanced over at it and saw the name on the readout. Pinpricks of unease poked her arms.

*Dad.*

Gripping the wheel tighter with one hand, she reached over with the other and hit the button to accept the call.

"Willie!" Her father's voice echoed through the little Toyota, filling the air with his cigarette growl and the imagined smell of cheap beer. "Been trying to reach you all week, sweetheart."

Willa tightened her fingers on the wheel and stared straight ahead at the road, determined not to miss any turns. "I've been working."

"That's my girl. Such a hard worker." The harsh rasp in his voice gave the words a sort of mobster effect, and she imagined him sitting there with a glass of cheap whiskey in his hand.

No, Pabst Blue Ribbon. It wasn't noon yet, and beer came before cheap whiskey. Her father was a man of principle.

"Wish I could be working." Her father sounded wistful and far away.

"How's the job hunt going, Pops?"

"Oh, you know."

Willa did know, which was why she always hated this conversation. Hated it but kept having it over and over again.

"You don't have to say it," her father said. "I know I wasn't supposed to quit one job without another lined up, but what can I say? The boss was an asshole."

Willa closed her eyes, then opened them again because she was driving and didn't want to die.

But she also didn't want to hear her father's excuses. The boss was a normal guy who wasn't a fan of his employees showing up falling-down drunk to operate a forklift. Clearly that made the guy an asshole.

Willa bit back that comment. "Did you make it to your doctor's appointment yesterday?" she asked. "The one I marked on your calendar on the fridge."

"Aw, hell." Another slosh of liquid. "I knew I

forgot something."

"Dad." Willa bit her lip and gave up arguing. What was the point? She'd just have to make a new appointment, maybe take time off to bring him there herself.

"Have you been staying away from the casino?" she asked instead.

She didn't know why she bothered asking. Yes, no, the answer didn't matter. The truth was that her father spent every waking hour there that he could.

"That's actually what I wanted to talk to you about," he said.

*Of course it is.*

Willa kept both hands on the steering wheel and stared straight ahead at the road, willing herself not to react. "Why's that, Pops?"

"Well, see, I could use a loan. Not a big one," he added quickly. "And only till I get back on my feet. Shouldn't take more than a week or two. Then I'll pay you back with interest."

Willa breathed in and out, gaze trained straight ahead on the asphalt. The sign for the Hart Valley Air Center flashed by in her peripheral vision, and she tapped the brakes. Dammit. She'd have to turn around.

"What happened to the last loan I gave you?" she asked.

"Damn cheating sonofabitch."

It was anyone's guess who he meant this time. Willa took a shaky breath and eased her car into the gravel shoulder off the side of the road. "I can't keep giving you money," she said. "I'm barely staying afloat as it is. My financial planner says—"

"Financial planner," her father said. "Man alive. You ever think back when it was just you and me without two nickels to rub together that you'd end up having a fancy financial planner?" The wistfulness of his chuckle sent sharp little daggers into Willa's gut. "Your mama would have been so proud."

*Past tense.* Willa took a deep breath. Now wasn't the time for that conversation.

"I might have a chance to bid a job for TechTel," she said slowly. "Mom's dream company, remember? She always wanted to work there."

"Isn't that something?" His tone made it clear he *didn't* remember. He had no idea what she was talking about.

It was just as well. Sometimes, Willa wished for the same big gaps in her memories.

"Anyway," she continued, "the financial planner is free. We have a trade agreement where I do his website and he helps me out with planning."

"That's my girl, Willa. Always got a plan."

She spotted a place to turn around and aimed for it, annoyed with herself for missing the entrance. Annoyed with herself for a lot of things, actually.

*I'm just trying to make sure I don't end up like we were. Like we lived when I was little.*

She wasn't cruel enough to say the words out loud, but she thought them. Thought them every single day.

"How much do you need?" She stomped the brake, sending gravel spitting out behind her tires. She hated those words for falling from her lips again. Hated herself for being weak.

It was easier than hating him. She couldn't hate

him. He was her father.

"Two hundred oughta do it," he said. "I'll pay you back, of course."

"Of course."

And Willa would wake up tomorrow to find herself living on a Caribbean island with her own private jet.

Gripping the wheel, she eased the car onto the shoulder and did a quick U-turn.

"I'll transfer two hundred tonight," she said. "Please work on the job hunt, okay, Pops?"

"You're the best daughter in the world, you know that?"

Willa did not know that. She also didn't know why she kept giving this man money when he was only going to piss it away.

"Take care of yourself, okay?" she said.

"I love you."

The low cadence of his voice, the sincerity of his words, had her heart twisting up in her chest. *This.* This was why.

"I love you, too."

And she did. As much as she hated to admit it, she loved the man who'd fed her and clothed her and kept her safe after her mother was gone. Not well— he hadn't done any of those things *well*. But he'd done them, if only sporadically, which was still a lot more than anyone else in her life had done.

*This* was why she worked so hard. To create the stability she'd so desperately needed back then and still wanted to this day.

She disconnected the call as she pulled in at the Hart Valley Air Center. Signs pointed their way to bases for the Hotshots, for the tanker planes she guessed must be those huge ones that dropped retardant on fires.

But Willa followed the signs to the smokejumpers, parking her car right next to a dorm facility where Grady had told her some of the younger guys lived. Not him—he had his own place, which he'd refused to show her no matter how much she'd pleaded with him.

"I'm saving myself," he'd teased, cupping her ass as he bent to kiss her on the front porch several nights ago. "For our real second date."

Willa had ground against him, eliciting a growl and a tighter ass grab from Grady.

"Why buy the cow when you can get the milk for free?" she'd whispered in his ear.

He laughed and swatted her butt before stepping back to put some distance between them. "Maybe I want more than milk," he said.

"We could just call this our second date and—"

"Whipped cream," he said, backing away from her as he headed for his truck. "Butter. A nice double-cream brie with—"

"What?"

"That's what I want," he told her. "More than just milk."

"Jesus, Grady." She'd let him go, not sure when a recitation of dairy products became such a turn-on. Just one more thing that had changed since she met Grady Billman.

Willa shook off the memory as she eased her car into a parking spot marked "Guest." She checked her makeup in the rearview mirror. It wasn't

much—just mascara and lip gloss—but her blue and
white sundress gave her an easy, breezy look. No
coincidence the spaghetti straps left her shoulders
bare. She'd caught Grady checking them out, so she'd
made an effort to leave them uncovered as often as
possible.

*Since when do you care what a man thinks?*

She got out of the car, reminding herself she was
just making the most of the short time she'd have
with Grady. That's what this homemade lunch was
all about, too. A long lunch on a workday, no less,
since that's the only time the air base was open for
public tours. Willa hadn't taken a long lunch on a
weekday in... Had she ever?

Clutching the small cooler in one hand, she made
her way toward the reception building. A warm
breeze fluttered the hem of her dress, swirling her
in a cloud of juniper berries and faint smoke. Must
be the wildfire up in Canada or maybe Northern
Washington. Grady had mentioned some of his
crewmates had been sent out to that one.

She stepped into the air-conditioned lobby and
made her way to a desk bearing a placard that said,
"Guests sign in here." A grandmotherly receptionist
in a red T-shirt stepped forward, wearing a name tag
that identified her as Lyla.

"Just fill out this form here." The woman
handed her a clipboard, and Willa scrawled all her
information, including her full first name. Christ.
She was surprised to see so many other names on
the sign-in sheet. Grady wasn't kidding about the
popularity of these base tours.

"You've got someone meeting you over there?"

she asked.

"Grady Billman," she said, annoyed with herself for feeling a flutter of excitement when she said his name. "He's giving me a tour."

"I'll page him to meet you out front."

"Thank you."

The woman hit a door buzzer, and Willa walked outside into the warm Central Oregon sunshine. She breathed deeply, picking up on a hint of ozone in the air that suggested rain was on the way.

Grady appeared like a mirage on the sweltering sidewalk, grinning as he approached. "You made it."

"You thought I wouldn't?"

"Wasn't sure," he said, mopping his brow with a yellow towel. "Sorry, we just got done with PT."

Which explained why he was shirtless. And why Willa had the sudden urge to drool down the front of her dress. No man should be built this perfectly, with sculpted abs and a broad chest and—

"You want it?"

She jerked her eyes back to his face. "What?"

"The tour." He grinned like he knew damn well where her mind had just gone. "You want the tour now, or did you want to start with lunch?"

"Oh. Either way." She hoisted the small cooler she'd brought from home. "There's ice in here, so it'll keep a while."

"Thanks again for doing that," he said. "You don't owe me food, but I appreciate it."

"You bought the pizza the other night, so it's only fair."

"That was damn good pizza." He smiled, possibly remembering what had happened after pizza.

And now she was blushing again.

"Come on," Grady said, taking the cooler from her hand. "We can set this in the break room, and then I'll show you around."

He led her to a small room near the entrance where a battered steel table held a napkin dispenser and a pile of paper plates. "Sorry about the mess," he said as two shirtless men wandered through with towels draped around their necks.

Kayla and Aislin would love this.

Willa kept her eyes fixed on Grady, pretty sure his abs could put everyone else's to shame. He tucked the cooler in a corner next to an older-looking refrigerator, giving Willa a chance to admire the muscles in his back. Had she ever admired back muscles before?

"Let me just grab a T-shirt and I'll show you around," he said.

"I don't mind," she said, her voice a little wobbly. "If you wanted to skip the shirt."

Grady laughed and walked to a bank of lockers in the hallway. He spun the dial on one of them as two more shirtless guys walked past.

"Yo, Billman. Oh, hey, Willa."

"Tony," she said. "Good to see you again. How was the concert?"

She knew damn well how the concert had gone, as well as how the rest of Tony's night had unfolded with Kayla in his bed. She hadn't stopped gushing about it since the following morning.

"Great," he said, grabbing a bottle of Gatorade from the fridge and twisting the top. "Tell Kayla I said hi." He wandered away as Grady finished pulling on a shirt.

"Sounds like our friends hit it off," Willa said.

"Yeah." Grady grinned, giving nothing away. "Come on, we'll start in the rigging room."

He led her down a hallway to a brightly lit room with tall ceilings and enormous counters lined up in rows. At one end, a guy with close-cropped hair and a black T-shirt was folding a giant parachute. He looked up and smiled.

"Hey, Grady," he said.

"Ryan, this is Willa. Willa, meet Ryan."

"Pleasure to meet you," she said. "You're the drummer, right?"

"Right." He grinned, and Willa could see right away why Aislin had picked him out of the crowd. She hadn't called him—probably hadn't even kept his number after Grady gave it to her—but he was definitely her type.

"You must have been at one of our shows?" he asked.

"At the Boyton Ballroom the other night," she said. "It was a great set."

"Thanks." He grinned at Grady. "I'm guessing this is the reason we had to play 'Smokey the Bear'?"

Grady grunted. "Something like that."

Willa moved forward to survey his work. "Can I ask what you're doing?"

"Sure." Ryan spread his arms wide. "This is where we lay out all the chutes and pack them. Gotta have a minimum of three years of service to work this job."

"We use Ram Airs here," Grady put in. "The square chute you see hanging up there. Most of us are trained on rounds, too, though."

Willa fingered the ropes, marveling at their thickness. "Is there an advantage to one over the other?"

Grady shrugged. "You can steer better with the square chute, but there's a steep learning curve. Takes a lot of practice."

"The army uses the rounds," Ryan offered. "More forgiving."

"You'll find advocates for both," he said. "Come on, I'll show you where we do repairs."

Grady's voice held a note of excitement she hadn't expected. He was passionate about his work; that was obvious.

"I should warn you up front that I might get called out," he said as he led her down a concrete hallway toward a room giving off an odd buzz. "They had some lightning strikes up in Northern Washington, so we're on standby to fly."

"Got it," she said. "I made sure lunch is portable, just in case."

"Thanks."

The buzzing got louder as they approached the room, and Grady led her inside. What in the world?

Grady turned to smile at her. "This is where the magic happens."

Willa surveyed the room in awe. Sewing machines, at least two dozen of them, lined the room in tidy rows. It looked like her high school home ec room, except all the machines were manned by grown men. Muscular, rugged men, a few of them with a faint sheen of sweat glistening on their bare chests.

One of them looked up and nodded at her.

"Ma'am." He looked at Grady. "Air-conditioning's busted again."

"Figures."

Grady turned to smile at her, and Willa realized her mouth was hanging open. She closed it, still too stunned to find words. "Knitting," she managed at last. "When I made that crack about playing music instead of knitting…"

"Yep." He grinned. "This is what I meant. Welcome to the largest sewing circle on the West Coast."

"What on Earth?"

"If you want to be a good smokejumper, you pride yourself on stitch quality," he said. "Bobby McKillop over there is a senior rigger, and Pete Jensen is a master rigger."

A guy with arms the size of tree trunks saluted, then went back to sewing. Willa watched, dumbfounded. "These are parachutes?"

"Chutes, harnesses, belts, jump suits—you name it," Grady said. "You know how I mentioned we're all control freaks?"

"Yes, but I didn't realize this is what you meant."

Grady grinned and ran his fingers over the fabric dangling from the ceiling. "Our lives depend on all that stuff, so we make damn sure every stitch is perfect."

"I had no idea."

"Most people don't," he said. "I'm sure there's stuff that goes on behind the scenes in your life that no one would ever guess at."

"Right." Willa nodded, reminding herself he was talking about work. Not her personal life, which was where more of the unknowns lurked. "This is the last thing in the world I pictured when you said you were a smokejumper."

"We're full of surprises." Grady smiled and took her hand. "Come on, I'll show you where we keep the gear."

He led her into another room, this one stacked high with shelves teeming with boxes. Hundreds of them, thousands, maybe.

"These are the packs we carry."

She turned to see him hoisting one off the floor.

"We jump first, and then these get tossed out afterward on cargo chutes," he explained. "We carry our own gear in the field."

"What's in it?"

"That's a two-manner," he said. "It's enough to keep two firefighters alive for two to three days. You've got tools, food, water, climbing gear, things like that. And we've gotta be able to hike a dozen or so miles with it, since that's often what it takes to get out to a road. To the pickup point."

"Who picks you up?" she asked. "A plane or…?"

"Usually volunteers," he said. "Drivers will get called out to the nearest town, wherever that happens to be, and we'll have to hike to get to them."

Willa tried lifting the pack. "Whoa." It was *heavy*. She could barely get it off the ground. No wonder Grady's shoulders were so strong.

"That one's about a hundred and ten pounds," he said. "There's a heavier one with a chain saw."

"A chain saw?"

"For clearing brush. With smokejumping, it's all about the initial attack. The idea is to knock the fire out while it's still small."

Willa shook her head, amazed by everything that went into his job. She hadn't had a clue. "So how does this work exactly?" she asked. "You get a call there's a fire, and then you go?"

"Or smoke," he said. "Sometimes not even that. Sometimes we get a call that there's been a lightning storm in Nevada or Montana or somewhere like that, and it's our job to go fly around looking for strikes."

"Like smoke curling up from the forest—that sort of thing?"

"Yep," he said. "The precursor to fires, rather than a big, raging gobbler."

"Gobbler?"

"Gobbler or gob—that's what we call the big fires," he said. "We're after the small ones. The smoldering bits in the remotest places that we're trying to keep from turning into big fires."

No wonder Grady grimaced at the mention of thunderstorms. "Is it usually lightning strikes that cause them?"

"That's common, but we see some human-caused fires, too."

"Wow, Smokey." She patted his abs, lingering a little longer than necessary as she smiled up at him. "You're kind of a badass."

He grinned, that mischievous, delicious grin that sent tingles running up and down her arms. And to other parts.

"Want to see how fast I can get my clothes on?"

Willa laughed. "Is this where I'm supposed to say I'm more interested in seeing how fast you can take them off?"

Grady smiled back. "Depends on which would impress you more."

Electricity crackled between them, their own private lightning storm with much more risk of collateral damage. Willa took a step back.

"I take it you have to suit up fast when a call comes in?"

Grady watched her face, clearly sensing a shift. "Yep. Come on, I'll show you the speed racks."

He led her into a room with rows and rows of garment hooks. "We need to be able to get our gear on in two minutes or less," he said. "Kneepads, ankle braces, leg straps, the whole nine yards."

She fingered the edge of a sleeve, marveling at the weight of it. "Because the pack's not heavy enough?"

He laughed and shrugged into it while keeping it on the hook. All part of the strategy, she guessed. "There's Kevlar in here," he said. "Protection from tree branches. That's one of the biggest risks out in the field."

Willa tried to picture it. Grady jumping out of a plane. Grady with those spiky things on his feet as he clambered down from a treetop. Grady in a blazing forest with a chain saw, making sure the fire couldn't spread.

She wasn't sure that's how it all worked in real life, but her mental picture was scary enough. "You said your dad used to jump?"

"Yeah, but he retired." Something dark passed over Grady's face. "Probably stayed in a little too long. It was hell on his body those last few years, but he didn't really have a backup plan."

Willa nodded, remembering Grady's own

comments about needing a plan for himself. "Sounds rough."

He shrugged. "It's part of the life."

"So what's are your ideas for after? For getting out earlier than your dad, I mean. Are there other jobs that interest you?"

Grady's face hardened, but he kept smiling. It was the strangest expression. "Maybe stripping." He rubbed a hand over his forehead, which seemed like a nervous gesture. "Those guys at Boyton seemed to be killing it that night."

Willa studied his face. "You don't like worrying about the future."

He shrugged. "You're right, stripping's no good. Maybe I'll be an astronaut?"

Message received. The subject was off limits. "All right." Willa cleared her throat. "So your brothers— you said a couple are smokejumpers?"

"Yeah, and one Hotshot." His whole body seemed to relax. "Those are the ground crew guys."

"Your dad must be proud of you."

"We're pretty tight," he said. "My whole family. But especially the ones who fight fires. We're all really close."

"I'd like to meet them."

He gave her an odd look, and she realized what she'd just said. Right. The two-date rule meant she didn't have a lot of meet-the-family moments.

"I'm sure they're good smokejumpers," she said. "Maybe I'll see them around."

Lame. Super lame, but Grady didn't react.

"Jake's out on a fire in California right now," he said. "And Paul has the next couple of days off."

There was an intensity in his eyes that made Willa take a step back. What was she doing here? She hadn't meant to make this feel like a budding relationship, and it definitely wasn't a date. So what was it?

She stepped back again, pasting a smile on her face. "We should go have that lunch now, you think?"

Grady nodded. "Sure thing." He shrugged out of the suit and offered her his arm. "Thanks again for bringing food."

They made their way down the hall in silence as Willa glanced at her watch. She'd been gone only forty-five minutes, but already it felt like ages she'd been away from work. She'd have to make an excuse to leave soon.

"It's nothing too fancy," Willa said as she started to unpack the cooler. "Roll-up sandwiches with turkey and avocado. I've got apple slices here, too."

"This looks amazing." Grady grabbed a chocolate chip cookie and took a bite. "Life's short; eat dessert first."

Willa fought the urge to grimace. "My father used to say that," she said. "Still does sometimes."

"I think I'd like your dad."

She said nothing, just focused on unpacking the cooler. But she could feel her shoulders tensing. "There's enough here if you want to share with the other guys," she said. "I made some extra sandwiches for—"

*Waaaaaaaaaaaaaaahhhhhhh!*

The siren was louder than anything Willa had ever heard, filling her eardrums and prickling the hair on her arms. She looked at Grady, who was stuffing a sandwich in his mouth as fast as he could.

"Gotta go," he said around a mouthful.

Boots thundered down the hallway behind him, and Willa picked up snippets of words.

*Northern Idaho.*

*Lightning strikes.*

*Hurry up, asshole.*

Grady dug fast through the cooler, grabbing cookies and apple slices and even an extra sandwich in a baggie. He finished chewing and tucked the food in the crook of his arm. "I'll be set for the ride if I can fit all this in my jump suit."

"Be careful out there."

He smiled and pulled her into his arms. "I always am."

The kiss was quick, but Willa's toes curled anyway, and the rest of her screamed for more.

But Grady was already backing away. "I'll call if I can," he shouted, jogging toward the hall. "Or text."

Willa rested a hand on the cooler and watched Grady surge into the rushing mob. "Good luck," she shouted. "Stay safe."

In the distance, she heard men shouting. Somewhere outside, a plane engine roared to life.

"I can walk you out."

Willa turned to see Ryan from the rigging room. "You're not going?"

"Nah," he said. "I'm not on the jump list till tomorrow."

She began packing the cooler, surprised to discover her hands had gone wobbly. "Want a sandwich?"

His eyes lit up. "Thanks!"

He unwrapped it and dove in while Willa finished packing the cooler. "Kind of a crazy life, huh?" she said, making idle conversation.

Ryan nodded around a mouthful of turkey and avocado. "It's rough on relationships," he said.

"Oh, we're not in a relationship," she said. "Grady and me, we're just…"

What the hell were they? She didn't have an answer, but Ryan didn't wait for one.

"Midsummer gets especially hard," he said. "It's hit-or-miss whether you see each other at all. Most of the girls I've dated get sick of it after a season."

Willa digested the information and did her best to look like she didn't care. "Sounds like an okay arrangement for me," she said. "I don't have room in my life for a guy who's hanging around all the time, distracting me from my work."

"Won't have to worry about that with a smoke-jumper." He reached for a cookie. "We're never around. Not even when you want us to be."

"Good."

Wasn't it?

Yes, of course it was. This was exactly what Willa wanted. A date or two for fun, some amusing banter, good sex—okay, *great* sex—and no attachments. This was what she'd been built for. Exactly the kind of relationship she needed.

"It's not a relationship," she said again, as much for her own benefit as his.

"Whatever you say." Ryan grinned as he stuffed the rest of a sandwich in his mouth, clearly not believing her at all.

# CHAPTER SEVEN

Grady trudged out of the forest and leaned his Pulaski against a tree. Peeling his jump suit collar off his face, he glanced over his shoulder to see Tony setting his chain saw on a stump.

"I'm thinking it's a Spam and Ritz kinda night," Grady said. "You?"

Tony took a long drink from his canteen and wiped his mouth with the back of his hand, leaving a smear of soot across his cheek. He looked like Grady felt—filthy, exhausted, but satisfied by a job well done.

"Saw some huckleberries down by the creek," Tony said. "Remember that Spam with huckleberry glaze that Jones made that time?"

Bobby McKillop staggered out of the woods behind Tony, limping a little on his left leg. He'd had a rough landing when they arrived two days ago after his tuck-and-roll took him right over a pointed rock none of them had seen. The jump suit had protected him from the worst of it, but Grady could guess the guy was sporting some badass bruises.

"I'm starving," he growled, dumping a full canteen of water over his head. "Whose turn to cook?"

"Abrams," Tony said as the young transfer from Montana joined them and dropped his combi at the edge of the campsite.

"What?" Ethan Abrams unzipped his jump suit and sat down on a boulder to take off his boots. "I've got kitchen duty, yeah?"

"Yep." Grady dug into his pack and pulled out a battered pot.

The rest of the guys produced the other necessities—a spatula, half a pack of crackers, a pouch of powdered Gatorade to mix with water.

With meal prep underway, Grady got to work washing up as best he could, using water from the nearby creek to scrub soot and dirt off his hands.

They'd spent forty-eight hours clearing trees and ground cover, eliminating fuel to starve out the fire. It was a small blaze, barely an acre, so they'd gotten it under control without too much drama. No high winds, no sketchy cliffs, no charging grizzly bears fleeing the smoke. They'd have to mop up in the morning, but for now they could rest.

"Who's got fuel?" Ethan asked as he fiddled with his one-burner stove.

"Yo." Tony threw him a can while everyone else busted out their tin camp plates.

Grady's stomach growled as he started shucking layers of clothes. He glanced up at the sky, admiring the pink and red streaks arcing through the clouds and clawing at the edges of the sun. The light was fading fast, but what a show. Forest fires did a lot of damage, but they made for killer sunsets.

"Everyone check your sleeping bags for snakes," Bobby called tiredly as he shook his out and laid it on the ground. "Buchanan was working the Tusk fire out near Whitefish last week. Said he found a baby rattler curled up right inside."

"Shit," Grady muttered, shaking out his own bag before claiming a flat spot a ways back from the others. Not that he didn't love his teammates, but a childhood surrounded by nine siblings all sharing rooms had left him with a fondness for sleeping solo.

Except that night with Willa. That was a switch.

His brain flashed on an image of her curled naked against him, her golden-brown hair tickling his nose. She'd felt so soft in his arms, so warm and lush.

"I'm gonna sleep hard tonight." Tony collapsed onto his sleeping bag across the camp, boots still on his feet. Grady glanced up to see his teammate checking his phone.

"You have service?" Grady asked.

Seemed like a less nosy question than "Did you hear from Kayla," though he kinda wondered about that. He wasn't in the habit of quizzing buddies about their love lives, but Willa's comment about her friend's fondness for Tony had him curious.

"Two bars," Tony said. "First time since we got here."

Bobby collapsed onto his sleeping bag and pulled out his own phone. "That'll do."

Everyone zoned out for a minute, checking emails, catching up on news, texting the obligatory "I'm okay" messages to family. Grady slipped his iPhone out of his jump suit pocket and checked the screen.

Nothing.

Well, a text from his mother. He fired off a quick note to her, letting her know he was okay and that the fire had been handled. While he was at it, he texted an update to the base commander, even though they'd already relayed the details via radio. It never hurt to be thorough.

He was about to shove the phone in his pocket when a text message popped up on-screen.

**Willa:** *Saw a headline about injured Hotshots in WA. Hope you're okay.*

Grady stared at the message a long time, lingering over every word like he sometimes savored the best bites of steak at the end of a meal. She'd been thinking about him. The idea of that made him giddier than it ought to. Would he seem too eager if he replied right away?

*Don't be a dumb-ass. She's worried about you.*

His thumbs left black smudges on the screen as he typed out a quick response.

**Grady:** *All good here. On a small fire in ID. Got it out quickly. Heading out to MT tomorrow.*

That always seemed nuts to anyone outside this kind of work. That you could wake up in one state, fly off and jump out of a plane into another, hike to a third state, get picked up and driven to the air base there, and then do it all over again with a jump in a completely different state. He had no idea where he'd be sleeping tomorrow or if he'd be sleeping at all.

"Here you go."

Grady looked up to see Ethan handing him a plate of Spam and…okay, he wasn't totally sure what *that* was. But it was hot and looked mostly edible, so he said thanks and took the fork and started shoveling food into his face.

"This is awesome," he said around a mouthful. "Nice work."

"Gonna have to make you camp cook every

night," Tony called.

"Shit, don't say that," Bobby muttered from the other side of camp. "He'll start spitting in it or something."

As the other guys kept bantering about dinner, Grady's phone buzzed on the ground beside him. He picked it up as a flush of heat washed through him when he saw her name on-screen.

**Willa:** *Glad you're okay. Looking forward to date 2.*

Grady smiled, then stopped himself. Date two would be nice. The day after that would be less nice. That would mean the end of his time with Willa, something he wasn't looking forward to at all. He thought about that as he chewed, then tapped out a reply.

**Grady:** *Does hiking count as a date?*

He shoveled up the last of his dinner and stood to gather plates, but Tony snatched his and started toward the creek. "You did 'em last night," he said. "You're on for breakfast, though."

"Deal." Grady sat back down and peeled off his boots. The sun was almost gone, so he might as well crawl into his bag. Night came fast out here in the woods, and he was exhausted enough to fall right to sleep the second his head hit the pillow. The ground. Whatever.

The instant his phone buzzed, he was wide awake again.

**Willa:** *Murder's not a big turn-on.*

Huh? Grady looked at the screen, then scrolled back up to his last message.

**Grady:** *Does killing count as a date?*

Shit. Damn autocorrect. Or maybe he should blame his sooty fingerprints, which sometimes caused the mistyped words. Probably ought to clear that up quick.

**Grady:** *Sorry, phone is an asshole. Does HIKING count as a date?*

He wriggled into his sleeping bag as Tony ambled back into camp and started packing away the cooking gear. The others had already crawled into their bags as stars pricked holes in the black velvet sky one poke at a time. A perfect crescent moon hung by a thread in the corner of his field of vision, and Grady rolled onto his back to admire it.

His phone vibrated again and he held it up to check the incoming message.

**Willa:** *Hiking? Because you haven't gotten enough exercise lugging a million-pound pack around the woods?*

He smiled and typed out his response, wondering if she was in bed, too. Did she sleep naked? She had with him, but maybe that wasn't her normal state. Maybe it had just been a convenience thing, since they'd woken up several times in the night to touch and stroke and—

**Grady:** *Hiking fire lines w/a heavy pack = not relaxing. Hiking river trail w/a beautiful woman = very relaxing.*

The response bubbles popped up immediately, filling Grady's chest with a surge of anticipation.

**Willa:** *Will be on lookout for beautiful women ;)*
**Willa:** *Also, no. Hiking is not a date.*

Then a pause like she was trying to figure out why. Grady kinda wondered himself.

**Willa:** *Exercise is NOT romantic.*

Hey, that worked for him. A little weird, but okay. Grady smiled as he read through her messages. This banter, it was nice. Not the same as talking with her in person, snuggled on her sofa with Willa's warmth tucked against his body. Still, he could get used to this.

**Grady:** *How's your week?*

**Willa:** *Workload heavy. Drama with Dad. The usual.*

That was interesting. She rarely brought up her father, and he thought hard about his response, not wanting to scare her away.

**Grady:** *Is your dad okay?*

**Willa:** *Fine. Work's crazy with RFPs. Trying to land Tranquility Villa and TechTel. Two companies I really, REALLY want.*

Two reallys? It sounded personal. Grady made a note of it, wondering if he should push. He'd love to know more, to understand what drove her so hard.

**Grady:** *Crossing all fingers and toes you succeed.*

**Willa:** *Thanks. Same.*

Grady looked at the words again, wondering what he could add. If there was any way to help relieve her stress.

**Grady:** *Massage. That's good for relaxation. Hey, spa date! Real date or no?*

Truth be told, he'd never had a professional massage. An old girlfriend used to hound him all the time about signing up for some couples' massage class. It sounded hokey at the time, but somehow it sounded more appealing when he pictured Willa stretched out on that table, her bare back tapering down to slim hips and her breasts peeking out around the edges of her ribs, just waiting for his hands to—

**Willa:** *Depends. Are you doing the massaging or are we talking day spa?*

**Grady:** *Whichever IS NOT a real date.*

He pictured her laughing, and it felt good knowing he was responsible for that imaginary laughter. Rolling onto his side, he waited for an answer, wondering if his teammates could see him over here tapping like a middle school kid with a crush.

**Willa:** *We'll talk when you're back if I still need to relax.*

Huh. Evasive. Or maybe not. Willa wasn't the type to play games, so maybe that's all there was to it. Either she'd feel like getting a massage or she wouldn't. She'd give him another date or she wouldn't.

This was not how dating usually went for Grady. How many times had the tables been turned, had the women in his life been the ones hounding him for more time, more attention, more dates? How had he become the pursuer of a woman who seemed like she could take him or leave him?

**Grady:** *I know something else that's good for relaxation.*

The instant he hit send, he second-guessed himself. Did that sound dirty? That wasn't how he'd meant it, so he hurried to text again.

**Grady:** *Meditation. My sister says it's been a game changer for her.*

There, that was good. Just a friendly suggestion,

something that might help her feel better. And that's what this was about, really. He wanted Willa relaxed and happy and—

**Willa:** *Uh...*

Grady frowned at his phone, trying to make sense of her response. He scrolled back up and nearly pissed himself.

**Grady:** *Masturbation. My sister says it's been a game changer for her.*

Shit. Shit, shit, *shit*. Damn autocorrect. Or dirty thumbs, whatever. He hurried to reply.

**Grady:** *Autocorrect, sorry. Meditation. It's supposed to be really relaxing.*

A long pause, then a response.

**Willa:** *I can assure you it's not.*

What? He scrolled back up, horrified to see what his phone had done this time.

**Grady:** *Autocorrect, sorry. Menstruation. It's supposed to be really relaxing.*

*Fuuuuuuuck.* His thumbs flew over the screen, correcting his latest faux pas.

**Grady:** *God donkey! M-e-d-i-t-a-t-i-o-n. My sister swears by it.*

He read his message three times and corrected the donkey thing to "goddammit" before hitting Send this time.

Willa responded with a series of smiley faces.

**Willa:** *I kinda liked your first suggestion best.*

Whoa. He scrolled through the messages to make sure he was remembering correctly. Yep, his accidental suggestion of self-gratification was first on the list, all right. He glanced around the camp at his teammates. No one was moving, but no way in hell was he going to be the creeper lying here in his sleeping bag stroking the salami while he sexted a beautiful woman.

He wished like hell he could call her, but phone sex on the fringes of a forest fire seemed wrong on multiple levels.

Little typing bubbles appeared on-screen, and Grady wondered if he'd taken too long to respond. If he'd made her self-conscious with his delay.

Her response popped up and he squinted at the screen, trying to make sense of it. There were no words. Just…emojis?

An avocado.

And an eggplant.

What the—?

Oh.

All right, he was no expert on erotic imagery, but the two veggies side by side like that were definitely meant to be sexy. The eggplant looked phallic while the avocado was…well, whatever the female equivalent was. That's what she meant, right?

Grady fumbled with his screen, scrolling for just the right images. A whale, a tiger, an alligator…*there*.

Locating the camel, he keyed it in, then hit the send button.

It took a few seconds, but her response popped up with a smile emoji.

**Willa: *Only one hump?***

Ha! She'd gotten it, even though he'd known it was a stretch.

He scrolled back through the damn emojis, locating the two-humped camel right below it. He sent that one, watching as the message went through.

Hell, he sent another. And another.

**Willa:** *That's an awful lot of hump. You sure you're up for that?*

"You have no idea," he murmured to himself. Before he could respond, she texted an emoji of a shower.

**Willa:** *I need to cool off now.*

He laughed, hoping the guys weren't still awake and watching. He'd never live this down. Sliding his thumb across the screen to search for images, he located one that showed a pair of hands extended palms-out. Probably a high-ten, but that could pass as a boob grab, right?

A few more seconds. Willa replied with a peach emoji. Butt cheeks? Had to be. Grady stifled a laugh. God, it had been a long time since he'd smiled this much with a woman. A woman hundreds of miles away, at that. It seemed crazy she could get him this riled up from a distance, and with cartoon emojis at that.

But there it was. He was fucking nuts about her, and this flirty chat was driving him even crazier.

He was still hunting for another flirtatious emoji when she texted again.

**Willa:** *I should sleep now. This was fun.*

Yeah. It was. Way more fun than Grady was used to. He rolled onto his back, wishing he could keep this going all night. Wishing she were here with him right now, breathing in the smoke-tinged night air and counting the stars overhead. He'd pull her against his chest, inhaling the scent of her hair and asking her questions about her life. He'd tell her about fires he'd worked and she'd tell him about her father and they'd fall asleep in each other's arms under the night sky.

**Grady:** *I miss you.*

He stared at the words for a long time, then deleted them. No reason to scare her off.

**Grady:** *I'm nuts about you.*

He threw a peanut emoji in there to make it wittier, but even that seemed too forward, so he deleted the words unsent and tried again.

**Grady** *Can't wait to see you again for*

He finished that off with a couple of wineglasses and a plate of food, figuring that was a tame enough visual for a date. And he did want a date with her, that was true. But he wanted more than one. More than two or three or —

**Willa:** *G'night, Grady.*

**Grady:** *Night.*

—more than she wanted from him, that seemed clear.

He put his phone down and settled in for the night, determined not to let it get to him.

# CHAPTER EIGHT

Willa tugged the blue dress over her head, snagging the merchandise tags on her ponytail as she yanked it off. "Ow."

"Here, let me." Aislin gently freed the azure silk from Willa's tangled tresses and hooked it on the dressing room door. "Red's more your color anyway."

Kayla stepped up with a flirty little crimson number draped over one arm. She eyed Willa standing there in her white cotton undies and made a *tsk-tsk* noise. "Tell me you have sexier underwear to go with this."

"I have sexier underwear to go with this," Willa parroted obediently, reaching for the red dress. "You guys, this is lunch with a five-year-old. Why are you making such a fuss?"

"It's lunch with *Grady* and a five-year-old," Kayla insisted, yanking the dress back so fast that Willa almost toppled over. "And you were told to look like a princess, so you're going to be the sexiest goddamn princess who ever walked the earth."

Willa sighed. "I'm thinking we should tone down the sexiness and swearing. I've never even met this five-year-old."

Aislin quirked an eyebrow as she perused the selection they'd assembled for her in the dressing room. "Cursing and dressing like a hooch would be okay if you were acquainted with the kid?"

Kayla responded before Willa could open her mouth. "She's not dressing like a hooch. She's going to look like a beautiful, magical princess."

Aislin grinned. "A beautiful, magical princess who's going to rock Grady's world."

"You guys are overthinking this." Willa plucked a pink dress off the hook and inspected the neckline. Way too sexy. She put it back and kept looking. "We're taking the kid to a princess tea party, not attending a royal wedding."

*And it's not a date*, she reminded herself, inspecting a flowy yellow dress.

It couldn't be a date with a kid as a chaperone. One of Grady's teammates had been injured in the field and refused the MRI his doctor ordered because it conflicted with a princess party held annually at a local teahouse. The single dad had hyped it all summer for his daughter and couldn't bear to let her down.

"That was nice of Grady to offer to take the kid to the tea thing," Aislin said. "Very chivalrous."

Kayla nodded and handed Willa the red dress. "Her name is Annabelle—how cute is that? Tony says Grady's family looks after her all the time. I guess they're pretty close."

"The upside of a big family," Willa put in, hunting for the zipper. "It's easy to absorb an extra kid when you've got a zillion brothers and sisters and grandkids."

"Still, it's a nice gesture." Aislin plucked the dress from Willa's hand and tugged down the zipper, then handed it back. "Though kind of a weird date, considering you haven't seen each other for two weeks."

"It's not a date." Willa tugged the dress over her head, grateful the fabric hid her face as she conjured another tiny fib. "And I like having Grady gone a lot. It keeps me focused on work."

She emerged through the neck hole in time to see her friends exchange a look. "It keeps you from getting too serious," Kayla said. "From admitting you're into the guy."

"I think it's awesome," Aislin said. "You're not ready for things to end so quickly with this one. That's progress."

Willa wasn't so sure about that, but there was no sense arguing. Better to change the subject. "How's it going with Tony?" she asked Kayla.

"Great." Kayla beamed, making it clear it was more than great.

Aislin reached out to help Willa with her zipper. "Are you guys getting serious?"

Kayla shrugged and helped Willa lift her hair away from the zipper. "Too soon to tell. He sure thinks Grady's great, though. Smart and responsible and skilled and—"

"Are you sure Tony's not in love with Grady?" Aislin smoothed a crease on the side of Willa's dress.

Kayla's smile morphed into a Cheshire-like smirk. "Positive," she said, the one syllable conveying every-thing Willa needed to know about how her friend and Grady's had been spending their time together.

"They're brothers-in-arms," Kayla continued, straightening Willa's hem. "The guys have mad re-spect for each other as smokejumpers, but it's more than that. They trust each other with their lives."

"Huh." Aislin looked thoughtful. "Which you're taking as a good sign we can trust him with Willa's heart?"

Willa rolled her eyes and turned to face the mirror. "Hello? I do have some say in this, too, you know."

"We're your fairy godmothers." Aislin grinned at her in the mirror. "Aside from making sure you look cute for your date—"

"Not a date!" Kayla insisted.

"Right, you'll look cute for your non-date." Aislin picked a blue dress off the hook by the door, considering it a moment before putting it back. "But we're here to tell you when you've met a guy who might be deserving of more than the usual treatment."

Willa gave up and surveyed herself in the mirror. Okay, fine. Her friends were right about the red. It was definitely her color, and the bodice hugged her curves like a dream. She fished under her arm for the price tag and blanched.

"It's fifty percent off," Kayla said, swatting her hand away. "And it's your early birthday present."

"My birthday isn't for months."

"A *really* early birthday," Aislin said. "Your half birthday."

Willa sighed. It probably said something that her friends were so determined to have her give Grady a chance. They hadn't been this passionate about any of her dates since…okay, *ever*.

A buzzing from beneath a pile of clothes sent Willa pawing through the heap of silk and linen to find her phone. Her father's phone number lit up the screen, and Willa closed her eyes. She hit the key to ignore the call and set the phone back on the bench.

It rang again immediately.

"Is everything okay with your dad?" Aislin's eyes filled with concern, but Willa brushed it off.

"He's fine," she said a little too quickly. "Just having some challenges at work."

Kayla's brow furrowed. "He got a job?"

"That's the nature of the problem," Willa said. "There is no work."

Her friends exchanged a glance that Willa couldn't quite read.

"You aren't still giving him money, are you?" Kayla asked.

"No." Willa didn't meet their eyes in the mirror.

Not lying, exactly. She hadn't given him anything since the two hundred last week, which was probably why he was calling again. Knowing her father, he'd burned through that in a matter of days. Two hundred was nothing in the broad scheme of things.

But it had been a lot when she was nine. Back when her classmates dared her to do a cherry drop on the monkey bars at school. She made it all the way around, hair flying behind her and squeals of excitement echoing from the cluster of girls as she let go of the bar and dropped.

Dropped right onto her butt. She put her arms out to catch herself, and that's when she felt something snap.

Her father had to leave work to come get her, his brow creased with worry as he drove her to the hospital. His voice was low when he spoke to the admissions clerk, but Willa could still hear. "We don't have insurance," he said. "But I have a little money saved. It isn't much, but—"

"Sign here, Mr. Frank," the nurse said, flashing a look of sympathy at Willa. "We'll get her all fixed up."

It wasn't till months later—long after the cast had come off—that Willa heard her father talking on the phone. "I don't have three thousand dollars," he murmured, his voice low as he covered one ear with his hand to drown out the street noise while Willa huddled just out of sight in the hallway. "Three hundred is all I have to my name, and I was trying to save for— No, that's not true. No, ma'am. They wouldn't let me apply for the payment plan because my credit— No, I understand."

Willa had crept quietly from the room. She'd always known her mother's absence left a huge financial burden on her dad. Yeah, his drinking didn't help, and neither did the gambling, but still. The sacrifices he'd made for her weren't something she could easily repay.

"Hello? Earth to Willa?"

She blinked her attention to Kayla, who was trotting back into the dressing room with a pair of strappy gold sandals with little kitten heels. "I know you can't stand wearing stilettos, but these will do amazing things for your legs."

Still rattled from the memories, Willa let her friends help her into the shoes, feeling more than a little like Cinderella.

She shivered, remembering how things ended up in the fairy tale. Sooner or later, someone would turn into a pumpkin. Sooner or later, Grady would get into his coach and go.

• • •

"Ladies." Grady pulled out a chair and gestured Annabelle toward it. "Your seat, madam."

Giggling, the five-year-old gathered her ruffled skirts and hoisted herself onto the chair with all the ceremony of a queen ascending her throne. "Thank you." Annabelle adjusted her tiara and regarded Grady with a regal air. "Daddy told me to say 'please' also."

Willa smiled and seated herself beside the little girl. "What nice manners you have."

"Yeah." Annabelle surveyed the restaurant where a dozen children in frills and ribbons were settling in with their families. "You also have to say 'excuse me' when you interrupt or burp or step on someone's foot."

Grady winked at Willa. "We'll cross that bridge when we come to it."

The little girl frowned. "What bridge?"

Covering a laugh, Willa sipped her water as Grady did his best to explain figures of speech. He was good with kids, that was clear. And his rhinestone tiara was on point, just like the sash he wore proclaiming him to be the "#1 Princess." God, the man was adorable.

"I've got about a million nieces and nephews," Grady had explained to Willa in the car on their way to pick up Annabelle. "It's the reason Bobby trusted me with this."

Not the only reason, Willa guessed. Grady practically radiated trustworthiness. How unlike her own father, who could be charming and charismatic but as reliable as a cheesecloth condom.

"Daddy says they only do the tea party one time a year," Annabelle was explaining. "And Grandma couldn't take me because someone had to drive Daddy to the doctor."

"That's right." Grady picked up the teapot and poured a little bit into each of the three dainty porcelain cups. "He was real sad not to be here with you, but it's good for him to get fixed up."

"Yeah." Annabelle frowned, looking unsure. "I like you well enough."

Willa stifled another laugh, wondering where the girl had picked up that line. "I like him well enough, too." That was an understatement of epic proportions, and Annabelle eyed her like she might suspect as much.

Grinning, Grady spread his napkin across his lap. His hand skewed the princess sash across his broad chest, and Willa resisted the urge to reach over and adjust it.

"Thanks," he said, still grinning. "I'm honored to have a date with two beautiful princesses."

Willa smiled and took a sip from her cup as Grady winked at her again. *Not a date*, he mouthed.

She laughed, sputtering her tea as Annabelle looked on in dismay.

"Grown-ups are weird." The girl picked at one of the tiny tea sandwiches and regarded Grady through her frame of perfect blond ringlets. "Did you get hurt, too?"

Grady shook his head, easily finding his place in the conversation. "I was on the same fire as your daddy, but I'm okay." He picked up his own teacup, which looked like a dollhouse prop in his big hand. "Your daddy's very brave."

"Yeah." Annabelle plucked a sugar cube out of the dish in the center of the table and nibbled a corner of it. "Was it a big fire?"

"Not too big," Grady assured her. "Lots of smoke, though."

Wrinkling her nose, Annabelle regarded him with a haughty look. "That's why you smell."

Laughing, Grady grinned at Willa. "Can't argue with that. It's tough to get rid of the smoke smell when you've been close to a fire. Would you believe I've showered four times already since I got home? Guess I should do it again, huh?"

"Yeah." The girl pointed at Willa. "Maybe she can help get behind your ears and stuff."

"That's an excellent idea," Grady said as heat flooded Willa's cheeks.

She focused on choosing from the platter of tea sandwiches so she wouldn't have to meet Grady's eye. It wouldn't do to find herself mentally undressing the man in front of a child.

"My dad stinks lots of times, too," Annabelle declared proudly. "He said you saw a bear this time."

Willa looked up in time to see Grady scrub a hand over his chin.

"That's true," he said. "But it was a long way off and not dangerous at all."

Willa sipped her tea, not sure whether he was trying to reassure her or Annabelle. Like Bobby's injury wasn't enough of a reminder how dangerous a smokejumper's job could be. How Grady could be gone at any moment.

*It's why you're not getting attached. One of a million reasons this can't go beyond two dates.*

Something Willa would do well to keep in mind.

She ordered herself to stay focused on the conversation. Grady was telling Annabelle about the different animals he'd seen on recent forest fires.

"...Lots of coyotes and a couple of bobcats," he was saying. "And birds. On this last fire, we had an owl that wouldn't stop hooting the whole night long." He hooted and flapped his arms like wings, making Willa smile and Annabelle dissolve into giggles.

"I like owls," the girl announced.

Willa tried to think of something to add. She didn't have nearly as much practice as Grady at being around kids. "Did you know owls are nocturnal? That means—"

"Owls are *not* turtles." The girl shook her head, making her curls bounce. "You're silly."

Grady burst out laughing, shaking his head as he refilled everyone's tea. "Can't argue with that."

Pleased with herself, Annabelle stared Willa down. "My mommy's dead. She died when I was a baby."

All the breath left Willa's lungs. She clenched her napkin in one hand, trying to find her voice. "That happens sometimes," she said softly. "It's sad when people die. Especially mommies."

Annabelle nodded, watching Willa's face. "Is your mom dead?"

Feeling Grady's eyes on her, Willa kept her focus on the girl. She fought to slow her breathing, even as her heart raced. "My mom—" Willa's voice cracked, and she sat up straighter in her chair. "My mom's gone, too."

The girl seemed to hesitate. Lashes fluttering, she reached over and patted Willa's hand. "That's sad."

"Yes," Willa managed. "It really is."

Annabelle nodded. "My dad says we can get a kitten after fire season. Hey! Can I go see the fish?"

"The fish?" Willa blinked, struggling to orient herself to the conversational style of a five-year-old.

"The fish." Annabelle pointed toward the corner of the restaurant, where a bright aquarium sat bubbling beneath bright lights. "I want to go say hi."

"Sure," Grady said, coming to Willa's rescue. "Just stay where we can see you, okay?"

"Okay!" Annabelle jumped out of her seat and took off running, making a beeline for the tank.

Grady sipped his tea, still watching Willa. "You okay?"

"Yes. Yes, of course." She took a bite of a tea sandwich, focusing all her energy on the taste of salmon and cucumber. "It's nice of you to do this for your teammate. His daughter's sweet."

"Yeah, she's a great kid. And he's had a rough go of it since his wife died." Grady watched the girl from across the room, eagle eyes trained on her frilled skirts. "Thanks for joining me. I knew it'd be more fun for her with a woman along."

"Don't mention it." She took a sip of tea, getting her nerves under control. "I've been crazy busy the last couple of weeks, so it's nice to get out of the house."

"Any new clients?"

She nodded, impressed he seemed genuinely

interested in her work. "One I'm really hoping to land. They've been on my radar a long time, and I'm finally getting a chance to pitch my services."

"Is this TechTel?"

Willa blinked. "How did you know that?"

"I pay attention when you talk." He grinned and popped a bite of shortbread in his mouth. "Don't look so surprised."

"I'm not; I'm just— Okay, I'm surprised." She laughed and dabbed her mouth with a napkin. "My work's not usually that interesting to other people."

"Everything about you fascinates me." He winced. "That sounded less cheesy in my head."

Willa smiled and picked up a gingersnap. "I think it's charming. Even more so, coming from a guy in a tiara and sash."

Grady grinned and straightened the rhinestone marvel on his head. "You like? If you play your cards right, I'll wear it in bed later."

Willa shivered. From anticipation? Attraction? Fear?

Maybe all those things.

Willing herself to stay calm, to keep her emotions in check, she glanced over at Annabelle. "I should go see how she's doing. Maybe she needs to visit the ladies' room."

"Sure, yeah. Good idea." Grady stood, the perfect gentleman, reaching across to help her out of her seat.

Willa's hand tingled where he touched her, kept tingling as she made her way across the room. She felt his eyes on her the whole way, liking it way more than she should.

# CHAPTER NINE

If Grady had any fears that lunch with a five-year-old would kill his chances of post–tea party romance, they evaporated the instant he stepped into Willa's house.

"I need you, Grady," she whispered as she pulled him toward her bedroom. "Please."

"Yes, ma'am." Her urgency surprised him, though maybe it shouldn't. Something had rattled her back at the teahouse. The questions about her mother, maybe, though he couldn't think about that with her tugging at the fly of his jeans.

"You're so fucking hot." He growled the words against her throat, tearing at her clothes with a hunger that equaled hers. They were like feral animals, nipping and panting and pawing at each other as they stumbled down the hall to her room.

Normally, he prided himself on restraint, but he was all over her. Kissing, touching, unzipping her dress the way he'd imagined doing for weeks. She felt so damn good, so right in his arms. It was like he'd been starving and Willa was there waving a big, juicy steak in front of his face.

When she drew back to pull the dress over her head, she looked at him with eyes blazing. "I'm glad you're okay," she breathed. "What happened to your teammate—to Annabelle's dad—I forget sometimes how dangerous your job is."

For the briefest moment, his fears flared into a

burning trash fire in the center of his chest.

*What if it happens to me?*

*What if my next jump is my last?*

*Where will I be in a year? Ten years? Twenty?*

He forced a smile and shoved those thoughts from his head. "I'm better than okay." His voice sounded strained, but he could blame it on lust, right?

That's what this was anyway. As Willa kissed him again, he let the carnal wave consume him. This thing with Willa, it was all about the here and now.

And right here, right now, he wanted her desperately.

He wasn't gentle as he tossed her on the bed. Last time had taught him that she didn't want sweet tenderness. She didn't want whispered words of admiration or slow, careful caresses. She wanted passion. She wanted greedy touches and hungry growls, and Grady was happy to deliver.

"Fuck, you're beautiful," he breathed as she sat up and threw the red dress aside, then let him lay her back on the bed. She slid naked beneath him, so gorgeous, his gut ached.

She moved her forearm across her breasts as a flush crept over her body. "I'm kinda missing the sexy underwear," she said. "My friends said I needed something red and lacy, but I didn't have it, so—"

"Naked works," he said, prying her arm off her breasts so he could bury his face between them. "You pretty much nailed the sexy."

Whatever she murmured next was lost in a blur of groans. She clutched the back of his head, panting her fondness for the things he was doing with his tongue. It was fucking nirvana. Every inch of her tasted like honey, and her skin was so damn soft. Just touching her like this was driving him crazy.

"I need to taste you," he growled against the underside of her breasts.

"I want that, too."

Normally he'd take his time, stay above the belt until he was positive she was damn good and ready. But holy Christ, she was ready. He could see that as he kissed his way down her body, licking her naval, her hipbones, every inch of flesh he could feast on.

Her legs parted, and he moved between them, dying to devour her. "Please," she panted, and he didn't understand at first. But she sat up and rolled to her side, moving so she faced his—

"Oh God." Grady groaned as she drew him deeply into her mouth.

She'd flipped them around so he could still slide his tongue between her slick folds the way he'd wanted, but she could suck him, too. It was his hottest fantasy come to life, and he couldn't get enough of it. He parted her with his tongue, barely holding himself together as her mouth worked magic on his shaft.

"Willa," he groaned as he flicked her tight bud with the tip of his tongue. "I'm not gonna last long like this."

But he couldn't stop. And neither did she. It was like they'd both been ravenous for weeks and couldn't keep their mouths from claiming each other, couldn't stop stroking and licking and tasting and—

"Babe," he warned again, almost past the point of no return. "Better stop."

She rolled away and onto her back, and he moved with her. Thank God he'd had the foresight to shove a condom in his back pocket, and he had it out and unwrapped in seconds. He sheathed himself quickly and moved between her legs again. Meeting her eyes, he saw an urgency there that matched his own.

"Please, Grady," she panted. "I need this."

And then he was inside her, moving and thrusting and claiming her with every part of himself. Dear Lord, she felt incredible, soft and tight and wet and so perfect around him. His eyes stung behind closed lids, and he honestly couldn't say why. He only knew he wanted her, that he'd never felt so complete before in his whole life.

The orgasm hit faster than he'd hoped, but she was right there with him.

"Grady." Her thighs clenched around him as her hips rose up off the bed and she arched tight and sweet against him. "Oh God."

He toppled over the edge with her, losing himself completely. What was it with this woman?

When he came back down, Willa curled against him like an animal seeking warmth. There was something tender in the movement, something achingly vulnerable, a side to her he'd never seen before.

"You okay?" he murmured as he planted a kiss along her hairline.

"Perfect." She laughed softly. "My hero."

And there it was again. The hero thing. He didn't really believe it, but it was a part of him, just like the job.

These pangs of terror, they didn't mean anything. Who the fuck cared what the future held, as long as he had moments like this?

Moments with the world's most beautiful woman cradled against him, her heart thudding fast and solid with his, reminding him that whatever lurked ahead didn't matter. Not in relationships and sure as hell not in life.

As he stroked a hand down her bare back, he almost believed it.

. . .

Grady woke up alone and not 100 percent sure where he was. He blinked a few times to clear his head, grateful to find himself in an actual bed and not on a forest floor with a rattlesnake wrapped up in his sleeping bag. What was that on his feet?

He sat up and looked at the foot of the bed where a black and white tuxedo cat lay curled in the tangle of blankets.

"Hey, kitty."

The cat didn't move and appeared to have all its legs, so this must be the deaf one. Earmuff? He reached down to scratch its ears, and the cat opened its eyes and stretched. After studying Grady a moment and finding him uninteresting, the cat lay down again and went back to sleep.

"Where's your owner?" he asked.

No response. Not that he expected one from a deaf cat. He patted the other side of the bed, surprised to discover it cool to the touch. Willa had been gone awhile.

He located his pants and boxers and pulled them on, not bothering with a shirt or shoes. A rustling in the corner caught his attention, and he glanced over to see Stevie the blind dog heaving himself to his feet.

"Hey, Stevie," he murmured as the big dog lumbered over to snuffle his hand for snacks. "Do you know where she is?"

If Stevie knew, he wasn't telling, but he did turn and walk out of the bedroom. Grady followed, impressed that the sightless beast didn't bump into any doorframes or even graze the towering bookshelf at the end of the hall. Grady slowed his pace, conscious of the fact that he hadn't been invited into this part of the house yet. Would Willa be pissed he'd gone wandering?

Unconcerned, Stevie ambled past the bookcase and disappeared around the corner. Grady hesitated, not sure he should wander this far. Then he heard a sniffle.

And another. And a soft hiccup that was almost a sob. No, it *was* a sob. He hurried around the corner where he saw Willa — *crying*?

She sat on the floor with her legs crossed and her face tilted down. Her hair made a curtain around her, and through it, he glimpsed tear tracks on her cheeks. He stepped forward to comfort her when he heard the noise.

"Rarrrrrrrrr."

The low growl snapped Grady's attention to the corner, where a massive gray cat sat perched on the end of a file cabinet. Even with its left front leg missing, the creature looked ready to strike. Willa jumped to her feet, swiping at her eyes.

"Grady." She dashed the heels of her hands across her cheeks again as she ran to the still-growling cat. "Barrow, stop it."

She swooped in and grabbed the animal, burying her face in its fur. The cat growled again, looking dismayed at being used as a Kleenex.

Grady stood there like an idiot, not sure what to say. "Are you okay?"

Of course she wasn't okay. Any moron could see that. He stepped forward to comfort her, but Willa stepped back.

"I'm fine." She pasted on a cardboard smile and tossed her hair as the cat snarled again. "Just watching one of those sad animal videos on YouTube, you know?"

Grady didn't know, since her phone was nowhere in sight. And her laptop was on the other side of the room, a screensaver flickering its evidence that no one had touched it for a good long while.

She must have seen him notice because her shoulders slumped a bit. "Fine," she said. "It wasn't that. I just—I didn't get a job I really wanted. This RFP I submitted recently, I thought for sure I'd get it, but I didn't, and I was bummed. Okay?"

"Okay. I'm sorry." He watched her face, pretty sure that wasn't the whole story but also sure he shouldn't push. Not now. "I know you work hard, so that must be disappointing."

"It's fine," she said again. "I'm totally fine."

"Do you need a minute alone or—?"

"No, I'm good." She forced a shaky-sounding laugh and held out the cat. "This is Barrow," she said as the cat growled again. "He's—uh—a little protective."

Barrow stared at Grady and hissed his greeting,

so Grady kept his hands shoved in his pockets. He ached to reach for her—Willa, not the cat—to offer comfort or tenderness or anything else she might need.

But she didn't appear to need anything. Not from him, anyway, so Grady kept his distance. "I think I met Earmuff," he said. "That's your other cat, right?"

"Right." The look she gave him was almost grateful, and he sensed he'd done the right thing by pretending everything was okay. "Wow, so I guess you've met everyone. Well, everyone except Carl the fish. Here, he's right on my desk—"

"It's okay," he said. "I'd rather wait."

She blinked at him. "You want to wait to meet my fish."

"Yes."

"Um—okay."

The look she gave him was like he'd just stuck lit firecrackers in his ears, but Grady didn't care. He leaned against the doorframe, taking in her rumpled hair, her sex-flushed skin, and wanting her all over again.

But mostly he wanted to know her, to be the kind of guy she'd confide in, who she'd invite into her life for more than just a few rolls in the hay. It was dumb, since this no-strings-attached thing had served him well forever.

That was before he met Willa.

He raked his fingers through his hair, conscious of her staring at him like he was nuts. "You said meeting cats and fish is second-date stuff," he said.

"I was kidding."

"Nope, you said it." He offered a sheepish smile

as the cat in her arms growled again. "And right now, I haven't met the fish."

She cocked her head at him, her puzzled expression shifting to amusement. "I suppose that's true."

"So I'm better off saving Carl for another time," he said. "To make the second date really count."

"That seems wise," Willa said, clearly not buying it any more than he did.

But she didn't argue. And right then, that seemed like the biggest win he could hope for. That and pulling her against his chest.

"Come here," he said, holding his arms open. "We don't have to talk about it, but I can at least give you a hug."

She hesitated, and Grady could see the conflict playing through her mind. Needing someone, accepting comfort from another person—that wasn't in her wheelhouse. Handling everything on her own was more her style.

But he saw the moment she relented. Saw it in her eyes that she knew he wasn't a threat, and a hug wouldn't make her weaker. It might even help.

"Sure." She set Barrow down on the floor, and the three-legged cat scampered away as fast as a three-legged cat could possibly scamper.

Some of her timidity was back as she stepped forward, almost like they hadn't hugged before. Like he hadn't been buried inside her more than once.

And then she was in his arms, burrowing against him. "Thanks, Grady."

"Don't mention it," he said, holding her to him, feeling her heart beat against his.

It felt like his biggest win so far.

# CHAPTER TEN

Willa rubbed her lips together in the mirror, then felt like a dummy for putting on lipstick to go mini golfing.

Which was *not* a date. Everyone knew mini golf wasn't a date, at least according to Grady. She'd threatened to Google it on the phone with him last night but got distracted when she typed in "is miniature golf" and autofill came back with "foreplay."

"You've been messing with my computer," she'd accused as she retried the search with the same results.

"I never touched your computer," he'd promised. "Speaking of touching things that belong to you—"

"Seriously, this is weird." Willa had gone through the rest of the search results again. "The second autofill suggestion is 'is miniature golf a profitable business?' Are there really a lot of people googling that?"

"Can we get back to the foreplay one?" he asked. "Because I just realized I totally missed my chance at a golf/foreplay joke. You know—*fore*?"

"Good Lord, I'm dating a twelve-year-old," she'd muttered even though the joke made her laugh.

"We're not dating," he insisted. "And miniature golf isn't a date. It's about as romantic as bowling. Which also is not a date."

"I know, I know," she assured him, secretly thrilled he was so eager to spend time with her that he'd make up these ridiculous rules so that she didn't have to break *her* rules. Or his. "Pick me up at noon."

Willa glanced at her watch now, aware that she was ready a full thirty minutes before he was scheduled to arrive. Might as well get some work done.

She sat down at her desk and pulled up the spreadsheet for Visit Hart Valley, the city's tourism bureau. One of her longest-standing clients, they made up almost a quarter of her income. That was scary. Her dad always warned her never to put all her eggs in one basket, surprisingly sound advice from a guy with the business acumen of a cactus.

Scrolling through her docs, her eyes landed on the RFP for Tranquility Villa again, and she had to force herself to keep breathing past the tightness in her chest. *Dammit.*

She'd wanted that job so badly. It wasn't the money, though that would have been nice. It was the chance to develop a website for one of the foremost providers of drug and alcohol rehab centers, a company she'd researched back when she tried to get her father into treatment.

"I don't have a problem," her father had insisted when she came to him at twelve years old with a brochure from Tranquility Villa. "And even if I did, I could handle it myself. I wouldn't need some damn facility."

But all the literature Willa had read said he *did* need professional help. That detoxing could be fatal without medical supervision and that odds of recovery were slim for alcoholics who tried going cold turkey on their own.

She never did convince him to go. They didn't have the money anyway. And now she'd failed at landing them as a client, which would have given her access to super-discounted services for family members—

"Stop it," she told herself. "Just keep working. Focus on the next client and the ones you already have."

Her little pep talk kept her going until she lost track of time. When the doorbell rang, she jumped in her chair and bumped Carl's fishbowl.

"Sorry." She straightened the glass globe and made a beeline for her front door while Stevie barked his fool head off.

"Hey," she said as she opened the door, her heart fluttering only a little at the sight of Grady standing there with a bouquet of—

"Beef jerky," Grady said, thrusting it out to her. "Because real flowers suggest it's a date, and this isn't a date."

Willa took the bizarre bouquet, marveling at the workmanship required to twist strips of beef jerky into a dozen perfect rosettes mounted on wooden skewers.

Stevie danced with joy at her feet. He might not be able to see, but he could definitely smell the treat to end all treats. Willa laughed. "This might not be a date, but Stevie's already half in love with you."

Proving her point, Stevie nudged Grady's hand with his big snout. Grady obliged, and Willa couldn't help envying the gentle stroking. "He's in love with my beef jerky," Grady said. "But I'll take what I can get."

Willa turned from the door. "Let me just put these in…um, what kind of vase do you use for jerky flowers?"

"Beats me." Grady kept scratching Stevie's ears with those long, strong fingers. "Someplace the pets can't get to them."

She ran back to the kitchen and tucked the jerky flowers in the fridge. After grabbing her sweater off a chair, she hustled back to the front door where Grady waited.

"Ready?"

"Yep." She bent to scratch Stevie one last time, assuring him he was the best dog in the world before following Grady out the door to his rig—

"Where's your truck?" Willa stopped in the middle of the driveway and stared at the big, shiny motorcycle.

Grady grinned as he turned to face her. "I always wanted a Harley." He swept a hand toward the gleaming piece of machinery. "Before you freak out, a buddy of mine was selling this for a great price. I couldn't resist."

"But—"

"Don't worry, I have an extra helmet. I even splurged and added the Bluetooth intercom so we can talk to each other if we want. Here you go." He slid the helmet onto her head, gently adjusting the chin strap as he looked into her eyes. "Are you okay?"

*Not in the slightest.* "Of course," she said, forcing a smile.

"I'm a safe driver, I promise," he said. "I took a motorcycle safety course last year, since I knew I'd be doing this someday."

He helped her onto the bike and showed her how to wrap her arms around him and lean with him on the curves. "I probably shouldn't have worn a skirt," she said into the intercom as he turned onto the road leading to the amusement park.

"What's that?" he shouted.

Huh. Maybe her voice hadn't triggered the intercom. "I said I want to marry you and have your babies."

She meant it as a joke, pretty sure he couldn't hear her anyway.

But he slowed just enough to send her heart racing, to have her thinking *what if?* Not what if he'd heard her, but what if she really could have that—

*No.*

That was stupid, almost as stupid as getting involved with someone who splurged on expensive meals or motorcycles, which was fine for him, but Willa broke out in hives whenever she wasn't cautious and frugal and saving and—

"Here we are," he called as he pulled into the lot. He brought the bike to a halt, then swung himself off and helped her do the same. As his hands slid from her waist, he skimmed his palm down and back up under her skirt, giving her butt a quick squeeze.

"The skirt was a great idea," he said, grinning at her. "So was the thong. We'll talk later about the marriage and babies."

*Aw, crap.* "I was kidding."

"I know." His grin didn't waver as he took her hand and pulled her toward the entrance.

The lobby of Hart Valley Fun Center buzzed

with joyful clamor. The crash of bowling pins, the laughter of children running past with lopsided party hats, the cheerful chirps from the video arcade—all of it combined to form a melody that was somehow familiar and foreign.

Willa never had a birthday party here, but she'd been to one once. She'd collected soda cans for weeks to save for a Dollar Store teddy bear that earned her admission to Lacey Simpson's tenth birthday festivities. Even now, she could taste the root beer on the back of her tongue, feel the buzz of excitement at having Lacey's mother check her seat belt and pay the friendly attendant for the go-karts.

"Two rounds of mini golf, please," Grady told the bored-looking teenager behind the counter.

"Pick your balls," the kid said without a hint of humor.

Willa chose pink, while Grady grabbed green. "To match your eyes," he said, winking at her.

She glanced at the ball and snorted. "If my eyes are neon green, I need to visit the ophthalmologist."

"Grab a putter and let's go."

He led her outside to the course, holding her hand the whole time. They made their way to the first tee, a pretty little Astroturf-covered spot with a windmill and a puddle she guessed was meant to be a pond.

"Would you like to go first?" He gestured to the tee, and Willa stepped up with her putter in hand.

"Absolutely." She got into position, even though she'd only done this a couple of times before. Not like anyone played mini golf seriously, so she might as well have fun with it.

"Fore!" she called, though they were the only ones on the course. The ball bonked off the windmill and meandered across the turf until it settled at the edge.

"Nice shot," he said, rubbing his palms together as he adjusted his grip on his own club. He stepped up to the tee, assuming a stance that told her he'd done this a time or two. His brow furrowed, and the look of intense concentration on his face told her he was taking this way more seriously than she'd expected.

*Thwack!*

The ball bounced easily off the windmill, then tumbled down the chute and around the water feature, almost like he'd planned it that way. Which he had, she realized, as he followed the ball with his eyes, frowning the whole time.

"Come on, come on," he murmured under his breath. "Shit. There's a breeze—"

"Oh no." Willa stared at him. "You're one of *those* guys."

He blinked at her. "What guys?"

"The kind of guy who treats every sport like he's a professional athlete."

He frowned. "No, I don— *Ah, come on!* Damn." Glaring at his ball, he grumbled something unintelligible and looked back at her. "What?"

Willa shook her head, stifling a laugh. "I rest my case."

A hint of sheepishness crept into his expression, but not much. "I like to do well."

She laughed and marched over to the ball. "And I like to have fun." With a solid whack, she sent her ball careening down the chute and across the green. It was a long way from the hole, but the sun was warm on the back of her neck and the breeze felt good ruffling her skirt. Making her way down the green, she turned back to watch Grady take his next shot.

"Focus," he muttered under his breath, and Willa stifled another laugh. He tapped the ball like a total pro, nudging it just gently enough so it went straight for the hole. It swirled around a couple of times, circling the edge until it caught on a loose piece of turf and went spinning off to the side.

"Dammit." Grady glared, seeming to forget she was there for a second. He shook himself out of it fast, turning to her with a smile. "Sorry. I guess I get carried away sometimes."

She slung her club over one shoulder, studying him in a fascinating new light. "You didn't mention this," she said, ambling closer to the spot where his ball had come to rest.

"Mention what?"

"That you take mini golf waaaaaay too seriously," she said. "This didn't come up when you listed your faults for me."

His brow furrowed a bit, but it was mixed with some of the earlier sheepishness. "I guess I never thought of it before."

"Is it just mini golf or all athletic pursuits?"

He stepped forward to join her, considering the question. "Probably all of it," he admitted. "We maybe shouldn't hit the bumper cars later."

"Noted." She glanced at her ball. "Would it drive you crazy right now if I picked up my ball and just set it in the hole?"

He stared at her like she'd just suggested butchering a kitten on the ninth hole. "Of course not." The twitch beside his left eye gave him away.

"Really." Willa stifled a smirk as she stepped forward. "What if I did it to *your* ball?"

"Why—" He stopped himself, looking pained. "No big deal."

"No?" Willa took another step forward. "What if I did this?"

She drew back her right foot and brought it forward, giving his ball a solid tap with the toe of her sandal. It bounced crazily back up the green, headed straight for the windmill.

Grady stared at her in disbelief. "You just kicked my ball."

She grinned up at him. "Is that a problem?"

"Pretty sure that's against the rules of mini golf."

Willa laughed, weirdly intrigued by this new side of Grady. A heroic hottie who wouldn't hesitate to risk life and limb to put out a fire but with a competitive streak so fierce, she could actually hear his teeth grinding together.

He stared forlornly after his ball, knuckles white as he gripped his club. "I don't like to lose," he admitted.

Willa looked into his eyes, charmed by his honesty even as his words struck a hollow chord in the back of her mind.

*That's what it's about. That's why he won't give up after two dates. It's not about you; it's about winning.*

Which was fine, really. He wasn't getting attached; she wasn't getting attached. This was exactly what she'd signed on for.

"Come on," she said. "Let's keep playing."

"Are you going to keep kicking my ball?"

"Let's do this," she began, smoothing her skirt down as a gentle gust caught the hem. "Any time you start getting all psycho about your golf swing or the breeze or anything else you think is impacting your score, I get to kick your ball."

He shook his head. "This is the weirdest date I've ever had."

Willa got into position to putt. "It's not a date," she reminded him.

Gripping her club with both hands, she bent her knees a little and drew it back to swing. She didn't hear Grady move behind her until she felt his hand on her ass.

"Excuse me?" she said, feigning dismay even as she leaned into his touch. She was damn glad she'd worn the thong.

His hand felt good there. She glanced around, grateful they had the course to themselves. All the families were inside playing arcade games and bowling, so he could put his hand under her skirt all he wanted.

He leaned in close, breath tickling her ear to make her shiver with pleasure. "Just relieving some tension," he murmured, giving her ass a firm squeeze. "Like one of those stress relief balls."

Willa leaned back against him, relishing his hand on her bare ass and the warmth of his breath on her neck. "You're treating my ass as your own personal squeeze toy?"

"Maybe more of a fidget spinner," he mused, rubbing his palm in a slow, languid circle over one naked cheek until she shivered with pleasure. "Is that a problem?"

"Nope." Her voice came out breathy and high, and she couldn't believe this was turning her on.

"Good." He released her ass cheek, and Willa tried not to miss the feel of his warm palm on her backside.

They continued playing, making the rounds from hole to hole with Grady gritting his teeth and glowering every time the ball didn't go where he wanted it to. Twice she had to kick his ball—once after he cursed at a stray bark chip on the green and once after he performed a particularly enthusiastic celebration dance over a hole in one.

"Have you always been like this?" she asked as he slipped behind her and cupped her ass again.

"Obsessed with your butt?" he asked. "Yep."

"Hypercompetitive," she said, swatting his hand away even though she kinda didn't want to. "I wouldn't have pegged you as a sports nut."

"I don't know that mini golf really counts as a sport," he pointed out as he took his turn teeing off on the next hole. "But yeah. I guess it came from having so many brothers and sisters."

"You said there were ten of you?"

"Yep. I'm smack-dab in the middle."

What would that even be like? Willa couldn't fathom it. "Do you see them often?"

"Every weekend," he said. "Well, not all of them. Whoever makes it to the family barbecue. It's at my parents' place every Saturday, but usually half of us have something else going on."

Willa shook her head, struggling to picture it. "I

can't imagine having that many brothers and sisters," she said. "Or having *any* brothers and sisters. That's just so foreign to me."

"What was it like being an only child?" He swung and hit the ball, loosening up now that they'd implemented their ass-grabbing, ball-kicking rules. "Did you get lonely?"

Willa stepped up to take her turn, grateful it required her concentration so she didn't have to meet his eyes. "I wouldn't say lonely," she said. "To be honest, my dad felt like a sibling half the time."

"How do you mean?"

She bit her lip, not sure why she'd brought it up. It wasn't like her to talk about her shitty childhood. "He wasn't the most reliable parent on earth." That was putting it mildly. "He'd forget to pick me up at school or buy groceries sometimes or—" She stopped there because Grady's eyes had gone dark, but she could have kept going.

*He'd forget to pay the electric bill.*

*He'd forget to buy me school shoes until my toes curled under from wearing sneakers four sizes too small.*

*He'd forget to come home for days on end.*

Willa's stomach clenched into a tight ball as she forced a smile. "It was a different sort of childhood," she said mildly.

"How did you get your name?"

"What?"

"Your name," Grady said. "You told me right after we met that Willa is short for William. That it was a long story." He shifted his putter from one hand to the other, studying her with those stormy gray eyes. "We've got time now."

She watched him measuring her, studying her face, gauging her reaction. She knew if she told him it was none of his business, that she wasn't ready to share, he'd respect it. He wouldn't hold it against her if she didn't feel like opening up.

"I was a surprise baby," she said. "I don't know all the details, but my dad told me I was completely unexpected."

Grady frowned. "Like—until you arrived?"

"Close," she said. "I guess my mom was almost eight months along by the time they found out. They were totally sure I'd be a boy. So sure, my dad made a bet with one of his poker buddies that he'd name the baby after him."

Grady grimaced. "Must have been one helluva poker game."

"Yeah. And William wasn't one to let my dad out of a bet, so…" She shrugged, studying Grady's face for a reaction. Was that pity or amusement? Maybe both. "It was easy enough to shorten it to Willa. That was my mom's idea, I guess. That, and my middle name—Marie, for her mom. My grandma."

"Were you close with your grandparents?"

"Not at all." She looked down at her golf club, tapping the head of it with her sandal. "Apparently my grandparents hated that they named me William—*hated* it. They'd only call me Marie, which drove my father crazy. But my mom, she wasn't great at standing up to her parents, so she'd call me Marie, too, whenever they were around."

The words tumbling out of her mouth sounded familiar, but it was someone else's voice. Even her friends had never heard this story. Not all of it, anyway.

Why was she telling Grady?

"After my mom was gone, it was just my dad and me," she said. "And he'd make up these stories for me about a girl superhero named William. She could fly and time travel and make herself invisible if she wanted to. And she always saved the day."

Willa didn't tell him how desperately she'd wish for those same powers. To be invisible. To rescue her father or herself from what they'd become. The prickle in the back of her throat signaled an unwelcome encroachment of tears, and she knew she needed to wrap things up.

"Your dad sounds like an interesting guy." He leaned against his club, all traces of competitiveness gone as he gave her all his attention. "It couldn't have been easy raising a kid all on his own."

"He did the best he could," Willa said, still fighting the tear-filled throat tickle. "Anyway, we were talking about your family. You're close?"

Grady didn't answer right away, and the way he was watching her face told her he had a pretty good idea they were edging into territory she didn't like talking about. She braced for him to push, but he surprised her.

"Yeah, we're close," he said. "I probably take it for granted that I've always got this support system around me. My parents are amazing, and I've always got siblings I can call if I need something."

"That does sound nice." The lonely longing in her voice should have embarrassed her, but it didn't. "I always wondered what it would be like to have a big, supportive family."

"It's nuts, but I can't imagine it any other way." He looked at her for a long time, like he wanted to ask more questions but didn't know how. "Come with me."

"What?"

"To Saturday's barbecue," he said. "It's the last one I'll be able to do for a couple of weeks before I take off again. You should join me."

She folded her arms over her chest and regarded him with the sternest look she could muster. "Meeting the family is definitely a date."

He snorted. "Since you haven't met my family, I'll give you the benefit of the doubt here."

"What do you mean?"

"Trust me—hanging out with my family is the *least* date-like experience you could imagine," he said. "More like a visit to the zoo or maybe an insane asylum."

Willa laughed. "Is it noisy?"

"Family dinners?" Grady snorted. "Like a freight train hitting a fireworks stand. Like a truckload of hyenas being driven in a flatbed with a broken horn. Like a rock concert amplified by—"

"Okay, okay," Willa said, laughing again. "I get it."

"Not to make it sound unpleasant," he amended as they walked together to the spot where their balls had landed. "My family's great. They're just…a lot."

Something hot and wistful twisted in her belly, and Willa looked away so he wouldn't see her face crease with longing. She had nothing to be sad about. The weather was perfect, and she was here with a good-looking guy. She had a beautiful home and career and—

"I'm serious," he said. "You seem curious about it, and it's free food. Come with me to the next one."

She laughed a little at the "free" part. He knew which buttons to push, though he couldn't know that wasn't the appeal for her. A chance to experience family—real, normal family—that's what she wanted to witness for herself.

"I accept," she said. "Thank you."

Grady grinned. "In that case, it's an un-date."

# CHAPTER ELEVEN

"You're taking her to meet your parents."

Tony said the words flatly, the same way he might have if Grady announced he'd be riding a pink unicycle naked down Main Street at lunchtime.

"It's not like that." Grady moved off the weight bench and wiped his face on a sweat towel before assuming his position as spotter.

Though he wasn't on duty, he liked to stick with his weightlifting routine on off days, so he'd come in early to join the guys for PT.

As Tony reached for the bar, he gave a snort of disbelief. "Taking her to meet your parents isn't like what?" he asked. "You mean in the same way it's not a date to have a tea party or go mini golfing or—"

"Shut up and lift," he muttered. He wanted to be annoyed, but the guy did have a point. The number of times Grady had taken a woman home to meet his family could be counted on one hand with five fingers remaining.

In other words, *never*.

It shouldn't be a big deal. His mom and dad were friendly, his siblings mostly okay. Yeah, they were loud as hell and nosy sometimes, but he loved the crap out of them.

So why hadn't he brought a woman home before? And why was he thinking of doing it with a woman who'd made it clear she didn't want anything long-term? Not with him, anyway.

He tried not to take that personally. It wasn't like he wanted anything long-term with her, either.

"Your turn." Tony got up off the bench and clapped Grady on the shoulder. "I'm just flipping you shit. You know I think Willa's great."

"She *is* great," he said. "And it's not like I'm looking to marry her or anything. I just like hanging out with her."

"And talking with her?"

"Sure."

"And making plans to do stuff together?"

"Of course."

"And nailing her?"

"Hey—"

Tony put his hands up in mock defense. "I'm just saying, that doesn't sound so different from marriage."

"The hell it doesn't." Not like his parents' marriage anyway, which always struck him as more of a strained business relationship than anything. How could it not be, with the stress of raising ten kids and paying the mortgage and dealing with a smokejumper's crazy schedule?

His mom used to swear she didn't mind, but Grady knew better. He'd seen the sadness in her eyes when his father would walk out the door to begin another endless shift. He'd seen the worry flicker across her face as she watched the nightly news for details on some forest fire raging out of control. Was his father there? Grady never knew, rarely had any idea which blaze his dad was working or even what state he was in that week.

Grady flopped down on the weight bench and

rattled off ten quick reps, barely feeling the weight.

"Slow down, Turbo." Tony laughed. "Do we need to get you one of those anxiety aids? A fidget spinner or something?"

*Willa's ass under a floaty little skirt…*

Grady stood up and wiped his face, deliberately not meeting Tony's eyes. "Fuck off and take your turn."

Tony laughed and mopped his brow with a towel. "Way to deflect, big guy."

• • •

"You seriously grew up in this house?" Willa trailed her fingers along the handrail of the steps leading to his parents' front door. Her eyes were all kid-in-a-candy-shop round, and Grady couldn't help reaching for her free hand.

"I straddled that railing when I was six and slid all the way to the bottom." He winced at the memory. "Nailed my nuts on the newel post."

"Ouch."

Willa pulled her hand off the rail and surveyed the yard while Grady tried to see it through her eyes. The house was well tended and large, but the shutters could use some fresh paint, and he needed to get with his brothers and plan a hedge-trimming party so their dad wouldn't get up on the damn ladder. The old man's back had been bothering him again.

Grady caught himself massaging his own low back and stopped. He'd landed hard on his last jump, and still hadn't shaken off the ache.

He focused on Willa instead, conscious of the nervous energy radiating off her in waves. It wasn't just the house—it was everything. What would she think of his family? What would they think of her?

"Someone in your family has a green thumb," she observed.

Grady followed the direction of her gaze. "The honeysuckle?"

"All of it. The wisteria, the weeping willows—it's beautiful."

He nodded and took it all in as though seeing it for the first time. The grass was bright green and freshly mowed. His mom's rosebushes were in full bloom, and there was a pack of tricycles at the edge of the lawn that belonged to his nieces and nephews. In other words, a pretty normal American house.

"My mom used to plant annuals when my dad would be out on fires," he said. "This whole area would be a sea of petunias and marigolds by the end of summer."

She turned and looked at him, her mossy-green eyes filled with way more interest than the situation called for. "He was gone a lot, like you are now?"

"Way more than I am," he said. "Smokejumper schedules were a lot crazier in the days before they started figuring out it was safer not to have us working around-the-clock the whole season."

"Did your mom get lonely or did she love having all that time to herself?"

A familiar pang hit Grady right in the chest. He kept his gaze on the yard so he wouldn't have to look at Willa. "She was lonely," he said. "She didn't sign up to be a single mom, but that's what she was most of the time. I know it took a toll on her."

*On us*, he thought but didn't say. He'd seen firsthand how his father's career had impacted their marriage. How the stress of family life had dulled the shine in his mother's eyes and left his father feeling frazzled and exhausted. The rare days Allen Billman had at home were devoted to kids' soccer games and trips to the orthodontist. Every penny, every hour of free time, got snapped up by someone else, usually one of the kids. Grady's dad had worked hard, no doubt about it, but had he ever once savored the fruits of his own labor?

Grady didn't want that for himself, and he sure as hell didn't wish it on any woman he brought into his life. Definitely not Willa.

*Stop thinking about the future. That's not in the cards for either of you.*

"I'll bet it was beautiful." Willa's voice jarred him back to the present, and he looked at her, trying to find his place in the conversation.

"What's that?"

"The flowers." She swept a hand toward the yard. "The ones your mom would plant when your dad was gone. Sounds like it would have been pretty."

Grady nodded, surprised to realize he hadn't thought much about those flowers. Not for a long time.

"Come on." He gave her hand a squeeze. "We should get inside."

Willa glanced at the front door, a faint hint of nervousness in her eyes. "I'm surprised they haven't heard us out here and come to check on us."

Grady laughed and pulled her toward the door.

"When a family this size gets together, they wouldn't hear a dump truck being driven through the dining room."

He pushed the door open, knowing there was no point in knocking. No one would hear anyway. The cacophony of voices led them down the hall and into the living room, where more than a dozen Billmans were shouting over one another.

His oldest sister, Angie, was in one corner hollering something about potato salad to Deb, his middle brother's wife. Deb kept nodding like she was following along, but she was distracted by her five-year-old twins squealing as they ran circles around the coffee table. A pack of his brothers-in-law stood six inches from the TV, trying to watch the Seahawks game with the volume cranked high enough to drown out the sound of his youngest brother, Jamie, playing guitar in the corner.

Grady's mom rushed in with a plate full of deviled eggs, not noticing Grady and Willa standing at the edge of the hallway. He watched her zip from the kitchen into the living room, dodging the obstacle course of her children and their offspring like a pro race-car driver.

"I think I got a little too much sriracha on these eggs," she was saying, "but why don't you try one and tell me—"

"Hey, Mom."

She whipped around fast, her face breaking into a huge grin when she spotted him. "Grady! You made it."

She shoved the plate of eggs at Grady's brother Abel, who stumbled backward but managed to keep all the slippery orbs on the plate somehow. "Hey—"

But their mother was already across the room, pulling Grady into a tight hug. "It's so good to see you," she said as she rocked back and forth, pulling him with her in a familiar maternal rhythm. "And this must be Willa."

She let go of Grady and turned to Willa, whose hand was outstretched to shake. Sheryl ignored it and went for the mom hug, squeezing Willa so tightly, she gave a little squeak.

"I've heard so much about you, sweetheart," Sheryl said as she pulled back. "Aren't you a pretty thing."

"Come on, Mom." Grady's middle sister sauntered over with a baby on her hip. "You'll embarrass her. I'm Stacy. And this is Audrey."

"Nice to meet you." Willa gently shook the baby's outstretched hand, earning smiles from both moms as she surveyed the insanity swarming the room. "I've never been around such a big family."

Grady's mom laughed. "Oh, honey. This is nothing. We don't even have half the clan here tonight. When the cousins and aunts and uncles show up, it's practically a riot."

"A riot made up of a lot of toddlers and pregnant women," Grady put in.

His mother laughed, backing away already. "Pardon me a moment. I need to go check the brisket."

His sisters hurried off to break up a squabble between their respective offspring while Willa stood surveying the scene like a tourist at a zoo. The twins careened past him, knocking into Grady's knees and making him stagger.

"Uncle Grady, look!" Clover—or was it Rose?—did a pirouette, then bounced happily in front of him. "We got our new cheer costumes, and Mommy said we could show you our makeup."

"Makeup, huh." Holy Christ, they looked like five-year-old beauty pageant contestants, what with the sequined skirts and spandex tops and—good Lord, were those false eyelashes?

"Don't ask." Grady's brother Liam ambled over with a bowl full of chips and a pained look on his face. "Competitive cheerleading. It's all the rage now in the under-five set."

Willa cocked her head and studied the front of Liam's shirt. "What does that say?"

He held up his arms and gave a resigned shrug. "Cheer Dad." He grimaced. "In bedazzled letters, in case you're wondering. Will someone please kill me now?"

Grady laughed and flicked a chunk of something—yogurt, maybe?—off the sleeve of his brother's shirt. "At some point, aliens took over the body of my hell-raising, biker-bar-owning brother and replaced all that badassery with the ultimate family man."

"Guilty as charged." His brother's eyes sparked with contentment as he stuck a hand out for Willa to shake. "Liam. Cheerfully emasculated by my two hellion daughters and the hottest wife in the world."

"Love you, too, baby!" called Deb from across the room. She flashed them a smile and skimmed a hand over her belly. The touch was brief, but Grady had been through this enough times to recognize what it meant.

"Holy crap," Grady said, lowering his voice as the twins perked up. "You—uh—spawning again?"

Liam beamed. "Yep. Two months along. Score another one for that badass Billman baby batter."

"Ew." Grady made a face as the twins kept right on dancing around his legs.

"Crap! Crap! Crap! Uncle Grady said 'crap.'" Clover and Rose swooped around, waving their adorable little starfish hands.

Willa was trying very hard not to laugh, but Grady could see the dimples forming in her cheeks. Good. He wanted her to enjoy herself here.

"Do not repeat that word," Liam scolded, shooting a look at Grady. "Uncle Grady is a bad example, but you're better than that, aren't you?"

"Nooooooo!" chorused the girls and went right on dancing.

Their father put a hand on each of their backs and nudged them toward their mother. "You've shown Uncle Grady and Aunt Willa your costumes. Now go see if Mommy has something to scrub that 'cr—that makeup off your faces."

The girls gave matching whines of distress but did what they were told and went scampering off in the other direction. Grady glanced at Willa, gauging her reaction to the "aunt" moniker. Her smile was big and genuine, and she looked completely charmed. Charmed and a little taken aback. His family could be overwhelming even to people who were used to being around that much chaos. He couldn't imagine how they seemed to someone who'd grown up without any siblings at all.

"Come on," he said to Willa. "Let's find the cooler. I'll introduce you to everyone else once we've gotten some liquid refreshment."

"Nice meeting you," she called to Liam over her shoulder as they headed for the dining room.

He led her past the big table with a zillion extensions in it and out a set of french doors onto the back deck. The hulking blue cooler that had been a mainstay at all Billman functions for the better part of two decades sat at the edge of the deck, and Grady led Willa to it.

"You'll need this," he said, tucking an icy can of beer into her hand. "Trust me."

"Looks like there's a bountiful supply," she said as she popped the top open.

"This isn't our first rodeo."

Three of his nephews raced past, their freckled faces striped with some sort of paint. Each little boy held a Nerf gun, and one of them whooped as they raced past. "We're superheroes, Uncle Grady."

"I can see that."

He pulled Willa back before nephew number four could crash into her as he chased after the rest of them, firing Nerf darts left and right. The boys took off down the steep slope of the backyard, shouting about force fields and superpowers.

Grady cracked his beer and turned to her with a smile. "Ready to go home yet?"

Willa shook her head, more than a little dazed-looking. "This is bonkers."

"Told you."

"And wonderful."

He studied her face for some hint of irony,

but no, she was dead serious. "Really? You're not overwhelmed?"

"Oh, I am." She smiled, and Grady's heart damn near melted. "But in a good way."

An unexpected warmth crept up through his chest. He'd hoped she'd enjoy it here, but this—this was more than that. She fit right in, which surprised him. "I'm sure they'll make you an honorary member if you like."

"I may take you up on that."

She sipped her beer as Grady watched the side of her face and wondered how long he could keep pretending he wasn't falling head over heels for her.

And how very, very bad that would be for them both.

• • •

After dinner, Grady retreated to the kitchen with Paul and their father for one of their most time-honored Billman family traditions.

"No one who helped make dinner has to clean up," his father explained to Willa as he shooed her out of the kitchen. "Go grab a drink and put your feet up."

"But I didn't help with dinner," she protested. "I only set the table."

"That counts," Grady said. "Out! Go on, I'm sure my mother's dying to interrogate you."

Willa feigned a look of terror, but he could tell from the flash of delight in her eyes that she was loving every second of it. Who'd have thought that only-child Willa would be so embraced by his over-the-top noisy, nosy family? Or that she'd enjoy the afternoon as much as she'd seemed to.

"Get your ass over here and start scrubbing." Paul snapped him with a dish towel, and Grady turned back to his duties.

"When are we going to switch to paper plates so this isn't such a pain in the ass to clean up?" he grumbled.

His father rolled his eyes. "When we stop giving a shit about the environment and the amount of trash this family produces." He piled a stack of plates next to the sink. "In other words, never."

Grady grinned and plunged his hands into the soapy water. He didn't mind, honestly. This was one of the things he loved about his family. In college, he'd gone to friends' homes for the occasional holiday meal and wound up dumbfounded to discover the females of the family shouldering the burden for both meal prep and cleanup. That would never fly in the Billman home. Here, everyone pulled their weight, and even the littlest kids had jobs to do.

"Your girlfriend seems great," his father said. "Totally held her own at dinner."

Paul laughed. "She didn't even flinch when the twins asked if you'll get married soon so they can be flower girls."

Grady suppressed the big, dumb-ass grin welling up inside him. It wasn't just the memory of Willa cheerfully telling the girls she'd have her secretary call theirs. No, it was what his father had said.

*Your girlfriend.*

He knew he should issue a correction but couldn't seem to bring himself to do it. He'd been careful about not scaring her away, not wanting her to think this dinner meant anything other than a free meal with a fun group of people who happened to look like him and share the same DNA.

But he'd be lying if he pretended not to like the sound of that.

*Your girlfriend.*

He liked it a helluva lot.

That…was a first.

"Hey, Dad," Paul said, reaching around Grady to grab a towering stack of dessert plates. "Did you go look at that sixty-two Bronco?"

"I did." His father's eyes gleamed as he toweled off the roasting pan Grady handed him. "She's pretty sweet. Needs a new catalytic converter, and the upholstery's a little torn up, but the body's in great shape. She'll be a good project."

A pinch of nostalgia caught Grady right between the ribs. Memories flashed up on the silver screen in his brain of his father out in the garage tinkering with his latest project car on one of his rare breaks from work.

Grady had been eight, but remembered it like yesterday.

"I thought we were going to spend time together this weekend, Allen," Grady's mom had said from where she stood on the other side of the garage, her voice soft and low.

Grady hadn't been able to see her face from where he'd been hunkered behind a stack of tires playing with his toy cars, but he'd noticed the quiver in her voice. Sadness, maybe, which he'd been hearing a lot lately.

He'd scrunched himself down low, not wanting to interrupt.

"I need time to myself, too, Sher," his dad had replied. His voice was low, too, but there was an edge to it. Something Grady heard almost never. "Seems like all I do lately is work and—"

"Exactly." His mom's voice had cracked on the words. "You're gone the whole summer, and the rare times you're home, we hardly see you at all. You're out here tinkering instead of spending time with us."

"That's not fair, and you know it." Dad had sounded more tired than angry, but Grady had held his breath anyway. "I spent all day yesterday running between Angie's soccer match and Nate's Little League practice. I got home in time to spend the evening showing Paul how to change the oil in his car."

Grady's mom had stayed quiet a long time. When she'd spoken, there'd been a faraway note in her voice. "I miss the date nights. Those years when you couldn't wait to get home to me and we'd stay up making love all night."

Wincing, Grady had scrunched lower behind the tires. He shouldn't have been listening to their conversation, he'd known that, but he hadn't been able to find a good way to make his escape.

"I miss that, too, Sher," his dad had said. "But this is how it has to be now. You knew when you married me that this is what it would be like. And I love the kids, don't get me wrong, but—"

"I know." His mother had sighed, and Grady could tell she wasn't angry anymore. Just sad. "Family is sacrifice."

"Family is love," his dad had countered, trying for wise certainty but sounding a little shaky. "I just sometimes wish it didn't mean losing every little bit of autonomy, you know?"

*Autonomy.*

At the time, Grady thought it had something to do with cars. With the projects his father liked to do out there in the garage but never seemed to have time for.

Even after he looked it up in the dictionary, he didn't get it.

*The quality or state of being self-governing. Self-directing freedom.*

It wasn't until years later that he began to wrap his head around it. His father had given up everything—hobbies, money, the little indulgences that made all the work worthwhile—for his career and his family.

It was then that Grady vowed never to do the same thing. He admired the hell out of his father, but he didn't want to become him. Not ever.

"Earth to Grady." Paul whacked him on the back of the head with a spatula. "You just going to stand there with the water running, or are you going to actually wash something?"

"Yeah," Grady muttered, glancing at his dad. "I'm on it."

His dad was studying him now, reading his thoughts as always. "You got something on your mind, son?"

"Just thinking about how hard it must have been," he said. "Juggling the family stuff and the job and all us damn kids."

Dad laughed, a familiar, booming sound that left Grady feeling homesick even though he was standing here in his own childhood kitchen. "Well now, I can't claim it was easy," he said. "It's gotten easier now."

"You mean for you?"

"For me and for your mom." Toweling off the cast-iron skillet Grady had handed him, he gave a thoughtful head tilt. "For smokejumpers in general, too. Schedules are different now. Better for family life."

"You thinking about that, bro?" Paul scraped a plate into the garbage disposal and stacked it on top of a towering pile.

Grady shook his head. "I don't think that's something I want." He glanced at his dad, remembering the way his shoulders had hunched that day after his mother left the garage in tears. The way Grady had watched his father for weeks afterward, wondering just how much this family had cost him.

"I don't think I have it in me to balance it all," Grady added, swallowing back the lump in his throat. "I think the casual thing is all I can manage."

His father watched him for a long time, then nodded. "If that's what works for you."

Did it work? It had for a long time, his whole adult life.

Willa's face flashed in his mind, and suddenly he wasn't so sure anymore.

# CHAPTER TWELVE

On the other side of the house, Willa was getting a lesson on welding. Welding, of all things. Didn't moms knit or bake?

Willa wouldn't know. Growing up without a mom had left her with lots of gaps in her memories and in her understanding of how family life worked. Familiar longing grabbed hold of her throat and squeezed, and it was all she could do to keep her focus on what Grady's mom was teaching her.

"We're just going to do a little light brazing at these joints right here," Sheryl explained.

When Willa had complimented the ornate fireplace grate in the living room, one of Grady's sisters had proudly announced it was Sheryl's work.

Sheryl had demurred. "It's just a little hobby I picked up to pass the time when Allen was gone for work."

That had earned a snort laugh from another one of Grady's sisters. "Ask her how long it took for her 'hobby' to become a lucrative secondary income for the family."

Sheryl had blushed prettily and waved aside her daughter's boasting. "I've been very lucky," she'd said. "It turns out ornate metalwork is a popular trend in all the vacation homes people are snapping up around here."

The oldest sister—was it Angie?—had rolled her eyes. "And talent has nothing to do with it."

"It's fun," Sheryl had reiterated with a little more steel in her voice this time. "It's just for me."

Now, out in the garage, Willa adjusted her protective goggles as she struggled to focus, to be a perfect pupil. "Brazing is welding?"

"They're similar, but brazing is a bit easier for beginners," Sheryl explained. "Lower heat and no melting of base metals."

"Got it." She wasn't positive she did, but she was eager to learn.

"We want to start by heating the brazing rod, just like this."

Willa obeyed, surprised when the brazing rod liquefied quickly and seeped into the seam between the two lengths of metal. "Wow, that's beautiful."

Sheryl laughed. "It is, isn't it? Just move the flame back and forth there like you're painting it."

"Is it okay that it's clumping?"

"Not a problem." Sheryl smiled behind her own protective goggles. "You can ease off the heat a little if you want, but those little bumps will get sanded down later anyway. There! Perfect."

Willa switched off the torch, just like Sheryl had showed her, and admired the angled joint on her own nearly completed TV tray. She had a new appreciation for Sheryl's talent. "You're a great teacher," she said. "My dad is going to love this."

"I hope it's handy." She plucked the torch from Willa's hands and started packing away tools. "We'll let it cool and do some cleanup on it later. You did a terrific job."

Willa wandered around the workshop, admiring some of the completed metalwork on display. There were tons of wall-mounted pieces showing herds of deer or ornate lettering that urged some unnamed deity to *bless this mountain home*.

Sheryl certainly kept busy.

Willa turned back to where the other woman was hanging her welder's apron on a peg. "You said you started doing this when your kids were still at home?"

"Most of them were." Sheryl turned, and in that instant, Willa saw a misty cloud pass over the other woman's face.

Willa held her breath. Had she overstepped? Or opened some door Sheryl didn't want to walk through? A lifetime of being motherless had left her awkward and uncertain in dealing with moms at all.

Sheryl nodded, like she'd decided something. "Allen was gone constantly when the kids were younger," she said. "You've seen Grady's schedule, of course."

Willa nodded. "He's gone a lot."

"It was much worse twenty years ago. So much worse." Sheryl leaned forward on her elbows, a conspiratorial posture that had Willa leaning in the same way. "They'd be gone for months at a time. Literally—there was one stretch I didn't see him at all for four months."

"You're kidding."

"Nope," she said. "That's the way it was then. And with a big family, we needed to keep the income flowing year-round, so he spent winters working fire season on the other side of the equator. Australia, New Zealand—he'd bring back a lot of stories and some great souvenirs, but we missed him like you wouldn't believe."

"I can imagine." Willa swallowed and tried to imagine not seeing Grady for that long. It surprised her how hollow the thought made her feel. "It must have been like getting to know each other all over again."

"It was," Sheryl agreed. "Anyway, learning to weld—having this little bit of autonomy—that's what helped get me through the worst of it." She laughed and looked down at her hands. "And I won't lie, the extra money helped."

Money. It always came back to money, didn't it?

Sheryl looked up, even though Willa hadn't spoken out loud. "It's about balance more than anything," Sheryl said softly. "Doing what you need to do to survive but making sure there's something left over for you. For the people who love you."

Willa nodded, hardly daring to breathe. Balance. Was this what mothers taught their children? She'd known Grady's mom only a few hours but already felt an attachment to her that went beyond this family dinner. She'd always wished for a connection just like this.

"Thank you," Willa said. "For the dinner and... well, for all of this."

Sheryl smiled. "You're welcome. We've loved having you here." She straightened up and untied the welding apron she'd donned over her clothes. "Are you close with your parents?"

A fiery hot knot cinched up in Willa's chest. "I— My mother's gone, and my father... It's complicated."

"I'm so sorry." Sheryl touched her arm. "I didn't mean to pry."

"No, it's okay." Something about the kindness in Sheryl's eyes cracked Willa's heart wide open. "I lost my mother when I was little. My father…it didn't bring out his best side."

Sheryl frowned. "Was he abusive?"

Willa shook her head and glanced down. "Not the way you're thinking. He was an alcoholic. *Is* an alcoholic. He's still alive."

If you could call her father's present state *living*.

Willa's words seemed to suck the air from the room. She didn't breathe, afraid she'd just branded herself as damaged goods. Or worse, that she'd inspired pity in this woman she'd grown to admire.

Sheryl held her gaze, not flinching, not judging, just looking into Willa's eyes. "That must be difficult," she said softly. "You're welcome to borrow our family anytime."

"Thank you." She dropped her gaze, afraid to let Sheryl see how deeply those words moved her. How badly she wanted to be part of this. "You have a great family."

Sheryl laughed. "I think I'll keep them." She turned and began inspecting Willa's TV tray, flicking a rag over the surface. "It's worth it, for the record."

Willa stared at the back of her head, struggling to keep up with the conversation. "What's worth it?"

"The struggle." When Sheryl turned back, her blue eyes were misty. "Fighting to balance it all— work, family, love, marriage, some sense of self— that's where you really find yourself."

"In the struggle?"

"Yes." Sheryl smiled. "It's hard, but it's wonderful, too."

Willa nodded, swallowing back the lump in her throat. "I can see that."

And she could. She really could. As she forced herself to breathe in and out, to act normal, her heart rearranged itself around this new notion of family.

• • •

On the drive home, Grady seemed quiet. Willa studied the side of his face, wondering if she'd said something to upset him. Or maybe something had happened at his parents' house.

Maybe it was none of her business, but she found herself reaching out anyway.

"You okay?"

He glanced over and offered a tired smile. "Yeah. Just a little wiped."

"You're back at the air center tomorrow, right?"

"Yeah," he said. "Probably an early flight. I'll need to get there before the sun's up, so I should call it a night."

"Oh. I thought—" She stopped herself, cheeks flaming. She knew better than to assume things, and how would she feel if he started making assumptions? It's not like they had any claim to each other. No plans carved in stone.

But it was in her nature to plan. To look forward to whatever came next. "I was figuring you'd sleep over," she admitted.

His gaze shifted to her face, and there was definite heat in his eyes. Raw, naked hunger. He wanted her, no doubt about it.

"Can I take a rain check?" he asked.

"Of course." She managed to keep her tone breezy, keep any hint of disappointment from her voice.

This was what she wanted. No commitments, no attachments. They'd only been on one real date. Why should she have any claim on his time?

When his hand slid across the console and covered her bare knee, her whole body blazed to life. "Thanks for coming tonight," he said. "My family loved you."

"I loved *them*. Thank you for inviting me."

His voice sounded weird and formal, so she didn't say anything else as he pulled up in front of her house.

When he killed the engine, he turned to face her in the car's dim interior. "You had a good time?"

She nodded, conscious of his hand on her knee. Of how badly she wanted him. "It must be nice being part of something like that," she said. "Belonging. Feeling like a member of a team."

"I never really thought about it like that," he said. "My family's great, but they're always just…*there*."

"That's what I mean." His hand moved up her leg, and she lost her train of thought for a second. "It's safe. Secure. Like there's always someone who has your back."

"You're right," he said, hand moving another inch and stealing her breath away. "Family's a great safety net."

*I want that.*

The thought flitted fast through her mind like a tiny bird, and she honestly wasn't sure if she meant family or what Grady's finger was doing along the seam of her knee.

A movement in the front window caught her eye, and Willa tore her gaze off Grady to see Stevie with his nose pressed against the glass. For a sightless dog, he spent a lot of time smearing snot on the windows and staring out at the street.

She turned back to Grady, touching the silver star pendant at her throat. "When did your mom start making money on her metal art?"

Grady blinked, surprised by the question, and Willa hurried to backtrack. "I'm sorry; it's none of my b—"

"No, it's fine." He sounded bemused. "Let's see, I must have been eight or nine, I guess. I just remember going to a lot of art fairs and farmers' markets and stuff."

"That must have been nice," she said. "For her, obviously. But also for your family. Having more security, I mean."

"I guess I didn't think about it much then." He scratched his chin, his other hand still anchored on her bare thigh. "Maybe I was too young. I do remember this conversation my parents had one night over dinner. My mom had just sold this piece to Sunriver Resort."

"Sounds like a big deal."

"It was," he mused. "They must have paid her a lot. Anyway, my dad kept smiling and holding her hand and he said we could start buying real ice cream. Not that crappy, generic ice milk we'd been buying."

Willa laughed, but questions were swirling around in her head. "Was he threatened?" she asked.

"By your mom making her own money?"

"Not at all," he said. "I don't think so, anyway. He always seemed proud of her."

Willa nodded, knowing she should drop the interrogation. She'd already been way too nosy.

"I like your parents," she said. "How they have each other's backs. How they've stuck together even when it wasn't easy."

Something passed through Grady's eyes. Nostalgia, maybe, or some other flicker of emotion. "You're right," he said. "Kinda different having an outsider perspective on my family."

*Outsider.*

He hadn't meant it as an insult or even anything personal. She tried not to let it sting. A car slipped past, slicing through the moment with the beam of its headlights. Stevie barked, reminding her of the travesty of his empty food bowl.

Willa nodded toward the house. "Can I talk you into coming in for a drink? I've got a nice Merlot that'll go great with beef jerky roses."

He laughed and squeezed her knee. "You and I both know how it'll end up if I come inside."

"How will it end up?" Her voice came out huskier than she expected, but the heat in Grady's eyes matched the lava bubbling in her chest.

"If I come inside, we'll end up with you on your back and me buried deep inside you, and it will be the best fucking feeling in the world."

"Oh." Willa shivered, touching her throat again. "And that would be bad?"

"It would be fucking fantastic," he said. "Just like it always is. But right now, the job comes first."

How many times had Willa said that herself? How many times had she told her dates that her career was first and foremost in her life, that she didn't have time for relationships?

There was no reason for it to sting hearing the echo of her own words in someone else's voice. No reason at all, except—

"So I'll see you when you get back?" she asked.

"Absolutely," he said. "I'll come straight here."

"No shower?"

He laughed and pulled her close. "We can shower together," he said. "Which, for the record, is not a date."

As he kissed her senseless, Willa wondered how long they could keep doing this.

# CHAPTER THIRTEEN

Grady's trip out to Northern California was uneventful, or as uneventful as jumping out of a plane into a fiery forest could be. He and the rest of the crew spent four days digging fire lines and sawing limbs in a thick, woodsy area sixty-five miles from the closest town.

There was no phone service, so no texting with Willa. He tried not to feel bummed about that. She was busy with her work, and he was busy with his. That's how it was supposed to be.

But still, he missed her. Missed the passionate glint in those mossy-oak eyes, the way her hair fell across her face when she bent to pet Stevie. He missed her teasing over mini golf and the dimples he saw so rarely that they felt like a hard-earned victory when he managed to coax them out.

By the time his crew finished mopping up the California fire, there was another blaze in Utah. Then Idaho, or was it Montana? They were all blurring together, a normal way of life for him and the rest of the crew as the summer grew hotter and forests got drier.

On day twelve, he finally got a chance to text her.

**Grady: *Taking a dinner break. I stink like you wouldn't believe. Miss you.***

He expected a sassy response, some joke about him smelling awful all the time. Alarm arced through him when he saw her response in all caps.

**Willa:** *OHMYGOD YOU'RE OKAY????*

He frowned at his phone, stirring Spam mac and cheese over the propane camp stove while Bobby collected water nearby.

**Grady:** *Of course. What's up?*

The little bubbles on the screen told him she was typing out a response before his had even gone through.

**Willa:** *It's been on the news. Two smoke-jumpers badly injured in NE Oregon. I wasn't sure where you were.*

Oh. Right.

He'd heard about it, yeah. It had been all over the channels, and the crews were pretty upset. He hadn't known either guy, both loaners from a crew in New Zealand. Even so, it gave him a sick feeling in his gut anytime something like that happened.

It hadn't even occurred to him that Willa would hear about it.

**Grady:** *I'm okay. Haven't had phone service, so I couldn't check in. Sorry you were worried.*

That wasn't totally true. A tiny, selfish little part of him liked that she was worried about him. That she thought of him at all when he was gone.

**Willa:** *Totally understand. Just glad you're okay. Stay safe.*

He typed back "you too," which was dumb. She worked at home, where the biggest danger might be tripping over Stevie. Smiling to himself at the thought of her big, doofy dog, he finished stirring the Spam and switched off the gas.

How nice would it be to curl up on Willa's couch to eat dinner together? Or fall asleep in her warm bed with Stevie on the floor in the corner and Barrow nestled between his legs.

But no, he couldn't think that way. If Willa was determined to avoid anything serious between them, then he needed to do better at keeping walls built up. It's why he'd turned down the sleepover invite before he left, even though he desperately, urgently wanted to fall asleep touching her body. It was better for both of them if they didn't get attached.

Right. Try telling that to his big, dumb heart. Or his brain, which kept drifting off to la-la land each night as he fell asleep under the stars. At first, it was normal stuff. Fantasies about snuggling Willa on the couch or riding the Harley with her arms and legs snug around him.

Then the fantasies took absurd forms. Willa joining him at more family dinners, an engagement ring sparkling on her finger. Willa round and lush with a baby—*his baby*—in her belly.

"For fuck's sake." Grady growled the words out loud as he dished up the Spam.

"Talking to yourself again?" Tony gave him a knowing look as he accepted his plate.

"Shut up."

It was ridiculous thinking about the future. Any future, but especially one involving Willa. He had autonomy. He had the here and the now, and that's all he'd ever wanted, dammit.

So why couldn't he shake the stupid, achy emptiness in the pit of his stomach? He shoveled in a heaping bite of Spam, hoping that might do the trick.

It didn't. Not even close.

• • •

On the morning of their last day on duty, Grady shouldered his pack to start the eight-mile trudge out to the pickup point. He'd never been so eager to get home, to climb in a warm shower and let the water sluice down his body while his hands trailed down someone else's. Willa's, specifically. How had that happened? How had his fantasies gone from a rolling slideshow featuring a dozen different women to a replaying GIF showing only one?

"Cheeseburger."

Ethan's voice jolted him out of his thoughts. Adjusting his pack, Grady picked up the thread of their usual banter about what they were most eager to get their hands on when they got back to civilization.

"Notorious IPA from Boneyard Beer," Grady said. He actually craved wine more than that, but the guys would give him shit for naming something too highbrow.

"A hot shower that lasts twenty minutes," added Bobby.

God, that sounded nice. Only in Grady's mind, Willa was there with him, her breasts dappled in droplets and her hair slicked back —

"Yo, Grady." Tony grinned. "You've got that look again."

"What look?"

"The one that says what you're most looking forward to has green eyes and won't go out with you more than twice."

Busted. "I'm going straight to her house as soon as I get home," he admitted.

"Going out?" Ethan asked.

"Nope."

"Because that would be a date," Tony supplied.

The guys snorted and guffawed as they kept right on trudging.

"We're staying in and ordering takeout Thai," he said.

Tony snorted. "Is that what the kids call it now?"

The other guys laughed, though Ethan gave a pained groan. "Pad Thai. Or no, pizza. That's what I want."

Grady glanced at his watch, counting down the hours until he could get to the one thing he wanted most.

By the time they reached the pickup point, they were all exhausted. Dusk was falling, turning the sky purplish black. While the other guys made small talk with the volunteer driver, Grady checked his watch and wondered how late Willa would be up. He should go home and shower first, maybe get a good night's sleep before turning up on her porch.

But when the truck pulled into town, he knew he couldn't wait that long. He had to see her.

It was ten p.m. when he trudged up the driveway to Willa's doorstep, dirty and bedraggled and so exhausted, he could barely stand. But the thought of seeing her again burned like an ember in his chest.

Her front door flew open before he even knocked. "You're back." She blinked at him in the porch light, green eyes luminescent as her hair fell loose around her shoulders.

"I'm back." He reached up and fingered the dainty little strap on her blue and white sundress. She was wearing the silver star necklace but maybe no bra. Fatigue gave way to something more primal as she moved aside to let Grady slip past her into the house.

"I missed you," he said as his arms went around her.

"I missed you, too."

Stevie sniffed the leg of his jump suit and backed away, but Willa grabbed Grady by the lapels and pulled him to her. The kiss was fierce and hungry and left them both gasping as they backed down the hall together. Somehow they made it to the bathroom, crashing into walls and knocking a hairbrush off her counter with a clatter.

"Strip," he ordered, though he was already doing it for her as she leaned down to turn on the water. The pretty cotton sundress went first as he tugged it over her head and tossed it on the bathroom counter. He was right about no bra, and her panties went next as he hooked his fingers under the lace and dragged them down her thighs.

Since he was down there on the ground in front of her, he wrapped his arms around the backs of her legs and nuzzled the warmth at her center.

"Grady." She gripped the top of his head, swaying as he licked into her. "Oh my God."

"This," he murmured, slipping his tongue inside her. "This is what I've been craving."

Not pizza or wine or any other comforts of home. Just Willa, slick and sweet on his tongue, gripping his fingers as he slid them inside her. Her hips moved in a slow arc as she fucked his hand, his face. Tongue buried inside her, he peered up to see her head thrown back in ecstasy, her breasts quivering with every panted breath.

"Holy shit," she gasped as she clutched his hair and came hard around his fingers.

He palmed her ass, bringing her down slowly. He could do this all night. Every last ounce of his fatigue had fallen away, and he stood up and reached for her hand.

"Shower," he said, hand under the spray as he bent to adjust the temperature. "Please tell me you've got condoms and I don't have to run out to my truck."

She grinned and pulled back the shower curtain. "Right there in the soap dish. I was ready for you."

"Thank God," he said and pulled her under the spray.

He knew he should take it slow, that he owed it to her to get familiar with him again. They'd been apart for two weeks, and besides that, they weren't officially together. But as he pressed her up against the wall of the shower and rolled a condom on with one hand, he couldn't think about anything but being inside her.

"Grady, hurry," she gasped as she wrapped her legs around his waist.

He drove into her in one slick stroke, making them both gasp. Then he held still, waiting until her eyes opened and she looked deep into his.

"This isn't a date," he said as he began to move slowly, in, out, with languid strokes that made her groan. "But someday you'll give me that second date. And then a third and a fourth and do you know why?"

Christ, why was he talking like this? About future plans, something he avoided like the fucking plague.

Willa's response was a strangled gasp, not a word at all. Grady tilted his hips, hitting that spot he knew would drive her mad.

"This is too good for just a handful of dates," he growled. "Too good not to last longer."

She cried out, and Grady drove in again, pounding until she screamed and dragged her nails down his slick back.

He let go, too, shutting his eyes as the water sluiced down their bodies and his legs quivered with exhaustion and his heart nearly exploded.

It crossed his mind to tell her then. To say he wasn't talking about sex, that that wasn't what this was about.

But as she came down and smiled at him, he forgot everything including his own name.

# CHAPTER FOURTEEN

Willa woke early the next morning, restless and brimming with pent-up energy. It took her a moment to figure out what was different.

She was naked, for one thing. And so was the big, muscular guy sharing her bed.

That was definitely different.

So was what he'd said in the shower.

*This is too good for just a handful of dates. Too good not to last longer.*

Had he meant it? Or was it just the heat of the moment?

It wasn't the first time a guy had suggested pushing past her two-date rule. But it was the first time she'd actually considered it.

She stretched, feeling deliciously warm and luxurious as she touched the edge of the bed with her toes. Then she curled on her side and lay there looking at him. Just looking, not touching, though her fingers twitched with eager energy.

Grady's dark hair was in dire need of a trim and mussed from going straight from the shower to bed. Willa smiled at the pleasure of it, breathing in the scent of campfire that still clung to his skin. It was always there, just the faintest hint of it, even though they'd scrubbed each other forever with sudsy vanilla bodywash.

*Marshmallows.*

That's what he smelled like. Campfire marshmallows.

A flood of memory rushed through her, catching her by surprise. A camping trip, one of the last times she remembered it being the three of them—her mother, her father, and her.

They bought a bundle of firewood at the grocery store, along with a ninety-nine-cent bag of Jet-Puffed marshmallows that left her mouth watering all the way to the campground. She wanted those s'mores.

Her father had whittled a stick to a sharp point, and her mother taught her to thread the end with a pair of pillowy marshmallows. She'd held the gooey white globs over the embers, giggling as they turned brown and toasty.

*We were so happy then.*

Years later, she'd learned they weren't camping for fun. They were camping because her father had lost his job again, and they were two months behind on their rent. They were camping because they had to, but right then, clustered around the campfire, it hadn't felt scary at all.

Grady stirred, and Willa stroked a hand over his chest. Part of her hoped he'd wake up and make love to her again, but that was selfish. He needed to sleep. He'd only been out for four hours, and she knew he needed to catch up.

She snuggled against him, burrowing into his heat. It felt nice, but she was too restless, too edgy to be comfortable.

*God, Willa. You can't even snuggle right.*

Yet another sign she wasn't cut out for intimacy.

She glanced at the clock and watched the numbers flip from 5:29 to 5:30 a.m. Kayla would be up. She was always up by five, and usually jonesing for someone to run with.

Willa picked up her phone and fired off a text.

**Willa: *Want company on your run?***

A few seconds later, a reply popped up.

**Kayla: *Who are you and why do you have Willa's phone?***

She smiled and typed a reply.

**Willa: Need to get up and move. See you at the end of my driveway in ten?**

Then she got up and quickly dressed in a sports bra and running shorts. "Come on, Stevie," she whispered. "This morning you're earning your breakfast."

Barrow and Earmuff were still dozing on the bed, too enraptured by Grady's heat to bother asking for breakfast. They had the warm curve of his knee and the deliciously toasty spot against his chest, and those trumped kibble any day of the week.

Willa could relate.

Could she learn to be more like her cats? Able to switch off and relax, to lose herself in the pleasure of another body's heat for more than an hour or two?

She sighed and headed for the foyer, pausing to clip Stevie's extra-short leash in place. His tail wagged and he followed her out the door, trusting as ever.

The sun was painting the sky a bright amber gold as she walked to the end of her driveway. Kayla jogged up to join her.

"Hey, girl." Kayla flipped her dark ponytail back, then frowned as her gaze skimmed over Grady's truck. "Tell me you don't have a hot, naked smoke-jumper in your bed."

"I don't have a hot, naked smokejumper in my

bed," Willa recited.

"Are you lying?"

"You told me to."

Kayla sighed. "You're hopeless. Come on."

She set out at a brisk pace, her bright-yellow running pants and orange top giving Willa a sunshiny beacon. Willa fell into step beside her, wishing she'd taken time to stretch. Maybe she should have suggested brunch instead of this.

"Same route as last time?" Kayla asked.

"Thanks," Willa huffed. "Familiar is best for Stevie."

Stevie's ears pricked as he recognized his name, and he gave a soft little *oof*. He was content to trot along between them, trusting they wouldn't run him into any tree branches or boulders.

After only a couple of minutes, Willa wheezed, already regretting her life choices. "Maybe we could slow down a little?"

Kayla laughed but kicked it down a notch. "So," she said, not winded at all. "When did Grady get back?"

"Last night," Willa huffed. "Late."

"He stayed the night again. Whatever you did to him must have knocked him on his ass."

"I think that was the forest fire," she said. "But I'll take credit."

Smiling way too cheerfully for so early in the morning, Kayla rounded the corner at the end of the block and started toward the park. "Seems kinda serious," she said. "If he's coming straight to your place instead of going home. Sleeping over instead of having you usher him out the door the second he rolls off you."

"I've never been that bad," Willa grumbled, deliberately avoiding the question of whether this was getting serious.

But Kayla didn't let it drop. "So it *is* turning into something more."

"More than what?"

"More than your usual two-dates-and-drop-'em ritual," she said. "This one seems to have sticking power."

"I didn't say that," Willa panted. "He just wanted to get laid."

"If he only wanted sex, he would have made sure to get some before he left."

Willa grimaced, partly from the pain of running but mostly because she wished she hadn't told Kayla about that. She'd been lonely those first couple of nights after he left and had shared more than she usually did. "You made my point," she said. "Can't be serious if he's picky about the timing of booty calls."

"That's your choice," Kayla said, not unkindly. "You're the one sticking with the dumb two-date rule."

"It's not dumb." She should probably add more, but she didn't have a good defense.

"Sure it is. What's your next date that's not a date?"

"Game night," she managed.

"Game night?" Kayla peered at her with renewed interest. "You invited him to game night?"

"Why is that a big deal?"

"Because it's been our tradition for almost ten years. Seems significant."

Willa gritted her teeth. How was Kayla not

winded? She could manage words like "tradition" and "significant" while Willa just wheezed and tried not to die.

But yes, she had invited Grady to game night. She'd asked him weeks ago, just after the mini golf non-date when he wanted to know when he could see her again. He'd plugged it into his phone, making a big show of flagging it as an "appointment" because it obviously wasn't a date if their friends would be there.

"It's just game night," she panted as Kayla rounded a corner and kept on running. "You're bringing Tony, right?"

"Yeah, but we're actually dating," she said. "Not according to some schedule, not with a giant rule book, *dating*. You should try it sometime."

Willa wanted to ask how serious things were getting with Tony, but she didn't have the lung capacity. Besides, she could see from her friend's glowing looks every time she mentioned the burly crew captain that Kayla was really digging Tony. But how did Tony feel?

The bigger question—and Willa knew because she was avoiding it—was how did she herself feel? Not about Tony and Kayla but about what Grady had proposed.

Could she really date him? Could he date her?

"So seriously, game night?" Kayla's words poked through Willa's thoughts and yanked her back to the present. "I don't remember you ever inviting a guy before. Not a guy you were sleeping with, anyway."

"Point?"

Kayla approached an intersection and looked

both ways before dashing through the crosswalk. Willa followed, struggling to keep her feet moving in the right direction, trying to keep Stevie pointed straight ahead.

"Don't you think that's significant?" Kayla asked.

"Nope."

"Well, I do," Kayla said. "It's the first time I've known you to feel that way about a guy," she said. "You went to his house for dinner, for crying out loud. You met his family."

Willa said nothing, though her brain bubbled around thoughts of the text messages she'd swapped with Grady's mom over the last two weeks. They'd started simply enough with Willa texting to say thanks for the dinner. Before she knew it, she and Sheryl were trading texts throughout the day about everything from welding to Grady's schedule.

She knew she should stop it—no sense getting attached to parents if this wasn't a long-term thing— but it was just friendly chatter, right? She'd stayed friends with plenty of guys she'd gone out with a couple of times. Connecting with Grady's mom didn't mean anything.

"Wills, I'm happy for you." Kayla slowed her pace another smidgen, probably noticing Willa was about to die. "I'm badgering you because I love you, and because I like giving you crap, but I'm serious. Grady's great for you. I think there's real potential there."

Willa swallowed hard, tasting iron in the back of her throat. If she died, maybe she wouldn't have to have this conversation.

But she knew Kayla well enough to realize that

she'd never let this go, so she settled for redirecting the conversation.

"Got a new client yesterday," Willa huffed. "Hart Valley Cheesemakers. Want to bid the photos for their site?"

Kayla glanced over and issued a dramatic eye roll. "And she changes the subject yet again."

Willa resisted the urge to flip her the bird.

"It's a good project," Willa said. "Good money, plus free product."

"Cheese," Kayla said with a reverence that bordered on sensual. "I'll definitely bid on that. Email me the deets?"

"For sure."

They plodded through the park with Stevie galloping along merrily. If only her dog could look less enthusiastic, maybe she could use him as an excuse to stop. "Gotta tie my shoelace."

Kayla stopped, running in place as she surveyed Willa's shoes. "Both look fine to me."

"That's my polite way of saying you're killing me." Willa slumped onto a park bench as Stevie came over to lick her face. "I give up. No more running."

Kayla laughed and dropped onto the bench beside her. She peeled off one of the fancy, plump-looking armbands she wore and offered it to Willa. "It's a hydro-sleeve. Drink. I brought one for each of us."

"Of course you did." Willa gulped deeply, grateful for her friend even if she was a pain in the ass. "Thanks."

"No problem." Kayla took a sip from her own. "So game night, huh?"

"Yep."

"We've always said it's a good chance to assess someone's character," Kayla reminded her. "Whether they cheat or take things too seriously or make up their own rules. What do you think we'll find out about Grady?"

"No idea." Her breath was returning. "He took mini golf pretty seriously, but that's different."

"Yeah, it is." Kayla grinned. "I like the part where you kicked his balls."

Why had she told her friends anything at all? They never let her live things down, especially not when it came to Grady. "Is Aislin bringing anyone?"

"Maybe her sister." Kayla made a face. "That's if she doesn't implode from the force of her own bitchiness. Bronwyn, not Aislin, obviously."

"Obviously." Willa chugged some more water. "So you and Tony, huh?"

"I like him." Kayla grinned. "I don't know if it's going anywhere, but I'm having fun. If it doesn't work out, I have a hunch we'll be best friends forever. In the meantime, we're having a good time getting to know each other."

So that's how normal people did it. They spent time together, just enjoying each other's company instead of assessing every possible risk involved in committing. What would that even be like? To date without fear of attachment and disappointment and the whole thing ending in a big, fiery ball of regret.

"You should try it sometime," Kayla murmured, reading Willa's thoughts. "It's fun."

A lump formed in Willa's throat, and she chugged some more water to force it back. "Come on." She stood up on shaky legs and handed the armband back to Kayla. "We should get moving."

Sympathy flashed in Kayla's eyes, but she got to her feet anyway. "And she's off and running again." She laughed as she trailed behind, then passed Willa with a smile. "You know, someday you'll find a reason to quit running away from anything that smacks of emotional investment."

Willa gritted her teeth and focused on slamming one sneaker in front of the other, over and over against the pavement. "Don't count on it."

But possibly, her heart already did.

• • •

Willa came home to find Grady in her kitchen, cracking eggs into a bowl. Barrow and Earmuff sat worshipfully at his feet, waiting for dropped scraps.

"Hey there." Willa mopped her forehead with the back of her arm and hoped she didn't look as awful as she felt. "Sorry I didn't leave a note. I didn't think you'd be up for a while."

Grady grinned, looking better than any man had a right to with bedhead and rumpled boxers. "I'm not very good at sleeping when it's an unfamiliar bed," he said. "Want scrambled eggs?"

"I'd love some." She brushed past him to fill Stevie's food and water bowls, not sure how to conduct herself in this scene of domestic bliss. Should she hug him or kiss him or squeeze his butt?

She settled for patting his arm as she got the

glass down and filled it with tap water. "Want me to make toast?"

"That'd be great," he said. "I didn't know where bread was, and I wasn't sure you'd be okay with me digging through your cupboards. Eggs seemed safe enough, since they're right in the fridge door."

The thought that he was so conscious of her privacy filled her with a strange mix of fondness and guilt. Of course he should feel fine about searching for bread when he'd spent the night in her bed.

But yeah, deep down, she was glad he knew to give her space. She rummaged through the freezer until she came up with a loaf of her favorite rosemary bread. "One slice or two?"

"Two, please." He glanced over in fascination. "You can freeze bread?"

"Of course," she said. "I do it every time there's a sale on this rosemary bread I love. I can never get through a whole loaf fast enough."

"Huh." Looking thoughtful, he whisked the eggs with a fork. "I'll have to remember that. It'll keep me from wasting so much bread."

Willa said nothing, even though her skin itched at the thought of anyone throwing away food like that. Maybe this was her good deed for the day, her chance to have an impact on Grady's chaotic life.

"Do you like your eggs a little gooey or drier?" he asked.

"Gooey, please," she said. "Want to throw in some cheese?"

"Hell yes."

Willa grinned, enjoying their easy chatter more than she cared to admit. She located a small block of cheddar and gave it a few strokes with the cheese grater before handing it off to him on a napkin. Then she buttered the toast and piled it on a plate while he dished up eggs and carried them to the table.

"There's sugar in that bowl right there and creamer in the fridge," she said as she nudged a mug of coffee toward him. "Thanks for breakfast."

"Thank *you*." He bit into his toast and smiled.

The scruff on his jaw made him look rugged and unkempt, like a sexy pirate. Something about the contrast of those stormy gray eyes and dark hair made her insides turn as squishy as the eggs.

"You're sexy in the morning," he said.

"I'm sweaty," she countered, hoping she didn't stink. "I'm not usually, but I got the urge to run today."

"Not enough exercise last night?" The naughty twinkle in his eyes told her he was more than willing to help her burn off more energy, and she shivered with anticipation.

"I have zero complaints about last night," she said. "I just felt like going for a run. Kayla lives a couple of streets over, and I have an open invitation to join her anytime."

"Ah, Kayla." He smiled and stirred some sugar into his coffee. "I'm probably not supposed to say so, but Tony's really into her."

"It's mutual," Willa said. "Did you know they're coming together tomorrow?"

Grady laughed. "My buddies don't generally share details about simultaneous orgasms, but I'm glad."

Willa rolled her eyes and tried to pretend she

wasn't amused by the juvenile humor. "Very funny. I'm talking about tomorrow. You know?"

The space between his brows creased in confusion. "What's tomorrow?"

"Game night." Willa's grip tightened around her coffee mug. "Remember? I invited you a couple of weeks ago. You plugged it into your phone?"

"Ohhh." He lifted his mug and took a swig. "That's tomorrow?"

"It is." It took everything she had to keep the shrillness from her voice. It wasn't like he was a husband who'd forgotten to pick up their kid at grade school.

*Not like your dad. He's nothing like your dad.*

"Shit, I'm sorry, Willa," he said. "I've got other plans."

Disappointment swirled in her gut alongside the eggs, and the mix was sour and leaden. "Something must have come up?"

"Yeah, this safety training thing out at the airfield. It's mandatory if I want to keep jumping this season."

"Oh." She tried not to let dismay show on her face. "On a weekend evening?"

"They had a bunch of others, but that's the one I picked." He chewed a bite of toast. "Base commander's gonna ground me if I don't get this done."

"Of course. I understand."

She was trying to, anyway. "So yeah, Kayla and Tony will definitely be at game night." She said it mildly, doing her best to pretend it didn't bother her that Tony had made time for it when Grady hadn't. "So will Aislin and her sister."

"Shit, sorry." He really did look sorry as he raked a hand through his hair. "I signed up for this particular session because my brother Jake—he's one of the other smokejumpers in the family? He'll be there, too. We don't see each other much, since we can't ever work the same fires."

"What do you mean?"

"It's sorta like in the military," he explained. "Hart Valley Air Center doesn't let siblings go out on the same jumps, because they never want a situation where parents lose two kids in one fell swoop."

Willa nodded, willing herself not to panic. There it was, another reminder of how dangerous Grady's job could be.

He must have read the worry on her face because his expression softened. "It's just a precaution," he said. "We don't lose people often."

Willa nodded and nibbled the edge of her lip. "Understandable."

He laced his fingers through hers. "What time does game night start?"

"Seven," she said. "Everyone brings snacks and something to drink, and people sleep over if they're not okay to drive."

"I'll be there," he said. "I might be a little late, but I can do it. The training should be over by eight, so if I skip grabbing a beer afterward with Jake—"

"You don't have to do that, Grady."

"I want to," he said. "I feel bad about forgetting. I don't want to flake."

There, he was trying. So what if he forgot and double-booked himself? He was making it right, and wasn't that better than her dad had ever done?

Ignoring the pinch in her gut, she pasted on a happy smile. "That sounds fine," she said. "We'll hold off on busting out the really good games until you get here."

"I can't wait." He leaned over and kissed her, just the faintest brush of his lips on her cheekbone.

But the effect was electric, and everything in her screamed, *It'll all be fine.*

Willa shivered, and it took her a second to realize why. Those were her mother's words, the thing she used to say when money got tight and her parents were fighting and Mommy would disappear for a few days. Or her dad would. Sometimes those stretches of time blurred together in her memory.

*It'll all be fine.*

How many times had Denise Frank said those words to her daughter, over and over again until Willa believed them?

And then one day, it wasn't fine.

Shivering again, Willa turned away to grab more coffee.

# CHAPTER FIFTEEN

"You want to grab a beer?" Grady's brother Jake stood tossing his car keys from one hand to the other, glancing out at the star-filled horizon. "It's still warm enough. They've got that new outdoor patio at the brewery."

Glancing at his watch, Grady shook his head. "I would, but it's game night at Willa's place. Rain check?"

He already felt like a huge asshole for blowing off Willa so soon after his declaration in the shower. What the hell had made him think he could be worthy of an actual relationship?

Jake flashed a knowing smirk. "You're giving up beers with your favorite brother for game night? It better be something good, like Naked Twister or Strip Battleship."

The thought of Willa sprawled on a Twister board wearing nothing but a smile was enough to send Grady's libido surging, but he held it together. "Doubtful, but I've never been before. It could be one big orgy."

"Dude." Jake laughed. "I need to meet this girl."

"Woman," Grady corrected without thinking. "And it's definitely not a sex party. She's been doing this game night thing for years."

"Huh." Jake looked thoughtful. "Seems like a big deal, then, if she's inviting you."

Yeah, Grady had thought the same thing. It's

why he felt like a jerk for forgetting, and why he was hustling to get out of there.

But hell, he hadn't seen Jake in ages. One more casualty of the job. "Did you hit the last family barbecue?"

"Yeah, we missed you," Jake said. "But we got to talk about you behind your back. Sounds like Willa was a huge hit."

"Everyone loved her."

Jake quirked an eyebrow. "Sounds like you're entering L-word territory yourself."

"Fuck off," he said automatically.

But part of him clung to that idea. Was it so far outside the realm of reality to think he could get there? That Willa could get there with him?

"You're late." Jake's words—and his punch in the arm—was enough to bring Grady crashing back to reality. "Get out of here. Go see your woman."

"Yeah." Grady dug his keys out of his pocket. "Good seeing you, man."

"You too."

He turned and marched toward his truck, light with the thought of seeing Willa in the very near future. But the distant future loomed a little darker. What would that look like for him? Was he kidding himself thinking he had anything to offer her in the long-term?

He did his best not to think about it on the drive to her place. It was after eight. Hopefully he hadn't missed too much of game night. He'd been looking forward to it and still couldn't figure out how he'd screwed it up on his calendar.

By the time he pulled up to her house, it was

eight thirty. The lights were blazing, and several cars lined the driveway. Stevie gave a startled "oof" when Grady rang the bell. Footsteps thudded through the house, and then the door flew open to reveal Willa looking flushed and lovely and not at all frosty.

That was a good sign.

"Grady." Her smile was warm, like she was surprised to see him. "I wasn't sure you were coming."

"Sorry I'm late." He held out the bottle of wine and she took it, studying the label. "It's a good one," he offered. "White Rose Estate makes phenomenal Pinot Noir."

She handed it back, and he braced for her argument. It was too expensive or not right for the crowd. "Thank you," she said instead. "Would you mind taking it into the living room while I find a corkscrew and some glasses?"

"Sure thing."

Pause. Just the briefest one. Then she stood on tiptoe to plant the softest, sweetest kiss on him. "I'm glad you made it."

"Damn," he breathed, conscious of his heart twisting itself into knots. "Me too."

She turned and hustled in the opposite direction before Grady could reach for her again. Did this count as a date? Now that he'd made his declaration about wanting more than two, he wasn't sure anymore. He also wasn't sure she'd want that, considering he'd managed to screw up the timing of this one.

With Stevie trotting beside him, Grady headed for the living room. Loud voices and laughter led the way, and Brandi Carlile drifted from the stereo.

Bodies sprawled around the coffee table, some cross-legged on the floor and others on the couch hunched forward over the game board. They all looked up as he ambled into the room.

"Yo, Grady!" Tony broke into a wide grin and reached up to clap his hand. "Thought you weren't going to make it."

Kayla was cozied up next to him, and the sight of the two of them together left Grady wistful. Would Willa feel like snuggling, or were they playing it cool? He had no idea where her head was at.

He nodded hello to Aislin, who was seated next to an icy-looking blonde who assessed him coolly. "White Rose Estate," she said, studying the bottle. "What year?"

Grady turned it around so she could see the label. "2014."

"The Vista Hills Vineyard or the Anderson?"

"Vista Hills," he said, grateful he'd gone with the one that ran sixty-five dollars a bottle instead of ninety-five. He had a hunch Willa would be more impressed by saving than by spending, though he had no intention of telling her the price of the wine.

"The Anderson's fabulous, but I prefer the 2015," the blonde said.

*Oh-kay…*

"I'm Grady," he offered. "Willa's…friend."

That got him a couple of snickers from the other people at the table, but the icy blonde just nodded. "I'm Bronwyn. Aislin's sister."

"We were just finishing up Pictionary," Kayla said, flipping her dark hair over one shoulder. "Pull up a chair and join us."

"Willa's sitting over there." Aislin pointed to a pile of throw pillows lying on the floor on the opposite side of the table, so Grady headed there and found a spot for himself in the pillow nest.

The table was littered with pieces of paper with pencil-scratch drawings, and Grady picked one up and frowned at it. "Who drew the penis with the hatchet coming at it?"

"Willa." Tony grimaced. "That's her rendition of a hot-air balloon."

Yikes.

"She has many talents, but artistry isn't one," Kayla offered.

He sensed her behind him before he heard her voice and recognized her touch the instant she brushed past. "Sorry the glasses don't match," she said, settling down beside him and putting a tray on the table. "At least I found a corkscrew."

"That's all we really need," Tony pointed out. "We can chug straight from the bottle—just pass it around the circle."

That got a laugh from everyone but Aislin's sister, Bronwyn. "It's an expensive wine, so I don't suggest that."

Everyone shifted uncomfortably. "Dude," Tony said, looking like he was annoying Bronwyn further by addressing her that way. "Kidding."

Bronwyn folded her arms over her chest and leveled a look at Tony. "Can I help it if I appreciate the finer things in life?"

Aislin's jaw twitched as she finished packing up the Pictionary pencils and pads. "And here we go," she murmured, so quietly Grady could barely make out the words. "Time to prove she's the smartest, most sophisticated person in the room, in case we forgot."

Grady stifled a laugh as Willa finished pulling the cork from the bottle. Her posture had gone rigid, so he reached over and squeezed her knee. "I'd be happy with Two-Buck Chuck out of sippy cups as long as the company's good."

Willa flashed him a shaky smile, and Grady let go of her knee. He wanted to kick himself for bringing the fancy wine. He'd been trying to make up for being late, but he'd only made her self-conscious. He jotted a mental note to dial back romantic gestures that could leave her feeling less-than or fretful about money.

"No wine for me," Tony said. "I'm driving."

Kayla smiled beside him. "I'll sit it out, too, in a show of solidarity."

Everyone else wanted some, so Grady took charge of passing glasses around while Willa poured. He was conscious of her beside him, aware of the warm floral scent of her shampoo and the soft tickle of her hair against his arm.

"What should we play next?" Kayla asked.

"Let Grady pick," Aislin suggested. "He's the newcomer, plus we can all judge him for his choices."

Everyone laughed except Bronwyn as Grady scanned the stack of game boxes off to the side. Scrabble, Scattergories, Life, Pay Day…

"How about Monopoly?" he suggested. "That's a classic."

He looked back at the group in time to see Aislin and Kayla exchange a glance.

"Uh…" Kayla's gaze shifted to Willa. "I'm not sure that's such a—"

"I love Monopoly." Tony grinned. "It's my chance to be the ruthless capitalist my grandfather always wanted me to be."

Bronwyn sighed. "I'll be the banker."

Of course she would.

Grady glanced at Willa, who was chewing her bottom lip. "You okay?"

"Yeah." She offered a weak smile. "I, um— sometimes take this game a little too seriously."

Grady laughed and slid an arm around her. "In that case, we're definitely playing," he said. "It'll make me feel better about the whole mini-golf situation."

Aislin shook her head, looking nervous. "Not like that," she said. "She's not cutthroat about it. She's just—"

"Intense," Kayla supplied.

"It'll be fine," Willa insisted, tilting her chin up just a little. "I haven't played in years, and that panic attack was probably just a fluke."

*Wait, what?*

Bronwyn was already pulling out game pieces. "How much do we start with?" She folded out the board, then handed the dice to Tony. "Everyone has to roll for turns."

While Aislin consulted the rules, everyone set about accepting their play money and choosing game pieces.

Willa chose the Scottie dog.

Grady wanted the race car but gracefully accepted the iron when Tony nabbed the car right out from under him.

"This must be an older game board," Grady murmured to Willa.

Her eyes flickered like he'd yanked her by force from some memory. "It belonged to my mother," she said. "It's from the seventies, I think. My grandparents gave it to me after…after she was gone."

Grady squeezed her hand. "I'm honored to get to play it with you, then." He picked up the iron and rolled it around on his palm. "Some of the older game pieces have been retired. This one got the boot pretty recently."

"*I've* got the boot," Kayla said, giggling as she held up her game piece. "This one's always been my favorite."

Grady set his tiny iron on the board next to Willa's Scottie dog. "They discontinued the iron after it got the lowest number of votes among Monopoly fans. Interestingly enough, the World Monopoly Champion—Bjørn someone from Norway—actually won using this game piece."

Willa stared at him, and Grady couldn't help noticing a little bit of tension had eased from her shoulders. Maybe having him here was helping.

*Don't flatter yourself.*

Willa blew a lock of hair off her forehead. "I don't know whether to be more impressed there's a World Monopoly Championship or that you can actually name a winner and the piece he used."

"The dude watches way too much television," Tony said as he smacked his game piece on the table.

"Says the guy who usually grabs the remote and

makes us watch weird reality TV shows," Grady countered.

Tony just laughed. "Guilty as charged." He shuffled his money into a pile. "Okay, let's do this."

Everyone else had their pastel paper cash divided into tidy piles by color or denomination. Grady glanced at Willa, who held hers in a death grip in her lap like she feared someone might snatch it away. Was this what her friends meant by *intense*?

He offered the dice to her. "Want to roll first?"

"You go ahead," she said. "I like to see what I'm up against."

Spoken in any other tone, the words might have sounded facetious or even flirty. But the way Willa's brow furrowed seemed like a good indication that her blood pressure was already mounting.

Maybe this wasn't a good idea.

Grady shook the dice in his hand and tossed them onto the board. "A four and a six," he said as he handed the dice to Willa, reveling in the warmth of her hand. "Beat that, baby."

She scrunched up her face in concentration, shaking the dice in both hands. "Six and a five." She let out a breath like she'd been holding it, then handed the dice to Aislin.

"How do you like the wine?" Grady murmured in her ear.

"I haven't tried it yet," she admitted. "I want to keep a clear head."

"For Monopoly?"

Aislin met his eyes over Willa's shoulder and shook her head. "We tried to warn you."

The game kicked off with Tony going first—a

three and a five. He ended up on Vermont Avenue and promptly bought it for one hundred dollars, then bought a little green plastic house to put on it. "I'm off and rolling," he said. "My life as an entrepreneur is just beginning."

Aislin went next and got a chance card that paid her a bank dividend of fifty dollars. "Must be my lucky day," she said.

Kayla snapped up Reading Railroad after rolling a one and a four.

Then it was Willa's turn. She rolled a six and a two, landing her right on Tony's square. He clapped his hands together and hooted. "Hand it over, doll. That's six dollars in rent."

Willa frowned and stared down at the money in her lap. "Renting is such a waste of money," she murmured. "If I could just *own* property—"

"It's a game," Grady assured her, giving her knee a soft squeeze. "And it's still early. You've got plenty of time to amass your empire."

Not looking reassured, she nevertheless handed her cash over to Tony.

"Thank you muchly," he said as he stacked the bills in his pile.

Willa stared at them like he'd taken the last doughnut in the box, and Grady wasn't sure whether to be amused or uneasy. Her handling of money in this game went beyond competitive. Even beyond the intensity her friends described. This was something else.

"Your turn," said Bronwyn unnecessarily. "Roll."

"Thanks," Grady muttered, scooping up the dice. His five and a six landed him on St. Charles

Place, and he went ahead and stuck a house on it. Hopefully, Willa wouldn't roll a three and end up paying him rent, too.

The game proceeded, with Tony amassing more houses and properties while Aislin drew a Community Chest card that declared she'd won a beauty contest for ten dollars.

"How fitting." Bronwyn smirked and sipped her wine. "Don't they have any career cards in there?"

"I have a career," Aislin said through gritted teeth. "Just because I'm not a lawyer—"

"More wine?" Grady offered, desperate to break up the tension.

Aislin shot him a grateful look. "Yes, please."

Bronwyn stuck out her glass. "Of course." She surveyed the board. "Why are we playing with an antique game, anyway? These prices are ridiculously outdated."

Kayla rolled her eyes. "Did you miss the part about this being Willa's family heirloom?"

It was Bronwyn's turn to look annoyed. "A Monopoly game? Sorry to burst your bubble, honey, but I don't think we'll be seeing you on *Antiques Roadshow* anytime soon."

Aislin had apparently had enough. "Show some respect," she snapped. "Her mother left when she was tiny, and when her grandparents came to tell her she'd died, they brought this box of her mother's things. That's all she has left of her. How about you try not being a judgmental bitch for once in your life?"

Everyone fell quiet. Even Bronwyn was shocked into silence. Grady felt Willa go stiff beside him, and he leaned closer, hoping she could feel the heat from his body. That she knew he had her back and wouldn't judge her for anything.

"Let's all take it down a notch, okay?" he suggested.

Bronwyn seemed to realize she'd crossed a line. As she murmured an apology, Grady watched Willa. It was like her sensitivity about money had melded with grief over her mother and formed a steel curtain around her.

He squeezed her knee and tried to get the game back on track.

"Kayla, I think it's your turn." As everyone returned focus to the game, he leaned closer to Willa. "You okay?" he murmured in her ear.

"Of course." She nodded, posture still ramrod straight as her hair tickled his lips. "This is fun."

Her voice wasn't very convincing, so Grady tried again. "We can choose a different game," he offered. "Or take a break if you want."

"I'm good, really." She turned and gave him a smile that didn't meet her eyes. "I need to do this every now and then, okay? To remember."

He nodded, not sure he understood but not wanting to push. To remember her mother or something else? He'd never heard that story before, the one Aislin told to shut her sister up, but it definitely gave him more insight into Willa. Who she was and how she became the way she was. It was the first time he'd realized how fragile she was under the tough exterior, and it made him want to cover her in Bubble Wrap. Or his own body, making sure no harm could come to her.

Kayla rolled and landed her game piece on the jail square.

"Don't worry," Tony said, snuggling closer. "I'll pay you a conjugal visit."

Willa was up next. She rolled a pair of twos and took the card for the Electric Company. "The mortgage value is seventy-five dollars," she said. "It's a sound investment, but it makes more financial sense if I could get my hands on the water company, too."

Tony nodded. "You could bankrupt someone in a hurry like that," he agreed. "Rent is ten times the amount shown on the dice if you own both utilities."

"I don't want to bankrupt anyone," Willa said quickly. "I'm just trying to have a solid financial strategy."

Tony rubbed his hands together, still playing the greedy capitalist. "Tell you what," he said. "If I land on the water company, I'll sell it to you for a small handling fee and you can—"

"No!" Willa shook her head like Tony had suggested they take a break and go burn down the neighbor's house. "That's against the rules, and besides—I need to do this on my own."

Tony's eyes flickered with surprise, but he recovered quickly. "No problem," he said. "Who's next?"

They kept playing, with Grady buying a railroad and Kayla eventually getting herself out of jail. Tony built a few hotels, Bronwyn drank more wine, and Willa's pile of money dwindled as she landed on a series of unfortunate squares that took her tidy pile down to just a few bills.

Aislin looked on in sympathy as Willa's next roll

landed her on a square that ordered her to pay two hundred dollars in income tax. "If you want, I can loan you some money, Wills," Aislin offered. "Just temporarily, to get through this part."

"Absolutely not." Willa stroked Stevie's ears, looking like she might be on the brink of having a stroke herself. "That's not allowed. You can't loan or give money to another player. It says so right in the rules. And I'm *not* accepting charity."

Grady leaned closer so their shoulders touched, unsurprised to find her whole body tense as coiled wire. "You should roll again," he said. "The dice landed partway off the board. Doesn't that require a do-over?"

Bronwyn frowned. "She would have had to do it right away, before she moved her game piece."

Grady resisted the urge to throw a handful of plastic hotels at her. "But if she didn't *know* that's the rule we're playing by—"

"It's fine, Grady." Willa bit her lip and handed over the last of her cash. "It's fine. I can get back on my feet with the next roll. I can do this."

The determination in her eyes convinced him to let it go, so he gave her knee a squeeze and picked up the dice. "I'll take St. James Place for one hundred and eighty," he said as he moved his game piece to that slot. Leaning closer to Willa, he brushed her ear with his lips. "Don't worry," he assured her. "If you land on it, you can pay me in sexual favors."

She laughed, but there was a tightness to it. "That's a considerate offer, but I'm not ready to turn to prostitution just yet."

Aislin flashed him a sympathetic smile. "Don't

feel bad, Grady," she said. "I once tried to sneak a fifty into her pile of money so she'd have enough to buy Atlantic Avenue when she landed on it."

"What happened?" He was almost afraid to ask.

Aislin's grin widened. "She socked me in the gut and knocked the wind out of me."

"It was an accident." Willa grimaced and shook her head. "I flinched when your hand brushed my ribs and my elbow sort of connected."

Kayla laughed and shot Grady a look that held a hint of challenge. "Still want to keep going?"

He glanced at Willa, who looked tense enough to claw through the legs of her jeans. Her fingers dug into her knee, so he took her hand and lifted it to his lips.

"Hey," he murmured.

She looked up with wide eyes, and Grady leaned close to murmur in her ear. "Want to treat my ass like your personal fidget spinner?"

She laughed, her body lurching forward and into his chest. Dimples pocked her cheeks, and her shoulders eased like someone had let the air out of them. "Yeah," she said, reaching behind to pat his ass. "Thanks, I feel better already."

• • •

Later that night in Willa's bed, Grady lay back in sweaty, satiated exhaustion. "Wow." He tried to catch his breath. "If I'd known Monopoly was such a turn-on for you, I would have brought a game board to our first date."

Willa blew out a satisfied breath and snuggled

against his chest. "It wasn't the game," she said. "The game's actually the opposite of erotic."

"Then what?" He kissed the edge of her hairline, grateful all the tension had gone out of her.

"Knowing you had my back," she said. "Having you understand why I felt edgy and that you wanted to help."

Grady wasn't sure he did understand, but the compliment made his ego swell.

"I'm glad I could help." His pulse kept hammering in his head, and he breathed in and out a few times to get it to slow. "We should do this all day tomorrow."

"Have sex?"

"Stay in bed." He trailed a finger down her spine and back up again, delighted to feel her shiver under his touch. "You and me, just like this." He grinned in the darkness. "That would be new."

"It would," she acknowledged. "And…nice." She met his eyes and smiled, and Grady damn near died with pleasure. "But I can't," she said. "I have some work to do for a client. It's a big project."

Grady digested that information, still stroking her skin. "Do you ever take a full day off?" he asked. "Like an entire day, no work at all."

"Of course." She shifted in his arms, hair tickling his chest. "Probably." She cleared her throat. "I mean, I can't remember when, but I'm sure I have."

And that told him quite a lot about Willa. The Monopoly game had done plenty, and so had the insights from her friends. This was how it was, getting to know her, like a treasure hunt of sorts. He was gathering all the sparkly bits, still trying to know her as well as he could. If there was one thing he'd learned, it was that she didn't let anyone in very easily.

He stroked a hand down her bare back and stared up at the stars scattered overhead, done in glow-in-the-dark paint. "I never noticed that before."

"Noticed what?"

"The constellations." He lifted a finger and pointed to her ceiling. "There's Ursa Major. And over there, that looks like Orion."

She rolled so they lay side by side, bare shoulders and hips touching as they surveyed her indoor solar system. "I stayed the night with a friend when I was nine." Her voice seemed distant, though she was right there next to him. "She had these cool glow-in-the-dark stars on her ceiling, and I wanted them so badly."

He reached for her hand under the covers, careful as he laced his fingers through hers. He was conscious of how rare this moment was, how unusual for her to let him in. "Did you ever get them?"

"Not like that." Hesitation gave her voice a little hitch. "The stick-on kind like my friend had were way too expensive. But after I told my dad about it, he took me camping."

He squeezed her hand. "That sounds nice."

She was quiet for a long time. So long, Grady turned to face her.

Willa kept her eyes on the ceiling, covers pulled over her breasts. "It sounds like homelessness."

Her voice was so soft, he felt sure he hadn't heard right. "What?"

"Homelessness," she repeated, not tearing her

gaze from above. "That's what we were. Homeless. It happened twice before my mom left, then more often after that." Her voice murmured low and even, like someone reporting the facts of a fender bender. "My dad would lose his job, and we'd get evicted and end up living in a tent for a while. Or the car, if it was winter."

"Oh, Willa." He rolled to his side to face her, cupping her bare hip under the covers. She didn't roll toward him, didn't take her eyes off the ceiling.

"I'm so sorry," he murmured, not sure what else to say.

"Don't be." She turned to meet his eyes, her gaze steady and unwavering. "It was a long time ago."

"Still—" God. What could he even say to that? Him with his parents still living in the big white house with its rose beds and three garages. They hadn't been rich, not at all, but they hadn't been homeless. Not even close.

"It's okay," she said, even though Grady knew it wasn't. "It was cold a lot and we were hungry, but there was this one night my dad pointed up at the sky and said, 'Lookie there. Told you I'd get you those stars. Anything you need, baby girl—you can count on your daddy to get it for you.'"

Grady stroked her hair, unsure what to say to her. "He sounds like a"—what was a good word?— "complicated guy."

"He was. Is." Willa pressed her lips together. "He's still alive. Obviously."

"Do you see him much?"

She glanced down at the edge of her sheet, fiddling with the hem. "Not as often as I should."

*Should.*

That word seemed to drive so much of Willa's life. Grady reached up and stroked a finger down her cheek, willing her to look at him again. When she did, her eyes were glittery in the darkness.

"He has to be proud of you," Grady said. "And even if he isn't, *you* should be proud of you. You've gone and made your own stars."

It sounded cheesier coming out of his mouth than it had in his head, but she gave him a shaky smile anyway. "I have."

She reached down and threaded her fingers through his where his hand rested on her hip. "Thank you."

"For what?"

"For not looking at me like…I don't know. With pity."

"Pity?" He brushed the hair from her face. "You're the least pitiful person I know."

This time, her smile seemed steadier. As her eyes held his, she unlaced her fingers from his and slid them to his cock.

He started to laugh, to tell her there was no way he could go again so soon. But he felt himself thickening in her grip and knew anything was possible.

"Christ," he hissed through gritted teeth as she stroked him. "What you do to me—"

"Make me see stars, Grady." The words were almost a dare, like a quest. "Please."

It should have sounded dorky, like something from a soap opera, but it was the hottest invitation he'd ever heard. As his blood bubbled to a boil and his dick throbbed in her grip, he rolled her onto her back and kissed her hard.

"Anything you want," he said when he broke the kiss. "Anything."

And then he set out to give it to her.

# CHAPTER SIXTEEN

Guilt finally drove Willa to visit her father, something she'd been meaning to do for weeks. She made excuses about the long drive or how busy she was with work, and those things were all true.

But the bigger truth was that she hated being around him.

She loved *him*—loved him with a fierceness that surprised her sometimes. But she hated who he'd become, who she remembered herself to be when she was around him.

Also, his house smelled like moldy cheese and wet newspaper, and he never kept the curtains open.

"Dad?" She pounded on the door, hoping he'd answer. Hoping she wouldn't have to break in the way she sometimes did.

"Hello? Dad, are you in there?"

Silence. Which could mean he was sleeping or passed out or—or—or—

"Willie!"

His voice sent a spear of alarm straight down her spine, and she whirled around to face him. As she took in his bedraggled appearance—torn jeans, inside-out T-shirt, five days' worth of scruff—her lungs deflated like two Mylar balloons.

"Dad." She took in the case of cheap beer he gripped in one hand, the unsteadiness of his gait. "You scared me. Where were you?"

"Aww, c'mere." He pulled her into a rough hug,

and Willa tried not to stiffen. The booze leaked from his pores, forming an eye-watering haze around him. "Can't I get a hug from my best girl?"

"It's good to see you, Daddy." She let her arms go around him, conscious of how skinny he'd gotten. Wasn't he eating?

She drew back, fighting to keep her discomfort masked. Her eyes stung from the fumes, or maybe that wasn't the only thing. They hadn't even set foot in the house yet.

As she glanced at the beer in his hands, she felt her fingers curling into her palms. Breathing deeply, she ordered herself not to lecture. Not to judge. It never did any good.

"You went to the store?"

"Yeah, I was running low on things."

"Things?" She scanned him for groceries, maybe a bar of soap or a carton of eggs.

He shrugged. "Money's pretty tight this month, you know."

It always started there. The request for cash would come soon, maybe before they made it through the door. Willa's guts twisted with guilt. She'd promised herself she wouldn't cave again, but she knew she would. She always did.

"You didn't drive, right?" she asked. "To the store?"

"Nah, I don't drive much these days." He shrugged again, averting his eyes. "Can't afford gas or insurance. Been thinking about just selling the truck."

Thank God for small favors. "That might be a good idea."

He straightened up suddenly, like he'd been shot

with an arrow, but the grin spreading over his face was less alarming. "Come on inside," he said, smile displaying the gap where a barroom brawl had relieved him of two teeth. "I've got something to show you."

"Okay." Willa took a breath, steeling herself. "I brought you something, too."

"No shit?" He grinned at the big cardboard box at her feet. "Lemme get that for you."

He stooped down and picked up the box, then turned to twist the doorknob. The set of his shoulders, the flash of dexterity—it was a glimpse of the man he'd been before.

*Before.*

As he pushed the door open, Willa bit back the urge to remind him to lock it. This wasn't exactly a safe neighborhood, though God knows he didn't have much to steal.

The smell hit her like a mushroom cloud. She held her breath until she couldn't anymore and then slowly breathed it in. Stale air and something new— maybe plastic?

She let her sinuses adjust, fighting back warring waves of nausea and nostalgia.

"Don't just stand there; come on in." Her dad shuffled toward the kitchen, so Willa followed and did her best not to gag. The stain on the sofa, that was new, and what the hell had he spilled all over the counter?

"Make yourself at home." He ambled into the kitchen and set the case of beer on the counter.

Home. If that wasn't irony, she didn't know what was.

Willa took a shaky breath. "Want me to make you a grilled cheese sandwich, Daddy?"

"Nah, no bread," he said. "Or cheese. It's been a rough week."

"Right." Willa hefted the cardboard box onto the counter, nudging his beer aside. "I actually brought those things. How about you have a seat and I'll make lunch?"

It was three in the afternoon, not exactly lunchtime, but her father didn't argue.

"That sounds real good, sweetheart."

Willa scanned the counters for the old cast-iron skillet, the one that had belonged to her mother's mother. That had been in the box, too. The one they'd brought her when they came to say her mother was dead and never coming home.

Her grandfather had looked her right in the eye as he said the words that day, gauging her reaction. She'd curled her fingers into her palms and fought to be strong, to show him she was a big girl who didn't cry.

Later, after he'd gone, she'd sobbed in her father's arms, howling like her soul had been ripped out while her dad stroked her hair.

Banging the skillet to jar herself from the memory, Willa turned on the burner. Her mom had learned to cook in this same skillet when she was a little girl. What would it have been like to have a mom teach her to cook?

Her dad wrestled a can of beer from the packaging and cracked it open. "I think I'll have one of these." Closing his eyes, he tipped his head back and drained half the liquid in a few gulps.

"Ahhh." He slammed the can down on the

counter, making her jump. "You want one?"

"No thanks." While the skillet heated, she got to work unpacking the box, filling his fridge with butter and milk and a bag of grapes she'd found on sale. Apples were cheaper, but he couldn't chew them anymore with his teeth in the shape they were now. She'd been hoping to land a contract with a chain of dental offices, which came with the perk of discounted services. But that hadn't come through. Not yet.

"Need help?" he asked, already wandering toward the living room.

"I've got it." She busied herself scrubbing a cutting board, keeping herself moving. Butter, bread, cheese, she worked methodically, blocking out the sound of the television flickering on from the other room and her father cursing at whatever was onscreen. Could be sports, could be the weather; it was anyone's guess.

"So how's the job hunt going?" she called.

"What's that?"

"The job hunt," she repeated as she sliced his sandwich in half and added a handful of grapes on the side. "Any leads?"

"Nah, not yet."

As she walked into the living room with the plate, she spotted him hustling to tidy the living room. To make things nicer for her. Her heart balled up tight as he stood up and squared his shoulders.

"Talked to one guy about doing some handywork at one of the elementary schools. He started asking about police records, though, so—"

"Right." Willa gestured to the couch. "Have a

seat, Daddy. Lunch is ready."

"You're too good to me, sweetheart." He touched the side of her cheek, watery eyes holding hers for a few beats before he took the plate and sat down. "Man, this looks good. Thank you."

"You're welcome." Willa sat down on the edge of a rickety-looking folding chair. Then she popped back up again, remembering her gift.

"I made you something." God, she hated the sound of her own voice. Like a nine-year-old scampering out of art class with a finger painting to tack up on the fridge.

Still, she hurried back to the kitchen and reached into the cardboard box she'd brought. "A friend of mine"—her voice lifted a little on the word "friend," not that her dad would notice—"a friend of mine has a mom who does welding. She helped me make this for you."

She carried the TV tray back to the sofa, setting it down in front of him like an offering. "This way you don't have to balance your dinner on your knees all the time." She picked it up and set the tray, grateful it seemed steady.

"Aww, shit." Tears glittered in the old man's eyes, and Willa swallowed hard against the lump in her throat. "You made this? For me?"

She had to look away. It was too much. The earnestness in his eyes, the delight over such a small thing.

"It was pretty easy to make." She swiped the back of her hand across her cheekbone, blaming the stale air for the unwelcome trickle of tears. She cleared her throat, willing herself to keep it together. "She had a bunch of different beginner projects in this book," she continued. "I got to pick one, and this seemed perfect for you."

"It is perfect," he agreed. "'Specially since I got a new TV."

Willa blinked. "What?"

The old man hooted, pleased with himself for shocking her. "Got it just yesterday."

He pointed over her shoulder, and Willa turned to see the monstrosity mounted on the wall. Holy crap, how had she missed that? She'd been so focused on groceries and stains and—

"Is that— Is it brand-new?"

"Sixty-five inches," he said proudly, failing to answer the question as he took another swig of beer. "Got it with the money you sent last month."

"But…that money was for rent." And groceries. And the debt collectors who always seemed to be banging on the door.

"Right, right." Her dad shook his head and picked up his sandwich. "Just wanted to treat myself a little, you know? It's been a rough month."

*It's been a rough month because you can't hold down a job and you won't get treatment for your drinking and—*

Willa bit her tongue. There was no point. She'd said the words over and over and over again until they could trip from her tongue in her sleep, and still it did no good. Her father wasn't going to change. Not ever, she knew that now.

She turned to look at him, wishing she could hate him. That would make things so much easier, if she didn't love him so much.

*Love is stupid.*

"What's that?" her father said around a mouthful of grilled cheese.

"Nothing," she said, embarrassed she'd spoken aloud.

"Mm." Her dad wiped his mouth with his sleeve. "Damn, baby. That's good."

"I'm glad you like it," she said automatically, positive he didn't notice the stiffness in her voice.

"Could you make me another one of these?"

"Sure." She started to get up, but he caught her hand in his gnarled one. His eyes locked with hers, and for the briefest second, she remembered the guy he'd been.

*Told you I'd get you those stars. Anything you need, baby girl—you can count on your daddy to get it for you.*

"Thank you for the present, Willie," he said.

"You're welcome." She swallowed back her emotions, all of them.

"You're a good daughter."

She nodded, not trusting her voice to say anything. He released his grip on her fingers, and she took a step back with her heart leaden in her chest. Turning toward the kitchen, she reminded herself how her feet worked. Left, right, left, right, one in front of the other until she reached the kitchen.

"Hey, would you grab me a beer while you're up?" he hollered after her. "I'm parched."

She closed her eyes and leaned against the counter, cursing herself for ever thinking it could be different. For thinking she'd ever escape the pattern. "Sure thing, Daddy."

• • •

From the moment she got home from her dad's house, Willa worked with an intensity bordering on mania. Sleeping became an afterthought. Eating, too, and any grooming that wasn't absolutely mandatory.

She juggled RFPs and redesign proposals. She analyzed color schemes and uploaded beta sites to the cloud. She coded web pages until her eyes crossed and Stevie nudged her hand with his wet nose, reminding her that both of them required sustenance beyond the coffee she brewed to fuel herself and the dog biscuits she tossed him so he'd forgive her for skipping his afternoon walk.

"Just a couple more hours," she assured him as her fingers flew over the keyboard.

Stevie heaved a sigh and threw himself onto his bed in the corner. Willa glanced over, wishing she could do the same. Wishing she could curl up in a ball and feel confident the bills would get paid, the clients would stay happy, the money would keep rolling in.

But she didn't trust any of that, so she kept working.

The texts from Kayla and Aislin were concerned but not frantic. They'd been through this before.

**Kayla:** *Running date? I'll piggyback you this time. Fresh air = good.*

**Aislin:** *It's not healthy to skip brunch. Café Lemony at ten?*

They accepted her perfunctory replies that she was slammed with work, that she couldn't take a break now. Not for a few days at least. Not until the roar of panic and self-doubt and fear quieted to a softer buzz.

It was Grady who grew worried. His texts were jovial for the first couple of days.

**Grady: *Interested in bowling? Definitely not a date.***

**Grady: *Forget bowling. Paintball?***

**Grady: *Okay, no paintball. Wild monkey sex?***

That one made her laugh, and also take a moment to tap out a quick reply.

**Willa: *Sorry, work's nutty. Rain check?***

That bought her a couple more days of solace, which she appreciated. It wasn't that she didn't want to see him. She was dying to, would give anything to drop everything for a movie date or just the chance to see him for an hour or two. To feel the way she'd felt when he held her in his arms after game night. Only she had to keep working. Just a few more hours, a few more bids, a few more emails to clients about future projects. She had to keep them happy, had to keep their business.

On day four—or was it five?—another text came through.

**Grady: *Tried calling, since this is awkward to ask via text. Is this you ghosting me? No hard feelings, but can you let me know?***

She knew she should answer. It was douchey of her to ignore him, to make him worry the way he was. Grady didn't deserve that, especially since he was due to fly out again in a few days.

Tonight. She'd text back tonight, just as soon as she finished this RFP.

A few hours later, he texted again.

**Grady:** *That sounded lame and needy, huh? Please ignore.*

Christ. What the hell was she doing?

But she kept doing it, ignoring messages from Kayla and Aislin, too. She worked with a crazed fervor, like she was possessed by a demon that knew HTML and Javascript and CSS but wasn't very good at personal hygiene.

Sometime later that day, the doorbell rang. Stevie barked and ran for it, his claws skittering across the hardwood. Hoping for rescue, probably.

"We'll go for a walk, I promise," she muttered. Raking her fingers through her hair—was that oatmeal?—she padded sock-footed toward the front of her house. "It's just FedEx," she assured him as she reached for the doorknob. "They're delivering that contract I—"

"Willa." Grady stood on her doorstep, brow creased in concern. "Jesus. Are you okay?"

She must have looked worse than she realized. Willa swallowed. "Grady."

He had no flowers, no wine, no beef jerky. Just a worried expression that grew more intense as he stared at her. "Christ, what's wrong?"

"What?" She smoothed her hair down and tried to remember the last time she'd changed out of these sweatpants. Wednesday?

"You look…gaunt." He was probably thinking another word—terrible? Horrifying? Insane?—but had the good sense to hold back. "Are you sick or something?"

Willa shook her head as guilt coursed through

her. "I'm sorry to worry you. I'm just—"

"Working, I know." Grady frowned. "Can you take a break for fifteen minutes?"

"What's happening for fifteen minutes?"

She half expected a sex joke, but the lines of concern etched deeper between Grady's brows. "I'm cooking you dinner," he said. "And if you don't have anything in your fridge, I'm running to the store while you take a shower."

"That bad, huh?"

He pulled her to him, wrapping his arms so tightly, she dissolved against his chest. "You've had me worried, Wills. You can't just drop off the face of the earth like that."

"I do that sometimes."

"Well, don't." He drew back and looked into her eyes. "Kayla and Aislin—they've been worried, too. They asked me to check on you. Thought I might have better odds of pulling you out than they would."

Her friends had a point. She started to reach for his fly. "You do have the magic wand."

"Nuh-uh." He circled her wrist with his fingers, bringing it up to his lips. Planting the softest kiss across her knuckles, he released her, then swatted her ass. "You need food and rest. Then we'll talk about your other basic needs."

"But—"

He caught her by the shoulders and turned her around, herding her toward the bathroom. "Go," he said. "I want to hear singing in that shower."

"Jeez," she muttered, marching toward the bathroom. "So bossy."

But as she closed the door behind her, she realized she was smiling. Then she glanced in the mirror, and her smile vanished fast. Lord, she did look awful. Her ponytail hung lopsided with the end of it snarled around the button of her flannel shirt. Stains dotted the front of her T-shirt like bad Rorschach tests, and a mascara smear marred the edge of her cheek. When had she applied mascara? Days ago.

No wonder he'd looked appalled.

Okay, so Grady had a point. Hygiene, basic nutrition—she should start there. She stripped off her hideous clothes and stepped beneath the shower spray, letting the water sluice down her back. The heat felt amazing, washing the kinks from her neck and the tangles from her hair.

Somehow, she lost track of time, because when she walked barefoot into the kitchen in clean jeans with a towel wrapped around her head, Grady was standing next to her counter.

Her clean kitchen counter.

"You did my dishes?" She stared at him. "You didn't have to do that."

"I also didn't have to bake a lasagna from scratch."

"You did that?"

"No, I said I didn't." He grinned. "But I did order one from Ernesto's. It'll be here in fifteen minutes, along with a salad and garlic bread."

Was this what it felt like to have someone take care of her? She couldn't wrap her head around it, couldn't stop feeling the prick of tears behind her eyelids. She blinked them away as she held on to the counter for balance.

"Thank you," she murmured. "I owe you."

"You don't owe me anything," he said. "This is what friends do for each other. Or fuck buddies. Or whatever the hell we are."

She took a step closer, resting a hand on his chest. "What are we, Grady?"

"I don't fucking know." His arms went around her, and he pulled her tight against his body. His big, solid, muscular body. "But I know I can't stay away from you."

Willa clung to him for a long time, breathing in and out until her heart rate slowed. Then she opened her eyes and drew back, going up on tiptoe to kiss him.

Her mouth was cool and minty from toothpaste, and his was warm and tasted like cinnamon Life Savers. Somewhere in the middle, everything felt right. Somehow, everything shifted into focus and the world made sense with him there.

When she drew back, her heart was hammering in her head. "I'm sorry I dropped off the face of the earth," she said.

"It's okay." He cupped her ass, holding her against him. "I thought you were blowing me off. Or you were hurt. Or kidnapped by aliens. I had to come see for myself which it was."

"And what's your assessment?"

He smiled and kissed her again. "That I'm nuts about you."

Willa laced her fingers behind his neck, kissing him again as she ground her body against his, reveling in his heat, his solidness. Grady's hands slid up her back, and he slowly unwound the towel from her head. Fingers threading through her still-wet hair, he molded her against him, claiming her with his mouth, his body.

"God, you feel good." He ground against her, using his body to turn her, to switch positions so he had her pinned up against the kitchen counter.

Willa didn't need any prompting. She boosted herself up, sliding easily onto the counter with his hands lifting her up by her hips. Twining her legs around his waist, she pulled him against her, grinding into the hardness between his legs. How long had it been?

How long had she let herself be sucked into the dark abyss of dread and fear and deadlines she invented all on her own? How long had she fed those imaginary wolves snapping at her heels?

Grady's hands slid up her shirt, making her forget, making her *feel*. Was that what she'd been running from? She didn't know. The only thing she was sure of was that his hands on her breasts left her reeling from pleasure that clouded out all the other sensations. All the fear, all the panic, all the uncertainty, gone with the stroke of his thumb over her nipple.

She moaned against his mouth and tugged at the hem of his shirt, hungry for the feel of his bare flesh against hers. Flames licked up the inside of her belly as Grady licked his way down her throat, breaking contact just long enough to tug her shirt off over her head. Groaning as his tongue circled her nipple, she speared her fingers through his hair and held him against her, held on for dear life.

*Ding-dong!*

Grady drew back, looking more than a little dazed. "And that would be the lasagna."

Willa groaned and slammed her thighs together, gritting her teeth. "I never thought I'd be annoyed by lasagna."

He scooped her T-shirt off the floor and pressed it to her chest, kissing her softly before stepping away. "I'll get the food. And then I'll make you come."

"In that order?" Her voice was high and quivery and not her own.

Grady grinned. "Any order you like."

• • •

Later—much later—after lasagna and a glass of wine for each of them, after frenzied sex that started on the dining room table and ended in Willa's bedroom, they stretched out on her bed, staring up at the stars.

"So here we are again," Grady said.

"Here we are," she agreed, snuggling against him.

He pressed a kiss to her temple, stroking her hair with his thumb and forefinger. "Feeling less stressed?"

"Considerably." She smiled as she burrowed against his chest, but a twinge of uncertainty tugged at her subconscious. "Mostly."

"Only mostly?"

She sighed, not sure how to explain it to him. "Sometimes I feel like I'm wearing a gorilla suit and trying to tread water in a pool filled with molasses."

Grady burst out laughing. "There's a description for you." He kissed her temple again. "I guess I get the picture, though."

"I want to relax, but I feel like the second I do, I'll

go under."

He didn't say anything for a long time. Just stroked her hair as his heart thudded steadily and softly under her ear. "When's the last time you missed a deadline?"

"What?"

"A deadline. When have you missed one? Or dropped the ball with a client or—"

"Never." She couldn't keep the scandalized tone from her voice. "My record with my clients is impeccable. I have a reputation for delivering on time—delivering *early*—every time."

"Okay," he said, not surprised at all. "Then do you think maybe—*maybe*—it would be okay to let your guard down just a tiny bit?"

Her fingers curled against his chest. "What are you talking about?"

"I'm not suggesting you spend your workdays chugging wine straight from the bottle while lighting contracts on fire," he said. "Just…it seems like once in a while you could take a day off. Refresh your brain, rejuvenate your spirit."

Willa opened her mouth to argue, to insist she did take time off—she *did*. Brunches with girlfriends, the occasional date with Grady, dinner at his parents' house—

"I'm not talking about a few stolen hours here and there," he said. "I'm talking about an entire day where you don't work at all. Or hell, it doesn't have to be a day. An overnight."

She anchored her elbow on the mattress beside him, propping her chin on her hand. "You've stayed the night here plenty of times."

"That's not what I meant." He rolled to face her

and brushed the hair from her cheek. "When's the last time you slept somewhere else?"

Tracing a finger around the little freckle at the edge of his shoulder, she gave him a small smile. "You've never invited me back to your place."

"True," he said. "Would you have come?"

"Probably not," she admitted. "It's hard with pets. And with a home office."

"How about a staycation?"

"A what?"

"A staycation. A night in a fancy hotel with room service and cushy robes and one of those fancy ergonomic dog beds so Stevie could come, too." He cast a look at the dog, who was curled on his bed in the corner. "We could leave after you finish work in the evening and come back before the start of your workday the next morning."

"So what's the point?"

"The point," he said, holding her hand up so he could kiss one fingertip at a time, thumb, index finger, middle finger, ring, pinkie. "The point is to give your brain a break. To recalibrate a little. Your home is your office, which means you're never off work here. Not really."

Willa thought about that. She imagined the big, cushy bed and champagne in an ice-filled bucket and Stevie gobbling gourmet dog biscuits. "It sounds expensive."

"Money's no object," he said, and Willa tried not to wince. "Okay, money's an object. But the manager's a friend of mine, so I get a discount. What do you say?"

Willa imagined giving herself over to a night of

bliss and relaxation in a peaceful hotel suite with a down comforter and big windows looking out over the mountains. She imagined basking in the same relaxation she felt now, only better. No home office buzzing down the hall, no niggling worry that she should hustle back to her computer to check in on her accounts or send that RFP or—

"What if I kidnapped you?" Grady asked, misreading her silence as reluctance. "Packed a bag for you, tied up your hands with a silk scarf, ushered you out into my car, and—"

"When can we leave?" Willa asked.

Grady looked down at her and started to laugh. "Anytime you want. Just say the word."

"Okay," she said. Hearing hesitation in her voice, she tried again, more firmly this time. "Okay. Let's do it."

# CHAPTER SEVENTEEN

"Holy cow." Willa turned a slow circle in the lobby while Grady watched, enchanted by the sight of her so completely awestruck. "This is unreal."

The tipped-back angle of her head left her hair trailing down her back as she surveyed the crystal chandeliers, the colorful murals, the fireplace surrounded floor to ceiling with smooth river rock. "It's so beautiful."

"It is," he agreed, not talking about the hotel at all.

Her green eyes flashed as they met his, and it was all Grady could do not to reach for her. Not to devour her right there in the lobby.

Stevie gave a soft "oof" and sniffed the air, eager for more of those fresh-baked dog biscuits the receptionist had tucked in their welcome bag. Willa twisted the leash around her wrist as she completed her survey of the space. "I've never stayed anyplace this fancy."

Grady smiled and pocketed their room key. "The lounge is downstairs. No live music tonight, but they've got a great happy hour if you're interested."

She swung her gaze back to his, biting her lip. "You seriously get this for free?"

He hadn't said free, had he? He didn't want to mislead her, but it was a pretty significant discount. "It's a pretty great deal," he said, not exactly lying. "Come on, let's check out our room."

He led her to the bank of elevators off to the side

and hit the button. The doors *whooshed* open, and they stepped inside with Stevie trotting beside them. Grady held the key card up to the sensor, and the doors closed behind them. "Going up," announced the jaunty voice with the slightest hint of an English accent.

Willa giggled beside him and shifted her shoulder bag. "I can't believe you didn't make a going down joke," she said. "You must be maturing."

"Don't count on it," he said as he slid an arm around her waist.

The doors opened again on the fifth floor, and he steered her toward the suite at the end of the hall. He'd paid extra for one of the nicest rooms, for the one with the view of the river and the park below. Just like he'd hoped, the curtains were open to frame the jaw-dropping views.

"Oh my word." She dropped Stevie's leash and rushed toward the window, peering out like a kid looking for Santa on Christmas Eve. Grady had never seen her this joyful, this relaxed.

"You can even see the mountains," she said.

Heart bursting with pleasure, he joined her at the window, resting a hand on the small of her back. "Looks like Stevie found his bed."

She turned in time to see the blind dog arranging himself on a plush pet bed lined in creamy faux fur. "How does he do that?" she asked. "Just knows right where the dog bed is, even though he can't see?"

Grady picked up a brochure off the dresser, skimming for details about the room. "It says here it's filled with some sort of special stuffing laced with dog pheromones. Who knew that was a thing?"

"Apparently the management team at The Hartford." Willa glanced toward the huge king-size bed in the middle of the room. "Maybe they've filled our bed with the same stuff for humans."

*Our bed.*

Grady liked the sound of that. He liked it a lot.

"Check out the dog bowls." He pointed to the corner where two enamel bowls sat on a place mat labeled Stevie in bright-red letters. "They even gave us color-coordinated dog doo bags."

"You mean rich people don't use gold-plated dog doo bags?"

Grady laughed and set his duffel down on the dresser. He'd never stayed in this room before, but he did get a chance to sleep in one of the downstairs rooms once. Alone, for the record—a favor from his manager pal after Grady played a show in the bar and wound up with a rowdy guest spilling beer all over his guitar.

Shoving his hands in his pockets, he ambled back toward the bed. "Wait till you see the pillow menu."

She turned to face him, her expression somewhere between incredulous and amused. "There's a pillow menu?"

"Two pages."

"You're kidding me."

"Nope." He moved toward the nightstand and plucked the laminated brochure from its spot beside the lamp. "Do you prefer feather or goose down?"

"I've never given it much thought."

He read through the descriptions, marveling at the level of detail. "Apparently the feathers offer slightly more support, while the down is fluffier."

"Good to know." Abandoning her spot beside the window, Willa wandered toward him with her skirt fluttering behind her. That was her idea—a little dress-up to go with their fancy night on the town. She'd even fixed her hair in some sort of nifty twist, describing it to him in a fake French accent that made him laugh and pull her into his arms.

She sat down on the edge of the bed, leaning back on her arms as she studied him under her lashes. "We have more pillow options?"

"Of course." He scanned the menu for more intriguing descriptions. "How about hypoallergenic?"

She laughed. "You saw me after a five-day work binge," she said. "Clearly, hygiene is not my top priority."

"And your circus of trained dust mites is grateful for it." He scanned his way down the menu, conscious of her bare legs crossing and uncrossing on the end of the bed. "How about buckwheat?"

"To sleep on or snack on?"

"Sleep. Apparently it's made from the husks of buckwheat seeds," he read. "Sounds very supportive."

"Sounds very itchy."

"Perhaps." He trailed a thumb down the page. "They have an anti-aging pillow."

"Stitched out of silk and fairy wings?"

He laughed and kept scrolling. "How about the lullaby pillow? You plug in your iPhone and music plays from these tiny speakers inside it."

"I think I'd be a little creeped out by a pillow that sings to me."

"How about a peppermint cooling gel pillow with memory foam?"

"Peppermint cooling gel?" She raised an eyebrow. "That sounds like something you'd have the concierge bring up if you forgot your toothpaste."

"Tatami?"

"Um—"

"'A very firm, traditional pillow used for more than two thousand years in Japan,'" he read from the card. "It's filled with tatami fibers that offer improved ventilation."

"Does it come with a side of sashimi?" she asked. "Because sushi's sounding pretty good right now."

Grady glanced up from the menu. "You want to go to dinner?"

"Soon." Willa uncrossed her legs, making her skirt ride up her thigh. He was pretty sure she'd done it on purpose. "We should definitely choose our pillows first."

Her voice had turned breathy and flirtatious, leaving Grady with little doubt what she had in mind for pre-dinner activities. He moved closer, settling onto the bed beside her as he continued to scan the pillow menu.

"They've got body pillows to snuggle with, if you're into that sort of thing."

She smiled and unfastened the top button on her top. "I was sort of hoping you'd be taking care of that."

Half the blood left his brain and traveled south as she crossed her legs again. The skirt slid up a couple more inches.

"How about a latex pillow?" His voice cracked a little as she undid another button on her blouse.

She laughed and put a hand on his thigh, gliding up and up and—

"In case we run out of condoms?"

Grinning, he tossed the menu aside and reached for her. "Not likely—I came prepared," he said. "But I'm willing to give it a go if you are."

With laughter dancing in her eyes and her hair floating around her, Willa dropped back onto the bed and pulled him down with her. "Let's give it a try."

• • •

Two hours later, they made their way down to the lobby. A mother and father with a young toddler stepped into the elevator on the third floor, joining them in the tiny space, and Grady wondered if the parents could tell he and Willa had just had headboard banging sex not ten minutes ago.

He smiled and squeezed her hand, and she glowed up at him like the most beautiful woman he'd ever seen. "Thanks for this," she murmured. "And for *that*."

*That.* He squeezed her hand again, pretty damn grateful for *that*, too.

"Going down," the automated voice announced, and Grady fought to keep a straight face. He loved that he and Willa had reached this point, that they had inside jokes that let them read each other's thoughts without a word.

Maybe he hadn't earned the right to call her his girlfriend—not yet, not quite—but wasn't this almost the same thing?

"Lobby," the voice announced, and Grady stepped aside to let the young family exit first. The dad rested his hand on the mother's back to usher

her out ahead of him, then turned back to hold a hand out for the toddler.

"Come on, Aidan."

"Wait." The little boy spun around at the threshold of the doors. "I forgot Gorilla."

Grady glanced at the lump of brown fur in the corner. He started to reach for it as the little boy tripped and stumbled forward.

The mother gasped. "Oh my G—"

"Got him." Grady slammed to his knees and opened his arms so the boy landed softly against his chest instead of face-first into the metal handrail anchored against the glass wall.

"You okay?" Grady peeled the little guy off to inspect him for damage.

The boy's brown eyes were wide with fear. "Uh-huh."

The kid nodded, dazed but unscathed, so Grady reached for the stuffed animal. "Looking for this?"

The mother released a breath in a soft *whoosh*. "Thank God you were there," she said. "What do you say, Aidan?"

"Thank you." The kid took the stuffed animal by the arm and stuck his thumb into his mouth.

"You're welcome." Grady got to his feet and dusted off the knees of his pants. "Have a good night."

When he looked at Willa, she was shaking her head. "I can't figure it out."

"Figure what out?"

"When you're not jumping out of planes to stop forest fires, you're either putting out restaurant fires or rescuing children," she said. "Is there an off switch for the hero thing?"

Her awestruck tone made it a compliment, but something tightened in Grady's chest. *Did* he have an off switch? Or would he drive himself into the ground the way his dad used to, taking everyone down with him?

Shaking off his fears, Grady slung an arm around her. "Maybe I'm bad luck," he said. "Maybe I cause people to light restaurants on fire or fall face-first into floors."

She looked up and smiled, which turned Grady's guts into a puddle of goo. "That's another thing I love," she said. "You're modest about it. You don't turn into some chest-thumping alpha male with a hero complex."

He tried to absorb the compliment, but his brain snagged somewhere back in the first part of the sentence.

*Love.*

She hadn't said she loved him. Not even close, but for some reason that word kept pinging around in his brain like a handful of rubber balls.

"What are you smiling about?" Her eyes held his with curiosity, and he realized he was grinning like a big dork.

"You," he said, because it was the simplest answer. "I'm glad we're getting to do this. I'm glad Kayla said yes to feeding the cats and I'm glad you said yes to letting me kidnap you for the night."

"Is it really kidnapping if I consented?"

"Not until I tie you up." He grinned as the hostess approached. "We'll save that for later," he murmured in her ear.

He felt the shiver ripple up her bare arm as she

followed the hostess to a quiet table in the corner. "Thank you," she said as the woman handed her a menu, then offered one to Grady, along with the wine list.

Leaving his menus on the table, he watched Willa's face as she surveyed the prices. She bit her lip, mossy eyes sweeping up one column and down the other. He braced for it, prepared for her to protest the high prices, to insist she only wanted a cup of soup.

Instead she set the menu down and smiled at him. "What are you getting?"

He hesitated. Was this a test?

The old Grady might have tried to impress her by suggesting a pricey bottle of wine, maybe recommending the lobster.

"Want to split an appetizer?" he suggested.

Her smile was tinged with relief and something else. Something that looked a little like the word that was still rubber-balling around in his brain.

*Love.*

No. That's not what this was. Not yet. But eventually, maybe—

"I'd love to," Willa said and reached across the table for his hand. "Calamari or bruschetta?"

"Calamari." Grady set the menu down and folded both hands around hers. "It's still happy hour, if you see any cocktails you like on that menu." Good Lord, what had he come to? Here he was deliberately being a cheapskate to impress a woman.

It wasn't the worst thing in the world, and it sure as hell was easier on his wallet.

"You can order off the regular menu, too," he

added quickly. "If you'd rather get—"

"No, this is perfect." She set down her own menu and smiled. "I want to try that Secret Garden cocktail with the fresh basil and lime."

"We'll make it two." He flagged down their server and placed the order, letting her know they needed a few more minutes to choose entrees.

"Take your time." She set down two tall glasses of ice water and a bowl of fresh bread with truffle butter, then vanished back to the kitchen.

Willa reached across the table and skimmed a fingertip over the knuckles on his right hand. "Thank you, Grady."

"You don't have to keep thanking me." He set his other hand on the table so she could touch that one, too. It felt good, that gentle touch, the delicate tickle of her fingertip.

"I just really appreciate this," she said. "You bringing me here. Urging me to relax."

"Is it working?"

She nodded, so beautiful in candlelight that Grady's fingers clenched into his palms. "I think it is."

"You're not sure?"

She glanced down at their hands, considering her words. "I start to relax," she said softly, fingertip pausing in the dip between his thumb and forefinger. "And then this voice in the back of my head starts whispering about how I haven't saved enough. How I'm only one medical emergency away from financial ruin. Or if I lost a few clients or had an accident where I couldn't work, I'd—I'd be destroyed."

Grady said nothing, recognizing this was a big admission for her. Yeah, he knew she worked hard;

he even had a loose grasp on the poverty behind it.

But he hadn't understood the fear. Not really, not like this.

"That sounds terrifying," he said.

She nodded, eyes sparkling with candlelight and maybe the faintest mist of tears. "It is," she whispered. "I'm not proud of it, being scared all the time. Being so afraid of losing everything."

Grady held very still. Her finger moved over the ridge of his knuckles, a slow, delicate bump and dip that sent a warm pulse of sensation up his forearms.

"You haven't met my brother Jake yet, right?"

Willa shook her head. "He wasn't at the barbecue, and I don't think he was at the base when I visited."

"Probably on a fire," he said. "Anyway, he's a year younger than me and he's been married before."

"But not anymore?"

Grady shook his head, hoping Jake would forgive him for sharing this story with Willa. His brother was a private sort of guy, but Grady knew without having to ask her that Willa wouldn't tell a soul.

"Jake's wife had an affair with some big-shot attorney in Portland."

"That's awful. Poor Jake."

"It's not uncommon in this line of work." Grady's vocal cords tightened, and he had to take a sip of water to keep going. "It's tough on spouses left alone all the time." He cleared his throat. "Anyway, by the time Jake figured it out, they'd built this whole case against him for emotional neglect—he was gone a lot, obviously. Anyway, they cleaned him out."

"Financially, you mean?"

"And emotionally. He had nothing left. No

savings, he lost his house—hell, they even kept the dog."

The horror filling Willa's eyes almost took his breath away. "What did he do?"

"He suffered," Grady said. "Drank too much, though I wouldn't say he had a problem. He holed up in his house and watched a lot of bad television. He cursed. He wallowed for a long damn time." Grady licked his lips, conscious of Willa's eyes on him. "And then he got back up and started again."

Willa stared, waiting for more of the story. But that was it.

"That sounds…"

She couldn't seem to find a word, so Grady supplied a few.

"Awful? Painful? Tough to watch and even tougher to go through?"

She nodded, hands balling together beside his. "Yes, all of that."

"It was, but you know what?" He didn't wait for a response. Just closed his hands around hers and kept going. "A couple of months ago, we got to talking. About life and setbacks and career choices. He told me he regrets nothing. That it sucked like you wouldn't believe to have to start over like that, but he's glad he did. That he likes his new life so much better than his old one, but he never would have known that if the rug hadn't been yanked out from under him."

Willa's jaw clenched. "You're saying I should start over?"

"Not at all." Definitely not—he knew that wasn't what she needed, or what she wanted to hear. "Just that you *could*, if you had to. And it would suck, don't get me wrong, but maybe you'd find some silver linings."

She held his gaze for a long, long time. "I'm not sure I could do that."

"You wouldn't want to, and I don't blame you." He held her gaze with his. "But you could do it. You're the strongest woman I know."

Her throat moved as she swallowed, and he could tell from her eyes that she was fighting to keep her emotions in check. "I don't feel very strong sometimes."

The waitress drifted over and set their cocktails down quickly. Seeming to sense it wasn't the right time to interrupt, she hurried away.

Grady picked up his glass and lifted it in a toast to Willa. "You're strong. So damn strong, I'm in awe of you most of the time."

"Thank you." She picked up her glass, too, and Grady clinked his against it. "Though I'm not sure you're right."

"I am. After all, you've resisted my relentless pursuit of multiple dates," he teased as he took a sip of the cocktail. "That takes some fortitude."

He expected a playful response. A joke about how he wasn't terribly irresistible or that such resistance required good taste rather than strength.

But Willa bit her lip and held his gaze with hers. "Maybe I'm tired of resisting."

Her voice was halfway between a flirty murmur and a grave confession, so he thought he'd heard her wrong at first. "Are you considering—?" Hell, what was he trying to ask? "Are you suggesting I've broken down your defenses?"

She laughed and shook her head. "You didn't break anything," she said. "Well, maybe the headboard in our room."

Grady grinned. "Nothing a little superglue can't fix."

"Right." Willa sipped her drink, then set the glass down beside the untouched bread basket. "My defenses are still intact. But maybe—*maybe*—I'm open to letting them down willingly. If you still want to, I mean."

"You're saying—" He stopped himself, not wanting to say the words out loud. He'd already put himself out there with her and still wasn't sure where they stood.

"I'm saying I'd like to make it official." Her smile was tentative but so damn sweet. "Dating. Boyfriend/girlfriend stuff. Whatever you want to call it."

She laughed, such a sweet sound. But there was fear in it, and in her eyes, too. It was mixed with hope and so much affection that he couldn't see straight, but the fear wasn't gone.

He set down his glass and squeezed her hands between his again. "We can take it slowly," he assured her, careful to keep his voice even. To keep from jumping up onto the fucking table and shouting in celebration. "However many dates you're comfortable with, whatever you want to label this thing between us—you can call the shots."

She nodded and gave him a shaky, fearful smile. "Okay," she said. "Let's do it. Let's date. For real, I mean. No more of these fake dates or dates that don't really count." She smiled bigger then, squeezing his hand. "I want it to count, Grady."

"God," he breathed. "So do I."

He let go of her hands and drew her close, kissing her for as long as he dared in a public place. When he drew back, they were both breathing hard.

"We could skip dinner," he began.

"No, let's not." Willa smiled. "Let's call this a practice date."

"Deal." Grady lifted his glass again, and Willa did the same. They clinked together with a sharp *ting* that echoed through the restaurant. The sound of celebration. Of hope and promise and good things to come.

# CHAPTER EIGHTEEN

"When does Grady come back?"

Kayla lifted her feet out of the basin of warm water as the nail tech began toweling her calves with a fluffy white towel.

The three of them were enjoying pedicures—Kayla's idea—at the beauty college with discounted services from student nail techs—Willa's idea—to celebrate Kayla landing a big new photography client.

"Friday." Willa tapped a button on the massage chair so the kneading knobs would move up and down her spine instead of punching her in the kidneys. "As soon as he gets into town, he's coming over with dinner from that fancy new personal chef service. I guess it's right by his house? Anyway, we'll eat together at my place, and then we're going to a star show at the planetarium."

"*The* star show?" Kayla gaped at her. "The one you've wanted to see for eons?"

"That's the one." She was trying to keep her voice from sounding too excited and failing miserably. "I don't know why I never went before, but I'm excited to see it now."

She didn't know why she hadn't gone before, but it could be any number of reasons. Too expensive? Too much of an unnecessary indulgence? Too much of a reminder of her father and how he'd always promised to take her, someday, eventually, when money wasn't so tight?

Why the hell had she held out this long?

She said none of this out loud, but the curious way her friends watched her seemed like odds were good they'd heard her anyway.

"Correct me if I'm wrong," Aislin said. "But this sounds like a date."

"It does, doesn't it?" Willa couldn't help the grin spreading over her face as she swished her feet through the warm water.

"So it is a date?" Leave it to Aislin to want it carved in stone.

"Yep." Willa nodded, still fighting to hold back the smile. "It's a date."

"A date." Kayla repeated the word like she might have misunderstood. Like Willa had just announced plans to shave her head. "Like an actual date?"

"Not dog walking," Aislin clarified.

"Or game night that's totally not a date," Kayla added.

"Or mini golf," Aislin added. "Or basket-weaving or sandwich-making classes."

"Or shower sex that's definitely not a date because you aren't leaving the house."

The nail tech rubbing Aislin's feet jumped a little at that and exchanged a giggly glance with the girl drying Willa's toes with a fluffy towel.

"Sorry," Kayla said to them, not looking too sorry. "Seriously, though, a real date? Like a *date* date?"

Willa sighed, second-guessing her decision to say anything but too damn excited about the date to complain too much. "I bought a Groupon for the personal chef service, so it's not super expensive," she said. "I already placed the order online. And Grady's in charge of the planetarium tickets."

"So you're finally doing it." Aislin shook her head slowly, like Willa had just confessed to joining a cult. A nice cult, but still a cult. "You're dating a guy more than twice."

Willa nibbled a hangnail and tried not to twitch as the student began massaging her feet. It tickled a little, or maybe that wasn't the sole source of discomfort. "It's not that big a deal," she said, knowing it was *exactly* that big a deal. "It's not like we're getting engaged or moving in together or getting matching tattoos. We've just agreed to keep seeing each other."

"I think it's great," Aislin said, possibly noticing Willa's discomfort. "Just take it one day at a time, Wills. He likes you; you like him—"

"And he makes you relax," Kayla added, sweeping an arm around the student-run spa. "Case in point."

"We've done this before, you guys," Willa reminded her.

"Yes, but not in the middle of a work week," Aislin said. "At four thirty with the agreement that you'll go out with us for cocktails instead of rushing back to work."

"Which could just be because that's happy hour and drinks are cheaper," Kayla added. "But we'll take it."

Okay, so the discounted drink thing had crossed her mind, but that wasn't all of it. Willa wiggled her toes and tried to remember the last time she'd felt this relaxed. "I'm trying, you guys. I really am."

"We know." Kayla flashed a smile. "Even Tony noticed a difference. The other night when you had us to dinner, he told me afterward that he can't believe how happy you seem with Grady." She lowered her voice and threw in a suggestive eyebrow wiggle. "He said Grady's acting pretty smitten, too. That he's never seen him like this before."

"Whatever he's doing," Aislin added, "he needs to keep doing it."

Willa did her best not to react, but she couldn't help it. Her brain sashayed right over to the memory of Grady drizzling maple syrup over her bare breasts and licking it off while he—

"Whoa." Aislin laughed. "From the way you just blushed, I'd say you're satisfied by more than just work/life balance."

Willa glanced down at her toes, watching as the nail tech swiped juicy strokes of bright red. She'd grabbed it the instant she'd seen the color was called "Campfire Flames," assuring herself she just liked the color. It wasn't that she was so nuts about Grady that she couldn't even get a freakin' pedicure without thinking of him.

Oh, who was she kidding?

Her subconscious wanted to freak out. Wanted to remind her this was dangerous, that she ran the risk of derailing all her plans.

But the rest of her sat grinning like a big lovestruck dork.

Thankfully, Aislin and Kayla had started chatting about some new Netflix show, so they didn't notice. They also didn't notice her phone pinging in her purse, so Willa reached for it.

Reached for it, then remembered Grady's voice. They'd been lying in bed at the hotel, her head cradled on his chest. She hadn't checked her phone for hours—understandable, considering what they'd been doing for several of those hours—though she could hear it vibrating in her purse across the room. Willa hadn't mentioned it, but Grady must have picked up on the trail of her thoughts to her phone stuffed in her bag on the other side of the room.

"Feels nice sometimes, doesn't it?" he'd asked.

"What's that?"

"Switching off," he'd said. "Giving yourself a break and letting calls go to voicemail, texts go unanswered for an hour or two."

As Willa had lain there with Grady stroking her hair, she'd considered his words. *Nice.* Was that what she was feeling? "Nice" almost didn't cover it. "Bliss" was more like it. Bliss with a side of anxiety, which might be the only way Willa could process bliss.

"Yeah," she'd finally whispered, snuggling up closer to him under the covers. "It feels great."

As Aislin and Kayla chatted beside her, Willa reached into her purse and powered off her iPhone.

She thought she'd gone unnoticed until Kayla gasped. "Did you seriously just shut down?"

Aislin peered around her from the other side. "Not possible. I've known you fifteen years and you always have your phone on. Even in the bathroom."

"Or at dinner."

"Or when having an endoscopy."

"Oh my God, I'd forgotten that," Kayla said. "Remember how the doctor told her to—"

"Enough." Willa laughed, though part of her

wondered if she really was that bad. If she'd been a lousy friend. No wonder she couldn't seem to make time for a relationship. "It's almost five. Isn't that when normal people shut down?"

"Normal, yes." Kayla grinned. "But you—"

"I'm trying to do better." Willa gestured to her feet as Aislin stretched out to give Willa a high five.

"Remind me to send flowers to Grady," she said. "Beef jerky ones."

"Forget the jerky roses," Kayla said. "Remind Willa to do whatever it takes to keep him around."

Willa's cheeks heated as her friends made kissy noises.

"I don't think that'll be a problem," Aislin said.

When the pedicure sessions were complete, they walked down the street to the Hartford Hotel and found a table in the downstairs lounge. Willa glanced at her watch. Five fifteen. She'd had her phone off for almost thirty minutes.

"Can you order me the Secret Garden?" she asked Kayla as she grabbed her phone and headed for the ladies' room. "And I'll split the calamari if anyone wants some. I had it the other night and it was amazing."

She waited for one of them to comment about her taking her phone with her to the bathroom, but no one said a word. God bless them for knowing there was a limit to how long she could be offline.

Pushing through the door to the ladies' room, she slipped her phone out of her purse and powered it up. When was the last time she'd been offline this long? Months, probably years.

It felt exhilarating. It felt terrifying. It felt—

"Oh shit." Her voice echoed through the empty ladies' room as Willa stared at the email from Scalemark Supplies, a new client she'd been courting for months.

*Ms. Frank,*
*We've been trying to reach you with follow-up questions about your RFP. The board of directors is narrowing the field down today, and we urgently need responses to the following…*

Shit, shit, *shit.*
She stumbled into a stall and locked the door behind her. Kicking the toilet seat down, she sat hard on the lid, thumbs flying furiously over her phone screen.

*Mr. Reynolds,*
*I'm so sorry for the delayed response.*

Delayed. For crying out loud, she'd barely been away for thirty minutes, and it wasn't like they'd told her the board meeting was today.

She considered typing something about being offline at the hospital visiting a sick friend, but her conscience wouldn't let her lie and besides, they had a point. The client was in decision-making mode. She knew better than to go offline at a time like that.

*I'm delighted to include the requested materials here. If you need additional information, you can call or text at your earliest convenience. Attached, please find…*

She spent a few minutes attaching the necessary

files because *of course* she kept those things on her phone. Of course she did.

Breathing a sigh of relief, she stood up and unlocked the stall door. Her hands shook a little as she made her way to the sink and washed up, pausing to splash cold water on her face. Her phone sat on the counter beside her, and when the screen flashed Grady's name, her stomach did a giddy somersault.

**Grady:** *Hey, sexy. Jumping on the plane soon. Miss you already.*

Her face flushed with warmth as she picked up her phone and typed a quick reply.

**Willa:** *Miss you, too. Looking forward to our date.*

**Grady:** *So am I.*

She glanced at her reflection in the mirror. Her friends were right: she did look happier. It seemed silly that something as simple as a text could have such a physical effect, but there it was, plain as day, in the mirror in front of her. That smile. That glow.

Grabbing her phone again, she typed.

**Willa:** *I'm doing pedicures and happy hour with Kayla and Aislin on a workday. Impressed?*

The reply bubbles popped up almost immediately.

**Grady:** *Very!*

She laughed as a gif popped up with cartoon cats applauding. Then more reply bubbles as he added something else.

**Grady:** *I'd be more impressed if you actually SWITCHED OFF, since it's after 5. But baby steps. Proud of you.*

She rolled her eyes as her fingers flew across the keyboard.

**Willa:** *I've had it off. Glad I switched on, since I got to hear from you.*

She started to add a couple of heart emojis, then stopped herself, feeling silly. She settled for a smiley face with heart eyes, then deleted that, too. She finally settled on a regular smiley face and the certainty that modern technology had seriously screwed with flirtation.

**Grady:** *Glad you're well. Miss you. Xoxoxoxoxo*

Willa fired off an *xoxoxo* of her own, then left the restroom with a little more spring in her step. As she walked across the restaurant, Kayla and Aislin shook their heads at her.

"I knew it," Aislin said. "She couldn't resist checking her phone."

"At least tell us it was for Grady and not work," Kayla said. "We might give you a pass for that."

"I was texting with Grady. It's the last time I'll hear from him for a few days." She held up her phone and made a show of shoving it in her purse. "And now I'm putting it away."

"Good for you." Kayla lifted her glass. "Cheers to Willa's new work/life balance."

"Hear, hear." Aislin clinked her glass and Willa followed suit.

"Cheers," she echoed, taking a sip of her drink. It was cool and citrusy and tasted just as decadent at this hour of the day. "And to calamari. Yum, this looks good."

As they all dove in, she forgot about emails and Grady and the client and everything else for a while. Was this how the rest of the world lived? Was this what it felt like to relax for a while and treat herself to a break?

Maybe she could get used to this.

By the time they left The Hartford, it was almost six thirty. She hugged Kayla, then Aislin, as they complimented one another's pedicures and promised to do it again soon.

"Anyone want to split an Uber?" Aislin asked. "I know we only had two drinks, but…"

"Yes," Kayla said. "Let's be responsible. Wills?"

"Definitely." She could come back for her car tomorrow, maybe even plan a running date with Kayla to get here. How about that for new and improved healthy choices?

She pulled out her phone to summon Uber, then froze. All the blood drained from her face.

"Wills?" Kayla's voice was tinged with concern. "What's wrong? Is it Grady?"

"No." Her voice came out in a whisper as her gaze swept over the string of missed messages. "I switched off my notifications. I didn't mean to. Maybe I hit the button when I shoved in in my purse or— Oh shit."

She fumbled the ringer back on, scanning the series of message alerts. The calamari curdled in her gut as she read the words.

*Please sign the attached nondisclosure form and return it ASAP.*
*Hello?*
*Need a response by 6.*

Willa glanced at her watch, already knowing it was too late. Dammit, dammit, dammit.

She tapped out a response anyway, then toggled her way to DocuSign to fill out the forms. Dammit, she knew better than this. What had she been thinking?

"Can we help?" Kayla asked. "Is there anything we can do?"

"I'm fine," Willa said, hoping it was true. "It'll be okay."

• • •

She lost the deal with Scalemark Supplies, and that sucked. Sucked *a lot*, and Willa shed a few tears while Stevie licked her face to assure her things would work out.

Which they did the next week when she worked double-time on a proposal for another new client that specialized in event planning. They loved her pitch and signed on for a complete website rebrand, giving Willa some assurance that the lights would stay on and her bills would be paid. She might even add to her nest egg, that emergency fund she tucked away for the kind of catastrophe that could bring everything crashing down around her. *Stability.* That's what she needed and what she continued to chase.

She redoubled her efforts at landing new business, crafting pie charts and doing heat map analysis free of charge to persuade newcomers to come on board. She stayed up late creating a mockup of an online order form a client could use for client intake.

She walked Stevie, too, determined to nail this balance thing.

"It's about balance," she remembered Grady's mother telling her. "Doing what you need to do to survive but making sure there's something left over for you. For the people who love you."

It did feel good, though she missed Grady terribly. She couldn't wait to see him again, to hold hands across the dinner table and gaze at the stars together in the Hart Valley Science Center's planetarium. She'd wanted to go since she was a little girl and felt dumb for never making the time. Not until Grady came along.

By the time Friday afternoon rolled around, she was jumping out of her skin. Grady wasn't due for another hour, but she got ready anyway, taking extra time with her hair and makeup. She even ran over to Kayla's to borrow some strappy little kitten heels and ended up borrowing an entire outfit. Dress, shoes, even a bracelet that sparkled with tiny crystal stars.

"You look amazing," Kayla told her. "Knock him dead."

Back at her own house, Willa glanced at her watch. It was after five. She frowned, uneasy to realize he was almost an hour late for the early dinner they'd agreed would kick off their evening together.

True, traffic could be crazy driving from southern Washington on summer afternoons, but it wasn't like him not to call or text. Hopefully nothing had happened. She set the table for the meal they'd ordered from the personal chef service, stomach rumbling with eagerness and maybe a few nerves.

Determined to stay busy, she went back to work.

Perched on the edge of her office chair, she did her best not to wrinkle the kick-ass linen wrap dress Kayla had loaned her. By five thirty, she'd started to freak out. The sky was sinking lower on the horizon, and her stomach snarled its discontent.

At a few minutes past six, Grady's truck swung into the driveway. Willa jumped up, pausing to light the candles on the dining room table as she hustled to the front of the house. Smoothing down her dress, she threw open the door.

"Willa." The grin that spread across his face sent a spear of heat to her belly. "I'm so sorry I'm late. I stopped to help a guy with a flat tire, and it took longer than I expected. It happened right in a dead zone, too, so I couldn't call or text."

"It's okay," she said, breathing him in as she threw her arms around him. He smelled like woodsmoke and shampoo, like he'd run home to shower but had been so eager to see her that he hadn't scrubbed all the pinesap from his hair.

"God, I missed you," he said.

"I missed you, too." She kissed the side of his neck, breathing in all that delicious heat. "So much."

He drew back to admire her. "You look amazing."

"Thanks." She grinned. "You're not so bad yourself."

Muscles stretched the front of his T-shirt, and he filled out his jeans like a dream. She was so busy admiring his body that it took her a minute to catch the guilty expression on his face. "What's wrong?"

"Don't kill me," he said, "but I didn't make it to the personal chef place before they closed. They left a message saying we can still pick it up tomorrow—

they'll keep it in the fridge or something. I'm really sorry."

He looked sorry, too. So sorry that Willa could almost ignore the growling of her stomach. "It's okay," she said. "We're going to need another plan for dinner, though."

"Got it." He wrapped his arms around her waist. "There's that nice Italian place right by the planetarium."

Willa forced a smile, trying not to think about the added cost. "They do have good garlic bread."

"If I call ahead and order, we can have the food waiting when we get there and then run across the street for the show." He nuzzled her neck, and Willa arched into him, groaning as goose bumps rippled up her arms. "Or we skip all of that and stay here so I can eat pizza off your naked body," he suggested.

Willa laughed, tempted by the offer. "Pizza delivery's at least an hour on a Friday night," she pointed out. "I can cook something, or we can—"

"Nope, no cooking." He tipped her head back and kissed her, distracting her all over again. "You've worked hard this week. It's playtime now."

"Mm, I like the sound of playtime."

Grady laughed and drew back. "Got your phone shut off?"

She hesitated, biting her lip. "I could just switch it to silent. What if—"

"Willa, it's after five." He glanced at his watch. "Way after five. Shit, sorry I'm so late."

"No, it's fine." She slipped out her phone and glanced at the screen. "I'll do it right before we leave. Promise."

He grinned and pulled out his own phone. "I can call Ernesto's right now and have food ordered before you come back from feeding Stevie and the cats. What are you in the mood for?"

"You," she admitted, hooking a finger in his belt loop. "But I'd settle for their eggplant Parmesan and a small garden salad."

"Done." He was already dialing. "Glass of Chianti?"

"Yes, please." She started for the kitchen, her brain churning over the change in plans. It seemed solid. Yes, it wasn't what they'd agreed on, but being flexible was part of this new balancing act. She could do this, could learn to roll with the unexpected.

Grady's voice rumbled from the other room. "Could we also get an order of tiramisu? Wait, make it two."

Trying not to fret, she scooped food into pet bowls as Stevie did a joyful tap dance at her feet. Grady really had thought of everything.

Grabbing her purse off the table, she pulled out her phone and checked one last time for messages. No emails from clients, no text messages about the RFPs she'd sent out earlier that morning. Was she really all clear?

She powered off the phone and held it up as she returned to the living room. Grady looked up and grinned. "Atta girl."

"Switched off and ready to play," she told him. "Commend me on my balance."

"Consider yourself commended." He pulled her in for a kiss that curled her toes, then slipped an arm around her shoulders.

"No motorcycle tonight, don't worry," he promised as he led her to his truck. "Ernesto's will have the food ready when we walk in, and we'll have just enough time to eat and make it to the show."

She snuggled up closer, reveling in his warmth. "My hero."

He gave a courtly bow as he opened her door and helped her into the cab of the truck. Then he ran around the front and slipped into the driver's seat. "It's good to see you." He turned sideways to pull her close, bumping his ribs on the steering wheel. "Ow," he said against her mouth.

"Are you okay?"

He answered by kissing her long and slow. His hand skimmed up her waist as his tongue grazed hers and every nerve in her body sat up and sang.

"I'm good," he said when they drew back from each other. "Better than good. I'm great."

"Me too."

He stuck the keys in the ignition with a shrug. "I did bang my ribs pretty hard on a tree branch a few days ago," he admitted. "I'm still a little bruised."

"Ouch." Willa winced on his behalf, surveying him for distress. "You're sure you're all right?"

"Positive." He started the engine. "Just need to be careful not to go leaning into steering wheels."

He started to release the brake, but Willa caught his hand. "Wait." She grabbed at the hem of his T-shirt. "Do you need to have it looked at or—"

"Nah, it's just a bruise." He flashed her a grin. "You can keep taking off my clothes, though."

She rolled her eyes, though deep down, she kinda wanted to. "One more kiss, and then we go."

"Deal." He pulled her close, avoiding the steering wheel as he slipped his hands into her hair and drew her against him. He kissed her deeper this time, making it count.

When they drew apart, they both were breathing fast.

"I'm rethinking the plan." His gaze flicked toward the house, and Willa felt liquid heat pooling between her legs. "We could just go back inside and ravage each other."

She laughed, not wanting to admit how much she wanted that, too. "Did you give them your credit card number for dinner?"

"Yeah, but—"

"We can't waste money," she said. "Or food. I'm starving."

Grady grinned. "We'll have plenty of time later for ravaging each other."

She cast one more longing look at the house. "On the other hand—"

"No, you're right." Grady released the brake. "The food's waiting for us, and you've wanted to see the star show forever. Only a few hours and we'll have each other's clothes off."

"Deal."

"Delicious anticipation," he said as he eased the car out onto the road.

Willa laughed and tossed her hair. "Not a bad way to kick off a weekend together."

"A whole weekend." He shook his head in awe. "Man, I must have done something right to get this lucky."

Willa laughed as happiness bubbled in her

chest and the house vanished behind them. She could almost shake the niggling fear that she was forgetting something big. That the monster was breathing hot and impatient down her neck, just like it always did.

# CHAPTER NINETEEN

After years of sleeping outside as a smokejumper, Grady had been positive nothing in the world compared to the beauty of a velvety-black night sky dusted with the glitter of stars.

He'd been wrong.

About so many things, but especially that. As he sat in that planetarium with his arm around Willa and her head tipped back to watch the play of speckled light dancing across the ceiling, he was certain he'd never seen anything so lovely in his life.

Not just the star show but Willa.

Willa with her face turned up toward the ceiling and her eyes filled with glittering stars and a wonder he might have called "childlike" if he weren't conscious of her very womanly, very soft body pressed warm and lush against him.

Afterward, as they walked out together with their hands intertwined, she looked up at him with eyes still twinkling. "Thank you," she said softly. "It was so much better than I imagined it would be."

"I'm glad." His heart squeezed in his chest.

"Not just the show but all of it," she said. "Dinner. The date. The fact that we've got more to come."

"I can't believe we get the whole weekend together." It was finally happening. He was finally getting what he'd hoped for, a chance to do things right with her.

She smiled up at him, swinging their hands

slightly. "What should we do for our third date?"

"Hmm." Snapping his fingers, he gave his best impression of a guy with a brilliant plan. "Don't tell, but Tony watches that dating show sometimes—*The Bachelor*?"

"What?" She laughed. "You're not serious."

"Dead serious. He records it and makes us all watch it Tuesday mornings if we don't get called out to fly."

"Oh, Kayla's going to love this."

"All the guys pretend to hate it," Grady continued as he led her down the street toward the parking garage. "But you'll always find six or seven of us clustered around the TV room watching like it's the State of the Union address."

"I thought I'd seen everything with your sewing circle," she said. "I'd pay good money to watch your little *Bachelor* viewing party. All those burly, shirtless smokejumpers—"

"Hey now," he teased, pulling her closer to him. "Should I be worried your fantasies involve my coworkers?"

"I promise you're the only smokejumper in my fantasies," she said gravely. "There might be a police officer, though, and definitely a cowboy—"

She squealed as Grady caught her around the waist and tickled her, fingers fluttering in the soft curve of her waist until they were both breathless and laughing. Her green eyes danced as she drew back and started walking again. "Anyway," she said. "You were telling me about watching *The Bachelor*?"

"Right." He forced himself to clear the lust from his brain so he could remember what the hell he'd been talking about. "I'm thinking we could nab some date ideas from the show."

"Like what?"

"Let's see," he said, trying to remember some of the more audacious ones he'd seen on recent seasons. "Helicopter dates are big. The couple gets in a helicopter and flies off to some exotic island for dinner. A dinner they never actually eat."

"You mean they just waste food?"

He shrugged. "I don't get it, either. Maybe they don't want to be caught on camera with their mouths full? Anyway, the food just sits there on the plate getting cold while they yammer on about who's not there for the right reasons."

Willa laughed and shook her head. "For the record, I plan to clean my plate completely on any of our future dates."

"I love that about you."

"And I'm thinking we should skip the helicopter dates, given your profession," she pointed out. "Can't have you spending more time in the air than you do on the ground."

"Good point." Grady racked his brain for more ideas. "Bikini pool parties," he said. "That's big on *The Bachelor*."

"Nothing says romance like being ogled and objectified."

Grady laughed. "There also seem to be a lot of dates where women fight each other with foam weapons while wearing wedding dresses. Either that or skimpy costumes."

Willa raised an eyebrow as they neared the parking garage. "I'm thinking *The Bachelor* might not be the best source of quality date ideas."

"Hmm," he mused. "Tony watches *The Bachelor-ette*, too. We've got plenty of options to choose from on that show."

"Such as?"

"Let's see." He led her around the side of the parking structure. "If I remember right, I'll need to compete in some sort of obstacle course that involves wallowing shirtless in a pit of whipped cream looking for a diamond ring. That's always popular."

"This has happened more than once?"

"Some variation, sure. Also, we're supposed to have conversations that include phrases like 'her and I's relationship.' Slaughtering grammar is an important part of dating in the Bachelor franchise."

"I'll have to work on that."

"Oh, and we're supposed to say 'falling for,'" he continued. "As in 'I'm falling for you big-time' because we're not actually allowed to say 'I love you.'"

He stole a glance at her face, curious how those three words would land in such a soft context. He wasn't saying them *to* her, just saying them, but still.

Willa didn't flinch and her smile didn't waver. Was he imagining her fingers clutching his just a little tighter?

"Should I be writing down all these stellar ideas?" she asked.

Grady steered her around a puddle of melted ice cream and took a deep breath. "For the record, it's true."

"What's true?"

"I'm falling for you." There. That was easier to

say than the big three, which were also probably true. Baby steps. "It's a cheesy phrase, I know, but I mean it—I've fallen hard for you, Wills. In case it wasn't obvious."

His heart thudded as he waited for her response. She didn't say anything right away, but when she turned to him, her face was lit by a smile. "Same," she said. "I've fallen for you, too. So hard."

She bit her lip, and Grady braced for a brush off. Some indication they weren't on the same page.

Then she smiled and his heart split wide open.

"Would you—" He hesitated. "Would you want to talk about moving in together?" He held up a hand in case she was going to protest. "Not right away—not anytime soon, I swear. I just—"

"Yes." Her smile widened. "You're serious?"

He laughed. "Yeah? It's something I've thought about, but I didn't want to freak you out. And seriously, we wouldn't have to do it soon. I mean, hell, I'd do it tomorrow." Okay, that was a little much. But he did like the idea. "Waking up together all the time?"

Willa laughed and brushed the hair from her face. "We'd need to have a plan," she said. "Logistics like your place or mine, and how we'd handle finances and—"

"And how many times a night we'd have scx?" He grinned and pulled her tighter against him. "Or who gets which side of the bed? And we'd definitely want to negotiate pillows. I'm thinking buckwheat?"

Willa laughed as Grady kissed the side of her neck. "I can't believe we're talking about this," she said. "This is nuts."

"But it feels right, doesn't it?" It did, just like Willa felt perfect in his arms.

She nodded against his chest. "It does. It really does."

Grady held her tight, soothing his own fears. Okay, so the idea of making plans was scary as hell, but he did like the thought of falling asleep together. Waking up and making love and—

And this. This right here, holding her in his arms under a streetlight for all the world to see.

"Come on," he said, drawing back. "Let's go back to your place and do this right."

Willa grinned. "It feels pretty right already, so I can't wait to find out what else you've got up your sleeve."

"My sleeve isn't where you should start looking." He flashed her a salacious grin, earning himself another giggle.

"Well, in that case," she said, trailing her fingers over the fly of his jeans, eyes widening when she found him more than ready to go. "We should hurry up and get home."

It was all Grady could do not to break the speed limit as they rocketed across town toward Willa's house, Willa's bedroom, Willa's bed. God, he wanted her. Not just her body but all of her. Her sharp wit and her kind heart and her laughter in the morning. The whole package, that's what he'd held out for all this time.

And yeah, the sex was amazing. No doubt about it, he wanted that, too.

By the time they pulled into her driveway, he was so desperate to have her, he couldn't see straight.

Blame the anticipation or blame her hand stroking his thigh, urging him to run the yellow light, to hurry, *hurry*, that she couldn't wait to feel him inside her.

How did he get this lucky?

"What is that?"

Blinking out of his sex-infused fog, Grady stared at her front door, where she was pointing. A small flap of pink paper fluttered from its post next to her peephole.

"Looks like one of those notification things when you get a package."

He turned back to her in time to watch all the color drain from her face as her mouth fell open in stunned horror. "Oh God." She threw open the car door and staggered out, sprinting up her walkway. "No. No no no *no*."

What the hell?

Grady jumped out after her, not sure what was happening. She reached her front door before he did and was already clutching the slip of paper in a trembling hand, her face filled with sheer panic.

"What's wrong? What is it?"

"Oh God," she breathed. "This can't be happening. I've been working so hard. I can't—"

"Slow down, Willa." He put a hand on the back of her neck, hoping to soothe her.

But she shrugged him off and turned with eyes blazing. "I can't believe I did that."

"Did what? What's happening?"

"You," she said, and Grady tried not to flinch. "They said this was coming, but I didn't know when, and I told them it wouldn't matter because I'm always home."

Grady stared at the paper, taking in the signature required line at the bottom. "They'll try again, won't they? Amazon's always doing that with my packages, or they leave them with my neighbors when—"

"No, you don't understand." She blinked hard, breathing in and out to calm herself, though Grady could see it wasn't working. "TechTel, the client I've been trying to land for months. They were sending me a hard drive with the files I need to complete the final test to land the job. There's a limited window to do the work."

Grady raked his hands through his hair, determined to fix this for her. "So we'll go pick it up tomorrow," he said. "First thing in the morning, you'll still have all weekend to do it."

"It doesn't work that way, Grady." Tears spilled down her face, and she clutched the delivery notice so tight, her knuckles went white and the paper crumpled. "This courier service—there's no local office, and they don't do weekends. They won't attempt delivery again until Monday. It's over. I'm screwed."

She crumpled then, just like the paper. He reached for her again, desperate to comfort her, to tell her it would be okay. There were other clients, other opportunities—

"I know you think this is no big deal," she said, drawing back. "More clients will come along, right?"

He blinked, too stunned to respond. "I didn't say that."

"You didn't have to. I can see it on your face. Mister Go With the Flow, Mister Learn to Have Balance. But this wasn't just any deal, Grady. TechTel—it's where my mother always wanted to work. Her dream job, the job she'd just landed when she met my father. I wanted to land this so badly. *Needed* it."

Her words heaved out in sobs so fierce, her shoulders shook. Grady reached for her hand, even as her words landed like fist blows. "Okay, I get it." He wasn't positive he did, but it seemed like the right thing to say. "It's personal. But there will be other jobs, right? You're always planning ahead, making sure you have lots of work rolling in."

He squeezed her hand, hoping to soothe her. He didn't understand her need to be twelve steps ahead of the game at all times, but he could be supportive. He could offer that, at least.

"You *don't* get it." Her voice wobbled. "TechTel, my mom busted her ass to get that job. It was the dream she gave up to have me, to marry *him*. This was my chance, Grady. My chance to land them as a client and make her proud."

"She'd be so proud of you already, Willa." He felt lost for what to say, but that seemed like a given. "Wherever she is—heaven—she's looking down and thinking what an amazing woman you've become. I'm positive about that."

She shook her head, her eyes wild and heartbroken. "You don't know anything." The paper slipped from her fingers, landing at his feet like an injured bird. "My mother's not dead, Grady."

His breath snagged in his throat. "What?" He stared at her, not comprehending, not breathing. "I don't— You said—"

"I said she left," Willa said. "That she was gone. And you heard the story about my grandparents sitting me down to say she'd died. Those things are all true."

Grady's head was spinning, and he wished he could grab hold of it with both hands to steady it, to process what Willa was telling him. "But she's not dead?"

"I thought she was," Willa said, dashing tears from her face. "For a long time, I believed what my grandparents told me. It was easier that way."

"Easier," he repeated, still not understanding.

"Easier than the truth," she said. "Which is that she didn't die. She just didn't love me enough to come back. She abandoned me—abandoned *us*, my dad and me—but she could have come back."

He wanted to reach for her, started to do it. But she stepped back and out of his reach. It stung that she didn't want his comfort, but this wasn't about him. He couldn't make it about him.

"How long have you known this? Are you in touch with her?" He had so many questions, but those ones hooked their claws in him.

"Two years." She dashed away tears again, seemingly frustrated that they kept falling. "For years, my dad would get drunk and say things like 'she'd come back to us if she could,' and I thought it was just drunk rambling. That he meant she couldn't because she was dead."

"I don't understand. She faked her own death?"

Willa closed her eyes. "I don't know, okay? I haven't spoken with her. She obviously didn't care enough to get in touch, and I assume she knows her parents told us she'd died."

It seemed like a big assumption to Grady, but that

wasn't the biggest issue here. "So your father knows she's not dead?"

"I have no idea," she said. "I hired a private investigator to figure it out myself. What's the point of bringing it up with him now?"

Grady frowned, not sure if she wanted a response. "Answers? Closure, I guess?"

She laughed, but it wasn't a happy sound. It was a brittle, dry laugh with angry cracks around the edges. "You obviously haven't met my father."

"No," he said softly. "I haven't."

Which should have told him something, shouldn't it? All this time he'd been letting Willa into his life, offering her his dreams, his fears, his family.

And she hadn't let him in at all. Not really.

He clenched his fists at his sides and ordered himself to breathe. Not to make this about him. "Willa, I'm so sorry." What a lame thing to say. "It's not your fault," he said. "No matter what happened, whatever the reasons, you have to know it's not your fault your mother left. That she didn't come back. That's on her. Not you."

She shook her head, tears dripping down her face. "It *is* my fault," she said. "Her leaving. Me losing my grip on my career. All of it, that's on me."

Christ, she was spiraling fast. He couldn't let her stumble down this path. He reached for her hand, and this time she let him take it. "Let's go inside," he said. "I'll make you some tea and we'll sit on the couch with Stevie and the cats and you can tell me all about—"

"No," she said, fingers curling into his palm as she squeezed her eyes shut. "No, I can't. I'm sorry, Grady.

I can't do this."

"It's okay," he said. "We don't have to talk about it if you don't want. I can just hold you and not say anything at all."

"No." She stepped back, shaking her head. "I need to make a plan. I need to rework my schedule and figure out if there's some way to bid for their next project. Maybe in a couple of years when they redo their site again, or maybe—"

"Willa, slow down." Grady slid his hand into his hair, not sure how to reach her. "Can we just take this one thing at a time? Maybe live in the moment just a little bit, give yourself a chance to process this."

It was the wrong choice of words. He saw it in the way her eyes blazed, the way her hands balled into fists.

"Easy for you to say." Her voice came out raw and brittle. "You throw money around like it's confetti, and anytime I ask about *actual* future plans, you make it into a joke."

Ouch.

But she wasn't wrong.

"Look, maybe I don't plan out my life and my future down to the absolute minutiae, but—"

"You don't plan at all, Grady." She took a shaky breath and a step back from him. "That's fine for you, but it's not how I can live. Don't you see? We're too different."

"What are you saying?" He knew damn well what she was saying, but he wanted to pretend a little longer that he didn't. That this wasn't crashing down around him while all he could do was watch.

Willa looked at him with sadness in her eyes. "I

think you should go."

He swallowed hard, lacing his fingers through hers. "Okay," he said, taking a few steadying breaths. "All right, you need to be alone tonight. I get it. How about tomorrow morning, we—"

"No, Grady, that's not what I meant." A tear spilled as she shook her head. "I can't do this. I can't date you. I was right all along; there's no room in my life for a relationship. I'm sorry I let you think that. Let myself believe it when I know deep down it could never work."

He stared at her. "You're kidding."

"I'm not. I lost focus. I never do that, and I can't do it again." Her shoulders shook with the force of all that grief. Years of it, grief that had nothing at all to do with him, with the two of them together. "There's too much at stake. I can't let my career slip. All the stability I've worked so hard to build. I can't give that up."

He fumbled for straws, fighting to find a way to salvage this. To give her some hope. "You'll get other jobs." His voice cracked, but he kept going. "Or maybe you can get an extension on this one. Maybe if we—"

"It's not just this job, Grady," she said. "It's about the big picture. The fact that every time I take my cyc off the ball for even one second, everything falls apart. *Everything*."

How was this happening? Not ten minutes ago, they were racing down the highway with Willa's hand on his thigh. He was this close to telling her he loved her, to holding her in his arms and making love to her again. They'd talked about moving in together, for crying out loud.

How had everything gone sideways?

Her hand was still in his, so he tried pulling her closer. If he could just get his arms around her, he could hold her and soothe her and tell her things would be okay. They had to be.

"I can't." She drew her hand back and stepped away from him. "I'm sorry, but I have to go. It's been wonderful knowing you, but—"

"Stop right there," he said, needing her not to finish that sentence. "Look, I'll call in the morning when you've had a chance to process things. We can talk then, and—"

"I'll have my phone off." She gave a choked little laugh. "That's what you wanted me to do, wasn't it?"

"Not like that. Never like that."

She shook her head and took another step back. "I shouldn't have let this happen," she said. "Shouldn't have let myself fall for you."

*Fall for you.*

The words that had meant so much just minutes ago hit like a slap. She said them like it was a sentence worse than death. "Maybe in the morning, things will seem better," he offered. "You'll calm down and—"

Shit, that was also the wrong thing to say. He knew from the way her eyes flashed, her nostrils flared.

"Calm down?" She folded her arms over her chest, hands still trembling. "This is all just a joke to you. A game. Win over the woman who doesn't want to be won, turn her life upside down. Was that the plan?"

"Jesus." The sting of accusation smacked him hard on the cheek. He shouldn't let himself react, but pride made his chest flare. "So this is my fault? I didn't exactly hold you against your will. I didn't drag you to that hotel or tie you up and force you to watch the star show. You chose those things, Willa."

"I did." She squeezed her eyes shut tight, like the words hurt her, too. "And now I'm choosing to undo them. I need you to leave, Grady."

He stared at her, eyes pinched shut, hair sticking to the tear tracks on her face. He could still reach for her, still save this.

Only he couldn't. He'd finally found a situation that didn't call for a hero. It called for a miracle.

"Go," she said again, eyes still closed.

This time, he listened. He took a step back, then another. There had to be a way to save this.

"Don't call me," she said. "I'll block your number, Grady; I mean it. It's not personal—I swear it isn't. This is just what I need."

Of course it was fucking personal. How could it not be?

"Okay," he said. "I'll respect your wishes if that's what you want."

*Tell me it's not what you want. Change your mind, please…*

"It's what I want." Her voice didn't shake at all. It was firm and strong and final. "It's what I want."

So that was it. Grady nodded, even though she couldn't see him. Even though her eyes were still pinched shut, blocking him out. "Goodbye, Willa."

He turned and walked to his truck, wishing on the stars and everything else that she'd call out to him. That she'd change her mind.

But he knew damn well she wouldn't.

# CHAPTER TWENTY

There was no saving the TechTel deal.

Willa knew that and accepted it. She got her hands on the hard drive Monday morning and sent it back with a note apologizing for the missed opportunity and thanking them for considering her.

They didn't write back, and she knew that was one door closing firmly behind her. She couldn't regret it, not really. Not if their expectations were so unrealistic, so demanding. If she'd learned nothing else from Grady and his family, it was the need to be gentler with her own mental health. Even so, she felt the loss of that potential business, of disappointing a potential client.

It wasn't the only loss she felt.

She knew there was no repairing things with Grady. Even if she wanted to, she'd said too many things she couldn't take back. He'd pursued her and won her and worked his magic until she came around, but he wouldn't do that twice. She'd made sure of that, even though the passing days left her wondering if she'd been too hasty.

"No." She said the word out loud to herself as she gripped the steering wheel harder with both hands. "It's better this way. You have too much at stake. Too much to lose if you take your eye off the ball."

Besides, they were completely incompatible. Yeah, it had been fun being with someone so spontaneous, so capable of living in the moment.

But who was she kidding? Willa needed to plan *everything*, to foresee every possible land mine and schedule her way around them. And Grady…well, planning wasn't exactly his forte. She'd loved that about him in some ways, but she had to be sensible.

And there was no sensible way for the two of them to be together. It was that simple.

The pep talk helped, but only a little. She was headed to see her father, which was a dumb idea. It sure as hell never made her feel better, but could she really feel worse?

"Dad?" She knocked twice on his door, then waited a bit. No response, but that wasn't unusual. She knocked again. "Hey, Dad, are you home?"

She tried the knob, which opened easily. The stale, greasy, familiar smells filled her lungs, but she pushed through the door and let a dusty slab of sunlight fall across the sofa.

Her father lay there slack-jawed with an arm over his face. Willa stopped breathing, watching for the rise and fall of his chest.

"Dad?"

He snorted and tossed his arm off his face, and Willa breathed again. As his eyes focused on her, he smiled. "Hey, sweetheart. What time is it?"

"Just after noon," she said. "It's Wednesday," she added, since he might not know that, either.

"Oh. Good." He sat up, rubbing his eyes as Willa glanced at the open spot on the wall where his TV had been. There were only wires and a hole in the plaster.

She opened her mouth to ask, then closed it again. That's not why she was here.

"Have you eaten today?" she asked instead.

"Yeah. Yeah, I had eggs and bacon and toast and orange juice." He planted his feet on the floor, toes peeking through the holes in his socks. Willa made a mental note to buy him some new ones.

"You're sure you ate?" She knew he was lying. Either he'd forgotten or he didn't want to worry her, which made her sad and angry all at once.

Mostly sad.

Turning away, she walked to the kitchen and set her grocery bag on the counter. Slowly, she began to unpack. "How about peanut butter and jelly?" she asked. "I'll have one with you."

"Sure. That'd be great."

She got to work laying out slices of whole wheat bread. She could give him that, at least. Protein. Fiber. A handful of grapes for more vitamins. She set them on two cracked plastic plates, concentrating on her work so she wouldn't have to meet his eyes.

"I wanted to ask you something, Dad." She could do this. Just like this, while her focus was firmly on the task of spreading Jif on slices of spongy bread. She couldn't do it looking at him; she knew that, at least.

"What's that, sweetie?"

"It's about Mom."

Silence. She knew he'd heard her, could feel the tension crackling from all the way over in the living room where he still sat. She didn't lift her eyes, couldn't look at him.

"Your mother," he said at last. "Thought you didn't like talking about her."

That was true. They never had. Not for a long

time, anyway.

*Just say it. Ask what you need to know.*

She looked into the peanut butter jar, steeling herself to put the words out there. To say them out loud after all this time.

"She's alive," Willa said softly. "Did you know?" Her voice cracked, and she couldn't make it say the rest of the words until she stood there breathing in and out for a few more heartbeats. "When Grandma and Grandpa came and told us she'd died, did you know she really hadn't?"

Long silence. Willa couldn't look up, couldn't meet his eyes.

But she felt his answer like a punch to the gut. "No."

She looked up then, daring herself to meet his eyes. To look deeply into those bloodshot brown irises as familiar to her as her own face in a mirror. She could read nothing at all in his expression, not a thing.

But the one thing she didn't see was surprise.

"You don't seem very shocked by what I just said."

Her father shook his head, slow and defeated. "Not much surprises me anymore, Wills," he said. "What are you asking? What is it you really want to know?"

"I'm asking if you knew she wasn't dead."

"No," he said again. "Not for sure." A pause, and that said so much more than he already had. "But I wondered."

She gripped the butter knife tighter, the smell of crushed peanuts making her eyes water. "You thought your wife—*my mother*—might actually be alive, and you never thought to do anything about it?"

"What was I going to do, Willa?"

The burst of life in his voice caught her off guard, and she dropped the knife with a clatter. She picked it back up again as her father lowered his head into his hands. "I wasn't enough for her," he said, his words aimed down at the floor. "We weren't enough. Why would I want you to carry that burden, too?"

Jesus.

She'd suspected as much, but it stung hearing him put the words out there, just lay them naked on the carpet like a corpse.

"So you let me think she was dead," she said softly.

"I let myself think that," he said. "It was easier that way."

"I see." She gripped the knife again, willing herself not to react with judgment or anger. Sadness was her overwhelming emotion anyway, so she let herself fall into it.

"Is that why you started drinking?" she asked.

He shook his head slowly, not lifting it from his hands. Like it had become too heavy for him to hold up anymore. "Maybe that's why I started," he said. "Who really knows?"

"You do," she said. "You're the only one who does."

He lifted his head, eyes flashing with something she couldn't quite read. "I drink because I'm a fucking drunk. That's what you think, right?"

"It doesn't matter what I think," she said carefully. "I'm not the one who can make the choice to change things."

Another snort from her father. "It's too late for that."

Where had she heard those words before? From her own stupid mouth, that's where.

*It's too late, Grady.*

And it was, wasn't it?

Her whole being fought the idea, both for her father and herself. She took a few calming breaths as she finished spreading peanut butter, summoning courage to ask the big one. The question she really wanted to ask.

"Why did she leave?"

He didn't answer. As the silence stretched out, she set the knife down again and looked up at her father.

His head wasn't in his hands anymore. He was watching her, rheumy, bloodshot eyes staring at her like he'd never seen her before.

"I don't know," he said. "Only she can answer that."

"You've spoken to her?"

"No. Never. I didn't even know for sure she was still alive."

But Willa knew. Had an address and everything, though she hadn't done a damn thing about it. She was too scared, too paralyzed by the past and her fears for the future, so she stayed stuck where she was, treading water, fighting for air.

That was how she'd been living, too, wasn't it? Her career, her relationships, her *life*—all of it was conducted in survival mode.

No more.

"I'm going to see her."

She hadn't planned to say that. Hadn't really planned to do it, either. But the second she said the words out loud, she knew they were exactly right. "I'm going to get some answers."

"Good." Her father nodded, anchoring his palms on his knees like he could draw strength from them. "I think you should. I think it's not healthy to let things fester."

It was her turn to snort. She opened the jelly jar and stabbed the knife inside, then pulled it out with a thick glob of strawberry on the end. Breathing in and out, she finished the sandwiches and set the knife on the counter.

Then she met his eyes again. "You need help, Dad," she said. "Real, professional help to deal with your drinking. I'm done."

He stared at her. It wasn't the first time she'd said those words to him, but it was the first time she'd said them with such force. The first time she'd meant them with every fiber of her being, and she saw in his eyes that he knew it.

She braced herself for the denial. The *I don't have a problem* or *I can stop anytime I want.* She'd heard the denials so many times, she could parrot the words right along with him.

"Okay," he said, nodding once. "Okay."

"What?" She must have heard him wrong.

"All right," he said, his voice firmer this time. "You go see your mom. You find out what you need to find out. And when you come back, we'll go."

"Go," she repeated, still sure she'd heard wrong. "You mean you'll go to rehab?"

He shook his head, lowering it slowly to his hands again. "I don't know where I'll get the money, but—"

"I've got it," she said. "If you're serious about going, I can make it happen."

"I'm serious," he said into his hands. "This is it. What they call rock bottom, right?"

Willa squeezed her eyes shut, feeling his despair right along with him. "Yeah," she said. "I think it is."

"I want it to stop," he said. "I'll go. Scout's honor."

For the first time in years, she actually believed him.

• • •

Why was she doing this?

Two years she'd known about her mother. Two years of knowing but not calling, not writing, not even telling anyone close to her that she knew her mom wasn't really dead.

Why now?

But as she gripped the arms of her airplane seat as it lifted into the air, she knew the answer. Knew it but didn't like it.

*Grady.*

He'd shaken something loose inside her, something she'd kept buried for years. How had he managed to do in a couple of months what she'd spent years avoiding? Not just the two years that she'd known the death was a lie but her whole life spent running from feelings of hurt and abandonment and sorrow.

She glanced out the plane's window as the landscape disappeared below her. Was this what he was seeing? She'd tried not to think about him, not to wonder where he was or what he might be feeling, but she couldn't help knowing his schedule. Right about now, he'd be getting on a plane with Tony and Jimmy and maybe Ryan and all the other smokejumpers she'd probably never see again.

The thought made her heart ball up like a wet tissue as the plane climbed higher into the clouds. So this was what flying felt like. It was scary and foreign and new, but the glimmers of sun streaking through cotton-ball clouds made her heart feel lighter. Why had she never done this before?

Before she knew it, they were touching down in Florida. Orlando, of all places. Willa had never been, never wanted to go, not even before she'd learned it was the place her mother had chosen over her.

Gathering her things, she trudged off the plane with her carry-on slung over one shoulder. No sense paying for a checked bag, and besides, she wasn't staying long. Just long enough to look Denise in the eye and ask her why.

*Why did you leave me?*

*Why didn't you come back?*

*Why didn't you love me enough?*

She tried not to look at the dollar amount as she signed the paperwork for the rental car. Tried not to remember how her business was blowing up in her face. After losing the TechTel deal, she'd worked overtime pleasing her other clients. It all felt like patchwork, like everything could fall apart at any moment.

Would she ever stop feeling like that?

Yes, yes, of course. After this, she'd keep her eye

on the ball. She wouldn't get distracted, let herself get carried away by frivolous things.

*Grady wasn't frivolous.*

Well sure, that's not what she meant. But relationships—the kind that seized your heart and soul and all your attention—those were for other people. Not for her. She'd always known that.

Double-checking the address, she eased the nondescript economy car into an open spot against the curb. 3268 Piedmont Court, just like it said in the PI's report. The house was squatty and brown and sagged a little on one side. A scraggly palm tree jutted up from a bed of pink rocks, surrounded by a sea of limp lawn pockmarked with scrubby tan patches. Even with the air-conditioning on full blast, she could feel the sticky heat from outside the car.

Maybe she should have called first, but then she might've chickened out. She needed to do this in person. Sometimes the element of surprise was what it took to ensure honesty, and that's what Willa craved most.

Hands shaking, she tugged the key from the ignition and got out of the car. She started to smooth her skirt but stopped. Did she really care about making a good impression on a woman who'd abandoned her husband and child, letting them believe all these years that she was dead?

But Willa did care, that was the hell of it. So she straightened her skirt and stepped onto the curb. She made her way slowly up the walk, hands shaking at her sides. Maybe her mother had moved. Maybe she was at work or visiting friends or remarried with sixteen children who—

*Rrrrrrrrring!*

She pressed the doorbell before she had a chance to back out. Deep breath in, out, in, out. Footsteps thudded inside, then the click of a dead bolt being unlocked. The door flew open and then—

"Whatever you're selling, I'm not buying."

The woman's bleach-blond hair made a frizzy halo around her head. Deep lines bracketed her eyes, her mouth, the spot where her dimples might be if she smiled. Willa knew those dimples. She saw them each time she smiled in the mirror, which wasn't often. She knew those green eyes, too, the same ones she'd seen lit from inside those months she'd been with Grady.

No one was smiling now. Her mother's face showed no flicker of recognition.

"Hello, Denise." Willa hesitated. "*Mom*."

The word came out parched and brittle. The woman's mouth opened, then closed again, then opened. No sound emerged. Not at first.

"Willa? It's you?"

Willa nodded, not trusting her own voice. Denise's eyes were familiar, but it was her voice she would have known anywhere. Even cracking with cigarette fatigue, it was the same voice Willa heard in her dreams, singing "The Itsy-Bitsy Spider" as she drifted off to sleep.

"Holy shit." Denise blinked. "Holy fucking shit."

Willa laughed. She couldn't help it. The whole thing was so absurd. "Yeah," she muttered. "Pretty much sums it up."

Her mother nodded, still in shock. "I never thought— I had no idea—" She stopped herself, shaking her head. "I'm guessing you have questions."

"A few." Understatement of the year.

Denise's brow furrowed. "Will you come in?"

Willa hesitated. She'd pictured herself standing her ground, talking to her mother on the porch.

But so much of her life wasn't turning out how she'd pictured, so she nodded. "Sure."

Denise stepped aside and Willa moved past her, breathing in the unfamiliar scents. Fabric softener, burned toast, maybe a hint of dog, though she didn't see one anywhere.

Nothing familiar at all. Not tied to her childhood, anyway.

"Right this way," Denise said, leading the way down a hall. "The place is a mess. Sorry."

Sorry? For a few magazines scattered across the coffee table or for a lifetime of worry and sadness and—

"Can I get you something to drink?" Her mother turned at the end of the hallway, gesturing Willa toward a couch in the tiny living room. "Tea or water or soda? I don't have any wine or beer or anything. Haven't kept alcohol in the house for years. I can't—" She stopped there, turned to face Willa. "I'm sorry," she said again.

This time, Willa felt sure the apology wasn't for the clutter. Remorse washed over Denise's face, and her fingers balled white-knuckled in front of her.

Willa looked down to see her own hands clenched in front of her. She released her hold, head spinning from the surreal quality of it all. "Why?"

What a clumsy question, so completely inadequate. The lines in her mother's face deepened like trenches as she crumpled in on herself. Denise gripped her own elbows, a form of self-comfort Willa knew well.

"Have a seat," her mother said softly.

She gestured toward a gray-and-cream-checked couch that held two twitchy-tailed tuxedo cats. One cracked an eyelid and peered at Willa as she sat stiffly on the edge of a cushion. A low, soft rumble-purr came from the other end of the sofa, and a wave of homesickness stole her breath away. Homesickness for a home she'd never actually known. How stupid was that?

"So." Denise sat stiffly on the edge of a faded navy chair, her knees almost close enough to touch Willa's. "You found me."

"I assume you didn't want to be found." Willa's voice came out tense and waspish, and she forced herself to take a breath. "Since you faked your own death and everything."

"I didn't— It wasn't like that."

"No? Then what the hell was it like?"

Denise looked down at her lap. "I wanted what was best for you."

Willa laughed, a bitter, dry, brittle sound. Of all the ridiculous things to say. "What I wanted was a mother," she said. "A mother who wouldn't abandon me, then let me spend my whole childhood thinking she was *dead*."

Denise closed her eyes, looking older than she had two minutes ago. "You're right," she said. "I deserve that."

"Why?" Willa demanded again, desperate now for an answer. A real one this time. "You owe me that much, Denise."

Her mother flinched but then nodded. Her mouth moved like she was weighing the heaviest words imaginable. When she finally spoke, her voice creaked like it hadn't been used in years.

"I loved your father," she says. "You need to understand that."

Willa said nothing. What could she say to that?

"And I loved you, too," she said. "More than anything. But I wasn't supposed to get pregnant. It wasn't meant to happen."

Willa clenched her hands together in her skirt to keep them from shaking. "What's that supposed to mean?"

Her mother took a ragged breath. "I'm bipolar," she said. "I also suffer from schizophrenia and chronic depression. The holy trinity of mental illness."

Willa stared. The words themselves weren't a shock, but she still didn't understand.

"The three conditions together can be a nightmare," her mother supplied. "But they get ten times harder with pregnancy."

Willa stared at her. "I don't remember any of this. You seemed like you had it together."

"You were five years old," Denise replied, shaking her head. "And I was broken. So broken that no one could have possibly put all the pieces into any semblance of normal. I wasn't holding it together at all, trust me."

Willa pressed the heels of her hands into her knees, trying to understand. "So you had me anyway, even though you weren't supposed to."

Her mother nodded. "Post-partum depression—

that's a real thing a lot of women face. But for me, it was hell. Years, not months. I couldn't function. Sometimes all I could do was lie on the couch sobbing while you cried in the other room. Once, I almost burned down the house. You were two and I just left the stove on and walked away. We could have died, both of us."

Willa held her breath. None of this was familiar to her, but the haunted glaze in her mother's eyes told her there was truth in those words. No one could fake that look.

"We were always broke," she said. "Your father, he did his best—tried to cobble together enough money for medications, for the kind of treatment I needed. But it wasn't enough. It was never enough."

Denise blinked hard, fighting tears with a fierceness Willa knew well. "I finally reached a breaking point," she said. "I pawned my wedding ring. It wasn't much, just a tiny little diamond."

"I remember that ring," Willa whispered. "You used to let me play with it."

Denise nodded. "I didn't get much for it, but it was enough to get me a plane ticket to Florida. To my parents' house."

"Grandma and Grandpa." The words were bitter and thick on her tongue. She hadn't thought of them in ages, hadn't seen them since that day in her living room when they'd come to tell her that her mother was dead.

"They had money," she said. "My father was a psychiatrist. You probably didn't know that."

Willa shook her head, trying to understand how that changed things. "They got you help."

"They paid for the rehab center," she said. "Inpatient treatment, almost a year in a lockdown facility. I was…I was not well."

A tear slid down her mother's cheek, and Willa fought the urge to comfort her. Anger bubbled under the surface of her skin, but sympathy swirled thick in the bitter mixture. "I could have visited you there. Or you could have called. Or—"

"The doctors said no." Her cheeks reddened, and she looked down at her lap. "My father…he said if I wanted to get better, I needed to do it without outside distractions."

"I was a distraction."

Her voice came out flat and hitched up on the last syllable.

*A distraction.*

She pushed aside the memory of saying that to Grady. That was different.

Her mother shook her head and met Willa's eyes again. "I didn't mean it like that. It just… I called your father once from the facility. He said—he told me you were doing great. Both of you, he said everything was fine."

Had it been? Maybe then, maybe at first. Maybe before the drinking started in earnest. "So then what happened?"

"I got better." Her gaze dropped to her lap, color flooding her cheeks again. "And then I had a setback. Heroin. It's common for people with mental health challenges to self-medicate; did you know that?"

"I did know that." Willa pressed her lips together, tamping down the anger. "I knew it because you left me with a goddamn alcoholic. We were homeless; did *you* know *that*?"

Denise's eyes filled with tears and shame. "I didn't," she said. "I mean, he always drank. Not like that. Money was his vice, not alcohol. The gambling debts, they were just getting worse. I knew I was more of a burden to him than a help. I couldn't work; I couldn't contribute. Hell, I couldn't even parent my own kid."

"So you just left," Willa said. "Without a call or a note or anything."

Denise flinched again. "I didn't know until afterward. That my father told you I'd died? I didn't find out for more than a year. I'd relapsed again and was living on the streets. By the time he told me, the damage was done."

So much damage. Willa could scarcely breathe. "Grandpa just—just—*lied*?"

"He thought it was best for all of us," she said. "He really did, you have to believe that."

Willa wasn't sure what to believe anymore. "You still could have called. Or written or something."

Denise shook her head, green eyes shimmering. "He convinced me it was best for you. That you didn't even cry when he told you."

The words felt like a punch to the gut. "I cried every night for *years*. Do you have any idea what that felt like?"

Denise's eyes filled, but she blinked back tears. "I was afraid if I stayed in your life, I'd do something awful. Burn down the house or overdose so you'd find me on the floor with a needle in my arm. I was so broken, Willa."

Willa clenched her hands into fists, heart twisting with equal parts sympathy and anger. "So was I."

She was still broken, wasn't she? The only time she'd started to feel whole was with Grady.

She pushed the thought aside, needing to focus this moment. "I needed you."

Denise bowed her head. "I thought you were better off without me."

"I wasn't."

Her mother looked down in her lap. "I'm sorry. I know it's too late, but I'm sorry."

*Too late.*

The words kept hitting her over and over. How many times had she thought them, said them out loud?

But she was here right now, wasn't she? And she had answers, a few of them anyway. The gaps were still there, hollowed-out craters of loss and regret and sadness.

Slowly, she reached a hand out and touched her mother's. Denise looked up, eyes searching Willa's, a flicker of hope in the green depths.

"Can you—?" Her mother's voice broke there, shaky and fragile. "Is there any way you can ever forgive me?"

Willa looked at her. Looked hard at the weathered face, the limp hair, the tired eyes. What good did it do to keep mourning the mother she'd been or hating the one she'd become?

"I forgive you," Willa said softly.

*Lip service*, she thought at first. But when she said the words out loud, she realized she meant them. "I forgive you," she said again, louder this time.

She still hated her mother. Hated what she'd done.

But more than anything, she felt sorry for her. Sad for everything she'd lost. Everything they'd *all* lost.

"Thank you." Denise lowered her face as another tear slipped down her cheek. Willa slid a hand into her purse and pulled out a travel pack of Kleenex. She handed it over, conscious of the fact that she was offering her mother more than a tissue.

"I thought I didn't deserve you," Denise said as she dabbed her eyes. "I'd made so many terrible choices that I thought I was finally making the right one by staying out of your life. Giving you a chance to be normal."

Willa choked out a laugh. "That didn't go according to plan."

Her mother studied her. "You seem pretty normal to me." She bit her lip. "No…mental health issues?"

Willa shook her head. "I mean, not that I know of. Some anxiety stuff, sure, but…" She trailed off there, wondering if there was more to it. If her parents weren't the only ones who could benefit from professional help.

Relief washed over her mother's face. "I worried. These things can run in families. That's another reason I never meant to get pregnant. I didn't even know I was pregnant until I was so far along."

"I know." Willa looked down at her hands. "Dad didn't talk about much, but he did tell me that."

Silence stretched out between them, but it no longer prickled with animosity. Just sadness and a soft swirl of relief. When Willa looked up, her mother was studying her.

"I don't regret it," Denise said softly. "Having you, I mean. I regret so many other things, but not that."

There was no room anymore for regrets. No point in accusations. Just a need to move forward, and that's what she would force herself to do.

"For years, I didn't check on you," her mother said, reading her thoughts. "My parents hired a PI a couple of times and told me you were doing well in school. That you seemed happy. It wasn't until a few years ago that I looked you up online. You're a business owner."

"Yes," Willa said, bracing herself for the familiar rush of worry about clients and deadlines and money.

It didn't come. There was no panic. Just a strange sense of…hope? "I'm okay." The words surprised her, and so did the truth in them. "I haven't always been, but I'm okay now."

"I'm glad." Her mother seemed to hesitate. "You're not married or…?"

"No." Willa pressed her lips together. "I'm not."

"Do you want those things?" Denise flushed. "I'm sorry; it's not my place to ask."

"It's okay. I—I guess I didn't think it was an option."

"Why not?" Her mother looked genuinely perplexed.

"Too busy," she said. "Building security, chasing deals, trying to keep things from falling apart."

Her mother nodded, understanding flickering in her eyes. "You get so focused on beating yourself up, driving yourself hard to succeed, trying to be stronger, to be better—you forget about why you're doing it in the first place. The things that make it worthwhile to get up in the morning and go about your day."

Willa opened her mouth to speak. Then she closed it. Was that what she'd been doing? She shook her head, not ready to wrap her head around that possibility. For fuck's sake, was she really looking to her child-abandoning mother as a source of wisdom?

But as a pang of hope hit her square in the chest, she realized she was.

Her mother must have seen the struggle in her expression, because she leaned forward in her chair. "Can I give you some advice?"

It must have sounded ridiculous, because Denise stammered a clarification. "I—I know I'm the last person in the world—"

"No, it's okay." Willa gave a soft, humorless laugh. "I'm in dire need of it right now."

Denise nodded, straightening a little. "Be gentle with yourself," she said. "And allow yourself to be happy. Don't fight it; don't decide that you don't deserve it. You do. You deserve the world, baby girl."

*Baby girl.*

She'd forgotten both her parents called her that. She'd forgotten what it felt like to have someone care so deeply about her. To have someone watching over her and wanting the best for her.

*You forgot until Grady reminded you.*

Emotion flooded her system, rushing through her until she couldn't catch her breath.

*Grady.*

Maybe she hadn't wrecked things beyond repair. If she could forgive her mother, if they could find their way to a second chance, maybe Willa could have the same with Grady.

It was Willa's turn to choke back the tears, to feel the flood of emotion clogging her throat. "I'm going to go now," Willa whispered, not sure what else to say. "I got what I came for, and I think...I think that's enough for now."

She stood up, and Denise stood, too, watching Willa's face with concern. "You're not just going to fly back, are you?"

Willa nodded. "Tonight, yes. I'm not staying." She bit her lip, hesitating. "But maybe I could come back sometime. Or you—you could visit me."

"I'd like that," Denise said. "I'd love it, actually."

"Good." She offered her mother a shaky smile. "That's a start."

It was. And for now, it was the best Willa could hope for.

# CHAPTER TWENTY-ONE

"Grady." His mother blinked at him from the front door, then broke into a smile. "What a surprise."

That made him feel like an asshole. He'd had plenty of that lately, so it was just another log on the pile.

"Hi, Mom," he said. "Sorry, I should come by more often when it's not family barbecue day, but—"

"No, it's fine!" His mom laughed and pulled him in for a hug. "We're always happy to see you, sweetheart. Come on in."

He let himself soak up the comfort of his mother's embrace, feeling like a kid again. And then feeling shitty again, because Willa had never had this. The comforts of home, two parents who were there for her always.

He'd taken so much for granted.

"I love you, Mom."

He said it from the depths of her hug, and she drew back to look him in the eye. He expected to see surprise, but all he saw was sympathy. "I love you, too, baby. Are you wanting to see your dad?"

He nodded, taken aback. "How did you—? I mean, why—?"

"Willa called." Sympathy deepened her stormy eyes to dark gray. "I'm sorry it didn't work out between the two of you."

"Right." Shit, he'd meant to tell them himself. He'd been planning to get around to it, but of course, he'd put it off. He hadn't even responded when they'd asked if she'd be joining him for family barbecue, which, of course, he'd skipped.

Because he was an asshole.

"How did you know I'd want to see Dad?" he asked.

"Because your father's been where you are right now," she said softly. "And he might have some thoughts to share."

Grady was too stunned to respond, so he let his mother take his hand and tow him down the hall to his father's study. He looked up as Grady entered, face breaking into a smile.

"Grady! I thought I heard voices out there." He got stiffly to his feet, and Grady resisted the urge to lend a hand. The same pride that led his father to choose his career, to stick with it for so long, would keep him from accepting help now.

"Hey, Dad." He clapped his father's back in a familiar hug, breathing in the familiar scent of woodsmoke he knew was all in his mind. His father hadn't been out on a fire for years, but sensory memory took over, and Grady hugged his father much tighter than usual.

"Your mom told me about Willa." His father drew back and cleared his throat. "Sorry to hear that. I really thought… Well, it doesn't matter now."

"What did you think?"

His father hesitated. "Have a seat."

They both sat, easing themselves into matching leather armchairs beside the desk. His dad aimed a remote at the television, killing the football game he'd been watching. Then he turned back to Grady.

"Your mother and I—we thought Willa might be the one."

Grady took a deep breath, desperate to cool the ache in his chest. "She was." The past tense hit him like a boot to the face. *"Is."*

His father registered the correction and nodded. "You're not giving up?"

Grady looked down at his hands. "She wants me to. Says it's over, but I just—I can't—" His voice shook, and he couldn't bring himself to look up. When he finally did, the steadiness in his father's gaze gave him strength. "I fucked up, Dad."

His father nodded, completely unsurprised. "Want to tell me, or you want me to guess?"

That surprised him, too. It also gave Grady a chance to avoid the ache of telling the whole dumb story. "I guess I'd like to hear what you think."

His dad folded his hands on his lap. "The job," he said simply. "To do it, you've gotta come to terms with the fact that every fire, every jump might be your last. And it's hard as hell to plan a future—for yourself or with someone—when you know deep in your gut there might not be one."

Grady breathed in and out. These words, these ideas. They'd been tumbling through his darkest thoughts for weeks. Hell, probably for years. But he'd never given voice to them before, not ever.

And now his father had.

"I thought I was doing the right thing," Grady said softly. "Urging Willa to live in the moment, be spontaneous. But I'm realizing I need to be more like her. To plan for a future instead of being terrified there might not be one."

His father offered a small smile. "That can be scary as hell," he said. "The job's not easy, and it's tough to accept that you can't do it forever."

"Yeah." Grady nodded, throat pinching tight. "I guess I've never wanted to think ahead. To accept that I need a backup plan for when I can't do this anymore."

Running his fingers through thinning hair, his father studied him long and hard. "I should have hung up my chute years before I did. And I should have been less afraid of admitting I was, well, *afraid*." He laughed, though it didn't quite meet his eyes. "How's that for irony?"

Grady tapped his father's foot with his own, not wanting to interrupt the conversation with a full-on hug. "You're the bravest guy I know, Dad."

He shook his head. "Bravery's overrated. I should have been focusing on compromise. On finding a way to put marriage and family at the center of my life instead of the periphery."

His father hesitated, glancing at the door. "Your mom and I, we had some rough patches. Did you know I moved out once?"

"What?" Grady sat back in his chair. "When? How did I miss that?"

"Easy. I was gone all the time anyway." His father gave a dark chuckle. "You were little, so I'm not surprised you don't remember. My point is, even the strongest relationships go through tough stuff. The test is in how you handle it. In whether you can bend and she can bend and somewhere in the middle of all that, you form this perfect bridge."

Grady kept breathing, still processing his father's

words. He clenched his fingers, a plan forming in his mind already. He laughed, conscious of the fact that maybe this was the key. Making a plan, finding a way to meet Willa halfway.

"I'm going to do it."

His dad cocked his head to the side. "Do what?"

"Win her back." Grady released his clenched fingers, feeling relief for the first time in days. He managed a small smile, and his father smiled back.

"Atta boy," he said, clapping Grady on the shoulder. "A man of action."

Grady laughed. "Even better. A man with a plan."

• • •

Grady scraped his fork through the last greasy pile of caramelized Spam and scallion pasta and loaded it into his mouth. He frowned down at the glossy page balanced on his knee and uncapped a blue marker.

"What the hell are you working on?" Tony stood up and started gathering plates from the rest of the crew.

On the other side of camp, Jimmy laughed. "That's Grady's arts and crafts project."

Grady kept his head down, tracing another box in bright blue. "I'm making plans."

Tony laughed and stacked the plates together. "Now there's a switch."

Something in Grady's expression must have told him not to push, because he turned back to Jimmy and started talking about Spam campfire muffins for breakfast. Grady missed most of what they were saying as he finished with the blue marker and picked up a red one. He'd been working on this for days, stealing a few moments here and there after the rest of his crew had turned in.

But tonight was their last night on this fire. They'd pack up camp in the morning, and Grady would have his chance. His one chance to make things right with Willa.

He couldn't blow this.

"—ever since Kayla and I broke up, we've been—"

"Wait, what?" Grady jerked his attention back to the conversation between Tony and Jimmy. "You and Kayla broke up?"

Tony leveled him with a look. "You've missed some things while you've had your head up your butt these last couple of weeks."

Grady grimaced, feeling like an asshole. "Sorry."

"Nah, it's no big deal." Tony smiled, not looking too broken up about things as he scrubbed the plates under a thin trickle of water from a canteen. "The whole thing was friendly enough. That's the problem, honestly."

"Huh?"

"We're better friends than lovers," Tony said slowly, as though explaining something to a dense first grader. "Not like you and Willa."

*Willa.*

Just hearing her name made Grady's heart ache again. He looked back at the pages in his lap, then picked up the yellow pen. He could fix this; he knew he could.

Making a few more marks, he thought about something he'd been wanting to ask the guys. Something personal, something he felt like an idiot asking.

"You guys have a rainy-day fund?" he asked at last.

Tony cocked his head. "You mean like a savings account?" He shrugged. "Yeah, sure. Not as big as I'd like it to be—"

"That's what she said." Jimmy snorted and slapped his knee, but Grady and Tony ignored him.

"But like if work dried up," Grady continued. "Or if you got hurt off the job or something and couldn't work for a few months."

"I've got about three months' salary socked away," Tony said. "I know it's supposed to be more, but I've got college loans and a mom who needs help sometimes."

"Right." And Grady had no one and a savings that would carry him about six days if he suddenly lost his job. "I met with a financial planner last week."

Tony's brows lifted. "No kidding? Did you see the guy I recommended?"

"Yeah." Grady cleared his throat, not sure why he felt embarrassed about taking control of his future. "He sure knows his stuff."

"Told you. How'd it go?"

"Better than I thought it would," Grady admitted. "I'd been putting it off for years, thinking all they'd say is that I'll never be able to retire."

Even Jimmy was paying attention now. "What *did* he say?"

"We came up with a plan," Grady said. "Not just for saving but for what I'll do when I can't jump anymore."

Frowning, Jimmy stabbed a fork into his pasta.

"You're never too old to jump."

Spoken like a rookie. Or like Grady before he pulled his head out of his butt.

"I've got plenty of good years, but I won't be one of those guys who stays in too long," Grady said. "I'm looking into pilot training."

"Shit, you'd be great at that." Tony grinned. "I'd fly with you any day."

"Thanks. That means a lot to me."

It did, too.

Just not as much as it would mean to earn Willa's trust. To convince her he could offer the sort of stability she deserved. The thing she wanted with a desperation he was only beginning to understand.

He flipped the calendar page again and made another mark, this time with his green pen.

An hour later, he closed the pages and tucked the last of the markers into his pack. Then he crawled into his sleeping bag and folded his hands behind his head. Staring up at the stars, he thought of Willa. Right now, she'd be home in her king-size bed with Barrow and Earmuff curled beside her and an ocean of glow-in-the-dark stars overhead.

*Win her back.*

That was his last thought before drifting off to sleep with all his hopes tucked in his pack beside his head.

• • •

The next morning, he was up before the others. He made breakfast and practically inhaled it before scrubbing up and jamming everything into his pack.

"Where's the pickup point again?" Jimmy asked as they set out trudging north.

"Little town called McKenzie Bridge," he said. "About five miles east."

Tony whistled. "Better get going."

The sun was still fighting to make its way up over the horizon as they hoofed it through the trees at a brisk pace. The ground was mostly level, and the forest wasn't all that dense. Smoke drifted in the air above them like an ethereal haze, but other than that, the morning was clear.

Grady put one boot in front of the other, focusing on the beat of his heart so he wouldn't think about Willa. About whether his plan might really work.

"A soak at Belknap Hot Springs." It was Jimmy who started the game this time. "That's only a few miles from McKenzie Bridge, right?"

"Hope you're planning to shower first," Tony said.

"Maybe."

"Sitting on the sofa watching TV and eating pizza," Grady offered. His chest tightened, but he pushed through the ache. Would they ever do that again? Curl up together on the couch and watch *Whose Line Is It Anyway?* with a box of cooling pizza on the coffee table in front of them?

Tony grunted. "The Cajun tots at Ramble Inn," he said. "Kayla's meeting me there when we get back."

"I thought you broke up," Grady said.

"Yeah, but we're still friends," he said. "Better friends than lovers, remember?"

Grady remembered. He also hadn't forgotten the rest of what Tony had said.

*Not like you and Willa.*

They'd had something so unique, even Tony had noticed. The thought made his chest ache, but it also gave him hope. He'd get back to town, drive straight to his house to shower, then over to Willa's where he'd—

"Hey, there's the truck," Tony called. "Guess we won't be waiting around this time."

Grady looked up, surprised to see they'd already arrived at the pickup point. A dusty green truck sat in a pool of sunshine. A pool that got brighter as the truck door opened and Willa stepped out wearing a blue dress and sunglasses. She slipped them off as she stepped toward him, her face brimming with hope.

Grady froze. He stopped walking, stopped moving, stopped breathing, and stood frozen between two pine trees. "Willa."

"Hi." The smile she offered was timid, not at all her normal smile. "Welcome home."

*Home.* He stood two hundred miles from his house, but here was Willa, and home was exactly what he felt in that moment.

He opened his mouth to ask questions—how, why, what on earth was she doing here?—but she spoke first.

"I've been second-guessing myself about doing this in front of your colleagues." She glanced at Tony and Jimmy as she stepped forward. It really was her—she wasn't a mirage. "I don't want to embarrass you. Or them."

"We're good." Jimmy grinned and set his pack on the ground. "We don't embarrass easily."

Tony rolled his eyes and grabbed Jimmy by the shirtsleeve. "We'll wait in the truck."

He dragged Jimmy to the truck and yanked him inside, shaking his head as he clambered up beside him. The door slammed shut, and then it was just the two of them. Grady and Willa.

Holy shit. He still couldn't believe it was her. "What are you doing here?"

"I came to apologize." Willa looked down at the ground, scuffing her sandal through the dirt. "I was wrong." She looked up, meeting his eyes this time. "About a lot of things, but mostly about you being a distraction. You weren't a distraction, Grady. You were the best damn thing that ever happened to me, and I was too wrapped up in my own anxieties to see that."

He stared at her, hardly daring to trust his own eyes. She was really here, really saying the words he'd never dreamed he'd hear from her.

"I did distract you," he said. "I'm sorry about the TechTel deal."

"It's not your fault," she said. "It was easier to blame you than blame myself and accept the fact that I'm human. That I can't keep running my life like I'm a machine. I have a heart and a soul and a body that aches to have you close to me, and none of the rest of it matters if you're not in part of my world."

He pulled air into his lungs, barely trusting his own eyes. She'd come all this way for him? "I can't believe you're here."

She laughed, though it sounded a little shaky. "I've been doing a lot of work. With a therapist, I mean—on myself. And I'm learning to give myself credit for creating the kind of stability I always wanted."

Grady took a step forward, not yet daring to touch her. "I understand now why that matters so much to you. Why it matters to *me* now, since we're in this together."

Her eyes widened, glittering with tears. "We are?"

Slipping his pack off, he dropped it to the ground and rummaged inside. "I was coming to your house tonight to apologize. To tell you I'd been selfish and to give you something."

She blinked. "What?"

He kept digging through the pack, tossing out sweaty socks and empty water bottles. "I made something for you."

A trickle of laughter filled the air as he tossed out a filthy T-shirt and another pair of socks. "Did you weave me a pine-needle basket or something?" she asked.

"No. Something better." At least he hoped it was. He straightened and held it out, hands shaking only a little.

Willa stared, then slowly reached out to take it. "A calendar?" She tilted her head to one side. "You made me a calendar?"

"Look inside." He couldn't keep the stupid burst of hope from filling his voice, his heart, as she flipped open the cover.

He watched her face as she turned the page to the current month, then beyond. Through summer and fall and winter and—

"What do all these marks mean?" She looked up

at him, curiosity sparking in her eyes.

"The green circles are long-term plans, weekends we'll spend together, that sort of thing." He swallowed hard, pulse beating in his throat. "The blue boxes are for spontaneous magic—times I get to surprise you with things."

She tilted her head, lips quirking in surprise. "You've scheduled spontaneity?"

Yeah, it sounded weird to him, too. But he could adapt, could learn to plan like this. "The dates marked in red are yours," he continued. "Well, it's alone time for both of us. But those are your times to tell me to fuck off, that you're busy making your dreams come true and you need space and time to do that."

Tears filled her eyes. She stared at him—just stared—as her hands began to tremble. "Oh, Grady…" Her voice caught, and she looked down at the calendar again. When she looked up, a tear slipped down her cheek. "You'd do this for me?"

He nodded as relief flooded his chest cavity. "Yeah," he said. "I never liked making plans because I never met anyone I wanted to make plans with." He swallowed hard, emotion clogging his throat. "But I want that with you. Long-term, short-term—I want all of it with you, Wills."

Another tear slipped down her cheek. She laughed and swiped it away. "You don't know how much this means to me."

Yeah, he did.

Just like he knew how much it meant to him that she'd taken time off work to come here, to meet him at the pickup point this way. His father's words echoed in his head as he took a step closer to her.

*The test is in how you handle it. In whether you can bend and she can bend and somewhere in the middle of all that, you form this perfect bridge.*

And now here they were, forming that bridge. "I love you, Willa."

Holy shit. He'd actually said it.

She laughed, looking caught off guard again. "I love you, too." She threw an arm around him, still gripping the calendar in one hand. "So damn much. And I missed you like you wouldn't believe."

"I believe it." He pulled her into his arms, so damn grateful to feel her against him again. "I've missed you, too."

He kissed her then, gently at first, then deepening it as she pressed against him, so warm and soft and sweet.

Dizziness swept over him as he drew back and looked down at her. "Sorry," he offered. "I smell like a campfire someone doused in sweat."

She shook her head and nuzzled closer. "You smell great to me."

Her gaze dropped to the calendar again and peered closer. He felt her stiffen as she noticed. "Wait." She drew back again, tracing a finger over the lines he'd drawn. "What are these two weeks marked in yellow in January?"

He grinned, pulse drumming in his ears. Leave it to Willa to notice. "Hypothetically speaking," he said, "I've always thought it would be amazing to plan a romantic getaway to Australia. That's the tail end of their fire season, so—"

"Seriously?" Her mouth dropped open. "I've

always wanted to go to Australia." She looked down at the calendar like she was still trying to make sense of it all.

"And the pink dot," he continued, pointing to a spot in the middle of that two week period. "Also hypothetically, that would be a really good time to propose to someone special on this hypothetical vacation."

He let the words hang there between them, knowing he'd gone way out on a limb. Knowing Willa didn't love surprises, so maybe this was one way to ease them both into this idea.

For him, it was a no-brainer. He was 100 percent sure he wanted to spend the rest of his life with Willa. No question at all in his mind.

But probably she needed a little more time to get there. To think through every possibility, process every red flag, plan everything down to the last detail.

He loved that about her. Loved everything, really, but especially that. The thing that made them so different was the thing he'd grown to love most about this woman standing in front of him with tears in her eyes and a marked-up calendar in her arms.

She wasn't speaking, and his heart lodged in his throat. "Willa?" He touched her arm. "We don't have to keep that on the calendar if you don't want," he said. "We could—"

"My hypothetical answer in this hypothetical situation would be yes." A tear slipped down her cheek. "But I'm okay with leaving it all up in the air." A blush crept into her cheeks. "That's one thing I'm totally okay with having as a spontaneous moment."

Grady grinned and pulled her into his arms again, crushing the calendar between them. "I love you so much," he breathed into her hair. "So damn much."

"I love you, too."

And somewhere in the middle, in that infinitesimal space between their bodies, everything was just right.

# EPILOGUE

*Six months later*

"G'day, Hot Stuff!" Grady grinned as he came through the door of their hotel suite in his jump suit. The fact that it was unzipped to the waist and he wore nothing underneath was not lost on Willa.

"You look like a stripper." Beaming, she stood to greet him, twining her arms around his bare torso. Damn, he felt good. "A hot Australian stripper."

"Is that a good thing or a bad thing?"

"A very good thing." She circled her palms over the muscles in his bare back. "How was work?"

"Great. Well, great as far as wildfires go. We got that blaze contained south of Brisbane. They've got more crews from New Zealand flying in to help, plus our teams from the States."

"And the pilot training?" She kissed the scruff on his jaw, then planted another kiss at the edge of his mouth. "Still liking it so far?"

"Loving it." He slid his hands around her waist, dipping one a little lower to squeeze her butt. "Almost as much as I love you."

She wriggled against him. "Sounds serious."

"Mm, very. Have I mentioned how much I adore being in Australia with the most beautiful woman in the world?"

Willa laughed. "Let me know when she's coming over and I'll get out of your hair."

Grady pulled her against him and kissed her long

and slow and deep. Damn, that felt good. Would she ever get tired of this?

She was pretty sure not. These last six months had been the best of her life, with each of them learning to flex just a little to make room for the other. She'd gotten better about switching off her phone, making a hard-and-fast rule about leaving it behind on their date nights.

*Scheduled* date nights. That was Grady's doing, his way of stepping up to the plate to plan some of the most romantic dates she'd ever experienced. A moonlight snowshoe adventure, complete with cocoa and a meteor shower. A silly game of naked Twister that left them both tied in knots and laughing until tears ran down their cheeks.

And Willa had learned the fine art of spontaneity. Sometimes it was as simple as swinging by the Hart Valley Air Center with a surprise picnic lunch. Another time, she agreed to his nutty plan to prowl thrift stores together, each choosing an audacious five-dollar outfit for the other to wear on a dinner date at the local truck stop.

And at no time did the world come crashing down around her because she took time away from work. She'd learned to plan for it, to schedule time off and communicate with clients. The downtime left her feeling sharper and more efficient than she had in her career.

"What are you thinking?" Grady drew back and reached up to sweep her hair off her face.

Willa smiled at him. "About how happy I am," she said. "And how grateful I am that your sister had all those airline miles to get me here."

Grady kissed her again. "The upside of having so many sisters and brothers is that there's always someone in a useful profession who can help you out in a pinch."

"I dropped a thank-you note in the mail to her yesterday," Willa said. "And a baby gift. I can't believe you have another set of twin nieces."

"The Billman family is good breeding stock, I'll give 'em that."

Willa smiled. "It's been nice feeling like part of the family," she said. "Being welcomed with open arms."

"They love you," he said. "Not as much as I love you, but a lot."

"I love them, too." She grinned and kissed him again. "And you, you're okay."

He grabbed her butt and squeezed. "Only okay?"

"Eh." She shrugged, mischief lighting her eyes. "You'll do."

He squeezed her butt harder, and she jumped back laughing. Grady chased after her, finally catching her over by the bed. He was just about to topple her onto it when her phone rang.

They both looked at it. "You need to get that?" Grady asked.

"Nope," she said. "I'm shutting down for the day. Work's done; it's time to play."

She'd had the good fortune to land several new Aussie clients, as well as a couple in New Zealand. She'd had meetings all morning, and it turned out the land down under was ripe for the sort of web development she offered.

And now it was time to enjoy this glorious—

albeit, *budget-friendly*—hotel suite they'd booked. It was Grady's first scheduled day off, and tomorrow they'd go snorkeling on the Great Barrier Reef.

Willa sat down on the bed and shot him an inviting grin. "Don't you love this mattress?"

"Very soft." He dropped onto the bed beside her, making them both bounce. "I have grand plans for this bed."

"I love when you talk dirty," she growled, brushing a kiss against his lips. "Planning is *soooo* sexy."

"I know your hot buttons."

He dotted a trail of kisses along her jaw as Willa nuzzled his ear. "You smell smoky," she said, burrowing her face into the crook of his neck. "I didn't think you were out on a fire today."

"I wasn't. Just helping to organize equipment. I can shower if you want, though."

"I don't mind." She kissed the soft warmth at the base of his throat, then drew back smiling. "Unless you *want* to shower. I could help you get some of those hard-to-reach spots."

"Tempting. Very tempting."

He kissed her one more time, then leaned back on his elbows to look out the window. White sailboats bobbed in the harbor, and Willa rubbed a hand over his chest as a pair of cockatiels flew past.

"I got to Skype with Stevie today," she said. "Kayla tried to get the cats to make an appearance, but they weren't interested."

"Did you tell Stevie he's a good boy and we'll be home soon?"

"Absolutely," she said. "Carl says hi, by the way."

Grady laughed. "I'm glad your fish and I have

bonded," he said. "Any word from your dad?"

"Aislin went to visit him yesterday," she said. "Took him some lunch and met with his new sponsor. He's doing great. Taking it one day at a time, just like he's supposed to."

She'd been nervous about leaving him so soon after his release from rehab. It was a precarious time to abandon him, and she'd nearly guilted herself into staying. But her friends had stepped up— Aislin, Kayla, even Grady's coworkers and siblings. Everyone rallied to make sure her dad was rarely alone, that he had a constant support system around him.

"I'm glad he's doing well. I know you didn't want to leave him."

"I knew my friends had my back," she said. "And I knew he needed to do this on his own. It's okay; I'll see him when I get home."

Grady smiled. "Speaking of home, there's something I wanted to ask you."

"Oh?"

She held her breath, wondering if this was the moment. The one he'd penned on the calendar all those months ago. She'd assured him spontaneity was great—even preferable—when it came to an engagement.

But she couldn't help noticing this day was smack-dab in the middle of their Australia trip.

Grady took both her hands in his and smiled into her eyes. "It's probably not a surprise that I want to marry you."

Willa's heart began thudding in her ears. She nodded, surprised to feel butterflies swirling in her stomach. "You've mentioned it once or twice."

Or a dozen times, which was fine by her. She was ready for it. This proposal—if that's what it was—but also the rest of their lives together.

"So I know I kinda killed the spontaneity there," he continued. "But I do still have one surprise up my sleeve."

He leaned over and slid open the drawer on the nightstand. When he drew his hand back, Willa gasped. A red ring box was nestled in the center of his palm, leaving no doubt what was about to happen.

As her eyes met his, her throat pinched with emotion. "When did you do that?"

"Don't worry—I didn't spend a gazillion dollars."

She loved that he knew that would matter to her. That she wasn't the sort of woman to want a big, flashy, expensive ring. That she'd care more about the budget, about making sure he could afford this.

Yet somehow, he'd still managed to surprise her.

"William Marie Frank," he said, smiling a little at the rare use of her real name. "Willa," he continued. "In less than a year, you've become the most important person in my life. You're my favorite board-game companion and showering partner. You tolerate my mini-golf play, and you make me laugh at least a hundred times a day. More than anything, though, you make me a better version of myself."

Tears clogged her voice, and she dashed one away from her cheek with the back of her hand. "I feel the same. When I'm with you, I'm the best person I've ever been."

He grinned. "And you were already pretty bangin'."

She laughed and swiped at the tears again. "I didn't expect to get all weird and emotional." Another surprise. A good one, the best kind.

Grady grinned and slid off the bed, dropping down onto one knee in front of her. "I can't imagine life without you. Will you marry me?"

"Yes." She choked out the word, nodding hard enough to send a fresh trickle of tears down her face. "Yes," she said again as she let her gaze drop to the ring for the first time. A simple, perfect circle with a small diamond and a plain gold band. "It's beautiful, Grady. Where did you…"

She touched the ring, memory flickering in the back of her mind. There was something about it…

"Oh my God." Her breath caught in her chest as she realized how she knew this ring. Why it was so familiar, so tinged with nostalgia. She met his eyes, looking for confirmation. "It's my mother's."

Grady nodded. "Yeah. Yeah, it is."

"But I thought—" She tried to recall the details of that conversation with her mother. "She told me she'd pawned it. That she sold it for a ticket to go back to Florida for treatment."

"She did," Grady confirmed as he slipped the ring from the box and held it out to her. "I asked her about it when she visited. When you were out running with Kayla? She told me the rest of the story."

"There's a story?"

He nodded. "Her parents," he said. "They convinced her she couldn't go back. Not to you or your dad, but they agreed she should have some sort of token. Her father called the pawn shop and bought it back from them. She's had it all this time."

"I can't believe it." Another tear slipped down her face. "I thought I'd never see it again."

He slipped it onto her finger. It was a little loose, but the daintiness of it was just right.

"We can get a different one if you want," Grady offered. "If you see it as a bad omen or you want something nicer or—"

"No, it's perfect." She held up her hand, making the tiny diamond sparkle in the light. "It's simple. Exactly what I would have wanted."

"Good." He grinned, looking relieved. "That's what I hoped. It seemed like your kind of ring."

She tilted her fingers back and forth, imagining her mother doing this same thing so many years ago. "I can't believe she kept it," she whispered. "All these years, it must have meant something to her."

"She kept it for you," he said. "She knew she'd probably never see you again, but she always held on to the tiniest hope."

She threw her arms around him, getting tear marks on his shirt. "You have no idea how much this means to me."

"I kinda do."

"You do, don't you?" She drew back and looked up at him, smiling into his eyes. "Thank you for loving me the way I am. For understanding and accepting the whole package instead of trying to change me into something I'm not."

"Oh, I think we've both changed for the better," he said. "That we're not too stuck in our ways to realize when we need to compromise."

She laughed and held out her finger to admire the ring. "Thank you, Grady. I'm so glad I found you."

He leaned down to kiss her, claiming her mouth with his. It didn't take long for things to heat up, just like they always did.

The next thing she knew, he was pushing her back onto the bed, his hand moving up her skirt as she wrapped her hands around his back and breathed him in. *Husband.* He was going to be her husband.

How had she gotten so lucky?

When they pulled apart, they were both breathing hard. "So this is forever," she said. "Really for real."

"Yep," he said. "Want Stevie to be the ring bearer?"

"We should probably set a date first," she pointed out.

"True," he agreed. "Weddings require a lot of planning."

She snuggled against him. "Or we could elope," she said. "I'd be okay with that, too."

As she said the words out loud, she realized they were true. An elaborately planned affair, a spontaneous ceremony at the courthouse, or something in between—it was all okay, as long as they were together. "Thanks for being the best date I've ever had," she said. "And the only one I'll need forever and ever."

"I like the sound of that."

She kissed him again, grateful she'd reached the end of her dating game.

And the beginning of the rest of her life.

# ACKNOWLEDGMENTS

Huge, heaping helpings of gratitude go to the folks at the Redmond Air Center in Redmond, Oregon, for filling my brain with gobs of great details about the lives and careers of smokejumpers. I'm especially thankful to Bill Selby, Sam Johnson, and Tony Selznick for sharing your time and your stories. Any fudging of facts or creative play with the details of the smokejumping world are totally on me.

I'm so thankful to the members of my street team, Fenske's Frisky Posse, for your creative ideas, your name suggestions, and your shared drooling over photos from my visit to Redmond Air Center (er, sorry, Sam... Also, it's a total coincidence that the guy on the cover kinda looks like you).

Thank you to Wonder Assistant Meah Cukrov for keeping my crap together, and for being an all-around awesome person. Thanks to Linda Grimes for your feedback and moral support. You're the best agency sistah and critique partner a girl could wish for.

And speaking of agents, I'd be nowhere without the support, cheerleading, and career steering of Michelle Wolfson of Wolfson Literary. It's amazing how much the industry has changed in our 12+ years together and also amazing that I still hyperventilate when seeing your name on my caller ID. Thank you for everything you've done, and continue to do, for my career and my sanity.

I so appreciate my readers, whether this is your very first time reading a Tawna Fenske book or you've devoured all 30+ titles in my backlist. I couldn't do this without you!

Much love and thanks to Cheryl Howard and Liana Ottaviano for loaning me your beloved Monopoly games for research. I promise I didn't do anything inappropriate with them. Much.

Thank you to the entire Entangled Publishing team, especially Liz Pelletier for the tipsy brainstorm session in Denver. I'm grateful to all of you for your hard work and dedication to making my books the best they can be. Big hugs to Jessica Turner, Melanie Smith, Heather Riccio, Heather Howland, Curtis Svehlak, Stacy Abrams, Meredith Johnson, Katie Clapsadl, and anyone else on the Entangled team who I might have inadvertently forgotten here. Love you guys!

Endless thanks to my family for all the love, support, and laughter. Dixie and David, Russ and Carlie and Paxton, Cedar and Violet—you guys are the best fan-damily I could have asked for.

And thank you to Craig Zagurski for continuing to rock the role of romance author husband. You're the hottest hero I've had the pleasure of meeting in real life, and I'm so grateful you're my happily ever after.

Discover Credence, Colorado, a small town
sure to leave you in stitches.

*Available now wherever books are sold!
Read on for a sneak peek...*

# CHAPTER ONE

Joshua Grady—Grady to all who knew him—didn't want much out of life. Just this ranch, Sunday night football, and to be left the hell alone. At thirty-five, with twelve years in the military, including a tour of Iraq and two of Afghanistan, he figured he'd earned the right.

He was a goddamn war hero. He even had a shiny medal and a fancy piece of paper from the government to prove it.

Unfortunately his uncle, who owned the ranch, had other ideas.

*New tenant incoming.*

Grady scowled at the text. Then scowled at the plume of dust advancing in the distance as a vehicle made its way slowly down the rutted road leading to his cabin. Jamming his Stetson on his head, he strode out to the porch, his big hands curling around the circumference of the rough-hewn wood of the railing as he sucked in the frigid December air. His scowl deepened, and Grady shoved his hands on his hips as the car rounded the bend and appeared from the center of the dust.

He blinked twice at the beat-up old van with lurid green and pink panels emblazoned with huge yellow flowers. *Jesus.* It was the Mystery Machine. And about as out of place here in rural Colorado as a tractor on Fifth Avenue. The vehicle pulled to a halt and the engine cut, and Grady half expected Scooby and the gang to tumble out as the door opened.

They didn't.

A woman slid down from the cab. Grady had been expecting a woman—Susan something something, his uncle had informed him when he'd arrived to get the cottage ready yesterday—but it didn't mean he had to like it. Living outside Credence meant not having to be sociable with anyone, least of all a woman who filled out blue jeans in ways that made him remember how much he liked women in denim.

Grady had decided a long time ago on a solitary life and was *not*, consequently, settling-down material, despite his well-meaning uncle's assertions about the joys of holy matrimony. He'd sure as hell stayed away from Credence during the summer when a nationwide ad campaign had brought busloads of single women to the small eastern Colorado town, hoping a few might stay and make Credence their home—and some of the Credence bachelors their husbands.

A couple of dozen *had* stayed, but he wasn't interested in any of them. Or this woman, either. He'd told his uncle repeatedly the last couple of weeks that he didn't want the cottage rented to some artist, and it was hardly his fault accommodations were scarce due to the sudden spike in population.

That ridiculous ad campaign hadn't been his idea.

But the land—several thousand acres of it—including the cabin *and* the cottage belonged to his uncle, and Burl Grady had the final say. Not that Burl had ever played that card until now, but it was the first time in three years Grady had regretted knocking back his uncle's very generous offer to sign over the ranch to him forthwith rather than waiting for it to come to him in his uncle's will.

He had enough money to buy his own damn ranch but his uncle had wanted to retire, and taking over the reins had been the one way Grady could think of to repay his aunt and uncle for stepping up during the worst time of his life.

Except now he had to put up with Little Miss Blue Jeans for a month.

She didn't see him as she walked toward the white fence that partitioned off the field to the front of the cabin, but Grady couldn't look away. She was hard to ignore. Her hair was contained in a bright-green knitted hat, so he had no idea whether she was blond, brunette, or redhead, but her knee-high Ugg-type boots and her sweet rounded ass swinging in those jeans were way more fascinating anyway.

Neither short nor tall, she was amply proportioned, a fact emphasized by her leaning on the top rail of the fence, which pushed out her ass. Grady shut his eyes. He'd never gone for skinny—he liked fullness and curves and this woman needed a flashing neon sign attached to hers.

Opening his eyes, Grady diverted his gaze, concentrating instead on seeing the vista in front, a sight of which he never tired. A couple of his horses grazed in the field on the grass that was getting sparse now, given the onset of winter. He'd need to feed them later but, for a moment, he forgot his chores and the angst about his unwanted guest and sucked in the deep, clean air of eastern Colorado.

The sky was a brilliant cloudless blue, the winter

sunshine more for show than effect, given it was a brisk forty-two, but they'd forecast snow for the next week, so he'd take the sunshine—weak or not. Too soon the sky would be bleak, tree branches would be a parched frozen gray, the fields blanketed in white.

Right now, there was still a tinge of green, and the sight of it filled him with a sense of belonging so profound it swept his breath away.

Even if there was a woman in blue jeans messing up the picture.

Blue jeans and no coat—just a thin-looking long-sleeve T-shirt. For God's sake, she was going to freeze to death out here.

As if she knew he was thinking about her, she moved back from the rail a pace or two and slowly turned in a circle, her face lifted to the sky, her arms outstretched. It was the kind of pose kids adopted when it was snowing, opening their mouths to catch some flakes. She wasn't opening her mouth, but she appeared to be trying to catch some sunshine.

There was nothing particularly remarkable about her face. She wasn't stunningly pretty or ethereally beautiful or even chipmunk cute. She was kind of average-looking. Not the sort of face that launched a thousand ships. More…girl next door.

That should have made him feel better. It didn't.

It was on her second turn that she spotted him standing with his hands on his hips, staring at her like some creeper, and she gave him a little wave. Grady didn't return it.

"God…sorry," she called. An easy grin spread over her face as she broke into a half jog.

"You must be Joshua." She pulled to a stop at the

bottom of the four steps, her warm breath misting into the cool air.

Her cheeks were flushed and her nose was pink and there was absolutely nothing average about her eyes. They were lapis lazuli, and they looked at him with such frankness, like they were assessing him and not just physically but mentally, cataloging and memorizing every single detail, even the ones he didn't want anyone to see.

"Grady," he ground out, feeling exposed and pissed off that this woman who couldn't even *dress for the weather* and was driving a *cartoon car* was having such an effect on him. "People call me Grady."

If she'd picked up on his surliness, she ignored it, tramping up the stairs to stand beside him, holding out her hand to shake, which Grady took reluctantly. "I'm Suzanne St. Michelle."

She pronounced it *Su-sahn Saan Meeshell*, which sounded very posh and very French and made Grady think about French kissing and then just kissing in general. He dropped her hand.

*What the ever-loving fuck?*

"Man," she said, her accent 100 percent New York as she half turned to the view and inhaled deeply. "You're really living the dream out here, aren't you?"

Grady gave a ghost of a smile. He'd learned a long time ago that dreams were made of dynamite and horseshit. She didn't appear to need an answer, though, as she chatted on.

"It's so easy to forget in the city that there's all this space and land and sky. It's so flat, and there's nothing for miles except fields and cows and horses.

They're such beautiful creatures, aren't they?"

Her question appeared to, again, be rhetorical, and she barely drew breath before leaping into a change of subject.

*Christ.* She was a talker…

"I bet the stars are magic out here, aren't they?" She paused to look at him this time but held his gaze only for a beat or two before she glanced back at the field and kept right on going. "Yep. No light pollution out here in the middle of nowhere. I bet it's dark as pitch in the middle of the night. It's the kind of sky that would have given van Gogh wet dreams."

She faltered slightly, barely a hiccup in time, just enough for her to frown slightly, like she knew she'd just said something a little inappropriate. But, flattening her hand against her belly, she forged on.

"And it's so quiet, no horns or traffic or blinking lights or sirens or crowds, or people for that matter. No background hum of chatter all around you. It's so…serene."

Yes. *Exactly*. Serenity. Something *Su-sahn Saan Meeshell* had pierced in about two seconds. Grady strapped on some mental Kevlar.

Suddenly, she turned back to face him with those startling blue eyes, pulling her woolen hat from her head. Fine, almost white-blond hair cascaded around her shoulders like a flurry of snow.

Yep…there went his serenity.

"So…" She inspected his face before dropping her gaze to take in his plaid flannel shirt, his well-worn Levis, and his even more worn boots. "You're, like, a…cowboy? The real deal?"

Grady was silent for long moments. Was that

another rhetorical question? When she continued to look at him expectantly, he answered. "I'm a rancher."

She wrinkled her nose in concentration. "What's the difference?"

"Ranchers ranch. Cowboys wrangle cows."

"Kinda like a shepherd?"

Grady blinked. "Sure." In the way a shark was kinda like a fish.

She was looking at him expectantly, those blue eyes trained on him as if she was waiting for him to elaborate, but Grady had just about surpassed his quota of words for the day.

"Okay then," she said after several awkward seconds of silence that she—*hallelujah*—didn't feel the need to fill up. "Your uncle said you'd show me the cottage?"

Grady nodded, grateful for something to do even if it did mean extending his time in Little Miss Chatty's company. He glanced at the van and tried not to wince. "Drive your…vehicle round back."

Thankfully she didn't talk anymore—no more questions or inane observations—she just took the two paces to the stairs and headed down. Maybe she'd used up her quota of words for the day, too? The thought cheered him as he followed behind her, his gaze looking anywhere but at the swing of her ass.

• • •

*Van Gogh's wet dream? What the hell, Suzanne?*

She cringed. But she'd always been the same

when she was nervous, even as a kid. Filling silences with pointless chatter. And Cowboy Surly or *Rancher* Surly had gotten the full verbal-diarrhea treatment.

As soon as she was done unpacking, she was calling Winona to demand an explanation. Her friend, who'd come to Credence after the first single-women campaign had gone viral and decided to stay, had convinced Suzanne a change of scenery would be good for her muse and, god knew, a Christmas away from her parents' sterile, minimalist brownstone had been too good to pass up. Hell, she would have visited Winona on *Mars*. But her friend really should have warned her about Grady.

Suzanne wasn't used to speak-as-little-as-possible-while-looking-all-sexy-and-brooding men. Men in jeans with hats and big-ass belt buckles who had rough hands and looked like they knew how to chop down a tree, ride a bull, deliver a calf, light a fire, and build a rudimentary shelter.

All before breakfast.

Men with rugged faces and beautiful lips, who looked like they'd forgotten more things about the birds and the bees than she'd ever learned.

She was going to need a handbook for Grady, and hopefully Winona had a copy.

But Winona had been right about one thing. Her muse was definitely stirring. It had crept up on her as she'd stared out over the field at the grazing horses. That itch, that…compulsion to put the scene down on canvas. To memorialize it in oil. And it had positively *slammed* into her like a sledgehammer as her gaze had connected with Joshua Grady.

Everything, from the way his height and breadth had dominated the porch, to the squareness of his jaw, the worn leather of his boots, and that shiny belt buckle riding low between his hips, had been inspirational. Suzanne hadn't painted anything original in well over a decade, but those first few seconds she'd clapped eyes on Grady had been an epiphany.

Now *there* was a subject to paint.

It was as if the heavens had opened and glories had streamed down and a giant hand with an extended index finger had pointed at Grady and whispered, *"Him,"* in Suzanne's ear.

The prospect had been equal parts titillating and terrifying because landscapes were easy, portraits not so much, and she hadn't been able to decide whether to throw up or run away and hide.

The universe, however, had delivered verbal diarrhea.

Pulling her trusty old transport van up outside the cottage, Suzanne slipped out of the car as Grady was stomping his feet on the welcome mat and taking off his hat. Opening the door, he said, "Ma'am," indicating that she should precede him.

*Hot damn.* He'd *ma'am*ed her. It wasn't the first time she'd been *ma'am*ed in her almost thirty years, but it had been the first time her clothes had almost fallen off at hearing it. There was something about the way this man *ma'am*ed that made Suzanne aware she had ovaries.

She walked into the cozy, open-plan cottage dominated on the far side by two large windows just as Winona had indicated. She knew instantly where she would set up her easel. Crossing to the windows—drawn as only an artist can be to light— she stared out over acres and acres of brittle winter pasture and, in the distance, a large section of wooded land.

"Bedroom's that way," he said from behind.

She turned to find him standing in the doorway, obviously not planning to enter. He pointed with the hand that held his hat to the left where she could see a bed through an open door.

"The heating"—he swiveled his head in the opposite direction, using his hat to again point to the far wall and the modern glass-fronted freestanding fireplace—"is gas." Switching his gaze to the kitchen area situated between the two windows, he said, "Kitchen should have everything you need. You have bags?"

Suzanne blinked at his obvious desire to be gone. It made her curious, and hell if it didn't make her want to paint him right now. From her vantage point, with the light behind him, he wasn't much more than a tall, dark shape taking up all the space in her doorway, but his presence was electric, looming.

But not in a threatening way. It was...spine-tingling, and her pulse skipped a beat, which made her feel like an idiot. She'd just met the guy. How freaking *embarrassing*.

"I...have so much stuff." Suzanne crossed to where he stood, determined to be businesslike to cover for her ridiculously juvenile response. "A couple of bags, a dozen canvases of varying sizes, about a zillion different paints, a box of books because there's nothing quite like the smell of a book, don't you think? My pod coffee machine because I'm such a caffeine junkie, and heaven help anyone who talks to me before my coffee every morning. Some CDs and a player, which I know is a little old-school, but Winona said the internet can be pretty spotty out here, and I *have* to paint to music because silence drives me nuts. Some groceries I picked up in Credence and—"

Suzanne stopped abruptly, aware suddenly by the ever-flattening line of his mouth that she was babbling. He was staring at her with an expression that left her in little doubt a simple "yes" or "no" would have sufficed.

He gave a brief nod and shoved his hat on his head. "I'll give you a hand." Then he turned on his heel and strode to her van.

It took the two of them fifteen minutes to unload everything. Fifteen long, silent minutes broken only by Suzanne occasionally directing him as to where to put something down. Sliding the van door shut with a muffled *whump*, he turned, his gaze settling on her face. The brim of his hat threw his face into shadow, which made him hard to read. But this close, she could see he had light-green eyes and some stubble. Short but enough to still feel rough.

"If that's all, ma'am, I'll be going?"

If that was all? Joshua Grady really *did not* want to stick around. Suzanne knew she was an average woman. Average height, average looks, average size fourteen who could probably stand to lose a few pounds from her ass and thighs—she was more pear than hourglass. Good teeth, nice smile, clear skin. She was...attractive at best. A six who could push herself to a seven, maybe an eight for a gallery opening or one of her mother's exhibitions.

She'd had boyfriends both casual and longer term—she was no blushing virgin—and she got along well with members of the opposite sex. But she wasn't the kind of woman to whom men *flocked*. She was pretty sure this was the first time she'd actually repelled one, though.

If only that turned off her muse. Unfortunately, *she* was a fickle little tramp and always had been. *And* she'd been MIA for a good ten years while Suzanne had reproduced other artists' works in the very lucrative field of museum and insurance-required reproductions.

Until today.

"Thanks so much, Joshua," Suzanne said. It would have taken her much longer to unpack the van without him, and it was appreciated. "May I call you Josh?"

The angle of his jaw tightened. "No."

Suzanne blinked at the blatant rebuttal and the morphing of his face from craggy and interesting to bleak and forbidding. But even more intriguing were the mental shutters slamming down behind his pale-green eyes. Shooting him her best flirty smile, she attempted to make amends. She could flirt with the best of them if required, and she'd never met a man who didn't appreciate being the object of a little flirting. "Well…anyway…I'd like to make you dinner to thank you for everything. What are you doing tomorrow night?"

Grady clearly *did not* appreciate the flirting.

His brows beetled together, a deep *V* forming

between them. "Look, lady." He paused and drew in a breath. "I know there was a whole single-women thing that happened here over the summer and that a lot of dudes around these parts are looking to get hitched, but I'm not one of them. I don't know what my uncle told you, but I am not in the market for a woman. Not for dinner or dating or a relationship or even a quick tumble in the sheets. I like peace and quiet. I like solitude. I've said more words today than I have all week. So you stay here"—he cocked his head at the cottage—"and I'll stay there"—he pointed at the back porch of his place—"and we'll get along just fine."

He drew a breath again, and Suzanne could do nothing but stare. It was the most animated his face had been since her arrival, and it was a thing to behold, his square jaw working, his eyes glinting with cold *steel*.

Suzanne blinked as realization cut through her artistic drive. Did he think she was here to… ingratiate herself with him? To…date him? Have *sex* with him? Did he think his uncle had pimped her out?

Did he think she was here to get herself *a husband*?

Jesus, what kind of Dark Ages bullshit was this? Sure, six months ago, the town may have been awash with single women looking for love, but Suzanne wasn't any part of that, and she most certainly wasn't here for a man.

A spike of indignation quickly flared into a slow, steady burn of anger. This dude's ego was as big as the whole damn ranch. And, flash of pain or no flash of pain, he could go and do something exceedingly sexual and anatomically impossible to himself. Suzanne narrowed her eyes, better to aim her death rays at him.

"Look, *mister*. This whole brooding cowboy act might work on some women, but I think I can *contain* myself around all your manly man bullshit, and here's a newsflash for you. I'm here to *paint* not *hook up* or trap some...*cowpoke* into putting a ring on it. All this *y'all* have"—she went deliberately *southern* as she gestured wildly around her—"is real charmin', but I'm a *New Yorker*. So yeah, you stay over there, and I'll try and resist the urge to leave love letters on your porch every morning."

She was breathing hard by the time she stopped, and her pulse was thumping like a jackhammer through her ears, but *man* was she ticked. He, on the other hand, appeared to be unaffected by her vitriol. Giving her a barely there nod, he pulled down on the brim of his hat.

"Ma'am," he said, then calmly walked away.

Suzanne watched him go, so damn pissed at him and his assumptions and how good his wide shoulders looked as he strode toward his cabin, she could barely see straight. Her muse, however, was popping champagne corks.

Which did not bode well.

Not for her *or* Joshua Grady.

*When a shy woman inherits a ranch, she'll have to find an inner strength to succeed—and open herself up to love—in this heartwarming novel from* New York Times *bestselling author Victoria James.*

# Cowboy for Hire

Sarah Turner has led a very sheltered life. So when her mother passes away after a long illness, suddenly she's left in charge of the family ranch with little know-how but plenty of will to keep it afloat. Determined not to lose her parents' legacy or newfound independence, she needs a hero fast—not to save her, but to show her how to save herself. But she's unprepared for the ruggedly handsome cowboy who answers her ad.

"Cowboy for Hire," the ad said, and Cade Walker is quick to respond. Betrayed as ranch manager by his former boss, he's looking for a new place to put down roots—without the pressure to prove himself again. Except when he meets his new boss, it's clear he's not only there to run a ranch but to also teach Miss Independent how to run it. But as they struggle to make the land flourish, they'll both need courage if they hope to find a family...together.

*From the author of* The Last Letter, *a gripping, emotional story of family, humanity, and faith.*

# GREAT AND PRECIOUS THINGS

## REBECCA YARROS

*How do you define yourself when others have already decided who you are?*

Six years ago, when Camden Daniels came back from war without his younger brother, no one in the small town of Alba, Colorado, would forgive him—especially his father. Cam left, swearing never to return.

But a desperate message from his father brings it all back. The betrayal. The pain. And the need to go home again.

But home is where the one person he still loves is waiting. Willow. The one woman he can never have. Because there are secrets buried in Alba that are best left in the dark.

If only he could tell his heart to stay locked away when she whispers she's always loved him, and always will…

*Great and Precious Things* is a heart-wrenching story about family, betrayal, and ultimately how far we're willing to go on behalf of those who need us most.

AMARA

an imprint of Entangled Publishing LLC